EXES & FOES

Also by Amanda Woody

They Hate Each Other

EXES & FOES

XOXO

by Amanda Woody

VIKING

VIKING
An imprint of Penguin Random House LLC
1745 Broadway, New York, New York 10019

First published in the United States of America by Viking,
an imprint of Penguin Random House LLC, 2024

Visit us online at PenguinRandomHouse.com.

Library of Congress Cataloging-in-Publication Data is available.

ISBN 9780593403143

1st Printing

Printed in the United States of America

LSCC

Edited by Dana Leydig
Design by Anabeth Bostrup
Text set in Franziska Pro

To anyone who has never felt "queer enough."
This one's for you, love.

CALEB

If I wasn't sure I preferred the sidelines to the spotlight before today, my classmate's fist sailing between my eyes pretty much sealed the deal.

"We shouldn't fight!" I croak, sidestepping and narrowly missing the incoming blow. Luckily, while I occupy an offensive amount of space vertically, I don't have much surface area to hit horizontally. I back away, nearly crashing into the sea of lunch trays congregating around us in the cafeteria. I guess it's not every day people can witness a fight between the captain of the shot put team and that one stick bug from their chemistry class. "If a teacher sees us—"

"Shut the fuck *up!*" Ian Summers snarls. He's the kind of guy most students don't like getting involved with, especially in a "let's kick each other's sacks" way. His muscular arms are meaty enough to ward off multiple vegans.

My attempt to disband the crowd with pleas like "You should eat your food before it gets cold!" doesn't work. Cheers and whoops echo through the spacious cafeteria, as if my toothpick arms stand any chance against Ian's bulky build. I'm a guy who looms, sure, but not in an intimidating "move it before I move you" way. More like the "disproportionate-limbed urban legend" way.

Basically, Ian could fold me like a lawn chair.

"What if we sit down and talk about our feelings?" I sputter out as sweat beads on Ian's temples. I'm talking out of my ass now, my focus distorted, because too many people are looking at me, whispering. "Breathing could help with your temper . . ."

Ian's ashy white face turns the color of beet juice. "What the *hell* did you say?"

I've already forgotten. The crowd's volume around me is ear numbing. So I merely stare at Ian, my tongue fumbling through words that won't save me. He shoves me with such force that I stagger to the edge of the ring, where several students reel back. In a flash, he has a fistful of my shirt and he's panting angry air in my face, the nostrils of his flat nose flaring.

"Piss me off again," he growls, "and I'll catch you outside."

My eyes flit over his shoulder. A girl stands on the inner curve of the ring, gripping her lunch tray with trembling hands. Seeing her reminds me of why I stepped in. Why I grabbed Ian's shoulder and wrenched him back. "Don't harass girls," I say sternly, despite the wobble in my voice, "and this won't happen again."

The thirty people encircling us go, "Oooooh."

"*What?*" Ian yells, his pale eyes flailing around the crowd. "I didn't do *shit!*"

"She asked you to leave her alone." It takes all my willpower to utter the words rather than disappearing in a puff of smoke *Looney Tunes* style. Because the longer I stand here, the more my ears open to the voices. The whispers.

Is that Caleb Daniels?

You forget this guy exists until he's standing over you.

Ian could crush this bitch into cocaine powder.

Maybe if I stop meeting Ian's alpha male gaze, his rage will shift from a boil to a simmer. So I step toward the girl he'd been harassing, leaving my back open to him in the hopes that he won't take advantage of it by slinging another blow at me. Before I can ask if she's okay, though, Ian speaks again, his voice dripping with amusement.

"You just wanted her first, right?"

The crowd of students freezes, clearly anticipating more entertainment to propel them through this tedious Wednesday. I'm not sure what he means until he continues through a sneer, his voice a taunting drawl.

"Can't blame you for wanting to sleep around with everyone. It's what you've grown up around, isn't it?"

The words crack through my chest and splinter my bones like a stroke of lightning. The garbled chatter surrounding us screeches to a stop. Wrath swirls in my stomach. The bones of my jaw snap rigid and tight.

Did you see what his mom was wearing?

Probably a teenage pregnancy.

My vision burns red as Ian's voice joins the reservoir of others lurking in the back of my head. What do they know about me? About *her*? I want to step toward him. To step away. To snarl in his face. To bite my tongue.

I don't get to decide which urge to follow through on.

Suddenly, curled knuckles slam into Ian's square jaw, snapping his head sideways and causing him to collide with the tile floor. He howls in pain, cradling his cheek.

"Lick dirt," a voice says, and people yell with excited delight. I look at the newcomer, my eyes bugging.

It's Emma. Fucking. Jones.

She rolls her wrist, her tangled strawberry blond hair spilling over the collar of her black bomber jacket. "Sorry to interrupt," she says while I'm trying to process her appearance, and she raps my shoulder in this overly familiar way that makes me scowl. Like she isn't speaking her first words to me since the day she deleted me from her life. "It's just that whenever I see Caleb Daniels losing a fight, I start swinging. You know?"

I scrunch my hands into irritable fists. Yeah. I know.

Ian scrambles to his feet, his jawline swelling under Emma's blow. "*You want to die, Jones?*" he shouts.

A combative smirk twists Emma's pale pink lips. *Please don't answer*, I want to say, because "making things infinitely worse" is an Emma Jones specialty.

But she's already engaging with a cool, amused voice—the kind she uses whenever she's seeking a last nerve. "Mocking Caleb's mom? Fucking yikes. Didn't your parents get divorced because *your* mom got caught railing the fifth-grade gym teacher?"

Oh no.

Thick veins bulge in Ian's neck. The crowd explodes with encouraging screams. Personally, I'd prefer to explode myself. Emma still has the useless ability to light a fire *just* when I've quelled one.

Ian storms toward us, and while I resist the urge to dive under the nearest table, Emma squares up with her five feet and six inches. "Ballsy," he growls, towering so Emma has to arch her neck to meet his incensed eyes. "Or are you only like this when your ex is in trouble? I'm sure he'll let you suck him off without putting on a show."

Another hum of *oohs*.

Emma meets this with sharp laughter. "Please. Caleb would never let something as unsanitary as a mouth near his dick."

It feels like a good time to pass away. To melt into the cracks between the floor tiles and live out my existence as a sentient puddle. "Don't bring my genitals into this," I plead, a sentence I hope I've now spoken for the first and last time. Over everyone's head, I see lunch supervisors wriggling through the multitude of students, trying to reach us.

Suddenly, Ian cusses and lunges for Emma, like he's going to grab her. All of my neurons fire at once, and I throw myself forward instinctively to separate them.

Don't touch her.

Ire burns in my blood. My nostrils flare.

Don't you dare touch Emma.

Before I can get there, Emma's knee smashes Ian between his thighs, proving once again that my only use in these situations is to stand aside and look awkward. As Ian collapses, wheezing, the two supervisors break through the throng of students, shouting everyone down while simultaneously glaring at us within the circle.

Just like that, my perfect high school record of unproblematic behavior is broken.

✗●✗●

I've been in fights before. But my experience with them back in elementary school usually involved someone kicking me around on the playground while I politely asked them to try the swings instead.

Confrontation has never been my style. If I'm good at anything, it's vigorously avoiding it and all other forms of attention so people won't notice me. For instance, whenever my friend Jas drags me to parties, I stand at a reasonable distance from her and the varsity volleyball team, drinking in drama and hoping nobody calls the cops on me. Or, say, at homecoming, watching people grind from afar is less dangerous than joining in and causing bodily damage with my razor-sharp elbows. During class, I'm the first person with an answer to a question, but why speak up when I could simply . . . not?

I'm not necessarily antisocial. I'm the class secretary. Talking to people is half my job description, even if I prefer the other half (taking notes, keeping things organized, using the power of my type-A personality). It's just . . .

Participating draws attention. And being seen is a nightmare, especially when the people looking up at me in awe can't whisper.

No way that guy goes to our school.

Someone should come get their dad.

Is that a college basketball player?

I learned how to brush them off, but that doesn't mean the words don't sting or remind me of painful moments from my childhood. And now I'm here, being shepherded to the main office because Emma decided to work her troublemaking magic. My chances of avoiding this situation plummeted to zero the moment she stepped in.

The lunch supervisor grumbles as she guides us forward. While Ian whines about physical assault, I grimace down at Emma. Her hands are stuffed in her jacket, and she's chewing gum obnoxiously, her dove white face unbothered. Does she care, even a little, that this is our first interaction in years?

Of course not. Considering she didn't care when she drop-kicked me out of her life in eighth grade without a single goodbye.

"Something to say, Legs for Days?" Emma asks, smiling vaguely in my direction. She still has those abnormally sharp canine teeth that make her look wolfish, like she's hiding something.

"Why are you still picking fights with people twice your size?" I demand, before realizing I probably shouldn't respond to that nickname.

Emma meets my stare for the first time. Her upturned eyes are as colorful as I remember—a smattering of green ringed with amber brown. "I injured his crotch, didn't I? Besides . . ." She steers her focus to the linoleum tile, like she can't stand looking at me, and she mumbles, "I said I'd always stand up for your mom."

A knife right to the chest. Fine. "I was de-escalating the situation," I say bitterly.

"Really?" She smirks. "Felt like I was watching you battle a grease fire with water."

Her amusement makes me grind my teeth. She can still crawl under my skin and make me itch with annoyance in a way nobody else can. "Next time, you don't have to step in," I tell her. "I'm not that same little defenseless boy from the playground."

Emma smiles briefly, like she's remembering something fond. Maybe she's thinking about how this situation is uncannily similar to how we met. "Like I said, he insulted your mom, and I had a violent opinion about it. Get your wagging finger out of my face or I'll crunch it off."

I didn't even realize I'd lifted my hand. How embarrassing. I lower it, because she'd bite it with the entire strength of her jaw, given the opportunity.

"How . . . is she, by the way?" Emma asks carefully, now watching the lunch supervisor, who looks like she's trying to stab Ian with her eyes.

I want to ask why she cares or say it's none of her business. I go with "She's fine."

Emma nods, apparently satisfied with this answer. Hmph.

Finally, we make it to the main office. The supervisor ushers Ian, Emma, and me inside, then orders us to sit in separate corners of the waiting area—a beige room contaminated with motivational wall posters. "Adams will be by soon," she says to the secretary at the half-moon desk before storming out.

Great. So I'll have to explain myself to the vice principal.

The fluorescent lighting hums as we sit in silence. Ian sprawls back in his chair, his hand cupping the front of his jeans (probably recovering from Emma's knee), glaring at her with such malice that it makes me shiver. Naturally, she appears unfazed and has pulled a soccer ball out of her bag, which she's dribbling between her feet. I'm not sure why she has it, since she got banned from the soccer field sophomore year.

After minutes of agonizing silence, the office door swings open, and there stands VP Adams—a woman with thick black braids who's always wearing abnormally tall heels despite the fact that she already towers over pretty much everyone in school. Her sharp eyebrows are joined at the center of her dark brown forehead, giving her a stern air that I've never been on the receiving end of. At least until now. "We'll start with Daniels," she says, walking toward the offices stretching into the hall behind the front desk. I guess that's my cue, so I rise, sling my bag over my shoulder, and brace for my fate.

CALEB

I must've dissociated through my conversation with Vice Principal Adams, because when I blink, I'm back in the waiting area, anticipating my sentence. Emma and Ian are being questioned together. The VP probably knows how to break up a fistfight, but I keep my ears pricked for screams anyway. The only noise I hear, though, is the secretary, who's on a personal call in one of the "sick kid needs to lie down" rooms.

I tap my shoes together, hating my apprehension. I shouldn't care about Emma's punishment. She's the one who stepped in and landed the first blow.

I said I'd always stand up for your mom.

My shoes click together faster. Dammit, Emma. Just *behave*.

Suddenly, I'm wrenched from my thoughts when someone slams through the main office door and staggers to the secretary's desk, panting like she's just sprinted a mile. *"Let the witness speak!"* she shouts. When she realizes no one's at the counter, she whips toward me, her hair flying around her.

"Uh, hi?" I say with an awkward smile, my fight-or-flight response having thrown me to my feet. It's not a creative response to this situation, but it's better than my other instinct, which was to launch my chair at her.

As she strides toward me, I recognize her abruptly. This is the girl Ian was harassing.

"I have to present my case," she says, the insistency in her inky black-brown eyes overwhelming enough to nearly swallow me whole. Tight spring twists twirl past her copper-brown shoulders. She's wearing a floral shirt with fluttery sleeves and pale blue jeans that hug the plump curves of her hips, and she's . . .

Beautiful.

Oh no.

When my brain registers this, my body betrays me by sending blood into my cheeks and revving my heartbeat. She's craning to see me, so I stagger back to avoid causing irreversible damage to her neck. "Your case?" I ask weakly.

She heaves a deep sigh, then begins to say . . . a lot of words. Very quickly. "I was in this daze after lunch, right, and didn't know what to do, so I sat on the floor in the corner of the cafeteria and ate my food. I went to class because I still didn't know what to do, but then I started panicking because, like, what if you get expelled all because this guy was being a cock to me? So I ran here during passing time to give my side of the story."

I take time to digest this exposition (and allow her to catch her breath). The first thing out of my mouth is "You sat on the floor for lunch?"

She blinks like I've stunned her. "Where else should I sit?"

I don't . . . Huh? "A table," I suggest.

"Can't." She gives me finger guns. "I have no friends."

It's such a relatable explanation that I can't help but well up. The only reason I have a lunch table is because Jas lets me sit with her and the other volleyball girls. "I'm sorry you got caught up with Ian," I say, because I'm not sure how to respond to her friend issue (relatable though it may be).

Her smile slices through the dreary day like a knife made of sparkling sunlight. "That's not your fault, Caleb," she says earnestly. "He was obviously looking for his prey of the day, and I was walking a little too close, looking a little too cute."

Wait. She said *Caleb*. Like, *me*, Caleb? "You know who I am?" I squeak out.

She cocks her head, curls cascading lower over her shoulder. "You're the class secretary, yeah?"

"Right, but most underclassmen don't know our names."

"Jesus," she whispers, sprawling her hands over the sides of her horrified face. "Do I really look like a baby-back bitch?"

I stare at her in bewilderment.

"I'm a senior—just transferred here last week," she says helpfully. "Sorry. That's what my old school calls underclassmen. I thought it was a universal thing, but your face tells me it's not. Oh, and I'm Juliet, by the way."

My face pales. How much of a dick am I that I forgot to ask for her name? She's *way* too cute, and I'm the pinnacle of mediocrity stuffed into the body of a linguine-limbed behemoth. Before my brain can string together a coherent sentence, I hear a faint sniffle.

Suddenly, Juliet is in tears.

Oh God. What the fuck? "I'm sorry," I wheeze, because it's absolutely my fault—

"What?" Juliet runs a knuckle under her eye, then gasps, like she didn't realize she was crying. "Whoops. Oh, that's embarrassing as hell. Sorry. This week has been . . . Uh, my eyes are still adjusting to city smog."

She gives me hoarse, flimsy laughter. And more finger guns.

I don't bother telling her we're in the suburbs and smog isn't really an issue here. That, and the fact that the "city" is small enough that it probably wouldn't be considered one if not for the small cluster of skyscrapers downtown. Instead, I pat my pockets until I find my handkerchief (yes, I have a patterned set at home, thank you), then hand it to her. Juliet accepts it with a grateful smile, dabbing her watery face.

"I've never seen a real human use these," she says. "You always carry this on you?"

"Of course." As any sensible man should.

"Anyway. *My case!*" she swiftly yells, causing me to stumble backward. She tosses my handkerchief to me, then begins to storm the hallway stretching behind the secretary desk, swinging her arms with intensity.

"Wait!" I call out, following her. "She's talking to Emma and Ian, so we shouldn't interrupt . . ."

"But what if she's handing out *punishment*?" Juliet demands. "I have to save Emma. And I'll show everyone I'm not a damsel in distress."

"No one said you were," I say weakly, but she's already shouldering open the door to Adams's office and screaming,

"I'm here to make my case!"

Vice Principal Adams blinks at Juliet from the propped position on her desk, her expression surprisingly neutral. I guess she's seen it all at this point. Ian and Emma sit before her, Ian quivering with rage and nursing his puffy face with an ice bag, Emma leaning back and looking insufferably amused.

"What, Higgins?" Adams asks with an audible sigh.

"I have a case," she repeats, and when she catches Ian's glower, she gulps, inching toward me. "I want to share my side of what happened."

"Summers harassed you, then Daniels stepped in to stop him, then Jones took a swing when he wouldn't back down?" Adams asks flatly.

Juliet opens her mouth. Closes it. Opens it. "That's the one," she says.

Ian begins to mutter obscenities again. Emma, though, is focused on Juliet, and there's an intrigued sparkle in her eyes.

"Thank you for your contribution, Higgins." Adams's expression never wavers, but she's kneading her knuckles into her temple. "Please return to the waiting area."

"Yes, ma'am," Juliet croaks, and she backpedals into my chest, promptly crushing my toes. She jumps away—which, ow—but what do I care, because she smells like coconut and vanilla. "Cheerio!"

With that, she closes the VP's door. Before I can say anything, she rotates toward the wall and slams her head into it.

"Hey!" I cry out, seizing her shoulders before she can do it again. "Why would—?"

"Kill me," Juliet rasps, patchy redness blooming across her forehead.

"Why? I mean, no," I say firmly, "but what's wrong?"

"I'm so awkward." She groans, and again, it's relatable enough that I resist the urge to beg her to date me, *please*, we were *made* for each other. "So much for new school, new me . . . How pathetic." She drags her feet toward the waiting area, moping.

"You're not pathetic," I say tentatively, falling in step behind her. I've had those thoughts about myself, but it's rare that someone's around to negate them. I want to be that voice for her right now, even though . . . well, we're strangers.

"Really?" She palms her eyes, like she's concealing new tears. "Because when Ian was hitting on me, I couldn't even shut him down clearly enough."

"*That's not true.*"

Juliet's perfectly sculpted brows pop at the sudden severity in my voice.

"It's not your fault that he overstepped your boundaries," I tell her as she begins to pace in front of me. "Please don't blame yourself, okay?"

Juliet's eyes rove me from head to toe. It's in a strange, meticulous way—not the "is he worth my time" analyzing I'm used to.

With my clammy palms, ashy white face, and . . . everything else, I'm probably failing whatever mental test she's conducting.

But then she snorts loud enough to make me jump. "What?" I squawk.

"Sorry. It's just . . . you've got a mature voice to go with your face," she says with amusement, nudging me with her elbow. I definitely don't notice that it's smoother than buttercream. "I feel like I just got lectured by my dad."

I can't say it's my favorite sentence of the day. I know she means well, but I've heard the sentiment before. Mostly by people seeking a reason to insult my mom.

He's so mature for his age. That's what happens without a support system at home . . .

"You hate me," Juliet says.

I wrench out of my pensiveness. I feel like every time she says something, she's giving me whiplash. "Huh?"

"I understand." Her cheery voice lowers with solemnity. "I'm used to people not being able to tolerate me, so don't feel bad."

Marry me, I nearly say, because I've used those exact words before when whining to my mom about my lack of a social life. Thankfully, I manage to sputter out something else. "I think you're great."

A shimmer returns to her pupils, and for a bizarre second, I think I'd do anything to keep them alight like that. Before she can respond, footsteps sound down the hallway. Emma is ambling away from Adams's office, hands nestled in her jacket pockets.

Immediately, questions buzz around my head like irritating bees. *What did she say? What's your punishment? Are you okay?*

I don't say anything. There's no reason to. Besides . . .

My eyes flit to Juliet, who's checking her pulse for some reason.

. . . I'm more interested in someone else at the moment.

Emma approaches with a sardonic smile—the same one from earlier that tells me she's about to commit some kind of heinous wrongdoing. I wonder if she ever uses her other smile. The one that scrunches her colorful eyes and brightens her facial features. The only smile that's ever kept me up at night.

"That was hot shit," Emma says, zeroing in on Juliet after hardly sparing me a glance. "The way you stormed into Adams's office. I could take notes from you."

Juliet emits high-pitched, wheezy laughter, close to what I assume a choking seal sounds like. "Really? I've only heard the *shit* part before, so this is pretty exciting for me," she says cheerily.

Can any one girl be so perfect?

"Anyway, thank you for violently beating the man who harassed me," Juliet says, scooping Emma's palms into hers. She's basically drenched in the shimmering glow of adoration. "You're a feminist icon."

Emma stares at her with what I assume is the same expression I was wearing when Juliet staggered into the office. Startled. Baffled. Fascinated. "We have English together, right?" Emma asks, noticeably squeezing her palms in return. "Juliet? I've been wanting to say hi, but you always book it out the door before I can reach you."

Juliet's throat bobs with a swallow. She's clearly believing whatever horse feces is spilling out of Emma's mouth. "I do a lot of sprinting between classes. Sorry. I didn't know you were trying to talk to me. I . . . feel like I've been invisible since I got here."

Emma offers a sugary-sweet, vomit-inducing smile, and says, "Everyone's probably nervous talking to the cute new girl."

Resentment burns in my blood. Of. *Course.* Like it isn't bad enough that I have to see her all over school since the breakup, but she also never browses a new corner of the building for relationships. Somehow she always ends up in my quadrant, our interests tangling, and I can never compete with her charming, carefree personality. Probably because I'm a six-foot-four titan with a passion for mops and a voice deep enough to earn me the yearbook election for "most likely to become a serial killer." That's not to say everyone I'm interested in will like me back, but whenever I start developing feelings for an acquaintance, Emma waltzes in and steals them away before I can even figure out if they're attracted to guys.

Adams finally arrives with Ian, who's still massaging half-melted ice over his face. "Go home," she orders him, and he shoots us a menacing glare. He must not want to further incriminate himself, though, because he leaves without a word. Adams rotates toward Emma and says, "Jones—"

"Wait!" Juliet rushes forward. "My case—"

"Relax, Higgins," Adams pleads. I wonder how often they've spoken, considering they're on a last-name basis after a week. Maybe Juliet has been coming here with questions since . . . well, apparently she has no one else to ask. "I have a clear picture of the situation."

"She already suspended us through the week," Emma says.

The word *suspended* rattles between my ears and heightens my blood pressure. I wish she'd look more distressed about it. I know school has never been her forte, but she's made it this far. Wouldn't she care if she were disqualified right before the finish line?

Juliet covers her mouth, like she can't fathom a worse punishment than being ejected from school. (I can't think of one, personally.)

I squeak, "And my punishment . . . ma'am?"

Adams waves her hand dismissively and says, "Go home and cool off."

Whew. At least this won't go on my record for all to behold when I apply for colleges.

Juliet is nearly choking with horror. "If you punish them," she says shakily, assuming a battle stance with her fists coming to chest level and her knees bending, "then punish me, too!"

Adams looks like she'd rather swallow glass than spend another second around us. "Go home for the day, then. To . . . reflect on today's events. Or something."

Juliet sniffles and nods, accepting her fate. She's so cute, I want to stab myself in the throat.

"Jones, stay back," Adams says, her frown shifting to Emma. "Daniels, Higgins, leave."

My emotional well-being is running on fumes, so I book it to the door, Juliet hot on my heels. Emma flops into a chair and watches us with narrowed eyes—whether because she thinks we're getting off easy or because we'll be alone without her, I'm not sure.

I said I'd always stand up for your mom.

I wrench my guilty eyes away. I can't take responsibility for her anymore. Besides . . . she doesn't want me to. That's why everything fell apart, isn't it? Because I'm too finnicky, stern, meticulous. Emma's always been the opposite. Disorganized, laid back, defiant. Our friendship never would've lasted into adulthood anyway. I glued Emma down when all she wanted was to take off running.

Maybe it's a good thing she broke it off. Before . . .

"We'll wait," Juliet whispers to her as we escape. That's not my preference, but if they're left alone for five minutes, Juliet will forget I exist, and I'll lose another chance to get closer to someone I find interesting. All because Emma has that confident smile, soft, shiny hair, and bold personality. Everyone falls for it.

Everyone.

As we enter the hall, I text Jas not to wait up after school. We were planning on studying at the library before she takes off for an away tournament. Unsurprisingly, I have a slew of messages from her.

JAS

Whore are you kidding me

I go to the taco line one time and you get into a whole

altercation

Caleb Daniels fighting in the flesh? Without me to witness?

I hear Emma punched him. How is that yt girl still covering

your ass after all these years

I roll my eyes and boldly ignore the texts, instead telling her I'm going home for the day before re-pocketing my phone.

Just in time to see Juliet collapse to her knees in the empty hallway.

"Juliet?" I ask in alarm, kneeling beside her.

"Suspended," she breathes, and suddenly, she's flopping onto her back on that nasty, grimy linoleum, staring, agonized, at the ceiling. "Is this what it's like to be a bad girl?"

I cough through a fit of surprised laughter. "You didn't get suspended," I remind her.

"I may as well have." She presses her hands to her face. "What do I tell my parents?"

"The truth?" I suggest, because I can't envision anyone being able to spin this against her. "Unless your parents are . . . victim blame-y or something?"

"No," Juliet says miserably. "They're perfectly loving and supportive."

Well. I want to tell her she should get off the floor before she contracts a disease, but I notice wetness gathering at the edges of her palms. She's . . . crying again? "Are you okay?" I ask, softer. Something is wrong, and I'm pretty sure it extends beyond the day's incidents.

"Peachy." Her voice is a brittle rasp. "The last few weeks have been magnificent. My brother is teaching halfway across the country. My mom moved us four hours away from the place I grew up, and none of my friends are texting me anymore. And now I finally have the chance to make a friend, and I ruin it by getting emotional."

A . . . friend? Who, *me*?

"Not at all!" I cry out. "Come on, stand up. This floor is disgusting."

Juliet works her way to her feet alongside me. I snag my handkerchief once more and lean in, pressing it gently to the edges of her swollen eyes. "Waterproof mascara is the shit," she whimpers.

"I'm sure it is." I offer a reassuring smile. "I'm sorry about your brother. Sounds like you're close to him?"

"I . . . Yeah." She takes a shuddery breath. "Terrell. He's my best friend. He was earning his PhD at the university nearby before we moved, so he was still living at home. Last month, he got a job in Boston, so . . ." She presses her head back to the wall, her curls flattening against the brick. Fatigue is overcoming her somber expression. "Then we moved, and my old friends don't seem to care about keeping up with me. So today is just the piss on top of my shit stain of a month."

"I'm sorry," I whisper, and I mean it. I can't imagine dealing with the complete upheaval of my life during senior year. "Do you . . . like hugs?"

I don't expect to say that last bit, but there it is anyway in all its creepy glory. I brace for a look of disgust or horror, but Juliet's eyes twinkle with playfulness. "Do you give your hugs to anyone who's sad, or am I special?" she asks.

I think my heart just exploded, but I manage to gargle out, "Special."

"Good answer." Suddenly, she steps into my chest and slaps her face against my shoulder. I catch another whiff of vanilla that warms my cheeks, and I fold my arms around her ample figure, hoping she can't hear the remnants of my detonated heart. "You're warm," she says, voice muffled but pleasantly surprised.

"It's the high blood pressure."

She laughs, tugging away from my grip. "Excellent hug. Eight out of ten."

Joking? She's joking? We're being humorous? "That's it?" I ask skeptically.

"You should squeeze tighter to make your hug feel secure," she scolds. "And make sure you're wearing a comfy sweater."

This conversation is so cute, I could succumb to the clutches of death. Judging by the way my body is revolting against this "talking to a pretty girl" situation, I just might. "Thanks for the feedback," I say.

She smiles, this one more genuine than the others I've seen today. Maybe my boldness comes from being part of student council—it's my duty to help people feel comfortable at this school. Maybe it's because talking to her has been uncharacteristically easy, or because there's finally someone around here who doesn't have preconceived notions about me or my mom. But I pull my phone out and ask, "Can I have your number?"

Juliet looks like I've just told her a jaw-dropping fun fact. "You . . . want to talk to me *more?*" she asks breathily.

"Of course. I think you're . . . um. Super." I cough through the nervous waver in my voice. Seriously? I couldn't think of a less awkward word? "So, if you want to text . . ." I hand my phone to her, allowing her to tap her number in. When I look at the name she saved, I see she included the sun emoji.

"Thanks." She smiles with enthusiasm. "You're a good person, Caleb."

Another burn rises into my face. "It's not a big deal—"

"Maybe not to you," she says with a wink.

Yeah. I could completely fall for this girl.

Emma

It's another suspension, which means another opportunity to be my mom's greatest disappointment. Wahoo! Yeehaw.

I slump back in my seat, sighing, resisting the urge to retrieve my soccer ball again so I can have a reason to look down at my feet. Adams towers over me in pumps, her wiry arms folded and tucked over the box braids cascading down her front, tapping her foot like she's expecting me to start sobbing about my difficult life. But she's never wrestled a tear from my eyes, so I won't let her win now. A few more months of this hellish torment and I'll be granted the freedom to drop-kick any asshole without adults ordering me to write double-spaced essays on why punching people is "immoral." This one is due on Monday.

"The fact that I'm still here feels like misogyny," I tell her.

Adams looks like she'd rather be peeling gum off the bottom of desks. Maybe I shouldn't be so annoying. She's just doing her job, and students like me make it harder. But she can't say anything that she hasn't already regurgitated to me in the past. *Why are you acting out? How are things at home? Is there anything you want to tell me?*

I won't apologize for what I did to Ian. How can she expect me to stand around while some filthy dick insults Ms. Daniels or harasses girls so far out of his class of peasantry, they needn't deign him a glance?

"This can't keep happening," Adams says gravely, bracing her palms against the waist of her blazer. At least she's skipping the lax, motherly "*talk to me*" phase of scolding I usually have to endure. Maybe she's finally given up on me. "If there's a problem, take it up with a teacher. Don't throw your backpack at people or taunt them into swinging or fill their bag with whipped cream."

"Shaving cream," I correct. Like I'd waste a can of Reddi-wip on some bigot.

Adams glares at me, her amber brown eyes unamused. "One more suspension, and we'll hold a disciplinary hearing to discuss expulsion."

Balls.

I'm so close to being done. I'd sooner drop out than start senior year over at some other school. Besides, I'm not *trying* to cause issues. They just . . . hunt me down. And force me to address them. In a manner one might consider . . . aggressive. Or uncouth.

Ugh. Uncouth? Really? I was only around Caleb for a few minutes today, and he managed to leave his residue on me.

As I seize my backpack and stand to leave, Vice Principal Adams tacks one more thing onto this shitty day. "You were already removed from the soccer team for your behavior," she says coolly. "Don't do anything else to remove yourself from this school."

It seems like an unnecessarily low blow. Like I would've forgotten the day I climbed on top of the defender and broke her nose sophomore year—a moment that turned my teammates against me and coined me the official menace of our class.

To be fair, Stephanie fully deserved my fist that day.

Why's that creep watching us practice again? Guess we should travel in packs so he doesn't try to—

No, no, nope. I shake my head of the remembrance as I stride into the hall, my jaw clenching. Moving on.

So, expulsion is next. All because Caleb Daniels stood there like an awkwardly proportioned stone statue when Ian insulted his mom. I swear the whole "Caleb's mom is a slut" rumor died back freshman year. She's not even one of the strippers at the club she's been employed at for years. She's a bartender who works night shifts and happens to be unapologetically confident in her body, to the point where other parents constantly accused her of trying to "seduce" them when she showed up for school events in her apparel. Still, even if she *was* up on stage with her entire ass out, who cares? Like, if men are going to be horny for you just for existing, you might as well profit from it, yeah?

I check my texts and huff.

ALICE

Not again: ')

Come on. It's not that often.

"Oh!" a voice exclaims to my left. "She set you free!"

Juliet Higgins and Caleb are outside the office, Juliet shuffling around with enthusiasm, Caleb stock still and stiff like . . . an awkwardly proportioned stone statue. He never learned how to properly stand so as to not terrify people or look clunky. I never had the heart to tell him that "pin straight and expressionless" is more ominous than he realizes.

As soon as we make eye contact—accidentally, on my part (his crisp blue irises and ridiculously long lashes have this maddeningly natural draw)—the nostrils of his narrow nose flare and his forehead creases. It's one of those *"I'm disappointed but also a little worried"* glares I got accustomed to back then.

I turn to Juliet, who smiles all toothy and cute. She's got that uncommon symmetry to her face, and this equally uncommon aura that brightens the hallway. It's been a while since I've met anyone like that. At this point in my dismal life, it'd probably be good to hang around someone like her to balance out the negative energy constantly oozing out of my pores. Sun-and-moon couples—isn't that what they're called? My best friend Alice comes the closest to being my "sun," though her cheeriness is a front. She likes being around people even less than I do.

"You really waited for me?" I ask, grinning. In my periphery, Caleb's almond-shaped eyes zoom between us with annoyance. He's not subtle. Even someone as pathetic as Ian could've seen the way he went doe-eyed when talking to Juliet. This girl has clearly captured his interest.

Mine too.

"Of course," Juliet says, bouncing a bit closer. "You were basically banished because of me. Least I can do is walk you out."

Banished? I'll use that from now on, because it sounds in-finitely more badass than *suspended*. Caleb didn't even get suspended, which is both fair and typical. Sure, he probably had the opportunity to punch Ian, but he's not like that. Never has been. Caleb is a gentle, kind person who huffs and wags his finger when he's upset.

It's one of the reasons we never should've become friends back then.

"I'm honored," I say, scooping Juliet's warm brown arm through mine and heading for the front doors of the building. Caleb scoffs, following us, his loud steps echoing around the hallway. "Though, getting punished had nothing to do with you and everything to do with me assaulting Ian Fuck-Ass Summers."

"Only because he was trying to get me to sit with him," Juliet says gloomily.

"It's not your fault he targeted you." I frown, because I hate when people blame themselves for things that aren't their fault. It's nearly as unbearable as when people blame *others* for things that aren't their fault.

"At least I met you guys," Juliet says, with an eager glance at Caleb. I peer back as well to see his pasty, lanky arms folded tight, one of his thick brown eyebrows creeping dangerously close to his hairline. "Talking to people has been, you know. An issue. Not the talking part, but the people part. Being annoying is this thing I'm really good at."

She sounds a little too joyful about being self-deprecating. But it's valid enough that my chest warms for her anyway. "I don't think you're annoying," I say softly.

"Just wait. Sometimes my friends would make this siren noise to tell me if I was being too obnoxious," Juliet explains, laughing. "Like, I just keep going. I have a lot of energy, I guess. That's why I jog between classes."

"Siren noise?" My voice comes weaker. That sounds . . . really shitty. Who the hell treats their friends like that?

My eyes lower. Not like I'm one to judge.

"Crap!" Juliet stops suddenly in the hall, nearly making me stumble, and Caleb has to do a jig to avoid trampling her. "I left my physics textbook in my last classroom. Ugh, and it's basically on the other side of the school." She pulls her arm out from beneath mine, which I allow with great reluctance, then begins backtracking down the hallway with a wave. "Go ahead—I don't want to keep you waiting. I'll text you later, Caleb!"

Caleb gives her this soft, warm smile in return. Hmm.

So then we're alone. The tension immediately begins to swell, so heavy it clogs my airway. I want to choke out an excuse to leave too, but he'll see through it. So we continue toward the school entrance together, where the security officers must've been informed of our departure, because they don't give us flack for leaving. The September heat bakes the asphalt, reflecting blindingly off of a sea of car hoods.

I can't read Caleb's energy. I used to be able to tell what he was thinking and feeling with a glance, but he's gotten better at hiding his emotions. Or I just . . . don't know him like I used to.

"You don't have to walk me to my car," I say when I realize he's tagging along with me into the parking lot.

He blinks down at me in surprise. "Huh?"

"You're parked in the first row," I tell him, quickening my pace in an attempt to leave him behind. "You always come to school a half hour early, right?"

"I . . . How would you know?" he demands. He keeps up with my strides without issue, being half leg.

Because it's you. "I always see your car in the front row. Only way you could get one of those spots is if you come early."

He sighs. But I really don't want him to accompany me to my car, because . . . well, he'll *see* my car. With all the drive-through bags, empty water bottles, wrappers, and mountains of clothes, he'd set the whole thing ablaze. Then drench us both in hand sanitizer.

I say, "Bye."

It's rude, but that's the only thing he'll respond to. Sure enough, Caleb clenches his fists, then spins around and storms back to the front row.

Finally, I arrive at my car. I drop into the driver's seat and insert the key, then crank, crossing my fingers. She groans, gasps, then comes to life with a mechanical sob of pain. Immediately, my dashboard lights up like the Las Vegas strip. My oil-pressure, engine-warning, tire-pressure, low-fuel, and airbag warning lights each vie for attention.

"I'll sneak home for money soon, Morgana," I mumble, patting the steering wheel.

Morgana makes a tortured *clunk* noise as I shift her into reverse. She's running low on whatever dark magic keeps her from spontaneously combusting.

As my car crawls backward, my phone buzzes. Quickly, I jam the gear into park to check who it is. Has Brooke finally answered my texts? It's been over a week, and she's been avoiding me at school, so I haven't been able to corner her. Ever since she moved in with her dad, she's been flighty about responding. I've been lenient, but come on. It's been over a year, and she still can't make time to hang out with me? We suffered through our childhoods together, cursing our fathers for leaving us with That Bitch. That has to mean something.

It's not Brooke. That Bitch is calling, presumably because Adams told her what I did and she wants to tell me how much she regrets birthing me.

I swipe away her call.

Now, where to go? Alice will be in school for a few hours, and I avoid going over to her house too often, because her parents ask questions (they're the nosy types). Driving around aimlessly isn't ideal with Morgana on her deathbed, and I've been banned from the soccer field, so I can't jump the gate until everyone's gone.

My next instinct is one I've tried kicking for years, but always remains, stubborn and persistent, in the back of my head.

Caleb's place.

Ugh. Why is it that every time I don't know where to go, he comes to mind?

I remember his expression from earlier. How enamored he was with the new girl. How soft his smile was. The barest hint of peachy pink in his face as he looked at her . . .

Oh. *Juliet.* Maybe I could get to know her better. Since she's new, she's not automatically wary of me, unlike most people. Whenever someone hears my name, their first thought tends to be, *There's the girl who causes problems and fights anyone who looks at her the wrong way.* Which is extremely untrue. Mostly.

Most people are guarded around me, and my run-in with the cops last year when my mom called them to hunt me down didn't help. Maybe I could've made a case against her for being the Fucking Worst, but as far as the police could tell, I was well provided for—a roof over my head, a mother who worried, plentiful food and resources. To them, I was just another runaway brat.

I ran again a few weeks later, when I couldn't stand to look at her smoky makeup and smell her nauseating perfume anymore. Thankfully, she hasn't called the cops again. Maybe she's realizing her life is exponentially easier without me in it, as she always claimed it would be.

It's rare I make friends around here, let alone cute ones. It's been a year since I've dated anyone, too, mostly because whoever said *yes* usually only did it to know what it was like to date someone with my reputation. It must not have been as thrilling as they'd assumed, because they all broke up with me after a few months.

The "concrete walls higher than the Eiffel Tower" issue doesn't help.

Juliet doesn't seem like the type of person who'd mind. I've seen her around school. She wasn't lying when she said she's a runner. The reason I've noticed her outside of class is because she's constantly jogging in the hall, like she's running late. It's earned snickers from people, but she either doesn't notice or doesn't care.

When the teacher introduced her in English . . . whew. I was instantly attracted to her. Her flawless makeup, her intense eyes, the golden shimmer of her body glitter. I wasn't lying when I said I've been meaning to introduce myself but could never catch up to her once she beelined from the classroom. She's comically fast, considering how short her legs are. Now, how could I get her number without waiting in the parking lot for her to leave school like some kind of creep . . . ?

Suddenly, a memory comes reeling back to me.

I'll text you later, Caleb!

Right. I can get it from him! Hoping he hasn't left the parking lot, I fling myself out of my car and sprint through the rows of vehicles gridded before me, making a break for the front lanes. The sun hammers my head, sizzling against the asphalt, and I remain silently grateful that I didn't apply makeup this morning.

A few rows ahead, I see him. Hands positioned at ten and two, posture straight, looking intently at the road like he's taking his driving test. "Wait!" I shout, needling myself through two cars. "I *need Juliet's number!*"

I fling myself into the middle of the lane in front of him, and

Caleb slams on his brakes in horror. His hood comes within two inches of my waist. He stares at me, fury contorting his otherwise soft facial features. I give him a weak smile.

He slams his car into park, then clambers out with all the grace of a wounded giraffe. "What the *hell*?" he snarls, stomping up to me. "I could've hit you if I wasn't paying attention!"

"But you're always paying attention." I take a few subtle steps backward, because I'm close enough to smell whatever oaky, musky lotion he uses. His wavy brown hair, always rumpled in spite of his persnickety personality, shimmers under the sun.

Dammit. What an annoying moment to notice these things.

"Can I have Juliet's number?" I ask.

Caleb stares at me. "What."

"I would like to obtain Juliet's number," I clarify.

His jawbone protrudes farther into his skin. "You want to cock-block me," he says flatly.

My mouth nearly falls open. I mean, it was obvious he liked her, but I didn't expect him to outright admit it. "I think she's cute, so I want to talk to her. Is that a problem?"

"Yes! Because . . ." Suddenly, he's squirming with discomfort. "If you start talking to her, I won't stand a chance."

I don't even know how to react to that. What the hell is he talking about?

Caleb looks like he wants to dive into his car and drive away, but he holds firm. "Whenever I'm interested in someone, you fly in like this majestic fucking eagle and take them away," he says, anger brimming in his voice. "They forget about me, and by the time you break up, they aren't talking to me anymore."

He has to be joking. "Since when have I stolen anyone from you?" I demand.

"Chris McNamara. Tessa Vasquez. Ariel Moreno. Derek Wheeler."

Damn. Receipts locked and loaded. Sure, I dated those people. I can faintly recall seeing Caleb around them, maybe even having a soft glow about him while they were talking. Maybe it's even true I remember Caleb *interacting* with them more than I remember . . . them. But that doesn't mean . . .

No. Nope. He's wrong. "So, you had feelings for these people that you didn't act on," I say, my voice tightening. "And during your hesitation, I asked these people out. Yet somehow I stole them from you?"

Caleb tousles his hair further, his face crunched with irritation. "It feels intentional," he mutters. "Whenever I get close to someone, you appear. Two days later, you're dating them. They lose interest in me because you're this fun, exciting person, and I'm . . ." His shoulders flex with a sigh. "Look, it's fine that you make moves faster than me. But sometimes it feels like you're making moves quickly . . . *because* of me."

My stomach churns, and every beat of my heart aches. How could he accuse me of taking potential partners from him *intentionally*? "I'm not," I say, though my voice is frail. "I wouldn't. I've ruined . . ."

I've ruined your life enough as it is.

I slam my teeth on my tongue, biting the words back. Maybe I should walk away and say, "Go get her, tiger." But he's wrong. And I like Juliet. Why should I forfeit a potential relationship because he's twisting situations around to meet his narrative? I know he's used to me screwing his life up, but that's not the case here.

How do we fix this? I know it's rare that he develops feelings for people (his sexuality is something he's struggled to label), but it's also rare for me to find someone who doesn't think they know me before they've even met me. With it being senior year, and increasingly unlikely that Mom will help me pay for college, my chances of finding people who might like me for *me* are dwindling.

I don't want to sacrifice getting to know Juliet. What can we do that'll give us both the opportunity to win Juliet over without me necessarily "stealing" her because I'm faster to develop feelings and ask people out? I guess the only way would be . . .

"She decides," I say tersely.

Caleb blinks at me, absorbing this. "What?"

"We both want to be friends with her, right?"

"I . . . Yes." He's looking more suspicious by the moment.

"So let's do that," I suggest, breaking my gaze away from his face before he starts griping and groaning. "We hang out with her separately and see if she develops feelings. If she does . . . maybe whoever she kisses first gets to ask her out."

I can almost feel the ick radiating off Caleb. I don't like the way the words taste, but how else do we make this fair?

"But that's just . . ." Caleb makes several disgruntled noises. "That's *wrong*. Turning someone's feelings into a game. What will you do if she's straight? Dump her as a friend?"

I purse my lips. Does he really think I'm that big of an asshole? Maybe he notices my face darken, because he scratches his pale neck and mutters, "It's been four years. How do I know you're the same person?"

Whatever. "We both think she's cute, and we want to get to know her," I say sharply. "Doing it like this is the fairest way of figuring out if she'd be interested in one of us."

Caleb paces in front of his car, running his fingers along his slender lips, thinking a little too hard, like always. After several tedious seconds, resolution shapes his features. "If it's the only way I'll stand a chance, fine," he says irritably. "Whoever Juliet kisses first, on the *lips*, can ask her out. And *she* has to initiate it."

He holds his hand out to make it official. His total seriousness makes my frustration waver, replacing it with amusement. I shake his palm with excessive force, smile, and say, "May the best bi win."

CALEB

I feel like I've made a pact with the devil.

Emma has this little smile as she shakes my hand and seals the deal on our . . . ugh. *Competition.* It seems gross, but I'm tired of losing to her, and Juliet is the first person I've been actively interested in for months. If agreeing to this tomfoolery allows me to take my time getting to know her without immediately losing her to Emma's charisma, I'll take it.

"So," she says, sweeping her strawberry blond hair over her shoulder. "About that number."

I almost forgot Juliet's number was the whole reason Emma had hurled herself in front of my car. "What about it?" I ask coolly.

"It'd be swell if you gave it to me." She flutters her lashes at me, maintaining her smile like it's going to win me over the way it used to.

"Good luck," I tell her, swinging open my driver's door.

"Wait!" Her eyes shimmer with anguish. "If it's a competition, we should both begin at the starting line, right?"

Like she hasn't started every other "competition" for people with a hundred-foot head start. "I earned her number, so you can too," I snip, ducking into my car and promptly ramming my forehead into the doorframe. *Ow.*

"You okay?" she asks, brows arching.

I'm *dandy*. I slam the door and shift into drive, waiting for Emma to step aside. She merely stands there, hands clasped in prayer formation, mouthing, *Please*. I lower the window, and shout, "I'm *not* giving you Juliet's number!"

Suddenly, she leaps forward, hoisting herself onto the hood of my car. "I'm suspended for the rest of the week!" she cries out, though I barely hear her through the steam spewing from my ears. "You get to see her Thursday and Friday. The least you can do is give me her number!"

I park and hurl myself out of the driver's seat, circling around to the hood.

"You changed your mind!" she says brightly, the fool. Fiery annoyance burns so thick in my blood, I feel it raising my body temperature.

"Five," I say, tapping my foot. "Four. Three."

Emma's eyes expand into little colorful moons. "You wouldn't."

"Two. One."

So be it, then. I seize her ankles, hoisting her toward the front of the hood. "Hey!" she croaks, and then I've got her around the waist, and I'm hoisting her over my shoulder. *"Caleb! It's just a number!"*

"And you can get it without stealing it from *me*!" I yell, slamming her onto her feet. She staggers back, disoriented, her face a vibrant pink hue.

"But if I wait until Monday, you'll have days to text her!" Emma advances on me, clearly noticing my phone in my front pocket. I snatch her extended wrists before she can grab at it. "I thought you were a rule follower! Caleb, please!"

She twists her wrists free, then jams her whole hand into my pocket and grabs . . .

The wrong fucking object.

"*Ah!*" she shrieks.

"*Ah!*" I shriek back, and I shove her instinctively, my heart wailing for a fire extinguisher, my whole body turning crimson. Her feet get tangled under her, and she falls, hitting the street. I . . .

Didn't mean to push her that hard.

"Sorry," she says feebly from her hands and knees, and I realize she's broken into a tremble. "I didn't mean . . . I'm such a piece of . . ."

Seeing her down there is enough to drive whatever just happened from my head. I kneel beside her and grip her wrists, flipping them. They're scratched up, and blood trickles into the lines of her palms. Her face is concentrated downward, but I'm close enough to see her eyes sparkling with tears.

"I didn't mean to," she whispers.

"I know," I say, despite my flustered vexation. I crawl into my car, grabbing a wipe, ointment, bandages, tape, and scissors from the first aid kit in my glove box. I sit cross-legged on the searing hot street next to Emma, tugging her hands into my lap.

"You should go," she says, squeezing her eyes shut as I wipe grains from the street off her hands.

"In a minute." So after all of that, she's giving up? I should be relieved that I've won this battle and don't have to sacrifice Juliet's number, but I'm still reliving the image of her colliding with the street. "Sorry for shoving you," I murmur.

"Don't apologize," she says quickly. "I just, like, assaulted you—"

"It was an accident."

Emma groans with embarrassment, which is . . . honestly entertaining. In all the years I've known her, she's never been one to get flustered or emotional. Now, out of nowhere, I'm seeing both of those sides of her.

I smooth ointment into her palms with my thumb, then wrap her hands in bandages and secure them with tape. "Should be healed in a couple days," I tell her.

Her mouth twitches, and I wonder if she almost smiled. "It's just like you to have all this shit stashed in your car."

"I like being prepared!" I say, huffing, and I climb to my feet, offering my hand. She examines it a moment too long before reaching up, allowing me to hoist her to her feet.

Emma looks like she's about to tell me something, but then, "Oh! What are you two still doing here?"

The voice causes us to whirl around. Juliet is ambling up the parking lot sidewalk, her physics textbook tucked under her arm.

Emma looks at me. Then at her bandaged palms. Then at Juliet. Not that it ever went away, but the tension between us suddenly heightens tenfold. She plasters an impish smile onto her face, steps forward, and says, "Hey, Juliet! Can I have your number?"

xoxo

I'm still grumbling when I get home. I got involved in a fight, got sent home, then the *Emma* thing, then I committed to a ridiculous competition for someone's heart, and on top of it all, my dad left me on read. *Again.*

I park in the complex lot, then climb the stairs to apartment 304, scowling.

It's a neat little space. "Neat" mostly thanks to me, since our precarious situation will spiral into disorderliness if I don't keep everything tidy. Beyond the entryway lies a split room—the left half being a living room equipped with a tattered couch and TV, and the right half being a kitchen just wide enough for one person. Down the hall rests two bedrooms and a bathroom Mom and I share.

She's not one for hominess, so I took it upon myself to hang scenic artwork on the walls. Paintings of beaches, scraggly mountaintops, sand dunes. We can't afford the time to go on vacation, considering Mom can barely take a day off each week if we want to scrape by with the rent. But having these paintings gives the apartment personality. And maybe hope that one day, we can visit these places.

Maybe we'd get closer to that dream if she stopped paying me a weekly allowance for everything, like grocery shopping, apartment cleaning, fixing up her car. I'm happy to do it—I *like* keeping things running smoothly—but she insists I'm basically working a full-time job, and the least she can do is reward me.

I just cleaned on Sunday, but I'm agitated. I need to do something with my hands. So I decide to clean again.

I whip out my rubber gloves, organize my supplies, and get to work. Mom's bedroom door is closed, which means she's either sleeping before her shift or getting ready for it. I hand-wash the dishes lingering in the sink, bleach the counters, scrub the stovetop and microwave, then retrieve our new WetJet (this is its first time touching the floor, which is kind of thrilling).

As I work on making the tiles sparkle, I get to thinking. If I'm going to . . . ugh, *win Juliet over* . . . I should plot. Try to organize moments when we'll be alone without Emma's interference. Emma is always two steps ahead of me in wooing people, so I should take advantage of the time I have while she's suspended.

My phone chirps. Immediately, I wrench it out, hoping it's my dad. He said he'd be better about communication, and he technically *has* been over the last year. It used to be I might go months without hearing from him, despite my best efforts to draw a simple *hey, kid* out of him. But since he committed to being more present in my life, he's been better about responding. It's been about a week since I invited him out to dinner.

It's just Jas answering my text.

I'll give Dad until tomorrow morning before following up. I'd hate to annoy him if he's just figuring out his work schedule or something.

Anyway. Maybe I'll ask Juliet to study with me at the library after school tomorrow. That shouldn't be weird, right? I don't know what she'd say if I suddenly invited her to my apartment when we've just met. And while we're studying, I'll find subtle ways to ask her about herself—her brother, parents, old school.

I store the mop in the closet and wash my hands, sighing. Hating that I can still feel the weight of Emma's scraped palms in mine.

A creaking noise approaches from behind, and I cock my head to find Mom ambling through the living room, dressed in work attire—a tank top that exposes her pearly white shoulders, form-fitting shorts, and nonslip sneakers. Giant hoops dangle from her ears, and her dark curls are scooped into a high ponytail.

"Morning, hon," she says, despite the fact that it's one o'clock. Her shifts usually start in the afternoon and end late at night, so her circadian rhythm's a little off. "Why are you home early? Did you get kicked out of school?"

She says it playfully. Little does she know. "I got sent home for getting into a fight," I say.

When the punch line doesn't come, her amusement drops, and she strides toward me, gripping my face between her excessively long nails and pulling it down to get a good look. "Where did you get hit?" she demands.

"I didn't," I say, squirming free of her clutch. "It was some ass-hole picking on the new girl. I stepped in, and he started swinging."

Mom claps my shoulder, her pale blue eyes bursting with pride. "Good for you, standing up for someone. That's my sweet little boy."

"Don't be gross about it," I mutter, though I can't hide my smile.

It's not often we get to hang out. She's home early in the day, sleeping or preparing for her shifts, and isn't around for long after I finish school.

"The asshole was punished?" she asks sternly.

"Suspended, yeah. I got sent home to 'cool off.'" I wish I were able to go to class, but I won't tell her that. She'd call me a loser and flick my forehead. "I wish I could've calmed everyone down, but then Emma punched him, so it was a lost cause—"

"Emma?" Mom's face brightens with intrigue. "You don't mean *the* Emma?"

I've made a grave mistake. I grimace, and her face splits into a luminescent grin.

"Tell me everything."

"There's nothing to say." I sigh, squirming past her in the kitchen entryway and continuing into the living room. I flop onto the couch and snag my laptop from the coffee table, flinging it open next to my textbook. Hoping she gets the message.

Either it sails over her curly ponytail or she purposefully swats it away, because she sits beside me, eyes glued to my face. "Tell me you're talking again," she pleads, her priorities clearly shifting far away from my educational success.

"Nope." My voice is sharp enough that her eyebrow arches. "She's just interested in the same girl I like. We're in . . . competition."

Blech. It sounds even worse when I say it out loud.

"We're not friends," I continue, hoping to hammer in the message. Every time I've accidentally mentioned Emma around her, I've regretted it. Four years ago, she seemed just as heartbroken as me when I told her Emma had cut me out of her life.

Mom analyzes me, like she's seeking lies in my body language. She won't find anything. There's no way I'd open myself to Emma again after what she did to me in eighth grade. I took enough emotional damage back then, and letting her in again would give her full access to the scars on my heart.

"Okay." Mom smooths a hand over my knee, though the lines in her forehead tell me she's not convinced. "We'll talk later. I'm heading in early to help set up for the night."

"I hope you have an easy shift," I say, forcing a smile.

She returns it, and though I used to think she couldn't fake them, I'm realizing more and more that she's probably just better at hiding it. She drags me sideways by my shirt so she can kiss my temple, then rises, heading to the door and snagging her purse.

Then she's gone, leaving me with too many thoughts and nobody to vent them to.

Emma

I sit tucked in my car, knees resting on the steering wheel, ass still parked in the student lot. I've been staring at Juliet's number, wondering what my first message should be. I've typed several variations, overthought all of them, and deleted them. Being cool and casual is one of my strengths, so why am I hung up on this?

But the stakes are high. Caleb is interested in Juliet too, and he'll give this his all. When he's done scrubbing his walls clean, he'll probably write out a meticulous, bulleted plan for winning Juliet's heart. Will he pull ahead if I wing it? I'm not a "details" person—will it feel forced if I try planning something?

My phone buzzes.

ALICE

Where are you staying tonight?

Ah. The dreaded question I'm usually good at dodging. **Home,** I lie, and send it. I'm not mentally fortified enough to deal with that. I'm suspended for the week, and though Mom works weird hours at her salon, I'll definitely have a moment to slip home, do laundry, and take a shower to avoid dirtying up Alice's bathroom.

Mom's face flashes before me. Her amused eyes, scolding tone, smug smirk.

Apologize and maybe I'll lend you money.

Only when I can lick Satan's frozen icicle dick.

Running away is the best thing I could've done for her miserable life. I'm sure she's elated, having the house to herself now that Brooke's moved out. I'm pretty sure Brooke's own insistence and worry was the reason she called the cops on me the first time.

ALICE

Are you actually going home

I tap **yep** and send it. My hands still sting from their kiss with the street. I hate it. The pain isn't bad, but every itch reminds me of who wrapped them. He had no reason to do that, especially after I sat on his car and accidentally . . . you know. But that's just who he is, because Caleb Daniels never changes.

My mind races back to the cafeteria, when he towered over Ian Summers yet somehow looked smaller. The way he forced every wobbly word out of his mouth during the confrontation. The way that, despite the apprehension sketched in his pale eyes, he didn't back down.

Maybe he'd changed a little.

I don't want to stick around for whenever school lets out, so I crank my car on. The engine doesn't explode—a sign of good fortune. I lug it into the city, past the stop-and-go traffic, the rectangular bank buildings that don't need to be that tall, the bustling shopping center and plazas. Morgana chugs under me like a train, and what was once a subtle vibration when I pressed my brakes is becoming noisy thunder.

I finally arrive at Mayberry State Park—a vast wooded area carved up by bike trails, playgrounds, and meandering streams and rivers. There aren't nearly as many cars as usual, maybe because it's a workday. Summer is still in full swing (piss off, September), so the leaves are solidly green or burnt brown. But it's still the serene place that comes to my rescue whenever I don't know where to go, so I won't complain about its mediocre state.

As I climb out of the car with my backpack, I yank my socks high up my ankles. A few months ago, I'd had an unfortunate run-in with that hussy poison ivy, who had me crawling home for calamine lotion and other remedies.

Caleb's stern voice pierces my head. *Where's your bug spray? What about sunscreen? You can still get burned through the leaves.*

I scowl, trekking into the woods across the carefully curated pathways. Over the years, I've managed to stifle his concerned voice into a low, barely noticeable hum. Sometimes it comes back in full force, sudden and unexpected, asking me to think things through. Even though it's been years, I can never fully get rid of him.

After following a maze of pathways I'd memorized, I find my getaway spot. The trees provide a fluttering, spotty canopy, the branches scraping together in a soothing white noise that joins the bubbling rush of the river. A few rocks are stacked at the bank, propped perfectly so I can sit cradled among them, facing the water, and draw my soccer ball into my lap so I can bounce it between my knees.

I make a mental note to get a soap bar when I go home. Maybe I can bathe out here. I rarely run into anyone in this neck of the woods. Though, knowing my luck, a family of five would come skipping through with picnic baskets and innocence right as I'm scrubbing my ass crack.

Hygiene has been my biggest frustration with being a runaway. Last night, I showered and brushed my teeth at Alice's, but I saw her mother's bewildered look when I shuffled out of the bathroom. There're always the locker room showers at school, but finding time to sneak there with supplies is a hassle, especially with the after-school activities and teams shuffling in and out.

I flip my phone, grimacing. So. Juliet. I should . . . plan something. Strategize ways to develop our relationship casually but quickly enough that Caleb doesn't instantly win her over. And he's fully capable.

Honestly, how could anyone not fall for him? He's kindhearted, responsible, sweet, and he'll put you first, *always*. Maybe he's bossy and a stickler for rules, and maybe he's clunky because he can barely operate his long limbs, and maybe he's intimidating because he slinks around like an axe murderer (because of the limb thing), and maybe his voice belongs to a thirty-year-old man. But he's perfect boyfriend material. His eyes are glinting swimming pools, his face invitingly soft, his smile warm. He even moisturizes. How many high school boys *do that*?

But, no, why am I thinking about him like this? I should be focused on Juliet, the girl I actually stand a chance with. Someone whose life I didn't fuck to oblivion back when I was a little brat. So first I pursue friendship with her, and if she indicates any interest in me beyond that . . . flirtation can commence.

So. How does one become friends with a person?

I knead my knuckles into my forehead, groaning. Alice Yang is my only friend, who I met on the middle school soccer team. We were both talented enough to play travel, but my mom didn't want to spend the money, and Alice's passion mostly rested in gaming. I was her favorite forward, she my favorite goalie. We started hanging out after a dicey game, in which the other team was playing dirty and we were ejected with red cards for kicking the shins of the girls roughing us up.

"Bonding through acts of violence" probably isn't an option with Juliet.

Screw it. I pull Juliet's number up, thumb out a message, and send it without deliberation. Thinking things through isn't my forte, so I'll do what I know best. Act cool and collected. **Hey Juliet! How are you doing after the shit show today?**

I wait, watching water bubble and froth against the stones jutting out of the riverbed, my soccer ball sitting still in my lap.

My phone vibrates. My heart does a shimmy of terror.

JULIET

Hey!! Thanks for checking on me :) Just crying on the bedroom floor. How's your knee after making contact with
Ian's ball sack?

I laugh, startled. I guess I didn't expect a person like Juliet to willingly type the words *ball sack*. **Knee is great,** I respond. **I'm proud of it for ensuring that Ian can't produce demon spawn.**

Juliet responds with five too many laughing emojis. **The world doesn't need more Ians,** she texts. **Thanks for your services.**

She has my kind of humor. I realize I'm rocking back and forth like some excited toddler, which is embarrassing enough to color my cheeks despite being alone. **Why are you crying? Can I help?**

I figured she was kidding, but her next text is **No, but thanks! I'll dry up eventually :)**

Hmm. I'm afraid of scaring her off by prying for more details, so I return to the previous conversation. **Be careful around Ian. He's a queerphobe. So if you're openly anything-that-isn't-straight-and-cis, he'll probably say some ignorant shit.**

My phone is quiet for a couple of minutes. My heart pounds in my temples, nearly drowning out the gurgling of the river. Maybe I took it too far?

Her text lights my screen. **Good to know, thanks!**

Well, that makes sense. It's not like she'll suddenly divulge her sexuality to me because I mentioned the word *queer*. Knowing my luck, she's probably straight, but I won't give up the idea of romancing her until she's making out with Caleb directly before my eyeballs.

Thankfully, the conversation doesn't peter out. I ask her more about herself, why she moved senior year. Apparently her mother was promoted to regional sales manager of a bank downtown and moved her family to be closer to her job. Juliet left a group of friends behind but doesn't go into detail about who they are or if she had any partners.

She asks about me too. I barely scratch the surface because that's what I'm used to. I live with my mom, I don't know who my dad is, and I have a half sister who moved in with her dad last year. Other than that . . . there's nothing worth sharing. To my surprise, Juliet recognizes Brooke's name—they're in the same Japanese III class.

Since when has Brooke been taking Japanese?

My phone is taking its last dying gasps, so I bid Juliet farewell. It's been a long time—years, actually—since I've gotten that swooping, butterfly feeling in my stomach. The last time . . . Well, I hope this won't end the same way.

I stuff my ball into my backpack and replace it with a notebook to jot down random reasons why physical violence isn't the answer (even if it's often the most effective). Scrap paper will do until I can visit the library to type out a double-spaced essay that I can hand to VP Adams.

Suddenly, I hear a shuffling noise, and my back pricks upright. Footsteps. I lurch to my feet and grip my backpack, preparing to use it as a melee weapon.

Then the figure steps through the slender trees concealing my hiding spot.

It's Brooke.

"So you do still come out here," she mutters, her words only faintly carrying over the bubbling stream. The trees cast little spotlights on her sandy skin, and her copper curls spill over a navy blue scarf despite the searing heat of the day. Looking at us side by side, most people probably wouldn't assume we share a parent. Different features aside, everything about her is more . . . refined. Smooth, glossy hair as golden brown as her eyes, high cheekbones, a full figure, a calming atmosphere. Then they look at me, the one with the wild eyes and ratty hair and all the curves of a prepubescent boy.

"Sister," I greet, my backpack dropping to the soil.

She ambles into my little clearing, stopping before one of the trees to my left. She scratches her nail against the smooth bark, brows pressed with a frown. "Mom told me you got suspended," she mumbles.

"She's still calling you to complain about me?" I ask, and though I try to sound amused, my voice is weak. When we were kids, Brooke was always on the receiving end of Mom's complaints, regardless of what they concerned (usually me). Probably because she never yelled back, rolled her eyes, or walked away. She took Mom's animosity in silence, which was just how that woman liked it. Before I packed my car up and ran the second time, I frequently heard her incensed voice through the walls of the house when she called Brooke to yell about something (again, usually me).

"You should stop doing things like this," Brooke says, focused too intently on the tree bark under her finger.

"Why do you answer her calls?" I ask, ignoring her.

Brooke's eyes flash with brief anger. "She has to let off steam somehow, right?"

"Let her scream at the empty house," I snap. "You shouldn't put up with her."

She merely grimaces, shifting around in agitation. I'm about to ask what her issue is, but then, "Whatever. Just stop riling her up."

Like my very existence doesn't rile her up. Like she isn't on the brink of a meltdown every time I breathe too loudly or leave my clothes in the dryer too long or don't properly close the jar of peanut butter. "So I should be a Goody Two-shoes who puts up with her bullshit?" I ask coolly, redirecting my attention to the swirling water.

The air ices up around her. It's an unnecessary dig, but I can't help it. Brooke ignores my texts, rejects my recent requests to hang out, but decides to come to the woods to nag me? Why does she want to be involved with Mom anymore, anyway? When we were younger, we used to fantasize about the day we'd finally move out. We would get an apartment and work full-time to support ourselves. We'd have a balcony and our own bathrooms, and we'd split the chores.

Then, two years ago, her dad came back into the picture. He'd always been in the periphery of our lives, popping in every so often while he struggled to get his life together. When he finally had things worked out, he became the kind of dad we'd daydreamed of having. A man who ruffled her hair, took her out for food, helped her with homework, sneezed remarkably loudly. Someone who wanted to be . . . involved.

Brooke's dad is nice. Before she moved out, he'd stop by the house on occasion. He'd smile at me, pat my head, ask how I was. He even invited me to dinner once.

But I'm not his kid. I don't blame him for keeping things surface level, especially considering I've always been a pain known for being a dick to authority figures. If there was any chance of him wanting to know me in an "adopt one kid, get one free" deal, I ruined that by being . . . well. Me.

"I'm not around to help anymore," Brooke says suddenly. I don't turn to her, but she sounds more solemn than angry. "At least when you got suspended before, I could be there to cool her down or help you clean up your mess. So all I'm asking is . . . remember that the things you do have consequences."

I'm sure it's coming from a place of concern, but I hate how stern she says it, as if she's my older sister rather than the other way around. Hearing all of this is just another reminder of how shitty I am at everything. Being a girlfriend. A best friend. A sister.

I leave her unanswered, giving her a taste of what she's been doing to me more recently. When I turn around, she's gone.

I sit by the creek for hours, moving to my car only when my butt bones are about to explode with pain from submitting them to a stone seat. While in Morgana's clutch, I watch the day melt away. Eventually, the sun is low enough, I can barely see into the trees. People filter out of the parking lot until I'm the final vehicle remaining, and the world is a velvety royal blue—the kind at dusk. Finally, I nudge Morgana back onto the city streets. She sobs all the way to my next destination.

It's an old-fashioned ranch house in a suburb. The cityscape clutches the horizon, looming over the neighborhoods, its lights clogging up the night sky. They haven't closed their shades yet, so as I pull up to the curb on the opposite side of the street, I can see them milling about inside. Brooke is carrying dishes to the sink while her dad wipes the table. They're grinning and appear midconversation.

I wonder if they cooked together. Brooke's the more talented one between the two of us. Maybe they'll watch a movie tonight. Or sit in the living room silently while Brooke completes homework and her father reads a book.

Ten minutes later, Brooke trails around the house and closes the blinds, cutting off my line of sight. My pathway into their lives.

I lean my chair back, snatch my pillow and quilted blanket, and get cozy. The great thing about summer (the only great thing, mind you) is that the nights are mild but still warm. Escaping the house is more harrowing in winter, when there aren't enough blankets in the world to shield me from its arctic chills.

I set my alarm to make sure I'll be up before Brooke's dad commutes to work. No way will I let them catch me snoozing outside their house.

I crack my windows, allowing the distant white noise of the city to lull me asleep.

CALEB

BACK THEN

The next kick wrenched the breath from Caleb's lungs. He sniffled, curling his fists into the wood chips as the boys snickered. The afternoon sun was blazing hot, singeing his nose red. The after-school program supervisors stood near the side doors to the redbrick building, chatting, paying no attention to the playground.

"Know what my mom said?" the ringleader of the fourth graders asked, stomping on Caleb's scrawny chest. "She told her friends that your mom is a *whore*."

The three boys burst into laughter again. Caleb wanted to shout at them—to explain that Mom always said you should love your body and wear what makes you happy and comfortable. Maybe people wouldn't say such nasty things about her if they knew that.

But the words iced in his throat, allowing nothing but short, raspy breaths.

"I bet she doesn't even know who your dad is," the boy said snidely. "How many ugly guys does she bring home every week?"

Caleb couldn't conjure a response, but it didn't matter. Suddenly, there was a loud, squeaky roar that sounded like a battle cry. The boy thinning the air in Caleb's lungs looked over in confusion.

Just in time to get walloped in the face by a bulky teal backpack.

"*Suck an ass!*" a shrill voice yelled, and Caleb gasped at the vulgarity, blinking through his blurry eyes. It was a girl from his second-grade class with tangled reddish-blond hair, ferocious eyes, and skin almost as pale as his. Emma Jones.

"Who's this brat?" the boy snarled, and Emma screamed again, whirling her backpack around and striking him a second time. As the boy stumbled, Emma seized a soccer ball from her bag, railing one bully in the face with it. The third boy pounced, but Emma kicked his shin, then spun around like a whirlpool, building momentum to smash his head with her backpack.

"*Bunch of ugly jerks!*" she bellowed.

If anything could get a supervisor's attention, it was a child screeching at maximum volume. Immediately, they rushed over. Caleb could only stare, frozen, as the boys collected themselves and turned on Emma. Though she was fierce and fought valiantly, she was still only a second grader, and the bullies were much bigger than her. The ringleader reeled back and punched her so hard across the face that she hit the wood chips. They were starting to kick at her by the time the supervisors finally arrived to yank them apart.

"Enough!" one barked. "What's going on?"

"She started it!" the ringleader cried out, whimpering. He pointed at his nose, which had been scratched by Emma's backpack zipper.

The woman's face was marred with a stern scowl. "Principal's office. *Now.*"

Caleb remained still, his body aching from blows. The boys' words reverberated through his head, itching his brain. Everyone was always saying nasty things about Mom and her breezy, comfortable clothes—even the adults. He *hated* it.

A shadow fell over Caleb, eclipsing the sun's scorching heat. Emma stood beside him, her hand outstretched, wood chips tangled in her hair. Her cheekbone was puffing up. "Come on," she said, wiggling her fingers.

Caleb didn't know what to say. Probably *thank you* would've been a good start. But he couldn't manage the words past the knot in his throat.

Emma grabbed his limp arm and pulled, peeling Caleb's back off the ground. "Your face is wet," she observed. Before Caleb could say something like *Tears are always wet,* Emma pulled a rag from her backpack and folded it, smearing it across his cheeks. "There."

Caleb's eyes were already moistening again. "Why . . . do you have that?" he croaked.

Emma stuffed the towel into her backpack. "To wipe my soccer ball after practice."

Caleb retched. Why would she use it on his *face*?

They followed the trio of fourth graders to the main office, Emma stomping the whole way, Caleb tiptoeing in the hopes that everyone might forget he was there. When they stepped through the doors, though, and saw Principal Cohen chatting with the secretary, emotion reeled in Caleb's chest. Suddenly, he was sobbing again.

"That loser's crying again?" one of the fourth graders muttered.

Emma made a guttural growling noise, and the boy yelped, ducking behind his ringleader. "Okay, but why *are* you crying?" she whispered, turning to Caleb. There were still wood chips in her hair. Caleb wondered if she would mind if he plucked them out. "They aren't hitting you anymore."

Caleb's chest heaved with quick, stuttering gasps. "Don't want to get into trouble . . ."

Emma tilted her head, looking at Caleb like he was a thousand-piece puzzle that she didn't know where to start with. She reached into her backpack, which made Caleb inch away. She wasn't getting that dirty rag again, right?

Emma pulled out a teal water bottle. Caleb wondered if it was her favorite color. "Drink it," she said. "You'll cry all the water out of your body and shrivel up into a pile of bones."

"Did you . . . drink out of it?" Caleb asked hesitantly.

Emma blinked her green-brown eyes and said, "No."

Hesitantly, Caleb flipped the lid and swallowed gulps of lukewarm water.

"Not today, at least," Emma said. "It's been in my backpack for a week."

Nausea rolled in Caleb's stomach, and he threw the bottle back at her. She had this little smile. Was she joking, maybe? Either way, it worked, because suddenly, Caleb could breathe again, and water stopped tumbling down his face.

The supervisor spoke to the principal, who talked to everyone individually in his office. When it was his turn, Caleb managed to explain what had happened—that the fourth graders pushed him around, and Emma . . .

Emma saved him.

She got suspended anyway. So did the bullies, who muttered that Caleb would get his stitches. Their parents picked them up from the office, each of them with choice words for the principal. Then it was just Emma, Caleb, and the secretary clicking on her computer. Caleb rocked in his chair, wondering what to say, until he realized Emma was poking at a bloody scratch on her knee. She must've gotten it when she fell.

Caleb smeared an arm over his puffy eyes, then pried open his backpack. He gathered hand sanitizer, a wet wipe, and a Band-Aid from the mini first aid kit he'd forced his mom to buy last year so he could keep it in his front pocket.

Emma watched with bewilderment. "What's that stuff for?"

"Emergencies," Caleb said with a hint of pride. Mom had told him it was *overkill*. Yet here he was, perfectly prepared. So take that, Mom. He knelt on the multicolored carpet in front of Emma's chair, examining the scratches. Then, after rubbing hand sanitizer into his palms, he used the wet wipe to dab the wound.

"You got weirded out by my water, but now you're touching my blood?" Emma asked, wincing as Caleb tapped sanitizer to her scratch, then smoothed the Band-Aid overtop it.

"You don't want it to get infected," Caleb said, wagging his finger.

"Oh. Okay."

Caleb washed his hands in the bathroom (blood was still gross), then hobbled to his seat and sat down. Emma was poking at the Band-Aid like she'd never seen one. Before he could tell her to stop, she spoke up.

"Why are you here today? I don't usually see you."

"My mom has work." Normally, he took the bus and stayed home with one of the babysitters, but both of them were busy today, so Mom was taking the second half of her shift off to come pick him up. "Um . . . how about you? Are you here every day?"

Emma sighed. "Yep, though my little sister gets to ride the bus. I'm so jealous."

Caleb furrowed his eyebrows. "Why don't you go home with her?"

"Mom doesn't want me home," she said simply. "So I stay here, and she picks me up around dinner."

Caleb squinted at her. She had to be lying, right? Moms weren't usually like that.

The office door opened, and a woman with a blond bob strode in, her makeup bold and colorful, her smile wide and unnaturally bright. "Samantha!" she said cheerily, approaching the secretary. "We have to stop meeting like this."

The secretary laughed nervously. "Good afternoon, Ms. Jones."

"Suspended, then?" The woman looked at Emma, her smile cutting uncomfortably deep into her cheeks. "I can't keep this one out of trouble."

Emma clutched the edges of her seat with white knuckles. What was she so afraid of? Her mother seemed . . . well, normal, for the most part. At least, she looked kind of nice.

"On your feet, missy." Ms. Jones maintained that jovial tone that was a little too loud for the quiet environment. Emma slung her backpack over her shoulder and trudged forward, avoiding Caleb's eyes. "I heard you pulled this poor boy into a fight with you. You should know better than to drag people into your messes, right?" Ms. Jones tapped the top of Emma's head with something that looked like stern fondness. "We want to make sure you don't end up like your father, sweetie. Remember?"

"She was t-trying to help," Caleb croaked.

Ms. Jones faltered, and in a flash, she was standing over him with a charming smile. "You're such a cute little thing," she said, reaching down and pinching his cheek. He was so startled that he couldn't even find the words to ask her not to touch him (something Mom always told him to say to strangers, even when he was trying to be polite). "I'm sure she told you to say that, hmm?"

"I didn't," Emma muttered, and Ms. Jones gave her a menacing look that was so brief, Caleb wondered if he had imagined it. In fact, he was pretty sure he had. Maybe this woman was a little off-putting, but she wasn't yelling at Emma or dragging her around. Maybe Emma was just being dramatic about her. Maybe there was another reason Ms. Jones wanted Emma to stay at the after-school program.

Another young woman stumbled into the office, her dark hair knotted in a sloppy bun and her face smeared with remnants of makeup. She wore a spaghetti-strap top and jean shorts, exposing flowery tattoos that sprinkled her skin. Her blue eyes cut through the room until they landed on Caleb, and she rushed to him.

"Baby, are you okay?" she asked gently, kneeling before him. She combed her acrylic nails through his hair, then stroked a purple splotch on his temple. He resisted the urge to fling himself into her chest and cry again. Why was he being such a loser today? "I'm sorry, honey. When the principal called . . ." She shook her head, sighing. "But I hear a brave girl stepped in to help?"

She turned her admiring gaze to Emma, who instantly looked away, blushing.

"Yes, yes, and her *help* is what landed everybody here," Ms. Jones said with a chuckle, her eyes roving Caleb's mother with a familiar disapproval Caleb had seen on other parents' faces when they looked at her.

"Um." Caleb forced volume into his shaky voice. "Emma got punched . . . She should put ice on it."

"*What?*" Ms. Jones snatched Emma's chin and pulled, revealing her swelling cheekbone. "Good Lord! Let's get home and take a look at that, sweetie. Poor thing. It'll be healed in no time, okay?"

Emma yanked out of her mother's grip, but the woman caught her wrist and began tugging her to the door . . .

"Thanks, Emma," Caleb sputtered out.

Emma glanced between him and his mom, her expression un-identifiable. In a blink, she was gone.

Mom scooped Caleb into a tight hug. "Let's head home," she murmured. "I'll make chicken wraps for dinner, and we'll get ice cream for dessert. Sound good?"

Caleb's eyes brightened. "Okay!"

She pecked his forehead and stood, nodding politely to the secretary. "Have a good night."

The woman watched as they approached the door. "Ms. Daniels?" she called.

"Yes?" Mom's pace faltered.

The secretary opened her mouth. Closed it. Opened it. She said, "We have a strict dress code, for future reference."

Mom looked at her apparel, then noticeably clenched her jaw. "I came straight from work. Apologies if my shoulders are too distracting to the little tots." Without waiting for a response, she drew Caleb into the hallway. He was kind of proud of her.

But the lump was back in his throat.

CALEB

I heave a relieved sigh, resting my arm against my forehead in bed. I revel in my victory of mustering the courage to ask Juliet to hang out. Then I crawl out of bed and pull on slacks and a plaid button-down. There's a student council meeting before school to discuss homecoming finalization details (since the president and treasurer are in fall sports and have after-school practices), so I want to look good. Not that anyone else cares. Most of them don't even notice me compiling notes in the back of the room, and that's how I like it. But that doesn't mean I should dress like some hooligan.

I discover Mom passed out on the couch, dark curls messily framing her heart-shaped face. She didn't even make it to bed this time. "*Tsk,*" I whisper, drawing a folded blanket over her shoulders. Originally, I planned to pull out the griddle and surprise her with pancakes, but I don't want to clang around in the kitchen and risk waking her, so I merely snatch a protein bar and head to the vehicle.

I invite Juliet to sit with me for lunch, though it's awkward since Jas and her teammates are out of state until tonight, so it's just me, her, and random people who don't talk to me. Juliet thanks us for welcoming her, then pries her textbook open and studies the lunch away for her quiz next hour.

Nothing to worry about. I can chat with her at the library.

The day passes agonizingly slowly, but eventually, the final bell rings. As I wait in the cafeteria, I draw a steadying breath, watching students pour out around me until it's merely a trickle. As the doors swing in and out, a frigid air swirls through the room, causing goose bumps to poke through my skin. Good old northern September weather—hot enough to melt concrete one day, then cold enough to need a winter jacket the next.

"I'm coming!" a sudden voice shouts, and I turn with a smile. Just in time to see Juliet, who's jogging toward me with a luminous grin, trip over a chair leg and smash her face into the ground.

"Juliet!" I cry out, dashing toward her.

Her head pops up, her curly twist braids in disarray, blood dribbling from her nose. "Handkerchief boy," she says weakly. "Good timing."

"Are you okay?" I ask, tugging the cloth from my pocket.

"Nose hurts a little." She wiggles it for emphasis, which is almost cute enough to make me smash my own face into the ground. My first instinct is to pinch the handkerchief around her nose, but that would probably be too motherly (and creepy), so I merely hand it to her. If she were Emma, I would've done it without hesitation. I would've said *slow down* and flicked her forehead, and she would've cussed but grumbled a reluctant *thanks*.

"You're smiling," Juliet notes, voice nasally from pinching. "At my pain?"

That's impossible, because whenever Emma crosses my mind, my face warps into a grotesque scowl. "Definitely not."

"I wouldn't blame you if you were," she admits. "I mean, that was funny."

"You tripping and hitting your face is not funny," I say sternly.

"No?" Juliet crawls to her feet, readjusting her backpack. "Guess I should be more dramatic about it next time. To the library!"

She sprints to the front doors.

I'm still on the ground, bemused. As I stand, I find myself chuckling. "Okay," I say, following after her.

X●X●

It is love. Love is what it is.

Juliet spreads her folders out at our table on the second floor, all of which are color coded to a specific subject and have their own tabs, highlighters, and sticky notes. It's so . . .

"Organized," I breathe, tears gathering in my eyes.

Juliet looks up, her nose now fully cleaned of blood. "Hmm?"

"Nothing! Just . . . wondering if you had a better day," I say, smiling nervously.

She shrugs. "Nobody got punched in the face, so I think so. Or, technically, I got punched. By the floor. But it was self-inflicted." She massages her round chin, looking pensively at the paneled ceiling through her voluptuous eyelashes.

What I wouldn't give to experience her beautiful mind for a day. "Everything else went okay, though?" I press.

"Yeah. Thanks for asking me to sit with you for lunch." She exudes a cheerful glow that nearly makes me forget it's overcast and chilly today. "Much better than eating with the mold in the corner of the cafeteria."

It's such a sad statement that I want to tear up again. How had I not noticed someone eating lunch on the floor before now? "You can sit with me every day," I tell her. Part of me wishes I were directly beside her so I could pat her knee or shoulder. But maybe I should deepen our relationship before leaning into physical cues like that.

"Thanks, Caleb," Juliet says with a beaming smile, and she turns her attention to the textbook splayed open in her lap. "For caring."

I don't expect that. "It's the bare minimum," I say feebly.

"Sure. But I'm a lot to deal with, so . . ." Her voice softens, and her eyes are unmoving on the paper below her.

"You're not," I insist, leaning toward her. Someone like Emma, on the other hand . . .

Dammit. Get out of my brain, Emma Jones.

Juliet laughs with strain. "Give it time, and you'll get sick of me." She flips the page, though I'm certain she hasn't absorbed anything from the previous. My eyes flit around the library, taking in rows of sleek wooden bookshelves, the window consuming the wall at her back that overlooks a pavilion littered with lounging high schoolers. A librarian is stocking shelves nearby, but otherwise, nobody is within listening range.

"Why would I get sick of you?" I ask, tentative.

Juliet swings her legs up into her chest. "All my friends do," she mumbles.

"I doubt that's true—"

"None of them have texted me since I moved." Juliet's face glazes with a painful indifference that doesn't suit her. "I should've expected it. They're always telling me that I talk too much, I'm too weird, I sound fake. Anyway." She flaps her hand, like she thinks this conversation isn't worth my time.

She's so desolate that my dismay is shifting to resentment. "Friends don't tear each other down," I say sharply. "Calling you annoying for being passionate about things you like? Calling your personality fake? It sounds like they're . . . I don't know. Projecting insecurities onto you. I know we just met, but I can tell you're a great person with a huge heart. I hope you won't let anyone make you think otherwise."

When I finish, I'm basically gasping for breath. Juliet is staring at me with wide eyes.

Oh *shit*.

"Sorry," I choke out. "I didn't mean to insult your friends. It just sounds like they were toxic, maybe?"

Juliet bursts into laughter, loud enough that the librarian gives us a cutting glare. Already, I feel embarrassment tingling in my cheeks. I almost apologize again, but she reaches out and seizes my palm. "I get why you're the secretary now," she says. "You're so good with words that you almost convinced me I'm not annoying. What a talent!"

She drops my hand before I can even process that she's holding it. Like that, she goes back to her physics book.

"You're not," I whisper, but if she hears me, she doesn't respond.

That's when *it* happens.

I hear a shuffling sound behind me, like someone's dragging their feet along the carpet, and a voice says, "Wow, you really are studying!"

My jaw latches shut before she even finishes her sentence. You've got to be fucking kidding me.

"Emma!" Juliet says, practically sparkling. "You decided to come!"

"Of course. I could use all the studying I can get," Emma says, walking into view. She's wearing jean overalls, a white shirt, and the cheekiest smile imaginable as she strides past me and hops onto the couch cushion to Juliet's left, dumping her backpack at her feet.

"What are you doing here?" I ask venomously.

"I asked Juliet to hang out, but she said she was studying at the library with you." Emma cocks her head at me, the little shit. "I've been having trouble understanding the symbolism in *The Great Gatsby*, so I thought Juliet could help."

"Oh, sure!" Juliet smiles at Emma, which makes me grind my clenched jaw. "I haven't read it yet, but we could figure some- thing out. It's about a gay guy thirsting after a rich guy thirsting after a rich woman, right? 'Old sport' and all that?"

Well, it's a better summary than anything I could've come up with.

They start talking about their English 12 class, leaving me fuming across the table. I'm in AP Lit, which has a whole different curriculum, so I can't contribute to their conversation. Their knees are brushing, and they're smiling and laughing, taking notes, making things up about the book, watching clips from the movie.

I can't stop myself from fidgeting. I'm *pissed*. When Juliet leaves momentarily to use the restroom, I shoot to my feet and loom over Emma, nostrils flaring.

"You came here to interrupt my time with Juliet," I growl, fists quivering.

"Obviously." She frames her face in her hands, smiles, and says, "I can't let you pull ahead of me so quickly."

I'm not sure if her admitting to her dastardly plan is better or worse than her playing innocent. Either way, I'm getting angrier, so I snap a finger in her face, seething. "If you want to hang out with her, make your own damn plans."

Emma opens her mouth, probably to retort with something witty to provoke me.

She chomps down on my finger.

"Ouch!" I squawk, wrenching it out of her mouth. Heat blisters in my cheeks as my index finger begins to throb. "What the *hell*?"

"You wagged," she says simply.

I shake my hand out, hissing. I should've known she'd try to surgically remove my finger with her dagger-sharp teeth, considering she used to do it years ago to try and "condition" me to stop pointing it at her. I'm about to scold her again (not that she'll listen), when my phone hums. My heart stutters.

Dad?

I reclaim my seat and scramble to open it. Jas is telling me the volleyball team came in third place. Good for them. I guess I should write off my request to have dinner with Dad tomorrow, considering he hasn't answered my follow-up.

"Who are you texting?" Emma demands.

I tear my attention away from my screen. "Excuse me?"

She's scrutinizing me with narrowed, suspicious eyes. "I haven't seen you make that face in years."

"What *face*?"

"It's like . . ." She gestures at me, like I'm supposed to know what that means. "Your eyebrows get all pinched, and you look tired and worn out, and you start leaking this ugly gloom. You're not talking to *him* again, right?"

I gaze at her in bafflement, wondering how she reached that conclusion by observing my face. It's been four years. Can she still read me that easily?

Before I can muster up a lie, Juliet returns, humming an out of tune song I've never heard. As Emma and I retreat to our respective studying, she glances between us, puckering her lips. If she feels the tension choking the air, she doesn't say anything. Just retakes her spot at Emma's side. All I can do is try to focus on my

AP Government and Politics notes. Every so often, I feel the pressure of eyes on me, and I look up, hoping it's Juliet.

It's Emma. From her wary expression, it's clear she hasn't forgotten about our brief conversation before Juliet's return. But it doesn't matter. She cut me away of her own volition, so she can't come prying. Rekindling my relationship with my dad has nothing to do with her.

Not anymore.

Emma

Someone's knocking on the door. I can tell I'm dreaming, because each pound reverberates through the walls of my empty house, smashing my eardrums like blunt hammers.

I don't want to answer it. But my feet scrape along the matted living room rug anyway, and my trembling fingers extend toward the knob. I twist, swinging inward. The sound of gushing rain and crackling thunder surges into the house.

He's sopping wet, shivering, his dark hair glued to his pallid face, his blue eyes stained crimson and shedding enough tears to rival the sky's. He's thirteen.

"Why?" he whispers.

I want to tell him that he won't understand. That I'm sorry. But the words are glued to the roof of my mouth. I want to take his shoulders, to wipe the tears from his cheeks, to do something, *anything*, but my hand won't pass the barrier of the doorframe.

Suddenly, he lunges out and seizes my arms in a tight grip, his eyes brimming with desperation. "*Why?*" he screams.

I wake to the feeling of someone's hand on my shoulder. I jolt upright, startled, and shout, "*Burgle someone else!*" before reaching into my combat boot and yanking out my pocketknife.

"*Jesus!*" Caleb chokes out. Older, seventeen-year-old Caleb's voice, in all its frighteningly deep glory.

"You have one too!" another voice says in delight. Juliet's?

Oh. The library. For a second, I thought someone was breaking into my car while I slept. "Sorry," I say, blinking through the grogginess of my nap. I guess I fell asleep studying (predictable Emma behavior). Caleb is poised five feet from me, clutching his pearls as if I pulled the blade out. Juliet is standing nearby, backpack hiked onto one shoulder, smiling brilliantly.

"It's getting late, so we wanted to wake you up," she says. "Also, your phone has been vibrating."

Swell. I lift it from the couch arm and discover I have twelve missed calls from my mom. As I'm swiping away the notifications, another call interrupts me, and I hiss with annoyance, putting it through. "What?" I snarl.

"It's me," a fatigued voice says.

Oh. "Brooke?" I ask, frowning. I wedge the phone between my head and shoulder, packing all the notes and books I was pretending to care about. Too bad I gave myself away by falling asleep out of boredom once Juliet turned to her physics homework. So much for trying to come off as intelligent and dedicated like my opponent.

"Can you talk to Mom so she'll stop calling me?" Brooke pleads. "She's been trying to get ahold of you."

To whine, of course. "I told you to block her number," I grumble, following after Caleb and Juliet as they descend the staircase to the ground floor.

A heavy sigh lingers in my ear. "Just call her."

She disconnects the call. I cuss, then look up to discover both Caleb and Juliet staring at me—Caleb with reluctant concern, Juliet with intrigue.

"Everything okay?" Caleb asks naturally. Caring despite it all.

"Yeah. Just . . . my sister. Being annoying." I hate their probing eyes, so I stare at the floor as we walk out into the chilly evening. I made sure to park farther out in the lot to prevent Caleb from seeing the disaster within. The sun peeks past the cityscape, beaming ginger light between the staggering skyscrapers, so hopefully he won't find it dark enough to accompany me to my car. He has someone else to walk with anyway.

I don't like the friction in the air, so on a whim, I twist toward Juliet and ask, "Can I pick you up for school tomorrow?"

Before Juliet can respond, Caleb scoffs. "Did you forget you're suspended?"

As if forgetting anything is possible around this guy. "I have a job interview tomorrow at eight," I say, keeping my attention on Juliet. "School is on the way."

Juliet brightens, if that's even possible. "Sure! Always wanted to try carpooling. It sounds exhilarating."

Hmm. I'll have to make it a thrilling experience so she isn't disappointed.

"I'll take you home from school, then," Caleb says before I can offer that, too. His blue eyes illuminate with an idea, and he continues with, "Actually, do you want to go bowling tomorrow night?

Jas and some teammates and their boyfriends are going. I had plans, but . . . uh, they're canceled. Want to come as my . . . friend?"

I have the feeling he was about to say *date*, which makes irritation prickle under my skin. "Sounds fun!" I say, jamming my thumb into the air. "Thanks for inviting us."

Caleb gives me the most malicious look he can muster, which might be terrifying if I didn't know him. Well, it's his fault for inviting Juliet somewhere while I was within earshot. For being such a smart guy, he sure does miss a lot of obvious opportunities. He should've known after this evening that I'm not above thrusting myself into his plans to thwart him from the inside.

He should've known this years ago, actually. That I'm not a good person. But he didn't. In fact, he constantly insisted otherwise, which was one of the reasons I had to . . . end things. Before I could get too swept up in believing him.

"I'll be there!" Juliet claps her hands, apparently oblivious to Caleb's cutthroat expression. "Can't wait to tell my family I got invited to an *event*."

We pause at Juliet's sleek, electric-blue sedan that somehow smells like new car *outside* the vehicle. "Thanks for the study date," she says, smiling up at Caleb in a charming, giddy way that sinks my heart, before she turns to me. "I hope I helped you with *The Great Gatsby*?"

Not even a little. "You were amazing," I say. "I definitely understand what the book is about now."

"Good. Hopefully the little gay gets his rich man in the end,"

Juliet responds, and boy, oh boy, I'm falling faster for this girl than I ever thought I would.

Caleb lingers, and I decide to let him have his goodbye moment alone so he won't follow me to my car afterward. I bid Juliet farewell and stride across the lot, glancing back only once.

Caleb is hugging her.

It's a gentle, careful embrace, like he's afraid of his own strength. Juliet laughs and says something like, *Ten out of ten this time!* I swallow around the knob in my throat, wrenching my eyes away. It's always going to fucking hurt, isn't it?

But . . . no. I can't let it. That's why I'm in this competition. Juliet is the kind of girl who can finally untether Caleb's fingers from around my heart. That's why I need to fight for her.

I slump into my driver's seat, eyes drooping with fatigue. I'm already in a shitty mood, so I might as well make my life even more miserable rather than wait for a happy moment she might ruin. I call my mom to give Brooke some reprieve.

"Emma Jones," she growls immediately. "Do you know how sick I am of getting calls from the school about your vile behavior?"

I'm too depleted to get riled up, so I grunt in response. Better she gets it out now on the off chance she resorts to calling the police again.

"You're lucky I'm not like your grandmother. Do you know what she would've done if I'd gotten *one* suspension, let alone *several*?" Mom barks. "You should be grateful you don't know what it's like to get a belt. But *no*. You take advantage of my kindness and do whatever the hell you want!"

Maybe one day she'll stop bringing up her shitty childhood every time we get into trouble. The whole "*I had it worse than you*" argument has never been effective, so I don't know why she still uses it.

"Your sister would *never* get into fights around school. Why can't you be more like her? She's got straight A's, *and* she's taking two honors courses. What are your grades like, Emma? Have you turned in a single assignment since the start of the school year?"

Her voice becomes a numbing mumble in my ears. I stare at the ceiling, sighing.

One of Caleb's hugs sounds nice.

CALEB

I should've known Emma's suspension wouldn't stop her from infiltrating my alone time with Juliet. Of course she randomly offered Juliet a ride to school before the thought crossed my mind.

Dammit.

I'm still muttering as I drive to school and crawl into the closest parking spot next to the building. The sun skirts low in the distance, bathing the brick school in burnt orange and scarlet. People slowly filter into the spots around me, filled with fatigued students who drag themselves into the building, earbuds in, shoulders slumped.

I tap my foot, waiting. We're getting closer to first period—where are they? Then again, I shouldn't be surprised, considering Emma's first language is tardiness.

Finally, I see them. They're walking down the sidewalk from the back of the parking lot—probably strategic on Emma's part, to give them more time to chat. She's dressed in an old rec-soccer crewneck and jeans, her hair gathered into a rumpled bun. *Job interview*, my ass. Juliet, in contrast, is wearing a white turtleneck tucked into a plaid skirt, looking adorable as ever.

I lunge out of my car and intersect with them right as they're passing by. "Hi," I say with as much cheeriness as the early morning allows, and they both reel sideways.

"Loud and awkward until you least expect him," Emma mutters, while Juliet breaks into a wide smile, setting my heart aflutter.

"Caleb!"

Even the way she says my name is perfect, the two most beautiful syllables to grace the air. "Where's your first class?" I ask, falling into step beside them. Emma's lip pulls into a sneer, like she's annoyed I'm interrupting their walk. Tough shit, considering what she did yesterday. "I can walk you to—"

"We'll take you there," Emma says joyfully.

My teeth snap together, and I glare at her over Juliet's head. "Aren't you suspended?" I ask coldly. "Which means you can't be on school grounds? And don't you have an essay due on Monday about the corollaries of punching people? And a job interview? Which, if you're about to go to one, I hope that's not what you're wearing." I try maintaining a light airiness through my spiel, though it takes effort.

Emma's upturned hazel eyes narrow to slits. "To answer those delightful questions," she says enthusiastically, "yes, I'm suspended, but who's around to care? And I do have an essay about the *corollaries* of punching . . ." The word drags across her tongue, and I know I'm being mocked. "But I have plenty of time before Monday. And yes, I have an interview. What's wrong with my fit?" She gestures to herself like she doesn't see the problem.

I groan, palming my forehead. "You can't show up to an interview in a sweatshirt. That's basic interview knowledge! And if you get caught inside, who knows what they'll do to—?"

"Hey, buddy, isn't your class on the other side of the building?" Emma interrupts, still insufferably pleasant. "Won't you be late if you take Juliet to class?"

"No," I snap, and I mean it. Though I'm cutting it close, my long strides can carry me across school in thirty seconds. "How would you know where my first class is, anyway?"

"My eyeballs grant me the gift of sight."

My nostrils flare. This morning is way too hot and crusty for her dry-ass personality.

"Top-tier banter, guys!" Juliet says, and it startles both of us. Somehow I'd nearly forgotten she was there. Maybe Emma feels the same way, because her ears burn red. "Anyway, this is great. I get chauffeured to school *and* an escort to class. Is this what the sovereigns feel like?"

"I'll carpool with you every day," Emma says earnestly. "I love driving."

I want to bash my head into a wall. How is she so much quicker than me?

"Aww, thanks." Juliet hits Emma with finger guns and says, "But maybe we can take my car from now on?"

"Oh . . ." Emma rubs her neck. "Sorry for the mess."

"It's not the mess," Juliet clarifies, patting her shoulder in a fond way that makes me clamp my fists. "It's more like your dashboard has several lights and sounds that probably shouldn't be . . . um, lighting and sounding."

Hmm. It seems like she's skirting around something serious. "What's wrong with your car?" I ask Emma.

"Nothing," Emma mumbles.

"Doesn't sound like nothing."

"Get your ears checked."

Thankfully, the vice principal happens to be chatting with the security guard at the front doors, and she immediately zeroes in on Emma despite her attempt to sidle up behind me. "Jones," she snaps. "Why are you on school property?"

"Terrible timing," I say solemnly, and Emma jabs my side, causing me to wheeze.

"Good luck on the interview!" Juliet exclaims, waving. The sight rejuvenates Emma, who winks at her, then flashes me a subtle middle finger before heading back to the parking lot. Charming.

Finally, I'm alone with Juliet. "So," she says while I'm trying to think of a conversation starter. "Did you do anything wild and exciting after we left the library yesterday?"

I went grocery shopping. Cleaned some more. Thought about her. Read through texts with my dad. "Errands," I say simply, walking with her up the staircase to the second floor.

"Sounds boring," Juliet admits. "I used to run errands with Terrell. He hates being an adult and talking to people, so he appreciated when I came with him." She gives a hefty sigh, her features dimming.

"Sounds like you didn't expect him to move across the country, huh?" I ask softly.

"Nope! I mean, the guy wouldn't even go to the bank without me being there for emotional support. I don't—agh!"

She trips on the last step of the staircase.

Unlike yesterday, I'm close enough to do something about it. Instinctively, I sling my arm around her waist, catching her. As I do, my palm presses into a tight material compressed around her midsection, which makes me feel invasive enough that I yank away immediately.

"Sorry!" I croak. "I didn't mean to grab you—"

"It's okay!" Juliet says breathily, but her eyes are frantic, wild, looking around the hall as if to make sure nobody's watching us. "I'm so sorry. I promise I'm more than my clumsiness. I swear I'm three-dimensional and very compelling. Dynamic, even."

I . . . don't know what she's talking about, but I say, "Yes, you are" in support.

"Walking is hard," she explains.

"I understand." And I do.

She smooths her clothes out and says, "You should get to class. Don't want you to be late because of me."

She hurtles down the hall, panting and gasping.

I'm not sure how or why, but I think I just screwed something up. "See you for lunch," I say weakly after she's long gone, and I turn to head to my class. I'm so distracted, I nearly bulldoze the pissed five-foot-one Indian girl standing inches behind me.

"Ho," Jas Deshpande says, thrusting her phone in my face. How long has she been waiting there? "First you avoid my texts on Wednesday. Then I see you walking into school with the new girl and *Emma Jones*. What the hell?"

Oh, right. How did I almost forget about the fight with Ian? "I . . . figured I'd tell you in person?" I say sheepishly.

Jas folds her muscular arms over her hoodie. She only returned from the volleyball tournament last night, so I haven't been able to catch up with her. Her hair is pulled into two thick black braids that dangle toward her rib cage, and she's wearing that familiar "I'll spike a ball into your ass no matter your excuse" expression.

"Can I explain on the way to class?" I plead. I've never been tardy, and I won't let my sulky best friend break my record.

She scowls but obliges and starts walking with me. She has US History across the hall from me, so unfortunately, I can't avoid this conversation.

"Emma and I are interested in Juliet, so we decided . . ." I falter, wondering which phrasing will sound the least dickish. "To hang out with her and see if she develops feelings for one of us."

"You're competing for her," Jas says. Cutting a clean line through my bullshit.

"I didn't say it passed the morality test." I feel her round dark brown eyes piercing through me, so I focus on the dull gray lockers to my right. "You know how hard the romance thing is for me. Every time I start developing feelings for someone, Emma appears, does a cartwheel, and snatches them away."

"And?" Jas clearly isn't swayed by my sob story.

"Having a competition is the only way I stand a chance," I say bitterly. "If Emma was free to flirt up a storm, I'd never be able to ask Juliet out. This way, Emma has to slow down and become her friend first."

Jas's russet brown face crinkles with distaste. I can't blame her, but frustration blazes my skin hotter anyway.

"I want to get to know Juliet," I say, gazing at the searing fluorescents in the tiled ceiling, hoping she won't give me the silent treatment after this conversation. "That's how I always am. That's why I lose to Emma. My process is slow, and hers is fast."

Jas appears thoughtful. Maybe she's conjuring another insult. "Make sure your competition doesn't overrun your feelings for Juliet," she says darkly. "You get overly passionate about anything involving Emma."

My cheeks warm, and I give a skeptical scoff. "This is the first time we've spoken since eighth grade, but yeah, okay."

"Spoken *to* her, sure. Spoken *about* her, no." Jas jabs an accusing finger at me, hiking one thick black eyebrow up into her forehead. "You bring her up whenever something remotely reminds you of her or when you need something to whine about. You even went to her soccer practices and games until she got suspended from the team."

Sometimes I wonder if Jas is really my friend or just my instigator of pain and suffering. "I don't talk about Emma!" I snap. The only reason I went to her practices was because I'd made an oath to never miss one. Even after our falling out, I felt a weird sense of duty to make sure someone was always in the stands for her. Just for her.

"You talk about her weekly," Jas says flatly. "And now that you're fighting her for the new girl, my torment will be endless."

"Find a new friend if I'm that unbearable."

"I can't." She sighs with misery. "Our friendship is like a show that should've ended three seasons ago. I'm not having a great time anymore, but I'm too invested to stop."

Jas is the worst person I know. Somehow I love her anyway. Hoping to steer the conversation elsewhere, I try to refocus on the fact that she's been gone the last few days. "Anyway, how are things with you? How was the competition?"

"My perfectly sane and morally upstanding competition went well," Jas says, her tone flat. I decide to ignore it. "As I texted you earlier, we got third place. I shared a hotel room with Leanna and didn't put my brush through her eye socket. My mom almost charged onto the court in her sari when someone spiked a ball into my face."

I shudder at the thought—Mrs. Deshpande is a soft-spoken, kindhearted woman, which makes it all the more terrifying to witness her wrath. "You played well, I hope?"

"Eh. You know me." Jas shrugs her wiry shoulders. "I'm mostly there for the free food."

The thought makes me smirk. Jas has never been a particularly competitive person, but volleyball is something she's always mysteriously excelled in. At her parents' encouragement (or begging) and the threat of college looming on the horizon, she decided to pursue the varsity team on the hopes of bulking up her applications. *It'll make my straight B's and lack of AP classes look more justifiable*, she'd claimed.

Mostly, though, she only participated because she liked the camaraderie of it all and the biweekly team dinners.

"Don't think that asking me about my tournament gets you out of the bullshit you just told me," she warns, sneaking an elbow between my ribs and causing me to wince.

"Look, I'm serious about Juliet," I say, my voice lowering. "It has nothing to do with Emma. I genuinely want to get to know her."

"I know, but if Juliet finds out, she'll think the only reason you befriended her was to beat Emma."

"So she won't find out," I say simply.

Jas taps her chin like she's deliberating something. Then, "I have an idea. One that could help you avoid this whole competition."

I scrape to a stop in the doorway to my classroom. We're ten seconds from the bell ringing, but she's piqued my interest. "I'm listening."

"You and Emma could fuck each other and leave Juliet out of it," she says brightly.

My face turns into hot magma. "Hate you," I choke out, and the last thing I see is her playful smirk before I slam the door in her face.

Emma

"You have many bad ideas, babe," Alice says, "but this one's the worst."

"I've had worse," I protest, walking beside her through the fractured bowling alley parking lot, hopping over potholes that shimmer in the late afternoon heat. It's back to being face-meltingly hot after yesterday's cold spell that cloaked the city and surrounding subdivisions in cool air and clouds.

I changed out of my clothes from earlier, per Caleb's interview advice, and I'm glad I did. Not only because he's probably right about looking professional or whatever, but because the temperature spiked a couple of hours later. The last thing I want is to be sweaty and smelly walking into this bowling alley to see Juliet.

The interview went . . . okay, I think? This was for a cashier position at a downtown automotive company. I'd been especially eager about it because one of their benefits is discounted pricing on car maintenance, like oil changes and tire rotations.

"Haven't you seen a movie?" Alice asks, snagging my shoulder before we can enter the building and swinging me toward her. Her thin eyebrows, which have been dyed gold to match her bleach-blond pixie cut, are so high up in her forehead they they're blending in with her hairline. "Like, even one? Anytime there's a competition, bet, or challenge involving feelings, it causes pain."

"I would've just asked her out, but Caleb told me that I *seduce all of his potential prospects*." I roll my eyes at the thought. I've been trying to wrap my head around the notion since he implied it.

"He . . . didn't actually say that, did he?"

"No, but it sounds like him, right?"

Alice offers light laughter, her raven-black eyes glinting with nervousness. "Okay, honey."

"I promised him I'd wait," I say, poking at my messy hair bun. I didn't get to shower last night, and my hair is annoyingly fine, so I can already feel oil accumulating. I'm also running dangerously low on cash from the last time I took money from Mom's stash, so a trip home is inevitable.

A job would help. This weekend, I'm planning on spending Saturday and Sunday at the library, both to type that essay for VP Adams and to submit applications to places I haven't yet spammed with my résumé. Most of my interviewers haven't followed up or returned my calls.

Alice is still wearing that awkward "I'm trying to be supportive, but this makes me want to die" smile.

"Worst-case scenario, I make a new friend," I reason. "A new, attractive friend who I can appreciate platonically."

"Oh, Emma. There's one far worse than that." Her chest pulls up with a sigh as she swings open the bowling alley door. Thrumming music pours out from within, rumbling through the parking lot. "It's that Caleb wins and they start dating. You have to see him holding Juliet's hand, kissing her, wrapping his arm around her. You can't bail because you're Juliet's friend." Alice gives me a solemn, desperate look that makes my heart twinge. "Even though you wish *you* were kissing those lips, you with his arm around you, you holding those hands."

She's being annoyingly theatrical. "Maybe you wouldn't be this dramatic if you pulled your head out of your screen sometimes," I say, scoffing.

"Video game narratives are very complex and compelling," Alice counters. "More so than a lot of books and movies."

"Okay, well, this isn't a book or a movie or a video game. This is my life, so you don't have to try to predict the ending of our competition like I'm some kind of entertainment for you."

Alice's eyebrows skyrocket, and I realize I sound like a dick, so I sigh, slumping forward.

"Sorry," I mutter. "Whatever. I've been rambling this whole time. What about you?"

She flutters her lashes at me. "You'll need to be more specific."

"Like." I gesture at her awkwardly. "What's up with you? Any updates on life stuff since I last saw you . . . two days ago?"

"Oh, Emma," Alice says with solemnity. "You know that I only exist to be the Robin to your Batman, don't you? What makes you think I have anything going on in my life other than you?"

". . . I hate you."

"Please don't. I would lose my purpose."

"*I hate you.*"

"But since you asked," Alice says wistfully, "I'm still organizing that collab with someone I've always dreamed of playing with, you know the one, and my parents finally gave up on me for getting a D on my Stats test, thank God, and yesterday I was so bored and lost without you to guide me that I went and made out with Hailey Lowell in the gym locker room, to which we then told each other we'd never talk about it again." She sighs, hanging her head back to gaze with yearning eyes up at the sky. "Maybe one day someone will tell my story."

I try valiantly to digest all of this. "This is two truths and a lie, isn't it?" I ask with fatigue.

"Yes! Can you guess which one?"

". . . The D on your Stats test."

"I wonder what made you say that," Alice says coolly, before quipping, "but yeah, you're right. It was a C minus. Though, my parents are still one thread away from abandoning me as their child."

"I would adopt you," I tell her.

She nods with a pensive smile. "Like Batman and Robin."

Yeah, this conversation is over. I amble into the bowling alley before she can find a way to bring this conversation full circle back to my competition with Caleb. It takes several seconds for my eyes to adjust to the darkened environment. Neon lights streak across the ceiling and frame the lanes, and UV light causes everything to glow. The sounds of bowling balls hitting polished wooden floors, pins colliding with each other, and the laughter of high schoolers ricochet through the building. There's an arcade beside the help desk, where a group of guys are going feral over a plushie in a claw machine.

At the back of the line, waiting to rent their shoes and lane, are Caleb and Juliet. Perfect timing. I sprint toward them, dragging a hissing Alice with me, and skid to a stop behind them. "Hey," I say eagerly.

Juliet spins around, her plaid skirt and curly black-brown twist braids twirling with her, and though she was probably already wearing one, I choose to believe her smile is that bright because she heard my voice. "You made it!" she exclaims.

"Wouldn't miss it. How was school? Sorry I couldn't keep you company during English." I give her a playful grin, and her following laugh is cute enough to make me squirm with delight.

"It's been a good day," she says. "Though, you never know when some boy will come along to drop-kick your happiness."

Caleb twists on his heel and glowers at me.

Don't I fucking know it.

But Juliet is looking over my shoulder as she says it, and when I follow her line of sight, I realize that . . . ugh. Ian Summers is one of the boys at the crane machine behind us. I guess when the seniors hear that a varsity team is getting together somewhere, they all have to follow.

"Oh, it's Emma Jones," a voice says, and someone steps out from the shadows behind Caleb. It's Jas Deshpande, who befriended Caleb back when they were paired alphabetically for the economics "raise a baby" project. Her cool brown eyes rove Alice and me with amusement, and she's twiddling one thick braid between her fingers. Even though she's the shortest person here, the way she holds herself, paired with her strapping athletic arms, makes her feel like a towering presence. "And Alice Yang. Two people who avoid group activities. I wonder what brought them out tonight."

Caleb shoots her a deadly glare, which tells me he probably told her about our plans to romance Juliet. Thankfully, Juliet is more preoccupied with examining Alice. "Oh my God," she whispers. "Are you a streamer?"

Alice smiles mechanically—a daily response to a daily question. "Yep."

Juliet's eyes instantly begin to glitter with excitement. *"The royalty herself."*

"Uh . . . I wouldn't say—"

"You're my hyperfixation!" she shrieks, hopping toward Alice.

I fight a snicker. Though Alice's channel earned her popularity around school, she's never pursued friendships outside of mine. Alice has many acquaintances, but even people who don't know anything about streaming act a certain way around her. It's difficult for her to differentiate between who's shallow versus genuine, so most of her relationships are surface level.

"Sometimes I have your streams up in the background when I'm doing homework," Juliet says, nearly out of breath. "You're the best at exploring and getting total completion. It's like you keep me relaxed but also make me laugh, and—"

Her voice cuts off, and her excited hands freeze midflutter. She folds them against her waist and calmly says, "Big fan."

Alice gives her a chipper smile and scratches the back of her short blond hair. "I'm happy you like the channel. It means a lot."

It's her stock response for whenever someone says they watch her, but this feels more genuine. No doubt she's already charmed by Juliet and falling madly in love with her. (It's technically a possibility. Alice succumbed to my gay agenda freshman year, the solidifying moment being when she walked out of a swim lesson in gym, and said, "You're right. It's tits after all.")

Thankfully, Juliet isn't her type. Alice prefers bigger butch girls who can snap her like a twig but mostly use their power for painting and gardening.

"Her setup is cool," I tell Juliet, glancing pointedly at Alice. "Maybe she'll let you see it."

Juliet sighs dreamily. Alice stares into my pleading eyes, her own impressively lifeless, before kindly saying, "Why don't you come over after we're done bowling, Juliet? It's nothing special. Just some lights and a glowing speaker."

Juliet clutches her collarbone like she's never experienced kindness before this moment. She sniffles and whispers, "I'm but a lowly peasant in your presence, queen."

"Uh . . . hmm. Don't do that." Alice swivels toward Jas and Caleb and says with an annoying amount of enthusiasm, "Why don't you come too? So nobody feels left out."

It's alarming how easily she can betray me like that.

"They're probably busy," I say with a strained smile, hoping to rectify this situation.

Caleb levels another glare at me. "I'm available." Because why wouldn't he be?

Jas shakes her head with genuine remorse, probably unhappy that she's about to miss whatever hijinks ensue. "I'm going to a party with the team later, but you guys have fun."

Alice claps her hands with apparent jubilation. "Me, Caleb, Emma, and Juliet. So eager to explore this journey of friendship." She shoots me a nasty look thinly veiled by a smile threatening to crack her cheekbones.

When it's Jas's turn to rent a lane, she gets two so "we can all bowl next to each other." Which sucks, because I can't escape Caleb, but it's also good because I'll be able to spend time with Juliet. We settle our belongings on the table between our lanes, and Alice and Jas depart to find their bowling balls. As I slink into a chair to tie up my rented shoes, enjoying the noisy atmosphere and sense of *togetherness* that Alice and I usually avoid, I hear a group of classmates from the lane beside us break into whispers.

"Isn't that Jones?"

"Better leave before she starts a fire in the bathroom."

"Shh! She'll beat your ass if she hears you."

My mood instantly deteriorates. This is one of the reasons Alice and I usually stayed in. If people weren't recognizing her and harassing her for pictures, they were muttering about me. Why did everyone think my only purpose in life was to cause issues? I glance up at Juliet, hoping she can't hear them. Sure enough, she's humming to herself, typing in our names on the two lanes—Booliet (I guess she's going for a Halloween theme, even though it's still September), Jas-O-Lantern, and Alicemetery on the left lane.

On the right, of course, is Emmaween (hmm) and Calebroomstick (I think she gave up).

"Just don't get a higher score than her and she won't fuck you up," someone says behind me, and the seniors snicker in response.

Suddenly, a loud slamming noise nearly startles me out of my chair. Everyone nearby quiets, seeking the source of the sound. It was Caleb. His hand is flat on the table next to me, and he's staring irritably at the whisperers.

It must be effective, because they continue bowling without another word. I stare at Caleb in perplexity while he props his foot on a chair to lace his shoes. Why did he do that for me?

I know why. Because he's him. That's always the reason.

Juliet is tying her own shoes now, so I reluctantly follow Caleb to the ball rack, propping my hands on my hips. "Never seen so many balls in one place before," I say with a grin, hoping to slice through the tension.

Caleb says, "They stock a variety for people who need different sizes and weights."

Well. Guess that's on me for expecting him to play along. But I'm no quitter, so I continue with, "What's your favorite type of ball?"

"Whichever has holes deep enough to fit my fingers." Caleb examines his massive palm in disgruntlement, then frowns at me. "What's wrong with you?"

"Nothing," I croak, laughter clawing at my throat, begging for release. He can't be serious. But he's deadpan, and there isn't the faintest twinkle of mischief in his bright blue eyes. "Anyway, can't wait to wipe the floor with your face."

I seize a sparkly teal ball that's slightly too heavy, but I don't care, because it's teal. If I stand here any longer, I'll start crying tears of hilarity, so I sprint away. I swear I catch the faintest glimpse of a smirk as I leave.

I find Juliet and Alice in conversation about a game that just came out, Juliet alight with wonder, Alice slightly self-satisfied since she got a prerelease copy. Jas is chatting with some volleyball girls near the vending machines, most of whom share her toned figure and authoritative energy. Which means I'm standing with my ball, alone, at the opening of the lane.

I take a few cooling breaths. It's fine that Alice and Juliet are talking. An amiable relationship between them will be valuable for whenever I wed Juliet. I approach the pins, swing back, and let loose. The ball rolls halfway down the lane before careening sideways into the gutter. To my dismay, I hear Juliet yell, "That was a practice shot! You got this!"

Of course she'd start paying attention right when I flub my first throw. Before embarrassment can reach my face, I swivel around and bow, causing both Alice and Juliet to clap for me. "I threw it into the gutter purposefully," I say, hopping toward the ball return.

"So you'll feel okay when you take your first turns."

"I appreciate your sacrifice," Juliet says with a grateful nod, and she snags her shimmering pink ball, climbing the steps to her lane. I spy the opportunity for a *moment*, and I grab my ball as well, meeting her at the lane to her right.

"Who's going to win this turn?" I ask innocently.

"You."

"Why's that?"

"I have astigmatism," Juliet says.

Oh. Uh. I can't find a way to make a joke about eye defects, so I say, "You saw my first throw, didn't you? But let's have some fun and bet on it."

Juliet's face lightens with intrigue. "If I win, what do I get?"

I rummage through my brain for an idea that isn't overtly flirty. *Loser has to kiss the other person's cheek* is probably too obvious. Damn you, Caleb, for forcing me to be subtle. But something like *loser has to buy the other person a snack* isn't meaningful.

"Loser kisses Caleb on the mouth," Alice says, and oh my god.

I'm going to drop-kick this fucker.

There's a horrifyingly loud thud, and Juliet and I spin around. Caleb has returned and just dropped his giant violet ball onto the tile floor. He's gazing at Alice in startled horror.

"Oh, that's *spicy*," Juliet says with a maniacal giggle.

"He . . . should consent," I croak, inundated with so many overwhelming emotions that I can barely separate them. Anger, frustration, disappointment (why does Juliet sound so keen?), maybe even amusement (Caleb makes funny faces).

"Good point," Juliet agrees. "Caleb, do you consent to be kissed on the mouth by the loser?"

I'm nearly shaking with embarrassment. I should be giving him a teasing grin, or poking fun, but I can only stand there in abject terror, awaiting his response. If he agrees . . . No. He *can't*. Both situations are lose-lose for me. If I win, Juliet will kiss him on his *lips*. If I lose . . . that means . . .

An image floods into my head. Thirteen-year-old me smashing my mouth against Caleb's, blood rushing through my veins, my body searing hot.

No, no, *no*.

Caleb's doing some mental calculation I'm not privy to. To my astonishment, he says, "I consent." He gives me a challenging, almost-smug look, despite his pasty cheekbones glowing pink. He knows the situation I'm in.

I have to win because I don't want to kiss him. But . . .

I have to lose because I can't give *Juliet* the chance to kiss him.

Fuck this *shit*.

"Here we go!" Juliet says, hopping into position with her ball, her curls bouncing with her.

"I believe in you," Alice calls from her seat, winking when she catches my livid expression. Is this her idea of punishing me for concocting the *competition* idea? How does she expect me to ever talk to her again? Juliet swings her arm back, and my muscles snap tight.

She drops the goddamn ball.

It rolls backward off the step, and Alice catches it with her foot. "That doesn't count, right?" Juliet asks, laughing feebly.

"Of course not," Alice says, her thick winged eyeliner crunching with a reassuring smile.

Caleb stands at the ball return, his wiry arms folded, observing Juliet with such fondness that it gives me stabbing chest pains. This *sucks*. Just get it over with, *please*.

Juliet unleashes the ball again (correctly, this time). It bounces comedically, but rolls to the end of the lane, colliding with four pins. "Yes!" she cries out, pumping her fist like she just got a strike. Maybe my unintentional plan of "make everyone feel better about their first throw by botching mine" actually worked.

Okay. I gaze at the pearly whites at the end of my lane, gasping through my breaths. Am I more afraid of giving Caleb the opportunity to advance his relationship with Juliet or of having to kiss him myself? And . . . oh, *fuck*.

Would Juliet kissing him for this dare count toward our competition? If she kisses him on the mouth, does that mean I just . . . lose? For *good*?

There are many bad things that have happened to me over the years, but this moment just might be the fucking worst.

"What are you waiting for?" Caleb asks, sounding abnormally cheeky. He does realize that he'll have to kiss *me* if I blunder this, right? Shouldn't he sound more panicked? Juliet stands on the lane beside me, rocking back and forth with excitement. Is she hoping

I'll lose? Win? Is she thrilled at the thought of kissing Caleb, or just at the idea of this competition?

I can't keep standing here, so I release the ball, hoping the Lord will make my decision for me. It streaks down the right side of the lane and smashes six pins. I stagger back, relieved but somehow more uneasy.

Juliet needs to hit three pins to win.

She steps up to the lane, and my fists are squeezed so tight I can feel my nails piercing crescents into my palms. Caleb shuffles around, obviously hoping for a gutter ball. Juliet tosses it forward. It rolls, rolls, rolls. I jam my eyes closed because I can't watch what happens next.

I hear the sound of pins collapsing.

"It's a tie," Alice says.

A . . . tie? I peek through my eyelids and realize Juliet and I have six pins each. I nearly collapse to the floor in relief. "Guess neither of us have to kiss Caleb," I say before Alice can concoct some precarious tiebreaker idea.

"Aww," Juliet says, hobbling back to her seat. I hate that she sounds disappointed. "There's always next round!"

Yay.

I slump into my seat, and Caleb passes me with his bowling ball without sparing me a glance. "Don't get your legs tangled out there, noodle boy," I say. He pierces me with a venomous look over his shoulder, then reels back and sends the ball flying.

It's a strike. Like this day can't get any worse.

It does, naturally, because Juliet congratulates Caleb by throwing her thick brown arms around his pasty neck and squeezing. Caleb looks so giddy about it that it makes me nauseous. Coming here . . . was a bad idea after all.

Jas returns from talking with her friends and steps up to bowl alongside me. I get six pins again. Just as she's flinging her ball into the gutter, a grating, aggravating voice rings behind me.

"Aww, so the new girl made friends with the class whore and little bitch secretary."

The lanes quiet around us. My blood is already steaming hot, sloshing around with the urge to assassinate. I whirl away from my lane, meeting Ian Summers's smug ice-gray eyes. His cheekbone is an ugly, splotchy yellow that contrasts horrifically with his tanned skin, which pleases me greatly. His question is directed at Juliet, but since he's looking at me, with his brawny arms folded over his broad chest, that means he only said it to see my reaction.

If he wants one so badly, I'll give him one.

I start storming toward him, but Alice catches my wrist. "Don't," she mutters. "He's not worth your anger."

The group of seniors muttering about me earlier is dead silent, watching the scene with bated breath. Caleb's stance is poised, taut, his narrowed eyes digging into Ian's face. It's quite a different approach from elementary school, when he tended to hide behind me whenever people picked on us.

Jas gives a noisy, petulant sigh, like this is the most boring thing that's happened to her all day. "Don't you have some father to disappoint?" she asks dryly, flicking a dismissive palm at him. "Be gone, little boy."

My mouth quivers into a smile. How did Caleb land such a badass as a friend?

Ian's lip crinkles at Jas. "Don't you have some clit to lick?"

"I'm not the token lesbian here, but good try." Jas gestures to Alice, who's literally wearing the lesbian pride flag stitched into her jean jacket.

"Hi," Alice says brightly, her black eyes stone cold. "Clit-licker here. You were saying?"

Ian's obvious frustration cools my rage just a bit. But then he sets his sights on Juliet, who's staring determinedly at the floor, and my urge to attack spikes dramatically. "Be careful where you bowl," Ian sneers at her. "These are the *queer* lanes."

He says it like any of us would be insulted by that word in our Lord's decade the 2020s. "Ignore him," I say, stepping toward Juliet and folding my hand over her clamped one.

To my surprise, Juliet shoots Ian a sharp, menacing glare. With a voice colder than the city's wintery nights, she says, "Then I guess I'm at the right lanes."

Oh.

My jaw nearly unhinges. Caleb's eyes become wide enough to fall out of his skull. Jas is smirking with pride, and Alice looks more delighted than I've seen in weeks.

Ian's posture tells me he's about to chuck a bowling ball at us. But he catches the eye of a security guard walking by, and mutters, "Disgusting," then storms away.

The relief causes all of us to slump. Juliet stares at where Ian just was, tears bubbling up in her eyes, fingers scrunched around her shirt. "Balls," she whispers, and suddenly, her eyes roll up, and she fucking *faints*.

Luckily, I catch her back before she can hit the floor, and I lower myself to my knees, cradling her head. "Juliet!" I cry, and for lack of anything more helpful to do, I fan her paling face with one hand. "Holy shit, *someone call an ambulance!*"

"I'm good," Juliet chokes out, and her eyes fling open. They're glazed but present enough that my anxiety dwindles.

"You just passed out!"

"True," she says. "I haven't eaten today."

She . . . *what?*

"When's the last time you ate?" Caleb demands, kneeling beside us and resting the back of his palm cautiously against Juliet's forehead. She blinks a few times at the ceiling and says, "I fell asleep when I got home from the library yesterday, and I forgot to pack my lunch today, so . . . like thirty-some hours ago?"

"Someone get this bitch a quesadilla," Jas snaps at the huddled group still whispering in the lane over, and they break apart, two of them rushing to the concession stand.

"Uh." Juliet looks blearily between Caleb and me. "Did I just . . . come out?"

Caleb and I exchange a glance, but before we can answer, Juliet gulps in a stuttering breath. Tears begin to carve dark trails down her cheeks. Before I can consider finding a napkin, Caleb is pulling out . . . Of course. A real-life handkerchief.

"Thanks," Juliet whispers, dabbing her wet face. I squeeze her knee because it's better than any words I can offer. Caleb is better at that, anyway. Comforting people rather than driving them away.

"Sorry if you felt forced into it," he says softly.

A tense smile comes to Juliet's face, and she straightens up out of my grip, putting her wobbly feet under her. Caleb and I prepare to snatch her if she collapses again. She merely flops into a chair. "Anyway, let's bowl, other queers," she says, injecting false chirpiness into her voice.

"You should eat," Caleb says in his stern, motherly voice, and he pokes his index finger in her face. "Does this happen a lot? What would happen if you passed out driving? What if Emma hadn't caught you? You could've hit your head."

Juliet examines Caleb with glowing eyes, like she's never met someone more admirable. I force a smile, hoping to trick myself into being amused because Caleb is being Caleb. But it slides away. It aggravated me sometimes when Caleb lectured me back then, but it still felt . . . good. Seeing him act like this toward others makes me squirm for whatever selfish reason.

Moments later, a chicken quesadilla arrives at the table, which Juliet inhales. Her eyes are tinted red, and it seems like something's weighing on her, judging by her fidgeting knees. Caleb, too, is studying her, the tip of his handkerchief poking out of his breast pocket.

My lip twitches into another smile. Fucking dork.

Once Juliet is sufficiently fed, we return to bowling. To my re-lief, nobody brings up the "loser kisses Caleb" idea again. Despite his gawky proportions, he's good at keeping the ball between the lines. I guess being straightlaced and staying in his lane are his forte, so I shouldn't be surprised by his adeptness.

Jas is the worst of us, despite Caleb's attempts to coach her ("Swing your arm like a pendulum—no, not like that—*no*, holy shit, Jas, do you know what a pendulum is?"). Alice and Juliet are decent enough to escape Caleb's lessons. Now that I've warmed up, my ball finds the gutter less and less.

It's . . . fun. I dreaded sharing space with Caleb, but being in a group makes it bearable. There aren't many opportunities to flirt with Juliet, but if Goal One is just to befriend her, we're doing okay. Slowly, she's regaining her energy and letting loose, laughing louder, yelling in excitement, rambling about her changing tech-niques. It's so adorable, I want to kiss her.

About halfway through our second game, I land my first strike. Juliet and Alice hoot and clap, and I whirl around, smiling with satisfaction, seeking Caleb for . . . whatever reason. Probably my com-petitive urge. But he's near the vending machines, talking to Jas, who looks unhappy and defeated. I realize with a start that he's changed back into his sneakers. What the hell? He still has four turns.

Caleb rushes to the doors, and then he's gone. Why would he abandon an opportunity to bond with Juliet? I bypass Alice and Juliet, both of whom give me high fives for something I've already forgotten about, and beeline for Jas.

"Where's Cal going?" I ask.

She's massaging the slight bump in her nose with weariness. "His dad invited him to dinner."

My back snaps tight and rigid. "His dad," I repeat, hoping I misheard.

Jas shrugs her toned shoulders.

That's just about the worst news of the day. I sprint for the front doors, shove into the parking lot, and skid to a stop when I see Caleb flinging open his driver's door in the front row. "Hey," I call out.

Caleb falters, peering over the roof of his car. His face pales, like he knows exactly why I came out here. "What?" he demands.

"You're still talking to that lowlife?"

Caleb's expression flattens, and he begins to lower himself into his car. No response? Really? My desperation mounting, I yell, "If you leave, I'll get closer to Juliet."

It's the only thing I can think of that might slow him down. If his father is who he's actually going to meet with, there's no insult I can hurl at the man that'll make Caleb see sense. So . . . I should use the competition, right? To make him stay? Even if I'm sacrificing the chance to bond with Juliet without his interference. Because even though I want to win Juliet over . . .

What if he gets hurt again?

It doesn't work. Caleb fixes me with a cold look, and says, "Fine."

Then he's gone, leaving me feeling as helpless and pathetic as I used to.

CALEB

"Been busy?" Dad leans over the diner table, grinning. "Any extra-curriculars? You're a tall kid—you pick up basketball?"

It takes my brain a while to process the question. Mostly because I'm sweating buckets from the sheer anxiety of being across from him. Dad lives thirty minutes outside of the city, but it's rare I see him. Usually because he's worried about gas money or he doesn't have time to make the trip. I've offered to drive to him, but . . . yeah, texting back isn't his forte. Not that I can blame him, considering how busy he is.

"I'm the secretary for student council," I say, twiddling my thumbs. "Jas nominated me and got the volleyball team to campaign for me."

Dad sips his Coke and waggles his eyebrows. "That some girlfriend of yours?"

I've told him about Jas before, but I refresh his memory anyway. "She's been my best friend for a few years."

"She pretty?" He plucks a soggy fry from the basket between us, plopping it in his mouth.

"Yeah. Anyway, how are you?" I ask lightly, because he'll ask me why I haven't made a move on her if I let the topic linger. Aside from the distant chatter of guests and clanging dishes from the kitchen, it's uncomfortably quiet in here. "How's the new job?"

"Eh, it's work." He glances out the smudged window beside us. He's been doing that a lot, like he's antsy about something or needs to be somewhere. He was downtown to meet with someone, the details of which he's been cagey about, so I abandoned the bowling alley to drive into the city and eat with him.

"So . . ." I scramble for another topic. It's been weeks since our last conversation—surely I can think of something he'd open up about. "Back in the dating scene?"

"There's a girl," he says, grinning.

I sense he wants me to tease it out of him, so I ask, "What's she like?" with as much enthusiasm as I can muster.

"She's a beauty." He stirs his drink with a longing sigh. Something I've noticed about my father is that he can never stop moving—whether it's physically, financially, or whatever-else-ly. His inability to commit to still moments was one of the things that drove him away from my mother. "Just stunning. Killer smile, blond highlights . . ."

"I meant personality-wise," I say, laughing weakly. "Is she nice?"

"Very nice." He winks at me, like we're sharing an inside joke (one I definitely don't want to be part of).

I don't bother asking if I'll get to meet her, because he's never tied down for long—either he loses interest or he pays them so little attention that they cut ties with him.

Dad steps away to take a call, so I busy myself with my phone. Juliet texted me sad-face emojis to express her disappointment at the fact that I left the bowling alley so early. I wish I'd been able to hold out longer. But I'm not sure when my next opportunity to spend time with Dad will be. I need to scoop up every chance I can get.

When Dad returns, he looks even more impatient, running his hands through his sandy-blond hair, his eyes darting around. Part of me wants to tell him he can leave, but I know he will if I give him the opportunity, and . . . I don't know. We haven't even been here an hour.

"I'm . . . interested in someone," I say, squirming to get comfortable on the stiff booth cushion. "She's new, just moved here for senior year."

As I expected, his face brightens with intrigue. "That's my boy. A good-looking guy like you won't have a problem snagging a lady. Is she pretty?"

"Beautiful," I say, my enthusiasm rising. I can't help it. It's rare Dad takes a genuine interest in things I'm doing, understandably. I'm not a particularly interesting person to be around. "She's gorgeous. Like, the 'takes my breath away' kind."

His eyes flicker with distrust. "Be careful with that type. They usually know it."

Uh . . . hmm. There's plenty I could say to that, but I'm not looking for a fight, and he'll probably say something like *It's a joke*, so I move along. "She's really sweet. But . . . do you remember Emma? My best—uh, ex–best friend?"

He squints skyward, as if combing through his memories.

"Little bratty girl with the mouth of a sailor?"

"Yeah!" I say brightly. "She likes Juliet too. So now we're competing, and whoever Juliet kisses first . . . wins, I guess?"

My father strokes the stubble hugging his jawline. Then, "It's good she ditched you when she did. I remember thinking she'd drag you through the mud."

I flinch. The remembrance of people constantly trashing Emma when we were friends rekindles my urge to defend her. "Why does everyone think she's a bad influence?" I mutter. "She got into fights with jerks, but other than that, she's a good person. Even if she's . . . sometimes misguided."

"Mm." That's the only thought he offers.

"Anyway, you got a new car," I say, peeking out at the sleek BMW out front. Moving along. "What happened to your other one?"

"Letting Jennifer drive it."

"Who?"

"My girlfriend."

I massage my neck, a stone sinking in my stomach. He probably took out another loan to pay for it. "I hope Jennifer's the one."

Dad gives a hearty laugh like I said something endearing. "Don't worry about me, kid," he says with another grin, and he leans over the table, ruffling my hair. "Your old man's got things figured out."

It's not the first time he's said that, but it does feel more genuine. He *has* been trying, evidenced by the fact that I've spoken to him more this year than any other year of my life. Which isn't enough to satisfy me, but . . . it's a start. I have to give the guy leeway to improve things, rather than cutting him out like I did years ago.

The server drops the bill off, and I scoop it up before Dad can, then say, "I'll get this." I have leftover allowance money from when Mom paid me for household chores.

"No, no," he says flippantly, reaching for the bill. "What kind of man would I be if I let my boy pay for my meal?"

"I'm the one who invited you here." I smile. *My boy.*

He climbs out of the booth and pats my shoulder. "You're a good kid, Caleb."

I try not to beam as he ties his scarf around his neck, bids me goodbye, then heads into the inky darkness of the evening. I watch his retreating back, estimating how much time will pass until I next see it, before heading to the counter to pay cash and tip. I trail out to my car, my mind zooming back to the bowling alley. I wonder who won the second game. Alice seemed the most adept of everyone, aside from me. Bowling has always come surprisingly easy to me, considering how much grace it requires.

I wonder if Juliet and Emma will get alone time at Alice's house.

As I settle into my seat, my phone dings. It's . . . Emma? I guess she unblocked my number at some point over the last four years.

EMMA

You said you wouldn't entertain that asshole anymore

Lovely. Her first text to me after all this time, and it's to annoy me. Before I can shift into drive, my mood ruined, she texts again.

EMMA

You promised.

Emma

Juliet obsesses over Alice's gaming setup like it's the sexiest thing she's ever seen. As she moves between the monitors, rainbow keyboard, stereo, ergonomic chair, and assortment of microphones and LEDs, I swear she's about to salivate.

I let them have their moment, leaning against the picture window overlooking the suburb. Fortunately I have something to do when Mrs. Yang enters the room with a tray of almond cookies and red bean mooncakes. She looks pleased, probably because Alice has finally brought over a friend who isn't me.

"Sorry to interrupt," she says, placing the tray on the center table before the sectional couch. "Don't mind me. Just dropping off treats from last week. Hope you ladies are having fun!"

Juliet flinches in the corner of my eye, like Mrs. Yang said something off-putting. The woman's gaze fixes on me for the briefest moment before she shuffles out of the room to a round of thanks. It's those subtle moments that make me antsy. I avoid eating Alice's food and using her shower too often, because I don't want her parents realizing I'm a runaway. Nonetheless, Mrs. Yang has a keen eye. I'm always anticipating the moment she might corner me and ask questions.

When she's out of sight, I snag a mooncake and bite into the intricate flower design, nearly drooling over the sweet, thick paste filling. Mrs. Yang usually makes them once a year to celebrate the midautumn festival. Apparently it's more widely celebrated with parades in bigger American cities, but the Yangs celebrate more intimately among extended family. In other words, this is my only chance to indulge until next year's leftovers.

Juliet is rambling off questions about the specs of Alice's computer. I catch Alice's eye with a violent wave, then point at Juliet's back, point at myself, and do a suggestive hip wiggle.

"A stroke?" she asks, deadpan. "You're having a stroke?"

I choke as Juliet swivels toward me, eyes wide with concern. "I'm fine," I squeak. "Just had a spasm."

"Right. Well." Alice stands from her crouched position beside the stereo and rubs her neck. "I'll just . . ."

She walks out into the hallway and closes the door. Way to be fucking discreet. At least she caught my signal to give us time alone, though.

Juliet looks Alice's setup over with another dreamy sigh, then hops over to the picture window, leaning against the sill. Her palms grip the edge, a few measly inches from mine. I nudge her pinkie, my heart rate already quickening. How do I make the most of this without being obvious that I'm into her? "Hey, you."

She smiles sideways at me. I don't know how her makeup is so sleek and unmarred after such a long day, especially one during which she fainted into my arms. "What a day," she says, reading my mind. "Just last week, I thought I'd be eating lunch alone the whole year and spending Friday nights watching rom-coms with Charles. Now I'm *out and about*."

My throat closes. Is that someone else in her family? Another sibling, maybe? A cousin? Or could they be . . . ? "Who's Charles?" I ask casually.

"My stuffed penguin, obviously."

Whew. This is a chance, so I say, "Just hang out with me on Friday nights, and I'll never let you get bored."

Juliet laughs, her curls spilling toward her shoulder blades. "What sorts of trouble will we get into?"

"The bad-girl kind," I say seriously, and she snorts. "You think I jest?"

She pokes her finger guns at me and says, "Yep. I haven't actually seen you do anything that lives up to a *troublemaker* reputation."

"I just got suspended for punching a person."

"To defend someone," she points out, sounding skeptical. "When you start running second graders over on a motorcycle in a leather jacket, then I'll believe you're some ruffian."

"Get to know me better and I'll show you my wild side," I say, sliding until we're shoulder to shoulder. I feel her body's warmth radiating against mine, and I resist the urge to link our fingers. She doesn't seem bothered by our proximity, which heats me even further.

Momentary silence overtakes us, but it's not uncomfortable. She's focused on the ceiling, and though she's wearing that smile that makes me feel warmer each time I see it, her eyes are clouded, like her thoughts are far away.

All at once, I remember what happened with Ian. How he mocked us, insulted us, and she felt the only way to defend us was to come out. It must be weighing on her, even if she's not showing the signs.

"Juliet . . ." I chew my lips to prevent anything invasive from popping out. Nonetheless, I get what it's like when you don't know who to turn to. Because people you care about are . . . busy. Or ignoring you. Or maybe you abandoned them in eighth grade, so why would they let you run back into their arms? "I don't know if I said this," I murmur, "but the way you shut Ian down was badass."

Juliet's smile turns fragile. "Thanks."

"Just know that I . . . *Caleb* and I . . ." I swallow, wishing I didn't have to bring him up. But showing her more resources than just *me* is the right thing to do, even if it gives Caleb more opportunities to have meaningful conversations with her. "We had each other when we were figuring things out. He took longer to understand himself, but we came to our conclusions a lot younger than most people." I tip my head at her, eyes softening. "Because we weren't alone."

Juliet stares at the beige carpeting. The longer I watch her, the more it seems like she's metamorphosing. Her bright, cheery demeanor is shattering, unveiling hints of somberness, of lethargy, beneath.

"Basically, if you need to talk, I'm here." I twist toward the window so I can look at something other than the gaming consoles. The suburban neighborhood is quiet, enveloped in a hazy golden glow from bedroom windows and driveway lights. The nearby city illuminates a wispy layer of pale gray clouds. "I don't know where you're at in your journey. You don't have to tell me. But if you feel frustrated because things seem impossible, I get it. I'm available. And . . ."

My fingers curl around the windowsill. Thinking about him—even speaking his name—is torturous. Despite that, I want Juliet to feel like she has multiple people who will be in her corner. People who will . . . understand.

"Caleb will be there too," I tell her. "If you feel more comfortable going to him, he'd be happy to talk."

Juliet doesn't speak. I chance a risky, apprehensive glance at her. She's smiling, but it doesn't reach her hollow, disillusioned eyes. I don't know what she's contemplating, but I feel like I'm seeing a whole different person.

"Thanks." Her voice has lost its lively tone. "Can I ask you something?"

"Anything."

"What's your relationship with Caleb?"

I reel back away from the window, alarmed. What does that have to do with anything? "Me and C-Caleb?" I sputter out.

"I can't figure you out," she admits, fixing me with a probing look. "One minute it's like you hate each other, and the next, you're smiling and bantering like friends. Are you exes?"

Juliet's words glitch and spasm in my brain, evading comprehension. She just . . . Juliet wants to know if Caleb is my . . . ?

Ex?

"No!" I blurt. "No, we're not, I mean . . ."

At the worst moment, my brain chooses to remember what it feels like to have Caleb's lips against mine. Startled but soft and sweet and—

Oh *God.*

"We're acquaintances," I choke out.

Juliet squints at me, clearly dubious.

"Okay, ex-friends," I admit. Though I'm nowhere near the corner of the room, that's where I feel like I'm cowering. "It just . . . didn't work out."

Look, I want to be Juliet's friend. I want to confide in her, feel comfortable around her. But this is too much too soon. I don't want to talk about this.

Maybe Juliet senses my reluctance, because she drags her eyes away, fanning out her palm to examine her nails. The paint is chipped on her middle and third finger, probably from bowling. "My friends wouldn't let me off the hook so easily," she mumbles.

"Hmm?"

"The queer thing."

Oh. Thank God we're back to that.

"If I said something like that—you know, the *I'm at the right lane* or whatever—my friends would've demanded to know what I was hiding." Juliet slumps against the window. "Marissa would've refused to talk to me unless I explained myself. Danielle would've been pissed that I hadn't said something sooner. Trav . . . might've broken ties with me."

She smirks, and it's about as cynical as I've ever seen her. It's raw. Unfiltered.

"He's that 'I don't care, just don't get in my face about it' kind of guy. But *in my face* to him just means existing publicly." Juliet rubs her thumb against the windowsill, like she's gathering nonexistent dust. "Anyway . . . thanks for offering to be there."

She meets my eyes, and there's genuine fondness that steals my words, captivating me.

I want to kiss her.

The moment dissolves, though, when her phone vibrates. I realize we're not in some romantic setting, but in Alice's gaming room. She's probably sitting out in the hall or something, letting us have our moment and sighing to herself. What a pal.

"It's Caleb," she says, affectionately enough that I feel a pang of jealousy. "He's just apologizing for leaving the bowling alley."

To think I almost forgot he left everyone to go see that loser.

"What's wrong?" Juliet asks, noticing my scowl.

"Nothing." I plaster a smile on my face, hoping it's half as convincing as the one she wears daily. "Did you check the closet? Alice has like eighty games in there. Maybe you've played some of them."

I steer her toward it. Juliet is nice enough to allow me to distract her.

The thought of Caleb nags me even after I drop Juliet off at home.

CALEB

BACK THEN

"You shouldn't go that high," Caleb scolded, watching Emma swing higher and higher until the chains on the swing slackened and snapped tight during her descent.

"Come on. I used to do this all the time." She grinned, her strawberry blond hair fluttering behind her. "I used to challenge you to see who could swing higher, but you never took the bait."

"The chain might break," he snipped.

"You're always afraid of something."

Caleb sighed, kicking at the wood chips. His sixth-grader legs had grown long enough to drag through the dirt, and he didn't trust the swing to hold his weight like it used to. But he and Emma had walked here because her mom came home earlier than expected, and she wanted to get out.

Caleb never understood their relationship. Emma didn't like talking about it, and shifted subjects whenever Caleb brought it up. He assumed what frustrated her the most was that . . . well, even *she* didn't understand why her mother treated her so unkindly. Especially in comparison to Brooke. The only guess she ever came up with was that it might've involved her dad.

"I don't know if he's even alive," she'd admitted at one point when they were on their backs in his bedroom, gazing at the glow-in-the-dark stars on his ceiling. "But whenever Mom starts yelling, she brings him up. Like, *You're just like your father.* I don't know why, but she hates him."

Caleb had been present for one of those arguments. He remembered Ms. Jones yelling something like *I should've known this would happen when your father left me with you!* He observed something strange as he stood nearby, feeling awkward and helpless. At the mention of Emma's father, tears had welled up in Ms. Jones's eyes, and her breathing had staggered with a gasping sob that Emma didn't notice.

Caleb only tried to bring it up once. Upon hearing this, Emma snarled, "My mom doesn't cry. She screams."

He figured Emma wouldn't care to hear his hypothesis—that maybe Ms. Jones didn't hate Emma's father at all. In fact, maybe the reason she took her anger out on Emma was because she cared about him a little too much.

Emma was a passionate, reactionary person who sometimes let her emotions get in the way of reason. Caleb agreed nothing could excuse that woman's behavior—her constant nitpicking, blaming Emma for things, comparing her to her sister. But wouldn't it help to know there was *some* reason for that behavior?

Caleb leaned his temple against the swing chain. He'd given up on approaching the subject with Emma, because unless it was three a.m. and she was half asleep, she kept her feelings on the situation bottled and corked.

His eyes wandered the playground. Aside from a few girls on the merry-go-round, the area was empty. He recognized them from middle school—maybe seventh or eighth graders? They kept peeking over and snickering, which reddened Caleb's face. Were they gossiping about him and Emma? Or . . . his mom? Those rumors came around every year, and though Emma threatened to beat anyone who insulted his mom, just knowing that things were being whispered about her—her job, fashion, lifestyle—made him ache.

"Here," Emma said, and something plopped into the wood chips in front of him. "Sugar should help, Mr. Melancholy."

Caleb looked at her with admiration. "Impressive word."

"Learned it from your dork ass," she said, winking.

Caleb leaned over, snatching what she'd thrown. A Reese's cup, his favorite candy. Emma had been carrying a bag in her backpack for months, and whenever Caleb got grumpy, she'd tuck one into his palm, and say, "You can eat it when you smile again."

He loved Reese's, so it tended to work. He didn't even mind that the wrapper had been on the ground (he was getting better about the germaphobe thing, having spent so much time around a naturally germy person like Emma). He peeled it off and nibbled the peanut butter and chocolate. A *much* better combination than mint and chocolate.

Not that he would've told her that. Last time he insulted mint chocolate, she refused to talk to him for a day.

Just then, they heard shuffling through the wood chips, and Caleb looked up to find the three girls from the merry-go-round approaching. He gripped at his shirt, bracing for anything while Emma scraped to a stop, flinging up wood chips with her toes. "What do you want?" she asked, narrowing her eyes.

"I wanted to talk to Caleb." The girl up front was pretty, with golden-brown hair and sparkly eye shadow. She was looking at him, which caused heat to flush his face. She really knew his name?

"Um . . . yes?" he squeaked.

She twisted her feet into the ground like she was nervous. "So, my name is Kenzie. We have class across the hall from each other for fourth hour," she said coyly. "I have an extra ticket to a movie tonight . . . if you want to go?"

Caleb could only stare. Was this real life?

"What are you chuckle-fucks giggling about?" Emma demanded, glaring at the girls behind Kenzie. "Is this your idea of humiliating someone?"

Kenzie shot Emma a bone-chilling look, and Caleb nearly joined her. "I'm not talking to you," she snarled, and when she moved her eyes to Caleb, her smile returned. "It's just some Disney movie that came out a few weeks ago. You could meet me at the theater around six?"

Caleb's heart was nearly flying into overload. "Yes!" he yelled, before clearing his throat and calmly saying, "I accept."

"Yay! See you there." She skipped off with her two friends, leaving Caleb smiling at his knees. He'd never been asked out before. It made him feel giddy and mushy.

"Don't worry," Emma muttered, stomping wood chips under her feet. "Next time we see her, I'll kick her cooch for you."

Caleb whirled toward her in a flash of anger. "Why would you say that?"

Emma's lip curled down. "Why would some seventh grader ask you out? Those girls had weird vibes. I think she's either going to stand you up or do something shitty."

Caleb crushed the Reese's wrapper into his palm, hating the sinking sensation in his stomach. Why was she so cynical about people? Sure, her mom never gave her a reason to depend on anyone, but hadn't they been friends long enough that Emma could start opening her mind and not be so stubborn?

"I'm leaving," Caleb grumbled, standing up.

"Your apartment is too far away to walk to it," Emma said irritably, but Caleb was already storming off.

He had a date to get ready for.

Emma

The coast is clear. For now.

I decide to risk it.

I screech to a stop beside my house and haul ass to my trunk, gathering as many dirty clothes as I can. I drag everything inside and stuff it into the laundry machine with detergent. Though I'd happily give them a long, thorough soak, I press "quick wash." The faster I get out, the better.

I sprint through the house, raiding the pantry for snacks, stealing another blanket from the living room as well as tissues, mini hand sanitizers, and other things I'm running low on. I fling open the hallway closet and find her tip shoebox.

Do I feel bad about nabbing a wad of hard-earned cash from her work as a stylist at a regal salon? The answer to this thought-provoking question is, of course, "Fuck no." I can't manage to get a job of my own, and I'm doing her a favor by staying out of her perfectly fluffed blond hair. I slide the money into my wallet, fling my current clothes onto the floor, and lunge into the shower.

Okay. Breathe.

I inhale, long and methodically.

Just breathe.

I allow myself a few moments of bliss as the hot water trails down my back. I glance at my phone on the bathroom counter through the fogged glass door. Caleb hasn't responded. Maybe I was too callous texting him out of the blue, but my fingers took over the screen. Thankfully, I erased a few more impulsive messages before sending them.

Why is he talking to that shithole again? After all the tears, fatigue, anger . . . after his difficult journey of severing his ties to that useless man . . . he's back to kissing the guy's feet? The thought is maddening enough to make me slam my fist into the tile wall.

Ow. Piss.

I shuffle into my bedroom to find an old pair of pajamas. The place is barren, aside from my dusty soccer trophies and boxes stacked in the corners. I guess Mom is using my room for storage now. I used to have movie and celebrity posters up, back when Brooke and I went through our preteen obsessions, but I stopped trying to hang them when I got suspended in sixth grade and came home to find them torn to shreds on my bedroom carpet.

This room is mine again until you earn it back, Mom snapped while I stared at the mess, teary with rage. Brooke was already on the floor, gathering the pieces, silent.

As I crawl into a faded T-shirt and checkered sweatpants, a sound turns my blood ice cold. The front door closing and the familiar click of heels growing louder against wood floor panels.

Shit.

My bedroom door slams open. She's wearing pumps that cause her to tower, and her alabaster white face is tight, twisted with ire.

For a few strained moments, we glare at each other. She's dressed in a trench coat tied at the waist, and her lips are cherry red. I can already feel the combative air rising, thickening the pressure in the house.

"So you're only going to come home when you need to steal my things, is that it?" she asks, her voice frigid.

Here we go! I don't want to deal with this, so I shove past her, storming into the bathroom to collect my dirty clothes off the floor.

"When will you learn that you can't spend your life being spoiled?" she snarls. "When are you going to do something to earn your keep? You spend years lazing around, failing school, fighting people, running away, demanding *everything* from me without putting in an ounce of your own effort."

I won't snap. I *won't*.

"Why aren't you grateful?" she demands, stomping after me as I head into the utility room. I click the washer off, even though my clothes are still submerged in soapy, bubbly water. "Why do you keep running from me, like I haven't given you the world?"

I gather everything into my arms. The dampness soaks into my T-shirt.

"I could make this house inaccessible," she says furiously. "You know how many mothers kick their children out? You know how fortunate you are that you can come back here to raid my food, steal my money, use my house?"

I grab my keys and wallet in the kitchen. I don't have arms for the bag of food I just packed, so I leave it, heading for the door, leaving a trail of foamy water in my wake.

"Brooke was never like this," Mom growls. "She understood how hard it is to be a single mother. She never took me for granted. But *you*?"

I stride to my car. Her footsteps echo against the concrete behind me.

"You've never appreciated me." She's still going, her volume piercing into the quiet neighborhood. "My mother never would've allowed me to get away with the things you've pulled!"

Once again, she can't go without bringing up my dead grandparents. How they used to beat her for talking back, lock her in the basement when she angered them. She thinks she's so much better than them because she hasn't swung her fists. Like she hasn't spent our lives yelling at us, making us feel pathetic and worthless and—

I need to get the hell out of here. I stuff my sopping clothes into my trunk.

"Are you even listening?" she growls.

I collapse into my driver's seat and lock the doors before she can consider seating herself on the passenger side. She yells through the window, but I'm already shifting into drive and booking it. My arms shiver, partially from the cold wetness of my shirt glued to my skin and my undried hair. Partially from something else.

Where to go?

Not Alice's. I just spent the night at her house this week, and both her parents are home, so they'll get suspicious if I show up looking like this. My relationship with Juliet is tentative, and I don't want to lean on her for help when she may not be ready to offer a shoulder. I can't hide in the woods at this time of night, and while I sometimes wander the city, it's too perilous in the dark.

When I look up through my windshield, I realize I'm sitting outside his apartment complex. His shades are drawn, but his car is parked here, so I know he's home. Maybe tidying things, scrubbing the floors, refolding his clothes. Maybe he's asleep. He's always been particular about his circadian rhythm or whatever it's called.

I shouldn't be here. So I drive away.

I end up in the outskirts of the city next to Brooke's house. Their blinds are closed, so I'm not sure if they're having a late dinner, movie night, or whatever. When I climb out of the car, the cool wind slices through my damp shirt.

Part of me wants to charge through their front door, find Brooke's bedroom, and flop onto her carpet so I can scream about what just happened. We used to come to each other whenever we needed to vent. It was mostly me kicking the air on her bedroom floor while she tried cooling me down, but sometimes she came to me too. She wouldn't say much. Just sit on my bed, texting her friends, frowning deeply. I'd throw on some retro nineties sitcom I knew she liked until the crease between her brows dissolved.

But she has a life outside of me now, and I don't want to burden her with my issues.

I fling open my trunk. Piece by piece, I unfurl my sopping clothes, laying them out to dry over my hood, roof, windshield, rear. The last thing I want is to start smelling like mold by letting them stay damp for too long.

But then I run out of space, and I still have a bundle in my arms. I stand in the choking blackness of late evening, infiltrated only by the dim radiance of the city and porch lights. The soft whistle of wind scraping through manicured yards is the only noise shattering the silence.

I stand there, immobile, the weight of my half-washed clothes growing heavier, the stillness of the neighborhood rattling in my ears.

Where . . . do I go?

The clothes slip through my arms and fall in a lump to the asphalt. I blink against the biting wind, my eyes blurring.

I don't know where to go.

CALEB

BACK THEN

Emma's house was within walking distance of the movie theater. So Caleb decided he'd go there instead of calling his mom because making her drive back after she'd just dropped him off was too humiliating to bear.

Before he could even sprint away from the theater doors, a cold voice called to him. "What happened?"

Caleb blinked through his blurry, teary eyes. People filtered in and out of the doors, many of them frowning and eyeing the goopy mess in his hair. Faintly, he heard incessant, high-pitched laughter trickling out of the theater, and he realized they were following him out. Like things couldn't get worse.

Emma was sitting poised and rigid on the corner of the water fountain in the middle of the paved plaza, holding a water gun. She took in Caleb's sticky hair, the wet stains on his shirt, the tear streaks on his face. "A slushy?" she guessed.

Caleb could only wipe his eyes and nod shamefully. Behind him, the laughter of the three girls coiled out as they followed him into the plaza. "I can't believe you showed up," Kenzie choked through laughter, grabbing her stomach. "Wait, your mom's coming back to get you, right? I want to see what she looks like."

"She'll jump out of her car in booty shorts and a bra," one of her friends said, and they laughed louder at the thought.

Caleb was frozen, his feet cemented by their amusement, their words circling his ears, shredding him in two. *Leave her alone*, he wanted to snarl, but the sound wouldn't come. Why did Emma bother teaching him how to defend himself when all he could do was stand there?

Emma dragged herself up from the stone fountain, sighing. He expected her to say, *I told you so*, considering that he'd left her at the park without a goodbye.

Instead, she said, "Move over."

Caleb was startled enough that he obeyed without question. Emma hoisted her Super Soaker water gun up and took aim at the three girls.

"Really?" Kenzie asked, smirking at Caleb. "Your girlfriend came to spray us with water? I'm terrified."

"First, I'm not his girlfriend." Emma's expression darkened. "Second . . ."

Her eyes caught Caleb's, flickering with familiar mischief that made him want to smile.

". . . it isn't water."

And so she sprayed them with Liquid Ass.

Caleb didn't know how many bottles she'd bought to fill a water gun. The stench was so powerful and overwhelming that nausea bubbled in his stomach and his mouth soured. The girls screeched and gagged, stumbling over each other, trying to shield themselves. People reeled away from the sight, throwing their arms over their noses, rushing into the theater or sprinting toward the parking lot.

"Emma!" Caleb cried out, staggering to her. She threw the water gun on the ground, seized his wrist, and yelled, *"Run!"*

So they ran. They ran and ran all the way back to Emma's house. When they coasted to a stop at the front door, their lungs ached with strain and Caleb's eyes stung with tears. He was laughing *hard*.

"Y-you really . . . ?" He keeled over onto the porch step, their horrified, disoriented faces plastered in his head. It felt *good*.

"Those ass-bags deserved it," she snarled, and more inexplicable laughter shot from his mouth like a canon, which made her smile. Caleb had a sudden thought he hadn't expected. It passed, fleeting, but lingered long enough that it stopped his hysteria and left him gazing at the evening sky, bewildered.

Maybe it was just the adrenaline.

Emma helped Caleb to his feet and brought him inside. Brooke was on the living room couch reading a Kindle, and when she saw him, she waved, her cheeks pink. "Come on," Emma said with a scoff, tugging him away before he could do anything more than greet her. "Mom's shopping, so we don't have to deal with her."

Caleb already knew Ms. Jones wasn't here, simply because the air wasn't suffocating.

Emma brought him to the bathroom and asked him to take his

shirt off, then lean over the tub. Caleb blushed, despite having been shirtless in front of her plenty, like when she'd snuck them into the community pool in the next-door subdivision. Something about this felt . . . different, though. Because of that random thought he'd had on the porch? He wasn't sure, but he did as requested and knelt beside the tub.

Emma pulled down the showerhead and turned it on. After accidentally nailing his face with ice-cold water, warmth dribbled over his neck. Now that he had calmed down, his gloominess was returning. Why had those girls done that? All of that just to point and laugh? Though, most of the people who picked on him didn't do it out of revenge or a personal vendetta. They did it because he was weak. An easy target.

"Sorry for yelling at you," he whispered.

Emma was uncharacteristically quiet. "Hold this," she said, handing him the showerhead, and she poured shampoo into her hands, lathering it through his dark locks. It was a little forceful, like everything Emma did, but . . . soothing. He even started forgetting about Kenzie's nasty smile when he'd entered the theater lobby.

Caleb closed his eyes tighter to stop the burning. "I'm sorry I'm so useless," he mumbled. "I wish . . . I could be like you."

Emma's fingers faltered in his hair. Then the shower clicked off, and she ruffled his head with a towel. When he looked up at her through his damp locks, her cheeks colored. She framed his face with the towel and drew him closer, forcing him to look into her round hazel eyes. "You're not like me," she said, poking his fore-head. "You're like Caleb. And that makes you perfect, you know?"

Caleb stared at her with uncertainty.

"You aren't useless," she continued. "You're nice. And gentle. We need more people like you, so don't say you wish you were like me. You're Caleb Daniels." She flicked his nose, and he wiggled it in protest. Ow.

"I'm easy to pick on," he whispered, averting his eyes. Being close to her . . . was causing something unfamiliar to tingle in his stomach. Not necessarily unpleasant.

"That's why you have me." She stuck her thumb into her chest. "I'll protect you. So keep being you, okay?" She leaned forward, bumping her forehead against his before he could scramble back. "Because I really like Caleb Daniels, and I don't want him to change for anyone."

Caleb didn't know what to say. Did she feel that strongly about him? He blinked quickly, hoping to stem the additional tears rising into his eyes. When Emma noticed, her smile weakened, and she pulled back. Caleb resisted the urge to re-close the distance—to feel the warmth of her skin against his. Strange. He'd never had that urge before.

"Sorry if I don't say that enough," she mumbled. "I'm not good at that kind of thing."

Caleb wanted to tell her it was okay—that he wanted her to stay Emma Jones, too. But a sudden banging noise at the front door interrupted the moment. A voice snapped, "Emma, Brooke, get out here! Why is nobody ready to help with the groceries?"

All of the softness in Emma's face splintered away with annoyance. "Sorry," she murmured.

"It's okay." Caleb scooped her into a tight hug, squeezing like his life depended on it. Maybe it did. "Thanks, Emma."

Emma must've been shocked, because it took a while before her arms came up to embrace his back. She whispered three words into his shoulder, three that reverberated through his head, over and over, following him all the way home that night, then the next, then the next, for weeks, months, years.

Always and forever.

CALEB

Bacon, check. Hashbrowns, check. Eggs, check. Right as I'm packing the food away, I hear that sound again. The creak of approaching footsteps. Mom is staggering through the living room in a T-shirt and stretchy shorts, yawning, her dark curls frizzed and spilling over her pale shoulders.

"Mom," I say sternly.

"Can't even wish me good morning before scolding me?" She smirks at my annoyed expression and peers over my shoulder, assessing the food. "My hard little worker, cooking breakfast at six thirty on a Monday morning."

"If I don't make food, you forget to eat," I grumble. The number of women who experience this strange phenomenon around me is inexplicably high. "Why are you awake?"

She crunches into a piece of bacon. "Wanted to see my sweet boy off to school."

"You should be sleeping," I say firmly. Sometimes I wonder where I get my sense of urgency and concern from. But I can't be mad at her. She's a capable adult who can take care of herself, despite my constant worrying.

"How are things with Emma?" she asks, scrubbing the egg pan in the sink until I hip-check her. She sighs, backing away to allow me space. "Has anyone pulled ahead in your competition?"

"Nope." I say that, though I'm sure Emma's already on her way to establishing a romantic bond with Juliet. It doesn't help that I abandoned the bowling alley to spend time with Dad, leaving Emma to move in even closer.

"I don't suppose"—Mom shifts with discomfort in the mouth of the kitchen—"you've reconsidered becoming friends?"

Here we go. "No," I say sharply.

"But what if you talk to her about—?"

"No!" I snarl, and I whirl on her, jabbing a finger into her bewildered face. "No, no, *and no.* She made it clear in eighth grade how little I mean to her. She dumped me in the trash and never looked back."

I spin toward the sink and scrub angrily at a frying pan. Is this the real reason she got up early? To berate me about Emma?

"I . . . Honey," she whispers, pressing her palms into my shoulder blades like she's attempting to loosen them with her touch. "I know you're still heartbroken. But . . . you were happy with Emma." She swallows, and it causes my throat to close. I hate how dismayed she sounds. "You used to tell me that one day, you'd marry her so she'd never have to go home again—"

"*Stop.*"

Mom steps back again. There's a dull, hollow ache in my chest. "We were kids," I rumble, shoving the food containers into the fridge. "I didn't know what I was saying. Emma decided not to waste any more time with me—"

"It was never a waste," Mom says tightly.

"Yeah?" I rotate on her again, nostrils flaring. How can she say that, like she didn't witness firsthand how Emma's betrayal shattered me? Like I didn't crawl into her bed every day after school for months so I could cry into her shirt? "It *feels* like a waste. I spent years with her. She was my . . . And she just . . ."

My nails stab indents into my palms. I try squirming around her to go back to my room, but she won't budge. All I can do is continue, exasperated.

"For *years*, I tried figuring out what I did wrong," I croak. "I thought maybe I was becoming too much like her mom, because I was always lecturing and coddling her. Do you know how much that hurt? To think I drove her away because . . ." The words are so thick I nearly choke on them. ". . . because I became too much like the person she hates the most . . . ?"

The sound disintegrates in my throat. We've rehashed this shit over and over and accomplished nothing. Mom massages her lips in that familiar way that tells me she has more to say. I don't want to hear it—it won't make a difference. I take her narrow shoulders, back her out of my pathway, and amble to my room to get my backpack.

"That's not true," she breathes. "Emma didn't break things off with you because of anything you did."

My stride scrapes to a stop, and I shift to see her. She's hugging her arms, her frosty blue eyes locked on the living room carpet. What's with the sudden guilty posture? "You can't know that,"

I say irritably, and I'm about to leave again, but Mom grabs my shoulder.

"I do," she says desperately. "I know."

Part of me feels like she's saying whatever to get me to stay so we can continue our conversation. But there's apprehension in her voice, like she's encroaching on a subject she's been forbidden from initiating. "Okay," I say, taking the bait. "Explain."

Mom draws a long, preparative sigh. "For a while, I've felt that telling you would only make it more difficult to heal," she says softly. "But now . . . if you have a chance to reconnect . . ."

"What are you talking about?" I ask, my chest pounding faster.

"Honey." A gentle, solemn smile touches her face. "Emma fell in love with you."

Every muscle in my body tightens. Seriously? To claim something like that, especially after I told her long ago about my . . . Isn't it just cruel?

"She came over one day while you were at a movie with a boy." Mom's voice is rigid but calm. "She realized she had feelings for you when you started showing interest in other people. I promised I wouldn't tell you."

I can't form words. This information courses through me in painful, disorienting shock waves. She's been sitting on this for *years*, even after our split? I don't know what to say, do, feel, or how to process this, so I merely continue to my bedroom, my legs wobbly. I gather up my backpack and head for the door.

"Caleb." Mom's voice is still quiet. Maybe she's realizing she chose the worst possible time to explode my understanding of the world. "Hold on—"

"Juliet is picking me up." She may not even be outside the complex yet, but Mom doesn't need to know that. "Make sure you eat before work. Bye."

So I leave because I can't spend time deliberating my disastrous past with Emma. There's only one person I want on my mind. The pretty girl I offered to carpool with to school. I'm about to get alone time with Juliet, and I won't let contemplative memories of Emma ruin that.

I wait on the front steps of the building for ten minutes before Juliet arrives. I offered to pick her up, since she's on the way to school, but she rejected me and said something like *Gender equality, I'll see you at 6:50!*

I climb into the passenger seat and prop my backpack between my legs. She's wearing pale ripped jeans and a honey-gold top with flutter sleeves. She smiles, her dark brown eyes highlighted in gold as well, and I'm so distracted by the sheer beauty that I miss what she says. "Huh?" I ask intelligently.

"Good morning," she repeats.

"Oh. Good morning."

She blinks at me a few times, then says, "Don't be embarrassed, Caleb. I look cute like this every day."

I cough on my spit. Can I be any more goddamn obvious?

Her chipper laugh revs my heartbeat. "Onward," she says, and she floors the car into the street. It's a fourteen-minute drive to school from my complex, so I have that amount of time to get her invested in a conversation. Maybe I should ask her about . . . ?

Emma fell in love with you.

Mom's voice assaults me out of nowhere. I blink, and a rush of images overwhelms me—Emma looking up at me, Emma smiling in that roguish way that warns me she's up to something, Emma filling the air with colorful words to make me laugh when I'm upset, Emma leaning against my back in her bedroom and whispering that nobody else will ever understand her.

"Caleb?" Juliet cocks her head at me. "Your energy is a little too intense right now. I mean, it's not even seven. You okay?"

"I'm . . . okay," I say, though it escapes my mouth in a wheeze.

"How was dinner with your dad on Friday?"

Yes. The perfect distraction. "It was good," I say brightly. "It's nice to see him every once in a while. Sorry I ditched you guys."

"Don't worry, we still had fun." She gives me a cheeky smile. "Though, not as much fun as when you were there."

She's probably lying (I'm infamous for my ability to kill joy), but it warms me anyway.

"I'd take any chance I could to hang out with my mom more, so I get it," she says, returning her attention to the road. It's spoken like a throwaway line, but the distance in her eyes tells me it's much more.

"She's busy?" I assume.

"Mm-hmm. Barely saw her before the promotion, and now . . ." Juliet exhales, reclaiming her smile. "She brought a blow-up mattress to her office in case she falls asleep there."

That seems excessive. "The woes of having a hardworking mother," I say, and on a whim, I nudge her shoulder. "My mom's got a day off a week, so we try to spend it together when we can. Do you have that kind of opening?"

"Mm. Sometimes." I notice her throat bob. "Her off days are usually spent running errands. I go with her when I can, but it's not very . . ."

"Fulfilling?" I ask.

She sneaks me an affectionate look that burns my cheeks and makes me want to kiss her. The thought comes out of nowhere, and it's not even possible when she's driving. Not to mention it's wildly inappropriate when she's sharing something private about her life. But I can't help but notice that she holds my gaze too long for it to be casual.

Emma must be early for once, because she basically materializes at Juliet's side as soon as we exit the vehicle. When I see her, the smile slides off my face and splatters onto the asphalt. Emma's dressed in leggings and a ratty T-shirt, her reddish-blond hair gathered into two ponytails draped over her shoulders. When we make eye contact, my brain flings me back to my conversation with Mom.

Nope. I can't think about that.

"Emma," Juliet says enthusiastically.

"Hey." With the purple half moons under her eyes, she looks exhausted. I hate that my protective instincts are flaring—that I want to ask if she's okay. But she wouldn't tell me if I did.

We walk to the school doors. It's a cool morning, but the air feels damp, so I can tell it's going to be muggy and irritatingly hot. Juliet fills the silence with details about this show she's been obsessed with and how she's been waiting for the US release of the movie, but none of her old friends would accompany her because it was "cringey shit." Though she initially begins to spill details with hesitancy, her voice comes louder, faster, when we don't push back. She stops fidgeting with her hands, and her trepidation gives way to passion and excitement.

I mentally bookmark this conversation. I'll find the courage to ask if she wants to go to the movie with me. But later—I don't want Emma inviting herself along.

"Oh," Juliet says suddenly. "Balls. I forgot my water bottle. One sec!"

She whirls around and sprints back to her car, leaving Emma and me in tense silence.

"You couldn't let me have this?" I ask indignantly.

Emma huffs. "You did the same thing to me when I dropped her off at school."

This is true. Doesn't make me less annoyed, though, especially after how we left things on Friday. "If you wanted more time with her, you should've texted her this weekend. Since you don't have responsibilities to worry about—"

"I was applying to more jobs," Emma snaps.

Hesitantly, I turn my eyes to her. She's tapping her foot, gazing off to the parking lot. Is that why she looks so miserable and exhausted? I spent the whole weekend running errands, assuming she and Juliet were bonding without me. How dire is it that she'd put job applications before Juliet?

"How's that going, then?" I ask.

"It's not."

"Why?"

"Because my résumé is shit?" She flicks up her index finger. "I suck at interviews?" Her second finger. "They think I don't have reliable transport?" Her third. "My resting bitch face?" Fourth.

"Do you look up interview questions before going in for one?" I ask, propping a hand on my hip.

"No. I mean, they ask the same stuff anyway," she mutters.

"Do you have work-related skills on your résumé? Like 'good communication' and 'time management'?"

Emma flings her arms into the air with exasperation. "What, I'm supposed to lie?"

"Yes!" I say, nodding sharply. It's just like her to do the bare minimum of research before diving headfirst into something. "To get a job, you have to gloat about how amazing you are and how much you want to work for them. When they ask why you want to work there, what's your answer?"

Emma rubs her sneakers self-consciously against the sidewalk. "Because . . . I need money?"

I slap my forehead. She can't really be saying that, right? Well, I don't want to spend more time around her, but if she has a job . . .

that's good for me, right? If she's working, she'll be spending less time with Juliet. "We could try mock interviews," I say, albeit reluctantly. "We ask you questions and prepare you for actual interviews. Send me your résumé and cover letter template."

Emma squints at me in bewilderment. "Résumé . . . *and* cover letter?"

"Your résumé lists your qualifications. Your cover letter explains to an employer why you'd be a good fit," I say impatiently.

Emma's mouth falls open. "They're two different things?"

My palm collides with my already-stinging forehead again. *"Emma."*

"Whatever!" she yells, dismissing me with a wave. "I didn't ask for a lecture."

"It's not a lecture." On a whim, I tack on, "I'm not even wagging my finger."

There's a heavy moment of silence. Then she snickers, and my shoulders relax, my resentment ebbing away as the air between us loosens ever so slightly. "You're lucky I never broke that finger," she whispers.

"I would've used a different one to criticize you," I say amusedly.

"Your middle?"

I consider it, an unwilling smile coming to my lips. "No, that would've been too vulgar. You couldn't even get me to say *hell* until sixth grade."

"But then it was a snowball," she points out, grinning back at me. It's not as sharp and mischievous as the ones she's been offering for the last several days. "You said *damn* one day, and two weeks later you were screaming *motherfucker* to the skies."

She's not wrong. I faintly remember the invigoration of inappropriate words when I stubbed my toe. "I blame you for my descent into impropriety."

Emma heaves a sigh. "At least that hasn't changed," she says wearily. "Your posh ass is still using irritating words."

"I'm not posh!" I squeak, which makes her head arch back with laughter. I squeeze my fingers together so hard my knuckles pale. What's taking Juliet so long? I hate how comfortable I'm beginning to feel, like I'm settling into an old atmosphere we used to share. Hoping to change the subject, I blurt, "Mom asked how Brooke is doing."

The air around Emma thins and cools. "She's fine," she says in a murmur. "Living with her dad."

She doesn't offer anything further. So I leave the subject and nearly melt with relief when Juliet reappears with a sparkly pink water bottle, smiling apologetically. I draw a deep breath. I'm going to ask Juliet to see that movie on Saturday. That's what I should be focused on.

Because my relationship with Juliet is the only one that matters.

Emma

"You hate it," I say.

Alice gives me that sweet, shit-eating smile that says everything I need to know. Scowling, I tear my outfit off and rustle through the pile I created on her bedroom floor. Thankfully, both of her parents are out this weekend—her father on a work retreat, her mother on a girls' trip up north—so nobody was here to judge me as I strolled in with heaps of clothing and staggered to Alice's room.

"You need a new wardrobe," Alice says, picking up a stained T-shirt between her index finger and thumb like it's contagious.

That earns an eye roll. "Sure, I'll just add that to the budget."

Alice gives me this long, tortured look. "Em . . ."

"No," I say immediately. I don't want to hear whatever advice she's about to solicit to my unwilling ears.

"I know she doesn't deserve shit from you," she says, ignoring me. "But would it be worth it to . . . apologize? Even if it's a lie. Just so she'll restock your wallet."

My jaw clenches tight enough to nearly crack bone. She must feel my lethal aura because she laughs awkwardly and rubs the short blond hair on the back of her neck.

"Just an idea, babe! But your deadly sin is pride, so I should've known better."

"You'll never catch me apologizing to that woman," I mutter, clawing through more clothes. Not without efficient methods of torture, at least. "There has to be something movie-date-worthy here."

"Right. *Date.*" There's something subtly amused in Alice's glittery black eyes, like she knows something I don't.

"Ye of little faith." I hold up a white tank top. "This and skinny jeans?"

"Do you have a decent jacket to wear over it that isn't a muddy windbreaker?" Alice asks skeptically.

Good point. I've been wearing that jacket on evening jaunts to the high school soccer field. A few attempts at fancy tricks have landed me on my back. In moments like these, I used to invade Brooke's room and beg her to let me borrow something nice and nonscroungy. She'd sigh, then tell me I should spend money on things other than T-shirts before flinging open her closet and arranging the perfect outfit for me.

I've been texting her pictures today, asking for approval or advice. So far, nothing.

Alice throws me a plaid cardigan from her closet. "Pair this with the top and jeans. And let's curl your hair so it looks like you tried. Also, I'm guessing you only have sneakers and cleats in your car?"

I smile meekly.

"Typical." She returns to the closet. "You're lucky we're the same size in everything but tits." As she flings cute ankle boots at me, I forgive her for the annoying suggestion about my mom.

I squirm into the outfit, leaving the plaid cardigan unbuttoned on my shoulders. I'm useless at styling my hair, so Alice works her magic, sitting me on a stool in the bathroom while she curls it and loads the room with toxic hair spray fumes. She even allows me to steal blush, eyeliner, and mascara. Makeup isn't part of my routine anymore, simply because it's annoyingly costly to replace.

"Okay." I twirl before her. "How do I look?"

Alice nods approvingly. "Like you're ready for a date that isn't a date."

"It's a one-on-one at a movie theater," I say irritably. "I even said, *Want me to be your date to that movie?* And she confirmed she's queer at the bowling alley."

"First of all," Alice snips, "anyone could say *I'll be your date* and mean it in a platonic way. Secondly, *queer* could mean eight trillion things." She narrows her eyes. "Best not to make assumptions until she's sticking her tongue in your mouth."

Wouldn't that be nice. I haven't felt the silky taste of someone's tongue in my mouth since last year.

Ew. Fuck. Okay, pure thoughts only from now on. I'll assume a heterosexual persona until further notice.

"I'll text you after our first kiss," I say.

Alice gives me a crooked smile, spinning her phone in her hand. I try not to think much of it, because she's been giving me the ick this whole week, ever since she nonchalantly mentioned that she and Juliet have been periodically texting.

I don't want to let her scare me, so I leave her pessimistic energy behind and take off for the theater with a thank-you and a plea for good luck. Juliet, Caleb, and I carpooled multiple times this week, which might've been horrible if Juliet didn't occupy our silent time by talking about the characters, plots, and romantic pairings of her show. Watching her rant and squirm over something she loves so much makes me want to giggle and roll around on the floor.

Wait. No. *Heterosexual.* I'm a dainty, quirky cishet woman whose only desire is to be pinned to a wall by the burly arms of a lonely farm boy with a mysterious past. I'm feminine but independent, confident but humble. I am not like other girls.

Attempting to think that way is useless. As I pull into the theater lot, my palms are sweaty, and my heart reels with excitement. I mean, she invited me to dinner afterward. How else am I supposed to take this?

I walk as sluttily as I can into the building. The ceiling domes over my head, and confetti carpet sprawls out before me, stretching toward a concession stand, bar, and numerous dim hallways. What should be a welcoming sight, though, is immediately destroyed by a well-dressed big friendly fucking giant.

"Execute me," I say.

Caleb's face warps with horrified disbelief. *"You?"*

"What do you mean *me*?" I demand, stomping up to him. He looks irritatingly cute in a collared maroon button-down and black slacks, his hair ruffled flatteringly, like he's been carding his hands through it. "What are you doing here?"

"Waiting for Juliet," he says with a scowl, his almond-shaped blue eyes burning a noticeable trail down my outfit. "And let me guess, you showed up to sabotage me?"

"I texted Juliet three days ago and asked her to see this movie with me. She even invited me to dinner!"

Caleb stares at me in incomprehension. "I asked her on Monday."

Before me? I feel a slight tear in the center of my heart. So that's why Juliet was relaying her show to both of us this week. I thought she was only filling me in, but . . . dammit. When I'd asked if she wanted company to the movie, she probably assumed I was asking to come with both of them.

"Salutations!"

The recognizable, radiant voice causes us to turn. Juliet is striding toward us in a checkered dress that hugs her ample curves nicely and swishes at her knees. My brain is spinning from the shock, the disappointment of it all. How did Caleb and I manage to mess this up so badly?

"Hey," Caleb squeezes out.

"Yeah," I say cleverly.

Juliet is nearly hopping in her high heels, her twist braids bouncing with her. "Thanks for coming. I've been so excited to . . . you know." She laughs, raining sunlight upon us lesser commoners. "I've been torturing your ears about it all week. Anyway, I'll get the popcorn!" She's already skipping off to the concession stand. "Can you find us good seats?"

Caleb and I exchange a wary glance, then head toward the

theater. I swear the walk through the doors into the faintly golden-lit room takes half an hour. "I can't believe it," I grumble as we climb the illuminated stairs toward the middle. There's hardly anyone here aside from a few couples and a group of college-aged guys toward the back. "Every time I think I'm getting time with Juliet, you *appear*. Don't you have drawers to organize or something?"

"I finished that earlier," he says defensively, earnestly, sincerely, in every way that makes Caleb himself. I pick a row halfway up, and though I'd normally sit in the middle, Caleb has always preferred the edges so he doesn't disturb people when his baby bladder acts up. So I sit in the third seat. Caleb opts for the first seat—a conscious decision to allow Juliet to sit between us, which simply means that he'd rather give us equal access to Juliet than sit next to me.

Fair. He hates me, after all. I've been acutely aware of this for years, but it doesn't lessen the ache in my chest.

Juliet arrives with a bucket of popcorn just as the trailers are beginning. She glances at the gap between Caleb and me, then plops down. "I know we're eating out after this," she whispers, "but I live only for theater popcorn. You have to ask for real butter and sea salt, though. You'll never go back—"

Someone hisses, "*Shh*" behind us—a college boy who tosses his middle finger up when I rotate to glare at him. The crushed, antsy look on Juliet's face throws me to my feet, because how *dare* some ugly frat boy with a backward cap make her look like that?

"The movie hasn't started yet, you asshole," I growl.

He lurches to his own feet in retaliation. "Want to come up here and say that again, bitch?" he asks loudly, shrugging out of his friend's pleading grip.

Other people are murmuring and staring. I'm about to make a verbal observation about his hairline when sudden movement draws my attention. Caleb is climbing the theater stairs, his face contorted with wrath—the kind that sends chills scratching down my spine. Since when could he look like that?

The boy sees Caleb approaching, and . . . yeah. Whether you know him or not, seeing that kind of fury on a six-foot-four guy's face is daunting. The boy takes an uneasy step back. To my astonishment, Caleb storms into their row and looms over the boy, causing all of his friends to tense.

"Sit down and keep that word out of your fucking mouth," Caleb snarls, his low, cavernous voice echoing through the theater.

With that, he thunders down the dimly lit staircase to our row, then folds into his seat. I can hear the boy muttering cuss words and his friends ordering him to let it go. Thankfully, he no longer seems interested in confrontation.

"Wow." Juliet's dark eyes sparkle with admiration. "That was the sexiest thing I've seen today, Caleb. Well done."

Just today? I think skeptically, peering over her shoulder. He's clutching his armrests with white knuckles, looking dangerously close to projectile vomiting. "Are people staring?" he chokes out. "Tell me they're not staring. That was terrifying."

Juliet and I exchange a glance, followed by uncontained giggling. Dammit, this guy is too freaking cute sometimes.

I wonder if Juliet is thinking the same thing.

"That was badass," I whisper to him.

Caleb gulps in a dramatically deep breath. His lips waver into an awkward smile.

"Learned from the best, Em."

Emma

The movie might've been interesting. If I'd watched it. At all.

Throughout the film, my eyes wander to the armrest I share with Juliet, then the one she shares with Caleb. I keep hoping I'll reach into the popcorn bowl at the same time as her, but whenever I stick my hand in it, I feel spindly fingers nowhere near as smooth and dainty as hers. So I smack kernels out of his hand, to which he flicks mine in retaliation, and we all but beat the shit out of each other's fingers until Juliet suddenly puts the bucket between her feet. Our punishment for distracting her, probably.

We leave the theater listening to Juliet gush about how "they did the arc justice" and "captured that scene so well." I adore listening to her ramble about things I only half understand.

But why does *he* have to be here to share this moment?

We return to our cars, which I guess should've been the first sign this wasn't a date. I lug Morgana through the cluttered, gridded city streets and find a parallel parking spot beside the restaurant, which I promptly drive past because fuck parallel parking. I discover a lot behind the building that looks free enough, so I shift into a spot. October has brought an ice-gray sheen to the air, and the clouds hang low enough to obscure the skyscrapers in fog. Light from the shrouded sun melts into the horizon, giving way to the glow of traffic lights and streetlamps.

I wait outside the restaurant, watching people barhop or amble to the shopping center, hugging my plaid cardigan and hoping this place isn't as fancy as it looks from the outside. Footsteps scrape up behind me, and I fling my fists out defensively. It's only Caleb, who observes my fighting stance with weary annoyance. His dark hair is even more tousled—he's probably been gripping it in frustration.

"Let's get a table," he says, swinging open the door. Sitting alone with him in a romantically lit restaurant sounds like a hellish nightmare from the depths of my subconscious, but it's chilly, and Juliet should be here soon. So, fine.

I amble to the host stand. There's fancy Italian music playing, like, the authentic opera kind that doesn't involve the moon hitting one's eye like a big pizza pie. There are candles, *real candles*, at the center of every table, and the environment is painted in dim gold that screams elegance.

"It's not as pricey as it looks," Caleb says, tunneling straight into my inner thoughts. "I looked up the menu before we came."

Good. I check my phone, squirming. Where is Juliet?

The hostess leads us to a booth situated next to a window, so at least I can stare at the street while we wait. We sit against the wall of our respective sides, clearly hoping Juliet will choose to sit next to us.

After a minute, Caleb speaks up. "Juliet texted. She stopped for gas and asked us to order the fried mozzarella. Her treat."

Yippie.

When the server stops by, we order waters and the cheese. I scan the menu and select a cheap entrée, though that doesn't stop me from continuing to read the fine print. Likewise, Caleb's focus is razor sharp on his menu, and I know he's doing the same thing— pretending he's absorbed so we don't have to make small talk.

Just when I'm about to squirm out of my mortal shell, my phone buzzes. *Brooke?* I think eagerly, but no. "Juliet?" I ask, connecting the call.

"—so sorry, I can't believe I'm doing this, I'm worse than the guy who called you the *C*-word to your face! Well, no, I'm obviously much better than that little-penis boy, but I *feel* like I'm worse—"

"Wait, slow down!" I plead, holding the receiver away from my ear with a wince. "Are you okay? What's going on?"

Caleb springs upright, alert.

Juliet gasps in a breath. "Sorry. I'm almost at the restaurant, but Mom called to say Terrell has news to share with us. And they're basically waiting on FaceTime for me to show up so he can talk about it."

I feel the blood draining from my body. "Ah," I say squeakily. "You're not coming?"

Caleb's marble-white face somehow pales.

"I'm so sorry!" she cries out, sniffling. "I even made you order fried cheese . . ."

"It's okay. Um. We'll eat it."

"Oh, good! I was trying to think of something we'd all like, and then I remembered how much white people love cheese—not to be stereotypical; I know some of you are lactose intolerant—okay, I have to go! Sorry again. Enjoy dinner!"

Aaand she's gone.

I tuck my phone away and begin to scramble out of the booth, because no, absolutely not. "No need to stick around," I say, but Caleb shakes his head, scowling.

"We can't leave without paying. And what are you going to do for dinner?"

It's a good question, not something I would've asked myself until I was halfway across the city with no destination in mind. Maybe I could snag something off the dollar menu at McDonald's. I'll have to go home soon, though, since I left all my food on the counter while fleeing, which means the cash I nabbed is dwindling faster than usual.

Caleb returns to looking at the menu. "Leave if you want, but I'm eating here, even if it's by myself."

Dammit. Does he have to say it like that? This is my chance to escape, but . . . the thought of him sitting alone, telling the server that his companions abandoned him . . .

Sigh. I settle back into the booth and text Juliet, telling her I can't wait to hear the news. Another conversation catches my eye lower in my texts.

You said you wouldn't entertain that asshole anymore.

You promised.

Maybe I should leave it alone, but how can I? After the years we dedicated to helping him loosen the choke hold his father had on him . . . what happened? "I thought you cut your dad out." I try sounding casual rather than accusatory, but his stiffening neck and crossed arms tell me he's already on the defensive.

"People change," he says, cool and rigid. "He's been making time to see me."

"Consistently?" I ask skeptically. "He's not inviting you to dinner one week, then dropping communication for months because of *other priorities*?"

"I've seen him a lot this year," Caleb snaps. "And he *does* have other priorities."

"Right," I say, rolling my eyes. "Like that time he promised to show up for your first basketball game and not only missed it but ghosted you for three months, then said he couldn't make it because his friend invited him to *watch a real game* at the bar."

Caleb's cheeks glow, and I immediately feel bad. Back then, though, sometimes blunt honesty was the only thing that got through to him. "I'm glad he didn't show up. I dropped out halfway through the season because I tripped in every game."

Lies, justification, misplaced faith. He's reverted to all of these things. By eighth grade, he'd given up on his father's empty words and promises. Caleb was . . . happier. Less concerned about impressing his father, about his texts going unanswered.

"Look, whenever you put faith in him, you end up disappointed," I mutter.

"He's changed," Caleb says, dagger sharp. "What would you know? You're behind on that relationship by four years."

Ouch. The moisture evaporates from my throat, leaving it dry and crusty. Now I *really* don't want to be here. Maybe I should apologize for bringing it up, but he's already continuing, his voice a deep rumble.

"Since you're nagging me about my dad, I guess I can nag you about your mom?"

I give him an incredulous look. Maybe he realizes what a low blow that is, because regret is already brimming in his eyes. "Fuck you," I say shortly, and I start climbing out of my seat—

"The fried mozzarella," our server says, blocking my exit and setting the appetizer on the table. "Still waiting for one more?"

I stare at her in dismay, trapped like a caged animal.

"Just me," Caleb says apologetically. "Sorry. I promise I'm a good tipper—"

"Lasagna," I blurt.

They look at me. So does the table beside us. I guess I screamed.

"I . . . request the lasagna," I say thickly, gripping the table to keep from toppling over in embarrassment. "I shall take the baked potato and house salad as my sides. You may hold the tomato."

"It's not a five-star restaurant," Caleb whisper-hisses to me.

"They have real candles," I whisper-hiss back.

"And mozzarella sticks."

"So? We're in America."

Caleb gives me this bewildered look, like he's just discovered a new species of human.

The server clears her throat, pens my order, then turns to Caleb. "For you, sir?"

"Don't torture yourself," Caleb says, his focus on me unwavering. "I'm used to eating alone, and it's better than spending an hour with someone you hate—"

"I have *never* hated you!" I shout.

Oops. I'm not sure where that burst of rage came from, but it's too late to backtrack. Caleb's balled fists tighten, and he glares at the fried cheese between us. "How would I know that?" he asks irritably. "You broke us up without any explanation."

Anger and guilt bubble into my bloodstream. "Don't assume things," I utter, blinking away the tingle in my eyes.

Caleb's eyes flash with rage, and I know I've said the wrong thing. "My best friend decides to never talk to me again, and I'm supposed to forget about everything we went through? About this person who changed my life? I'm not supposed to try to figure out what I did wrong?"

I want to disappear under the table, where nobody can look at me, talk to me, or touch me. "Y-you . . . didn't do anything wrong." Every pained, croaky word claws at my throat, desperate to remain unspoken. "I . . . It was my—"

"I recommend the shrimp linguine," our server wheezes out.

We whip toward her in terror. I guess we both forgot she was waiting for our orders. "Shrimp linguine sounds delightful," Caleb squawks.

The server sprints away.

Caleb instantly turns to his phone. I seize some mozzarella sticks and munch, fumbling for my own. It's awkward and wildly uncomfortable, but we get through the wait without exchanging words. I stare at my unanswered messages with Brooke, trying not to reflect on his words. I should've left when I had the chance.

When the food arrives, I'm so nauseous I can barely choke it down. Which sucks, considering it's the best lasagna I've ever had. "Thought you didn't like shrimp," I say, eyeing the pasta Caleb's twiddling around his fork. "Because of the texture."

He grimaces. "I panic-ordered."

That nearly makes me laugh. "Checks out."

He gives me this stern look that actually manages to lighten my mood. I push my lasagna toward him and gesture for his meal. His jaw flexes with uncertainty.

"I like shrimp," I say, snatching his plate and stuffing a forkful into my mouth.

Caleb sighs but offers a brief smile of appreciation before digging in. I'm impressed. Years ago, he never would've eaten food that had my "spit" on it. "That changed in eighth grade," Caleb mutters.

I blink at him in puzzlement. "Huh?"

"Your *spit*," he says, and I burn ruby red when I realize I accidentally voiced my thoughts. "I realized I didn't mind it back in eighth grade."

"Really?" I slant my head, frowning.

He pokes at the top layer of noodle on the lasagna, his throat bobbing. "I stopped caring as much about germs . . . after you kissed me."

Oh God. Oh *fuck*.

What do I say to that? I want to fling myself out the window. I want to choke to death on this shrimp. How do I run away so I don't have to acknowledge that?

Thankfully, a flash distracts us both, and by the time we look over, our server is gone and has left us one bill in her wake. Whew. "Too late to ask her for separate checks?" I assume.

"We've tormented her enough, I think. I'll get it." Caleb swipes the book out from under my approaching fingers.

"This isn't 1926," I say snippily. "I'm a capable, independent—"

"I'm paying because you don't have a job, not because you're a lowly woman."

I scowl but relent. Mostly because I need to preserve Mom's money. I have no idea how much upkeep my car needs, but I need to spend cash on it soon, lest it fall apart while I'm on the expressway and I have to Fred Flintstone it to some gas station.

As soon as Caleb gets his debit card back, I lunge out of the booth and say, "See you."

"Wait," he orders, snagging my plaid sleeve. I hate the two pangs that strike my heart—one of guilt, one of inexplicable hope. He stands, reclaiming the upper atmosphere. "I'll walk you to your car. That parking lot isn't well lit."

I almost tell him I have enough internal rage to body anyone who tests me, but I nod, because he'll insist. It's probably not worth mentioning that I used to protect him in the past, because he was always too unsure of himself to stand up in his own defense.

Caleb has grown in several ways, without me being there to hinder him. As I knew he would.

Caleb gives me a soft nudge between my shoulders that makes every fiber of my body tingle. He escorts me to the parking lot, his shadow stretching over mine as we amble to my car. I sigh, relieved that this is over, and unlock the doors. "Thanks for dinner," I say. "If Juliet abandons us again, I'll cover that bill."

I hope he'll give me a pity laugh for trying to lighten the mood. Instead, his face is contorted with horrified disgust. All at once, I realize my mistake. My interior lights illuminate the disaster that's been steadily accumulating over several months. The empty water bottles, wrappers, takeout bags, clothes, scattered toiletries, and schoolbooks and . . .

"It's not what it looks like," I say uselessly.

Caleb doesn't seem to hear me. "One option," he breathes.

"Um . . . and that is . . . ?"

"We burn it"—he turns on me with wide, insistent eyes—"to the ground."

"We can't," I say, though nothing would make me happier than to start anew. "I need transportation."

He flings open the passenger door, seizes a plastic bag from . . . some forgotten moment in my past, then shoves discarded trash into it. "Unbelievable."

"Leave it alone," I order, fumbling for the bag, but he hip-checks me, causing me to stagger sideways. "Caleb!"

"What is this? What's going on?" He picks up a Ziploc filled with . . . Oh God. Moldy toast crust. His index finger pops out, and I know I'm in deep shit. "I can't *believe* you're still not eating your sandwich crust. It's the healthiest part of the bread! Are you back on your 'junk food or nothing' diet? Where are you getting nutrients from? And *how* could you let your car get this bad without cleaning it?"

He's wagging it in my face. Maybe I should be annoyed that he's berating me, but the sound of his strict concern is clenching my chest. I don't know why. I guess . . . it's been a while since someone cared. At least to his extent.

"Seriously, what have you been eating since I stopped making you lunches?" he demands, snatching up more trash. "And what's with these blankets and pillows? Do you *live* in here?"

My body stiffens before I can stop it.

It's like Caleb's turned to stone. A new, dangerous energy hovers around his shoulders. "Emma," he whispers, chilling enough to erect goose bumps.

"Gotta blast," I splutter out. I slam the passenger door, then vault my car hood and scramble into my driver's seat.

"Wait!" Caleb sprints around to my side, but I lock the door, forcing him to bang on the window. *"At least let me deep-clean your car!"*

I fling my vehicle in reverse and hot wheel it out of the parking lot. When I look in my rearview mirror, I find him galloping toward his car.

He's going to follow me.

Naturally, I get stuck at the first red light I see, which gives him time to slink into his car and pull up behind me. My eyes find his in my mirror, and I see he's glaring, his expression ferocious enough to make me gulp. There's only one solution.

I drive around until he gives up.

Oh, do I try. I take random turns, exceed the speed limit, and swerve around corners, pushing Morgana to the brink despite knowing the risks. I'm not sure how else to get away from him. Caleb won't stoop so far as to break the law to follow me, right?

But there he is, right on my rear, eyeing me like a slab of meat on a cooking stone.

I don't know where I'm going. The city lights become a blur in my mirrors, and soon I'm driving along random suburban roads, targeting roundabouts to confuse him. My car dings at me—is it the low gas, tire pressure, washer fluid?—but I don't pay it attention. "I believe, Morgana," I say, patting the dashboard with nervous fondness.

I veer onto an unmarked dirt road. No way he'll follow me this far, right? He'd risk getting dust all over his car.

A moment later, his headlights flood my vision. He's still pursuing, and I know it's not just because he wants to deep clean my car. I worried him. It's so dark now that I can't see him through his windshield. We're far enough outside of the city that there aren't incoming headlights or additional cars. Now I *really* can't lose him.

My phone vibrates in the cupholder. Shivering with anger, I swipe the call and put him on speaker mode. "Leave me alone!" I yell.

"*Please* stop the car so we can talk."

"No!" I can't let Caleb wriggle his way into this situation. His heart has always been bigger than whatever feelings he harbors toward someone, which means he'll want to help me, despite everything I've done to him. And that . . . would be too painful. "My life isn't your business, so—"

Thunk. My car jolts like I hit something heavy.

Then the whole thing shuts off.

My heart staggers to a stop. Panic shudders through my body. My headlights. My engine. I can't see. The road is too dark. I'm still moving. Shit. *Shit.*

"Emma?" Somewhere in my fright, Caleb's steady voice finds me. "Why did your lights go out?"

I can't speak. I'm still moving at forty miles an hour. The only light providing vision is from Caleb's car, illuminating the edges of the road.

"Turn your hazards on, okay?"

Hazards. Right. My hand finds the button.

"Pump your brakes and pull over."

Brakes. I push down on them. There's resistance, but I manage to slow the car and curve to the shoulder of the road. I shift into park and sit there, stunned, numb. What just happened? I don't know . . . what to do.

There's a tap on my window. Caleb's shuffling around outside my door. Without thought, I push it open, and broken, frail words tumble from my mouth. "Turned off. My car. It . . ."

Suddenly, Caleb leans over me, close enough that his soft, dark brown hair grazes my cheek. He unbuckles my seat belt, then takes my trembling hands, lifting me onto my feet before I can tell him, *No, I'm fine, just let me deal with this.*

"My car turned off," I repeat pointlessly. "It just . . ."

"Hey. Look at me." Caleb catches the frame of my face in his sprawling palms, tugging it up, forcing me to meet his pale blue eyes. Oh God, those gentle eyes. I . . .

I can't get lost. I try tugging away, because it's the only thing that might save me from falling, but suddenly, he's wrapping me tight in his arms. I don't realize I'm sobbing until my face meets his shoulder, and my tears are accumulating into a puddle on his collared shirt. I clutch his back, uneven gasps raking my chest.

"Deep breaths, Em." He combs his fingers through my stiff, curled hair, careful not to catch any knots. He works through the ends, then trails down between my shoulders, drawing a tentative line toward my waist. He nestles his chin against my head, and in that moment, I remember why I fell in love with Caleb Daniels and why I'll keep loving him always and forever. "Just relax. I'm here."

I'm here. Why? After all this time, why is he still *here*?

I'm close to melting in his arms, telling him everything, begging for his forgiveness and asking him to never let me go again because nobody cares about me the way he does, so fully and unconditionally. I never want to leave this moment, this feeling. I want to keep him.

So I wrestle away.

I smear my hands across my face, eliminating the tears that escaped without permission. I want to tell him to leave, that I'll call a tow truck, but he's already climbing into my car. He cranks the key in the ignition. The engine whines, and my headlights flicker. Smoke isn't pouring out of my hood, so that's a good sign. One more crank, and Morgana finally comes alive, rumbling warningly.

"Tire pressure is low," Caleb says. "You've got twenty miles of gas left. How long has your engine light been on?"

I scratch my head, blinking with lethargy. "Couple days."

He arches a skeptical brow.

"Few months," I whisper.

He gives me a once-over, then asks, "Are you okay to drive?"

I'm still shaking wildly, but I manage to nod. I have to stop being so pathetic in front of him. The more vulnerable I am, the warmer he looks. The more he wants to be there for me.

To my surprise, he holds out his car keys. "Follow behind me," he instructs. "Let's get this to the nearest gas station so we can fill the tank and tires."

I want to tell him he doesn't have to do . . . any of this. He doesn't have to stick around or switch vehicles with me so I'll feel safer. But it won't make a difference, so I jog to his car. I have to move the seat closer to the peddles by about thirty inches and readjust the mirrors a substantial amount before I can see anything out of them.

Caleb begins to limp my car toward the city. Drawing deep breaths, cooling myself down, I follow him.

"Thank you, Cal," I whisper.

Obviously, he doesn't hear me.

CALEB

Emma doesn't crash my car on the way to the gas station, so there's that. She pulls into a parking spot near me and sits motionless as I tug out my debit card and cash for the gas and tires.

I stare at her dashboard, sighing. The airbag and check-engine lights are on, and she's in desperate need of an oil change. A sudden image of Emma's face, bemused but soaked in tears, infiltrates my mind. The helplessness in her eyes. The flush in her cheeks. Her fractured sentences. The way she fell so trustingly against my chest . . .

The gas pump clicks, startling me out of my stupor. I replace the pump and give Emma a thumbs-up. We drive to my apartment complex, where Emma parks my car next to hers, then mumbles a thank-you as we switch keys. Before she can head to the driver's seat, though, I catch her elbow.

"Please don't drive that until I look at it tomorrow when there's sunlight."

Emma bites her trembling lower lip. "You've done enough," she whispers.

That's not true. I haven't done enough for Emma Jones until there's nothing left I can possibly do. I don't bother explaining that to her, though, so I merely say, "I'll get you pajamas, and you can spend the night."

"What?" Emma's eyes widen with alarm, and she backs away. "I can't *sleep* here."

"I'm not letting you sleep in your car outside my apartment," I say sternly, clasping her wrist and tugging her toward the stone staircase. As we enter the apartment, I murmur the words that have been lingering in my head for the last hour. "Is that . . . what you've been doing? Sleeping in your car to avoid your mom?"

She stares at the kitchen floor tiles, deadpan.

I stride to my bedroom and fumble through my dressers, her following behind me. The sight of her deflated shoulders makes my heart ache. I hate that it makes me feel anything. "How long ago did you . . . move yourself out?" I ask carefully.

"Last year."

A lump swells in my throat. I pick out an old T-shirt and shorts that won't be outrageously big, then toss them to her.

"I don't sleep anywhere unsafe," she says, reading my thoughts. "I usually park outside of Brooke's house in this nice suburb. Sometimes I pin my blankets over the windows—"

"Stop," I plead. The more she speaks, the more anxiety prickles at my skin.

"I . . . sleep in Alice's room sometimes. In a sleeping bag." Emma must notice the tension building in my shoulders. "It's fine."

A spark of frustration escapes into my words. "*I'm seventeen and living out of my car* doesn't sound fine."

"I don't have a lot of options!" she snaps, her voice breaking.

I have several opinions, but I don't want to continue arguing with her when she's upset, so I merely nod toward the bathroom door, and say, "You can get changed. Use the shower if you want."

"I . . . Okay." Suddenly, she looks defeated again, like she's lost all strength in her body. She retreats to the bathroom and closes the door.

Okay.

I swap my clothes for sweats. When Emma emerges, her hair damp and her face newly burnt with the remnants of tears, she finds me in the kitchen scooping ice cream. "Tell me you still like mint chocolate chip," I plead.

She looks at the bowls on the counter in befuddlement. I try ignoring the fact that my shirt practically crawls to her knees, which makes it look like she's not wearing pants, which gives me this rare tickling sensation in my stomach. I scowl as I plop another scoop into her bowl. Seriously? We've grown apart, and yet I'm still somehow . . . ?

"Don't you hate mint chocolate chip?" she asks.

"It's okay."

"So your mom is the culprit," she says with a smirk, wandering to the counter. "I knew she had good taste."

I decide not to confirm or deny that, because I don't know if I have the capacity to answer further questions right now. I watch as Emma rubs her eyes with a yawn. Her stature is normally so uptight and proud, so unafraid and confident. Now it's like she's slowly curling in on herself. I plop a heavy dose of whipped cream on her dessert, then slide the bowl toward her. She's smirking.

"What?" I ask suspiciously.

"It's just like you to lecture me about eating junk food and then scoop me a bowl of ice cream."

It's just like you. The words poke into my heart, but I ignore it, bringing my own (more meager) bowl to the couch and flicking the TV on so we don't have to sit in silence. We watch *The Golden Girls*, licking our ice cream spoons. Mint chocolate chip . . .

Is actually horrible.

"Thanks," Emma murmurs. Her legs are folded into her chest, and she's balancing her empty bowl on one kneecap.

"Has that happened before?" I ask. "Your car turning off?"

"No."

"And your mom . . . isn't helping you pay for upkeep?"

"No."

I knead my temple. I've heard firsthand the things Ms. Jones has said to Emma—the way she compares her to her sister, the way she scratches and claws at Emma's self-worth. But she's always financially provided for her kids. So, what, Emma ran away and her mom took it as an opportunity to make her fend for herself?

Emma stands, takes our bowls to the sink, washes them out, and places them in the dishwasher with a familiarity that makes my chest tighten. When she returns to me, her fists are scrunched around my shirt, and her expression is severe. "I'll take the couch," she says firmly.

Keeping my eyes above her collar, I say, "Take the bed. You've had a shittier day."

She squirms with discomfort.

"I'll drag you," I threaten.

She scoffs loudly. "And use physical strength against a gentle lady such as I?"

I propel myself to my feet, and Emma skitters back toward my room. Maybe she remembers how easy it was for me to hoist her off my car the day we met Juliet. "Fine," she says irritably. "Thanks. Um. Good night."

She closes the door.

The usual silence overtakes the apartment, aside from the hum of the TV. It's late enough that the upstairs neighbors aren't running after their kids. I flip open my laptop on the coffee stand and look up Emma's vehicle information. Then I retrieve my tool kit, car jack, and safety glasses from the utility closet before setting my alarm.

I snag a spare blanket and pillow from the hallway closet and sprawl out on the couch. Trying to erase her teary, desperate expression from my head. Hating that some part of me wanted to keep holding her as she wrenched away—to wrap her up tight and keep her there until she stopped crying.

I wonder if Emma finds my bed comfortable. The mattress is old but relatively big—enough so that we both could've fit on it.

But that seems like a bad idea. So the couch it is.

CALEB

BACK THEN

Emma's eyes were forests. The soft wood of bark, the crisp green of summer leaves, the sparkling gold of sunlight. Had they always been so colorful?

"Cal?" Emma smashed her brows together, looking up at him with suspicion. Caleb had finally grown to be two inches taller than her, so they were no longer at eye level. For some reason, he sort of liked that.

He blinked, coming back to his senses. "Heh?"

"You're staring."

Oh. He wrenched his eyes away, hating the warmth tickling his cheeks. They had come to the park with his mom for a Saturday lunch and left her behind on the picnic blanket with a risqué romance book while they went to explore. Every time a strange noise sounded from the woods, Caleb squealed and staggered back while Emma lunged in front of him, balling her fists.

Years later, he was still a coward. But maybe that was okay, so long as he had her.

They crunched along the leaves and twigs of the pathway to the open field. Caleb didn't realize he'd lost focus again until he felt an elbow poke his side. "You're quiet today," Emma said, fiddling with her fingers in that "you're making me nervous, but I won't admit it" way.

Caleb chanced another look at her and regretted it instantly. Her eyes were doing that shimmering thing again. Forests. The kind you could get lost in. And *getting lost* was something he'd been doing all day. He didn't understand what was different—it wasn't like they hadn't walked in the park before. So why . . . ?

"Hey. Daniels. *Hello.*" Emma waved her palm in front of his face. "You okay?"

"What's it feel like to have a crush?" he asked.

Emma stared at him. Caleb stared back. Then his face got fiery hot, and he threw his hands up defensively.

"Sorry, that was weird!" he cried out, and Emma threw her arms around her stomach, bellowing with laughter.

"Why the hell are you thinking about something like that?" she asked, grinning.

"Just wondering." His voice was barely audible. They'd talked about crushes before, but Caleb wasn't sure he'd ever legitimately had one. Sometimes, he felt like the whole school was in on a giant joke he wasn't part of. They talked about sex, romance, hotness, with an enthusiasm that didn't feel real. What was so great about it? The sex stuff sounded gross, and the romance stuff sounded like things he already did with Emma, like going to the movies, having dinner together, sharing a bed . . .

"You've had crushes, right?" Emma asked, poking her finger at him. A warm breeze fluttered through the leaves and branches, tugging at strands of her hair. "Like Nadia from my team. You said you really liked her."

Well, he really liked the pretty, intricately patterned hijabs she wore. She swapped for a different one every day, and they were usually stitched with eye-catching designs like stars, checkers, and flowers. Oh, and she always smiled when he waved at her from the stands, unlike some of the other girls who snickered and whispered when Emma wasn't paying attention. Of course he liked her.

"For me . . . I know I have a crush when I get this butterfly feeling in my stomach," Emma said, softer than Caleb had expected. Rather than swinging her eyes between the trees, as she was prone to doing, she centered them on the ground. "When I see them, my heart beats faster. I wonder what it would be like to hold their hand and kiss them. I want to make them laugh and . . . protect them."

Butterfly feeling . . . ?

Caleb fanned a palm over his rib cage. The heat in his stomach, the rev of his heart, the urge to stay with her, the ache he felt when she left . . . He'd never experienced these sensations before. Over the last year, his emotions had grown stronger, to the point where he started noticing the shiny balm on her lips. The points of her canine teeth when she smiled. The forest in her eyes.

Was it normal for best friends to notice these things about each other?

The trees broke apart, spilling into an open field where kids played tag and teenagers tossed a football around and his mom was reading on her back, her dark curls splayed out chaotically around her narrow face. At the sight of her, Emma smiled and sprinted forward, collapsing next to her on the blanket they'd sprawled in the grass. Mom laughed and fished in the picnic basket, drawing out a cookie—clearly, it was the first thing Emma had asked for.

"Cal wants one too," Emma said when he caught up to them.

He hadn't voiced this. He'd been trying to be more responsible lately, and he already had three cookies, which was more than the amount he'd allotted for himself. What was Emma tempting him for?

His mom plucked another chocolate chip cookie out and waved it in his face. The smell was delectable, and it was warm enough that the chocolate was melting. It was the perfect cookie, really. "Okay," Caleb said in resignation, taking it. Emma winked at him, all smiley, her lips stained with chocolate. Caleb wanted to hand her a napkin. He thought he might also want to wipe it off her lips with his thumb. And then maybe even . . .

Huh. That was new.

Caleb flipped away from them and nibbled his cookie, hoping neither of them had noticed that he was blushing deeply.

Emma

I don't wake until noon. Which is a lie—I'm technically up at eight, then at ten. But I'm in Caleb's room, and his white sheets smell fresh and crisp, with a hint of lavender. Everything is spotless and organized, not a single item out of place. His pale blue walls are decorated with paintings of landscapes. Places he mentioned he'd like to visit one day—scorching beaches, frosty mountains, open skies where the city smog doesn't choke away the stars.

I drift in and out of sleep, the whir of his fan a comforting white noise. It's been a long time since I slept on a mattress.

Eventually, I start feeling guilty about occupying his room, and I slide onto my feet, peeking into the hallway. Ms. Daniels's bedroom door is closed. Hopefully I can sneak out before she sees me, because otherwise . . . I don't know.

I just don't want to see her.

I shamble into the living room just as Caleb is striding through the front door in a stained T-shirt spattered with oil, carrying a toolbox and car jack. Safety glasses sit atop his hair. His skin is smeared with whatever my car shat on him while he worked on it.

"I . . . thought you were just looking," I say weakly.

Caleb wipes his sweaty forehead. His degree of dirtiness tells me he's been out there a while. "I bought oil compatible with your

car and replaced yours. Your fuel filter was clogged, so I cleaned
and reinstalled it, which turned your engine light off. Your airbag
light is on—you might need a new clock spring." He plops his tools
down, then begins to pry his gloves off while I watch, mesmerized.
Caleb . . . is dirty. Dirt. On Caleb. And sweat.

He looks *good*.

"I can't change it without special tools, so you should make an
appointment with a mechanic," he continues, oblivious to my enamored gaze. "Get your muffler repaired, too. It could leak exhaust
fumes into your car."

I'm both dazed by this sight (Caleb Daniels is *dirty*) and overwhelmed with everything he just said. All I can say is "Oh."
Obviously a *thank you for spending your Sunday morning repairing
my car* is in order, but I can't find the right combination of words,
and they won't be enough. They never are.

Caleb rubs his neck, then says, "I'm going to shower. You can
stay if you want."

He squirms past me, then grabs clothes from his room and disappears, leaving me standing there petrified. Though Caleb's tone
was light, I know he doesn't want me around. I should leave before
I weigh heavier on his shoulders.

I grab my keys and basically hurdle over the staircase railings to
get away from the apartment. I'll figure out how to repay him later.
Right now, I just need to get out of his hair. If I stay . . . I might say
or do something I'll regret.

But then I get to my car.

It's still a rusty sack of shit, but it's a *clean* sack of shit. My clothes have been folded in a woven basket, the floors are visible, and my blankets and pillow sit tucked atop my passenger seat. My toiletries are organized in a plastic basket that must be his.

Morgana comes to life without sobbing. The muffler is still an annoying rumble in my ear, and the airbag light glares at me, but otherwise . . .

She's going to make it.

I take a gasping breath of relief. It's so much more than I realized. I *can't* leave now. Not without making him breakfast or something. I jog back up to his apartment and try bursting through the door, until I realize I foolishly locked it behind me. "Wait!" I cry out, pounding on it. "Caleb, let me in! *I'll scramble your eggs!*"

He's probably in the shower and can't hear me. But then the door clicks.

Ms. Daniels pokes her head outside, her eyes bleary, clearly having just risen from sleep. Her hair is knotted into an explosion of brown waves atop her head, and chunky classes sit on her skinny white nose. She's in her late thirties, but she looks more like a college student who stayed up late studying.

I consider fleeing before she can process my presence. But her ice-blue eyes widen, and her slumped figure snaps upright. "Emma!" she says. "Oh, honey. Come in!"

Honey. The word awakens a familiar warmth I've tried to forget over the last few years. "I . . . actually," I say, my brain working to hand me an excuse to leave, "I forgot I need to . . . escape."

Shit.

"What did you say about scrambling my son's eggs?" she asks, gesturing for me to step inside. Reluctantly, I do.

"I was going to make him breakfast," I mumble. "He did work on my car . . . Figured it's the least I can do."

"No wonder he was sleeping on the couch. You were in his bedroom?"

I swallow hard. "I didn't want him to feel like he couldn't sleep in his own—"

Ms. Daniels cuts me off with light laughter. "You know how he is," she says, wrapping an arm around me and guiding me into her kitchen. I resist the urge to lean into her touch. "Whether you're a friend or enemy, he'll give up his bed for you."

"Yeah," I whisper. That's Caleb. Always giving, giving, giving.

Ms. Daniels hands me a basket of ruby-red strawberries. I rinse them in the sink while she pulls out eggs and bacon. Moments later, the crackling of greasy meat is almost enough to drown out the silence.

I grab a knife from the utensil drawer, then get to work on slicing the fruit.

"You know," she says, and my grip tightens around the handle, "Caleb's favorite part of the day used to be here before school. Making your lunch perfect was exciting enough to get him out of bed." Her lip flinches upward. "He says you used to come to school with Pop-Tarts and chips when left to your own devices."

I don't know what to say. I go with "Oh."

I scrape the strawberries into a bowl, then snag a spatula and begin stirring the eggs on the stovetop while Ms. Daniels flips the bacon. It's becoming . . . comfortable. I hate that it feels like no time has passed, even though it's been four years since I blocked her number. There was no other way to keep her from contacting me, and seeing her messages made my stomach burn.

If you want to talk to someone, I'm here, baby girl.

The walls of my throat feel thick and sticky. I wish there was more tension in the air. This ease is depressing.

"Brooke doing okay?" she asks eventually.

"I think so." Even if she's been avoiding me.

"You think?"

I should've just said *yes* like a normal, noncryptic person. "She moved in with her dad last year," I say, keeping the information minimal. But she's a mom (a good one), so she knows what to ask next.

"She started a new life and left everything behind?"

I've been avoiding that acknowledgment for a while. Nice that she can say it to my face point blank without hesitation. "I guess," I mutter.

"And your mom is still pretending she's the pinnacle of perfection?" she guesses.

"Always."

"Seems you're turning out okay, though."

I'm not sure that's true.

Maybe she notices my dubious expression, because her smile widens and she says, "You're doing good, Emma. Despite it all. You should be proud of the person you're becoming."

I drop my spatula, causing liquidy bits of egg to splatter onto the stove. What the hell? How can she say that when we haven't spoken in years? Why would she have faith in the person who ghosted her son after calling him her best friend?

I'm not her daughter. She's not my mom. She never has been, even when I convinced myself otherwise.

The bathroom door down the hallway opens, and I've never been so happy to see that lanky bastard. His hair is slicked back with shower water, his skin washed of grease and oil. He looks cozy in sweats. "Mom?" Caleb's dark eyebrows shoot high into his forehead as he looks between us. "Uh, what's going on here?"

He doesn't sound mad, which makes this worse. It feels too . . . nice. Whenever I slept over back then, I'd wake early and fumble around his kitchen to surprise him with breakfast as a thanks for always making me lunch. I was always too noisy, though, or burning things, which roused Ms. Daniels from sleep. She used to join me in this teeny kitchen, teaching me how to cook or arrange breakfast burritos and slice up fruit.

It made my heart sing. *When I marry Caleb, you'll be my mom for real*, I said to her once.

How fucking embarrassing.

"I . . . should go," I whisper, and I shuffle out of the kitchen, snatching my shoes. "Thanks for everything, Cal."

I book it before either of them can sneak in another word.

When Caleb texts me later to ask where I'm sleeping tonight, I lie.

CALEB

"I'm *so* sorry about my sudden and unexpected departure on Saturday" is the first thing Juliet cries when I climb into her car on Monday morning. In a group text with Emma and Juliet (one I'm reluctantly part of), we decided it was best to meet at Juliet's house on our way to school, since she lives the closest and doesn't require backtracking. She's scrutinizing my expression, her eye shadow glittering under the interior lights. "How was dinner?"

"Um . . . it was a dinner," I say weakly. How else should I explain it?

"I'd hope so." Juliet nods. "I'd feel betrayed if I went out to dinner and ended up with lunch."

The back door swings open, and I yelp, preparing to hurl my backpack at our assailant. But it's only Emma, who slinks into the seat, her hair tucked into a sweatshirt hood. Her powder blue sedan with the rusty tires is parked nearby in the street. "Yo," she mumbles. The purple under her eyes is more pronounced, and her face is pallid.

"Emma!" Juliet greets, peeking over the headrest at her. "I'm so sorry about my sudden and unexpected departure on Saturday."

"Huh?" Emma looks at her blearily. "Oh. No worries. What was Terrell's news?"

Apparently he won an award for teaching excellence. In October. Good for him.

We head to school. I pick up my conversation with Juliet but can't help my glances backward. Emma's leaned up against the window, her eyes sealed shut. Juliet looks between me and her rearview mirror with concern.

"You sure everything went okay on Saturday?" she whispers.

I nod, but in truth . . . I'm not sure anymore.

X●X●

The rest of the week passes without any indication that something happened on Saturday night. Emma and I continue ignoring each other and only talking to Jas, Alice, and Juliet at lunch. As the days pass, Emma seems to rekindle her flames, and returns to less-than-subtle attempts to woo Juliet with her charm.

It seems like Juliet is steadily feeling more comfortable around us. Every day, she speaks a little more—rambles a little longer. She dreams of cosplaying her favorite show and book characters at conventions with friends who actually want to go with her. When she isn't cooking with her dad, running errands with her mom, or calling her brother, she's playing video games and reading.

Not at the same time, she clarifies. *Nobody should have that kind of power.*

It's nice to see her . . . warming up. Juliet has always been warm in her mannerisms, but it's clear she held back for fear of scorn. When we're alone, she seems even more comfortable. On Tuesday, we walk to the library to study alone since Emma earned detention for throwing a box of tissue at Ian Summers's head during English.

In her defense, Juliet says when I groan, *the little wanker was whining about having to read three female authors in a row.*

Our "studying" ends up being "talking over open textbooks." Juliet curls up by the window and notes that the days are cooling down. This spirals into us discussing our favorite seasons, then Hallmark Christmas movies, then the overabundance of heterosexuals in media, then favorite queer characters. Juliet never mentions her own labels, but she seems relaxed. The first time we said *queer* around her during a brief conversation, she froze up, like it was a forbidden word. Now she's more at ease with using it.

I feel like we're becoming . . . you know. Friends.

It's difficult to tell where Juliet stands with me versus Emma. I always find myself closely watching and overthinking her body and verbal language around us. But then I question what, exactly, I'm overthinking, and who, exactly, I'm watching. I realize at one random point that I'm instinctively trying to determine how *wooed* Emma is by Juliet. Which is useless information, so I try deleting the part of my brain attempting to figure that out.

I text Emma daily to ask where she's sleeping. She claims she's returning home when her mom is in bed, but whenever she shows up to Juliet's house and it's her turn to drive, I notice her blankets and pillows are disheveled on her seats. I want to challenge her claims, but I can't without proof. So I have no choice but to hope she's not lying.

On Saturday, Juliet texts me that Alice is doing a chill stream with friends. I was intending to walk around the mall with Jas, but we shift our plans so I can prevent Emma from getting alone time with Juliet.

When we arrive, Alice and Juliet greet us with sparkling smiles. Emma, however, looks at us with startled repugnance. I guess nobody told her we were coming.

Alice fluffs up her short, dyed blond hair and thickens her winged eyeliner, then begins her stream and introduces everyone to her fancy camera with her fancy microphone. Everyone but me, at least, who has zero desire to have one thousand . . . now three thousand . . . now *five* thousand people watching me. The chat box begins to scroll faster as more people join to watch, spamming emojis and calling her pretty. I decide to stand near the plush couches in the center of the room, away from where Alice's webcam is angled but close enough that I can see the screen.

The four of them take turns venturing through an old game Alice already played on her channel to completion. Alice, of course, plays the game well enough that she might as well have designed it. As she warms her chat up, Juliet hops over to me, and I bump her in greeting with my elbow—which basically means I accidentally skewer her and rip the air out of her lungs.

"I'm sorry," I croak, steadying her. "I just meant to tap you."

Juliet is laughing overtop me. "It's okay. You're a growing boy."

I don't know how that's supposed to explain my dagger elbows, but I accept it anyway. We watch as Emma and Jas lean over Alice's shoulders, asking questions about the weapons and environment and world. Well, it's not technically alone time, but it's as close as I'll get to having any with Juliet.

"This is nice," she whispers.

I cock my head. "What is?"

"Just . . . this." She folds her arms around her chest, like she's giving herself a hug. The smile disintegrates from her face. "It's nice."

She doesn't specify, but I'm pretty sure I know what she's thinking about. I wonder how many times she found herself trapped in a room like this with people she considered "friends," tiptoeing through her sentences, swallowing her words and enthusiasm so as to not seem annoying or weird.

I wrap an arm around her shoulders and give her a squeeze of support, hoping she knows that I'm in her corner.

Juliet eventually leaves my side to get closer to the screen during Emma's turn. Emma's tactic, unsurprisingly, is to scream and sprint straight at enemies to clobber anything in sight. The chat seems particularly entertained by this.

"People love when Emma sits in during streams," Alice tells me, pausing by the couches on her way back from getting a snack tray. She's watching Emma with soft, fond eyes that cause my jaw to clench instinctively. An eighth-grade-Caleb reaction slipping through, I guess. "Everyone's always asking if we're girlfriends."

"Have you . . . considered it?" I ask, lowering my voice so those crowded around the monitors won't hear.

Alice gives me a deeply skeptical look. "Have you considered dating Jas?"

I shudder. Hell no. Half of our relationship would be her ver-
bally abusing me. Much like she does now, actually.

"She's not my type," Alice says, shrugging. "And I'm not hers."

"She likes cute girls with a sharp tongue. You fit that bill pretty
well."

"No, that's *your* type." Alice claps my shoulder, then whispers,
"Emma's type is *anyone Caleb Daniels shows interest in.*"

I stare at her, my mouth hanging open.

Pardon?

She's already back in front of the camera, telling Emma to get in
line for another turn. When Emma climbs out of the seat, she looks
flushed and riled up, like she's ready to fight the nearest person. I
can't help my smirk. Back then, playing games with Emma was
an overwhelming experience. Her competitive nature was always
intense, to the point where she would roll around and groan and
punch the ground with frustration if I wasn't playing with enough
passion. Teasing her annoyance out of her by purposefully being
bad was pretty amusing.

"Try a cookie," I tell her, picking one up from the tray.

"Hmph." She snatches it and nibbles. On a whim, I pat the top
of her head. I don't know why I notice when the tension between
her shoulders melts away.

Jas's method of playing is stealth based, in that she hides in
bushes and then gives up when none of the enemies get close
enough for her to silently kill them. "Meh," she says when I tell her
the chat is probably bored, flipping her coarse black hair over her

shoulder. "They get to look at me. That should be good enough for them."

"Your turn, Juliet!" Alice says, gesturing to the chair.

Juliet chokes on . . . her saliva, I guess, because her glass of water is out of reach on the windowsill. "No," she squeaks. "Just because I play video games sometimes doesn't mean I'm good."

"After spending ten minutes watching Jas crawl around in grass, there's no way you'll be less entertaining," I say, grinning when Jas smacks my shoulder.

"But I don't want to waste anyone's time," Juliet whispers.

"No such thing when you're with friends."

Juliet looks at me with wide, glistening eyes, like I've said something she's never heard. Emma takes her palm, guiding her to the chair and sitting her down. "You're hot and funny, babe," Emma says with a reassuring smile. "People will love you. See? Even chat is rooting for you."

Everyone looks at the monitor. Chat is rapidly scrolling across the screen.

Let's go Juliet!!

She's so pretty wtf

You'll do great

What foundation do you use?

DATE ME JULIET

Juliet blinks rapidly, like she's tearing up. "Okay," she says quietly.

Of course she's great, far better than she claimed to be. Emma, Alice, and Jas shout their support, egging her on as she ducks and dodges around enemies, landing critical shots, and I can't help but join everyone to better see the screen. Even if it means I'm within view of the camera.

There's a massive, beaming grin on Juliet's face now. Half of chat is still spamming her name. The other half is demanding to know who the giant thirty-year-old man in the back is. We keep cheering, making jokes, rooting her on.

By the time she pulls herself away from the game, her cheeks are glistening with tear stains. Happy ones, I think.

Everyone in the room silently agrees not to mention it.

DAD

Sorry I've been MIA for a while, caught up with work.

When Alice suggests we spend our evening in a karaoke room downtown, my first instinct is to say, *No, please, God, no*. But then Dad texts me back, and I'm suddenly in such a good mood that I say, "Hell yeah." Since Alice's parents are out to dinner, she stuffs a backpack full of their booze, mixers, and Solo cups.

"Are you sure we should drink?" I ask as we gather on the sidewalk to trek into the city. Downtown glows in a halo of gold, looming over the little subdivision, beckoning to anyone seeking an evening of entertainment. "It seems . . . risky."

"Caleb." Jas places a hand on my arm, looks deep into my eyes, and says, "Take a break from being the mom friend. We'll be okay."

Hmm. I've been in groups before—mostly with Jas's volleyball teammates. Maybe I won't have to be as concerned with these people.

"Try not to take on the responsibility of everyone," Emma says, her fists stuffed in her black jacket. She thumps her strawberry blond head against my shoulder, then starts down the sidewalk. "Let's all behave so Caleb Daniels can let loose."

I watch her retreating back, trying to think up some excuse to complain. Jas shrugs, and says, "Let's be delinquents," then follows her. Alice gives me a mischievous wink, like we're in on some joke together, before skipping off.

Juliet's arm slinks through mine. "Shall we?" she asks.

I become very aware of my pounding heart. Her eyes are sparkling and bottomless, like always. I find myself wondering what it would be like to kiss her. Her lips are full, soft, shiny. I imagine tucking a strand of hair behind her ear. Tilting her chin up, tugging her onto her tiptoes. The scent of mint chocolate chip on her lips . . .

Wait. What?

I clear my throat, returning Juliet's smile. "Let's go," I say.

Arm in arm, we head off after the others.

Emma

The karaoke entrance is a dingy, dimly lit alleyway on the edge of the city.

"Murder den?" I ask, eyeing the fogged glass door. "We're here for slaughter?"

Alice snickers. "Relax. The best karaoke places are off the beaten path. Now . . . men first!" She gestures at Caleb, who looks like he's anticipating that people may drop out of the sky to mug us.

"The burden of testosterone," he mutters, swinging the door open and tromping in. We fall into step, peering around his shoulders. A single fluorescent light hangs above the desk, where two women are speaking behind the counter. Behind them stretches a daunting hallway, and in front of them sit empty pieces of worn furniture.

Juliet takes up the gauntlet of talking to them, and requests a reservation for five. Then, we're following them down the horror-movie hallway and into a dark side room that at least twelve people have absolutely been dismembered in. Several neon light strands stretch across the crooks of the walls. A massive screen and microphones sit before a U-shaped couch, along with a touch-pad to select songs.

As soon as the women are gone, Alice breaks out the goods—

rum, vodka, orange juice, Coke, and Sprite. "And one last thing I didn't pack!" she says, pulling out sanitizing wipes. Caleb nearly glows with happiness, grabbing them and beginning to wipe the room down. I won't admit that I snuck them into her bag before we left.

"So," I say to Caleb as Jas and Alice debate whether rum is better than vodka. My goal for the night was originally to lure Juliet into singing a romantic duet with me, which will end with our eyes linking and our breath hot and yearning on each other's lips. Now I'm adding "get Caleb fucked up" to the list. "What are you having on your 'Caleb Daniels loosens up' night?"

He eyes the alcohol with wariness. "I've never . . . had drinks."

"I know. Because you babysit everyone and you don't want to be tipsy or you'll blame yourself for anything bad that happens," I figure.

Caleb's hand flinches, like he's resisting the urge to wag his finger.

"We'll all take care of each other," Juliet says, rubbing Caleb's shoulder. I can't help but notice her palm linger, and a twinge of jealousy rips through my chest. "If we die a death most foul, I'll shoulder the blame. And then I'll hand it to Alice, who brought us to this shady-ass location and supplied us with alcohol. Woo-hoo!"

She twirls to the booze table.

Caleb takes a deep breath, steeling himself. "Okay. *Here I go.*"

His determination nearly makes me double over with laughter. Fucking dork.

I allow him a taste of my rum and Coke, to which he screws his face up with disgust. Of course he'd need something sweeter and gentler on the taste buds, so I mix him a fruity, less-heavy-handed concoction that he's able to tolerate. In the back of my mind, I know I shouldn't waste what little money I have from Mom's stash on frivolous things like some hole-in-the-wall karaoke place.

But I've been taking a lot of losses lately. And this . . . sounded like fun.

Alice and I take the mics, singing a poor rendition of a duet with a soprano voice that's far too high for Alice and a baritone that's far too low for me. Jas then blows me out of the water with that one Zac Efron / Zendaya song from that one musical movie about that one problematic guy. To be fair, I'm basically guessing my way through the tune, but it's horrific enough that I instantly hand my mic to Juliet when I'm done.

"No, I'm good," she says with panicked laughter. "And by good I mean extremely bad. If I start to sing, we'll end the night with a concussion, and it will be my concussion, because you all have knocked me unconscious to escape."

"I'll sing horrendously on top of you," I promise, seizing her palm and . . . what the hell. I massage her fingers and slap a flirty smile onto my face. "I'll be so obnoxious that nobody will think twice about your voice."

"Please don't," Alice pleads, and Juliet grins, squeezing my hand and effectively setting my face on fire. Then, she gulps down her vodka and seizes my microphone.

"Let's do it."

She and Jas do "Don't Go Breaking My Heart." I snag Juliet's elbow and pull her up, forcing her to dance with me. Her laughter cuts in and out of the microphone, and then Alice is up, showing off wild dance moves clearly not from this century. Hoping the walls are soundproof, we bellow lyrics, switching the microphones between us, pouring more drinks while pacing ourselves with the water jug. Caleb watches from the couch in amusement, birdie-sipping his Solo cup.

After an hour, my forehead is hot with sweat, and my hair is up in the wildest bun imaginable. Every blink tilts the world. I figure I'm at my limit, proven correct when Alice snatches the rum from me and says, "Water, miss ma'am."

Right. Water.

Juliet is a giggling, bumbling mess, cuddling up at everyone's sides. Jas sways in her seat, her face carved with a smirk. Alice keeps dissolving into uncontrollable laughter caused by . . . pretty much anything. I'm doing a lot of running around, dancing, and rolling on the floor. But that's not just me, right?

While Alice and Jas sing "Ain't No Mountain High Enough," I swivel around on the floor to face Caleb. He's sipping his third drink, staring unblinkingly at his phone. I can tell immediately who he's texting from his strained but hopeful but tired but eager expression. "Your dad?" I ask.

Caleb blinks through a haze to look down at me. "Yeah."

"What's wrong?"

"Nothing. Just . . . his schedule keeps changing."

Maybe I should take Caleb's lack of involvement in the night as a win, since I've been given several opportunities to sing with Juliet and look lovingly into her eyes (she looks lovingly back, though I can't tell if it's romantic). But . . . God, he looks so dejected. "Turn your phone off," I order.

Caleb grimaces.

"You haven't done one song," I complain, grabbing his knees and knocking them together with irritation. "What happened to our 'Caleb Daniels lets the hell loose' night?"

"I like watching," he says defensively.

"Of course you do, because we're four attractive and sweaty girls who—" I sputter off when Juliet suddenly chokes on her drink to my right. Caleb and I stare at her in alarm as she catches her breath.

"Sorry," she hacks out. "Carry on."

She goes back to drinking, but she's noticeably tenser. Did I say something weird? I didn't realize I was talking loud enough that she could hear me.

Well, whatever. I scramble to my feet and wrench Caleb's wrists. He doesn't budge. "Stand up," I plead.

"I prefer sitting," he huffs.

Jas and Alice's song ends, and the next one we have queued begins to play. I steal both microphones and stuff one into Caleb's unwilling palm. Then I kick my voice as deep as it can go, and suddenly, I'm singing Aladdin's part in "A Whole New World," only it's basically an octave lower than it should be.

Caleb chokes on a snort. I'm feeling bold, so I flop into his lap and drape myself dramatically against his chest, seizing his chin, pulling our faces closer so he can't escape my horrific rendition.

Before the chorus, I wrench the mic away from my mouth and hiss in his ear, *"Loosen the fuck up, Caleb Daniels."*

He massages his temple, and I realize how close we are. It's not just our faces—I'm literally *sitting on him,* my back pressed to his front, my head nestled into the crook of his shoulder, my hair splayed over his shirt. Worse, I'm very warm and very buzzed, and he looks very, very pretty from this angle.

I have to get out of this situation before I do something I regret, so I slide onto my feet and begin to sing dramatically again. He smears a hand over his face, sighing.

"Come on!" I moan, pulling at his palm uselessly. "Sing with meeeeee . . ."

"No."

"Please?"

"No."

"Pleaasseeee?"

Caleb hurls himself onto his feet, startling me backward. He looks pissed now, and I wonder if I've pushed him too far in my drunken coaxing. He lifts the microphone, and for a second, I think he might throw it onto the floor.

But then, he begins to sing. No, *scream.* He's launching the words into my face, trying to sound angry, but everyone is already laughing hard enough to wipe the exasperation from his eyes. A moment later, we're shrieking in each other's faces, each of us trying to be louder than the other. He has the kind of voice that might normally shake the walls, but since I took Aladdin's part, he's trying to lift his voice into Jasmine's high pitch. Which means his words are cracking all over the place, and it's so funny, I can't even finish the song because I'm sobbing with laughter.

The music dies out while we're all trying to breathe. It's the worst version of "A Whole New World" to have ever been uttered.

"Okay," Jas croaks, wiping her eyes. "My ears are bleeding. I vote that Caleb can only sing male parts from now on, and we can only sing female parts. Sound good?"

"Yes," I say, my voice scratchy with strain.

"Yes," Caleb says, massaging his throat.

"No," Juliet says.

Everyone swivels toward her. She looks between us with bewilderment, then squeaks with surprise, like she just realized what she said.

"I mean, yeah!" she corrects. "The boy sings the boy parts, and the girls . . . *we* sing the girl parts! That's how it works! Gender and all that!" She gives us finger guns individually while emitting unnatural, high-pitched laughter.

The whole room is still quiet, especially because we don't have another song queued up. Juliet's eyes are two gigantic orbs that move between us in panic.

"What?" she asks dimly. "Why are you all looking at me? Let's get back to drinking and singing."

She swigs from her cup. When nobody says anything, she bursts into laughter.

Then she sprints for the door.

My body reacts for me, throwing me toward her and catching the crook of her arm. "Wait!" I plead. "Juliet, don't—It's okay!"

"It's definitely not!" Juliet shouts, tears glittering in her eyelashes. "It was the rambling of a drunken fool! I have to go puke or something." She wrenches away from me, heading again for the door. No. *No.*

I toss my arms around her shoulders, wrestling her back.

"Emma!" she cries out, trying to shove at me. "I don't know why I brought up the gender stuff, honestly, it's not . . . ! I'm not . . ." Her voice breaks.

I hug her tighter, fighting her resistance. Her struggles fade away, and she takes giant, gasping breaths, slumping against me. I smile, nudging a tear off her cheek with my knuckle. "Want to talk about it?" I ask quietly.

Juliet turns her eyes between all of us, like she's trying to determine if anyone here would think negatively of her. Slowly, she ambles back to the U-shaped couch and sits on the middle cushion, allowing Caleb and me to sit beside her, then Jas and Alice to sit on either side of us.

"This is a good group," Jas says, tentative. "But we can drop it if you want."

"No, it's okay," Juliet mumbles, focused intently on her thumbs. Several more seconds pass before she feels comfortable enough to start talking again. "So, like. I've been thinking for a couple years . . . Terrell is the only person I've told. But I'm pretty sure I'm nonbinary. Like, a she/they kind of person." She clears her throat, blinking harder. "I know that probably seems weird because I'm . . . you know. Feminine. And I like 'girly' things, like wearing makeup, dressing up, whatever." She squirms, and I settle a hand on her knee. That seems to destress her. "It's just . . . I don't always feel like a girl. I've been wearing a binder to see if that helps, though I haven't felt a difference . . ."

A fleeting expression crosses Caleb's face—one of realization, I think. We make eye contact, though, and it disappears.

"I'm pretty sure liking feminine things doesn't have anything to do with your gender," I say, giving her knee a reassuring squeeze. "Like, your gender and presentation can be two different things, yeah?"

Juliet swallows loudly. "Yeah."

"I know I'm cis or whatever," Caleb admits, his voice low and calming. "But I don't think every trans or nonbinary person has to have, like, body image issues to question their gender. Just because you're comfortable being 'girly' doesn't mean you can't be nonbinary."

"They're right," Alice says brightly. "So don't invalidate yourself, okay?"

Juliet looks between us with an appreciative smile. "This is weirdly easy," she murmurs. "My friends from my old school would've laughed at me. Said it was just a phase. I don't even want to know what they'd say if I asked them to use other pronouns. Holy shit . . . what a bunch of dick sluts."

None of us expect that, because we all reel back with laughter. Juliet's smile widens, and she looks so . . . relieved. Happy. She's beautiful.

Jas peers around Caleb's shoulder, and asks, "So, you want us to use both she and they for you?"

"Uh, maybe when we're alone?" Juliet asks, clicking her heels. "I don't want anyone else to know. Terrell has been trying to convince me to come out to my parents, but . . ." She sighs, her eyes glazing. "They've always said they're allies, but, like. Gender and sexuality are two different conversations, you know?"

"Okay," I say with a reassuring grin. "We'll toss in theys and thems in private."

Juliet gives me a grateful nod.

"That was really fucking cool," Alice says, lunging to her feet. She sways a bit and says, "Celebratory shot!"

"Wait, it's not a big deal," Juliet squeaks, but Caleb claps their shoulder.

"It's a *huge* deal."

So we take that shot and get back to singing. Juliet flings their arms around like they've never felt so free in their life. Caleb, too, finally lets loose, his stiff movements melting away and the bothered pinch disappearing between his brows.

I'm not worrying either. Not about how much money I'll have to fork over for having a night out or about hunting for a car mechanic or about whether Juliet is spending more time talking to Caleb than to me.

Alice's parents are in bed by the time we get back to her house, so she's able to return the alcohol to its appropriate pantry drawer without answering questions. Nobody can drive, so she lays blankets and pillows around her bed for us to claim.

"Sleep here, Juliet," Jas says, patting the blanket to her left against the wall. Where neither Caleb nor I have access to her. (Not that I was planning on getting in her space, but if she accidentally rolled into my arms, I wouldn't have pushed her away.)

"Okay!" Juliet flops down, humming.

Caleb grumbles, and Jas offers an icy smile that chills my bones. She must despise our competition as much as Alice does.

I sneak in a shower while everyone is getting situated, since I'm not sure where my next one will come from. After my run-in with Mom, I've been more reluctant to go home, even for quick jaunts. I dress in Alice's pajamas, and when I return to the bedroom, everyone is lying in silence, the only sound being the whirring fan. There's one space left on the floor beside Caleb, who's sprawled on his back, conked out. The thought of sleeping near him makes me squirm, but at least we're not alone. So I snuggle into the blankets, keeping to the outer edge.

But then I hear rustling, and suddenly, weight presses against my spine. Caleb has shifted across the floor and nudged his head between my shoulder blades. His every breath is slow, long. Warm. I can feel them through the thin material of my shirt.

It's how he used to lie during sleepovers. Curling up, nudging his head into my back, like he was unconsciously trying to get closer to me. I command myself not to roll over onto his face in my sleep.

It doesn't matter. I'm not going to sleep anyway.

Emma

BACK THEN

Having a best friend was pretty damn cool.

Caleb Daniels was a little wimp, but Emma loved it. If anyone said something nasty to him, her *best friend* (it felt funny saying that), she chased them around the playground until they apologized. She didn't mind getting sent to the office for using "dirty" words, as Caleb called them. Or . . . well, her fists.

Caleb made her delicious, balanced lunches, and it was . . . sweet. Mom never made their lunches because they were "lucky" she kept the fridge stocked and they should "put in the work" to feed themselves. Emma didn't fully understand why Caleb liked her enough to keep doing this, but was afraid that if she asked, he might realize there was nothing good about her after all and leave.

Emma started going over to Caleb's apartment more after school. She rode the bus with him and sat behind the driver, where Caleb felt the safest. Sometimes Ms. Daniels kept an eye on them, and sometimes she left a babysitter in her place. When they were together, they played fun games in Caleb's room or kicked her soccer ball in the yard behind the complex.

Emma preferred when Ms. Daniels was around. She was funny,

smiled warmly, and never made Emma feel like she was taking up space. Ms. Daniels hugged Emma when she left, kissed her forehead before they went to bed during sleepovers, and made a mean grilled cheese. Sometimes, she brought them to Mayberry Park or the ice rink.

When Mom picked Emma up, she never lingered, except to apologize. "Sorry to dump her on you," she always said to whoever was watching them. "Hopefully she wasn't a pain."

"Emma is never a pain," Ms. Daniels always replied.

One day, both the babysitters were busy, and Ms. Daniels had a night shift, so she asked Emma's mom to watch Caleb until she could pick him up around ten o'clock. It had been seven months since Emma and Caleb met.

It was the first time he would be in her house.

Caleb rode the bus home with Brooke and Emma, which was a new experience. Usually, if she couldn't go to Caleb's apartment, she was stuck at the after-school program while Brooke took the bus home alone.

Brooke and Caleb had met a couple of times, but this was their first full interaction. Emma made sure to sit behind the bus driver, and scoffed when Brooke squeezed them into the seat by sitting on the outside edge. She twirled her waist-length curly princess hair, asking Caleb questions about his mom, favorite subject, and *ugh*. Couldn't she leave him alone? And why was she so pink?

Caleb didn't seem to mind, though Emma wished he'd stop smiling so much.

She was almost annoyed enough to forget that her mom was home.

They ambled to the one-story house with the navy blue front door, though Brooke got stopped by one of the neighbors to grab a tray of freshly baked cookies. Good. Maybe Emma could sneak by her mom without her noticing they were home. "Let's go to the basement," she whispered.

Caleb frowned, obviously having hoped she might show him around. Emma nudged the door in and listened. It sounded like her mom was in the kitchen, clinking plates. She gestured for Caleb to follow, and he did, tiptoeing inside.

They crept across the matted living room carpet toward the basement door. Caleb was so busy looking around that he didn't notice a TV-tray rack, which he slammed his knee into. "Caleb!" Emma whispered, but it was too late. Emma's mom emerged from the kitchen, a towel draped over her shoulder. Her scowl was quickly replaced with that beaming, fake smile she slapped on whenever guests were over.

"Hi, you two," she said vibrantly. "I didn't hear you come in."

Emma wanted to grumble that yeah, that was the point, but Caleb stepped forward first, and politely said, "Hi, Ms. Jones. Thanks for letting me come to your nice house today."

"You're a sweet boy." She winked, then said, "It's a wonder you spend so much time around my daughter."

Emma felt the words jab deep into her chest. Caleb gripped his backpack straps tighter, his brows furrowing. "Let's go,"

Emma said, but her mom was speaking over her.

"How was school? This one didn't drag you into trouble, right?" She jerked her head at Emma, to which Caleb shook his own.

"No. Um." His eyes brightened, and he said, "We played soccer during recess. She's really good!"

Her mom arched a stern eyebrow at Emma. "Don't tell me you're pulling this boy off the playground so you can practice soccer. Have you asked him what *he* likes to do during recess?"

Emma couldn't find the words to confirm. Her ears were turning pink.

"She always asks," Caleb squeaked out. He was inching toward Emma like he was preparing to shield her from her mom's cutting glare. "I like playing soccer with her."

Her mom looked dubious. "Well, don't let her walk all over you, sweetie. She's like her father, this one." She swiveled toward the kitchen and whispered, "Useless," then walked away.

Like her father. Her mom loved sliding in digs like that, saying that Emma received all her negative qualities from him. Whenever she spoke of him, her fists clenched, and her face paled, like the words were painful.

Caleb was frozen, staring at where Mom had just been talking to him. Emma hoped he wasn't rethinking their whole friendship. "Let's go downstairs," she encouraged, tugging his sleeve. He followed her to the basement, silent, but when they were out of earshot, Caleb hurled his backpack onto the carpet with an angry huff.

"She's wrong!" he snarled, and suddenly, he was pacing. "You're brave and make me laugh and make me feel better when I'm upset. Just because you're bad at making lunches doesn't mean you're *useless!*"

He was more frazzled than Emma had ever seen him. She did something neither of them expected. She laughed.

"What?" Caleb's face colored as she gripped her stomach. "Emma, stop laughing!"

"Sorry." She wiped her eyes, grinning. "Seeing you get angry is funny."

"Why?" he demanded.

"You're Caleb. You're nice and sweet and stuff," she explained. "I'm the one who's angry and nasty. Not that you're being nasty. It's just funny."

Caleb's eyes darkened, and he drew farther away from her, his lower lip puffing out. "You're not angry and nasty," he mumbled. "If you were, I wouldn't be your friend. You're nice and sweet, too."

Emma was so stunned she couldn't even find a joke to respond with. And that was usually her forte. So she merely laughed again.

The basement door swung open suddenly, and they peered up the staircase to find Brooke's head peering through the crack. "You're being loud," she whispered, with a pointed glance at Caleb, like she was trying to warn him as well. "Be careful."

Emma cupped her hands around her mouth, then screamed at the top of her lungs. Sure enough, the footsteps upstairs grew louder, like Emma's mom was now stomping around the kitchen instead of walking.

Brooke's face gnarled with fury, and she hissed, "You make everything worse."

She slammed the door, leaving Emma to huff and Caleb to stand there awkwardly. Whatever. "What do you want to do first?" she asked, tossing her backpack onto the floor. Hopefully they could pretend none of that happened—

"Don't listen to her," Caleb said. His expression was severe, his mouth pursed. "I . . . I'm sorry I didn't believe you back when you told me she was horrible to you. I guess she's only nice when other adults are around, huh? But just know that she's wrong about you. Okay?"

Emma couldn't do much more than look at him, her mom's voice a bothersome echo in the back of her head. Had she made sure to ask him what he wanted to do today? Had she made sure to give him that extra candy in her pocket? Had she made sure to say thank you during lunch?

She smiled, and said, "Okay."

CALEB

My head is spinning. Alice's room is pitch black, so it must still be night. As my eyes adjust, I faintly see Jas and Juliet lying in the opposite half of the room. Which means . . . ? I twist my head. Emma is lying on the blankets beside me, fingers tapping her pillow in a methodical way that tells me she's not asleep.

"Why are you awake?" I mumble.

Her silhouette shifts with a shrug. "Floor is cold."

I stare at the moonlight trickling through Alice's blinds. *You used to be the warm one*, I almost say, but I bite my lips. No need to remind her that I used to curl up against her back during sleepovers so I could leech her warmth. "Have my blankets," I say, nudging them toward her, but she pushes against them.

"You're skin and bones. You'll die of hypothermia."

"I'm a healthy amount of lanky," I hiss.

"Whatever, string bean." She rolls so her back is to me.

"You . . . you can't insult me and then—"

"Hey," a blunt voice says across the room. "Mind shutting the fuck up?"

I gulp. Sorry, Jas. I shuffle closer to Emma and open my bundle of blankets, draping them over her. "What the hell?" she whispers, but I slap a hand to her mouth.

"*Shh.*"

Maybe I'm still tipsy.

"Sharing body heat," I breathe.

Emma coughs. "Oh."

I'm steadily becoming aware that we're only half a foot from each other. Her back is so close, her waist so available and magnetic, I have to hold my palm down to prevent myself from slinging it around her. Her shiny hair, which smells fresh and flowery, is tangled in a way that tells me she probably lay down while it was wet. I can't let go of my fingers or I'll twist them around her locks.

"Are you staring?" Emma asks.

I choke on my inhale. "*No.*"

She flips toward me, then startles me by stroking her thumb under my eye, a tiny smile furling her lips. "You're buzzed," she whispers.

I wonder what lotion she applied after showering, because her palm smells as nice as her hair. Which is weird to wonder, but I can't direct my thoughts anywhere else when she's right *there*. "No, you," I shoot back.

She snickers, then pats the top of my head, like she used to. "My gentle little Caleb, all drunk and sleepy. Have sweet dreams."

Hmm. That sounds pretty good, even though I don't like whatever the hell she just called me. "I'm six foot four," I mumble, eyes falling shut as she brushes her thumb once more against my cheek. I think Jas offers another cuss word. Emma's hand remains where it is, framed around my face.

I zero in on the rise and fall of her breath beneath the blankets, images from the night whirling through my head. It was fun. I want to thank Emma for helping me forget about my dad—for forcing me to loosen up.

But she's probably already asleep.

Emma

It's going to be a fucking amazing-ass day. Not only did Brooke finally answer my texts, but I successfully invited Juliet to hang out one-on-one this Saturday.

I spend most of the week after school at Alice's house, at the library (Caleb and Juliet like to study), or at my nook in the woods. I wasn't sure what Juliet and I might do on Saturday, but just as I was concocting something romantic and intimate, they texted me.

JULIET

Can we do it at my place? And bring pajamas :)

A sleepover. With Juliet. Be still, my heart.

There's no way in hell I'm telling Caleb. This is my chance to finally try and advance our relationship. Whether that's to Friendship Level Five or More Than Friends, we'll have to see. On top of that, Brooke invited me for coffee. I'm passing up an opportunity to study with Juliet and Caleb in the library, but if I don't catch her now, I might not see her for another year.

On Thursday afternoon, I chug Morgana to the local coffee shop, rehearsing my twenty-foot-long list of questions for her. I leap through the drenched parking lot to the front door. Rainwater soaks into my sneakers, but I'm too eager to pay it attention. I push into the shop, and the door swings shut behind me, cutting away the torrential rain.

It's a cramped local place with rustic brick walls and a high unfinished ceiling that captures every noise. I find Brooke at a rounded table in the back, her copper curls pouring over a lavender purple scarf and button-down jacket. She's fiddling with a to-go cup, her face drawn. Heavy.

"My long-lost sister," I say as I approach, giving a dramatic bow. "How ist thee?"

Brooke forces a laugh that doesn't reach her large honey-brown eyes. Something is definitely wrong. Already, I feel my chipper mood dissolving, my mind deliberating worst-case scenarios. I sit across from her and shed my jacket, until I realize she's not doing the same.

"Somewhere to be?" I ask, eyeing the to-go cup.

"Just . . . wanted to make this quick," she murmurs.

Quick? That really doesn't sound good. I know I'll regret asking, but I lean forward, folding my hands on the table, and ask, "Did something happen?"

"No." Her voice is tight, and her skinny, lightly tanned fingers squeeze her coffee cup. She won't meet my eyes. "I have . . . a problem."

"Which is?"

"You."

I stare at her blankly. I've already determined the direction this conversation is going, and it's causing blood to pump in my ears and drown my thoughts. I wish I'd gotten a drink from the barista so I wouldn't have to watch bitterness shape her normally calm, docile face.

"I've started this new life with my dad," she says, twisting the pink stud in her ear. "And it's . . . great. He cares about me. He cooks us dinner or pays for takeout without complaining about how expensive I am. He asks me how my day is because he wants to know, not because he wants to complain about his own day."

She inhales slow through her nose, then breathes out quietly through her mouth. It feels like she's been rehearsing this. Somehow that makes me feel worse.

"I know now what I was missing out on," she mumbles. "Mom fucked me up. I . . . I *hate* her for everything she did to us. To me. The pressure to be perfect and live up to her expectations, to listen to her go on and *on* about everything she *hated* and how hard it was to have kids who aren't paying rent . . ."

Brooke latches her jaw shut. Steadying herself.

I keep quiet.

"I've tried keeping her out of my life," she continues. "But she won't leave me alone. Every time she calls me, it's not because she misses me. It's because she wants to complain about *you*."

Brooke snaps her gaze to me, her teeth gnashing.

"Why do you have to provoke her?" she asks, her volume staggering upward. "Why don't you just *stop*? Every day in that house, you antagonized her when all she wanted was for you to shut up and behave." Her back straightens, her nostrils flare. "Do you know how often I covered for you, calmed her down, so she wouldn't make that house even more miserable? Do you appreciate *anything* I did to keep her off your back? Do you even realize how many times she threatened to kick you out?"

She sounds so desperate and angry. I've never heard this level of emotion from my sister. She's . . . been hanging on to this.

"You made everything more difficult," Brooke says, her voice breaking. Suddenly, the hardness in her golden brown eyes fractures, revealing despair underneath. "I *hated* that house. I *hated* hearing you scream at each other all day and night. Why couldn't you just take what she threw without punching back? Isn't it obvious she needs help? That she's traumatized? I wanted to bring up therapy, but I couldn't because . . ."

She slams her fist on the table, tears collecting in her lashes.

". . . every time I tried, you'd *piss her off*, and she'd completely close up again!"

Pain pulses through my body—each word an agonizing blow to my face, chest, rib cage. I feel myself sinking into my chair, lower and lower, becoming small enough that I could fit into her clenched palm.

"You're my big sister!" she cries out. "You're supposed to help, not make things *worse*! You're supposed to protect *me*! But I spent those years watching your back, looking out for you, keeping Mom from boiling over whenever you did something to annoy her." Brooke took a gasping breath and screamed, *"Fuck you!"*

She lunges to her feet, looming over me, tears gliding down her flushed cheeks. If people are looking at us, I can't see them. My vision is white around the edges, fuzzy. There's so much whirling around in my head that I can't decipher any of my thoughts quickly enough to hurl something back at her. I want to tell her that she's wrong—it never mattered whether or not I antagonized Mom, because she was going to lash out anyway. I want to growl that she doesn't understand because she was always Little Miss Perfect who could rarely do wrong in our mother's eyes. That it's not *fair* for her to expect me to hold my tongue and cower while that woman beat us down, over and over. That I thought, maybe by my pushing back, *maybe*, Mom would be less inclined to lash out so she wouldn't have to deal with me.

That she was able to flee, and she left me there alone.

"Even now, I can't escape because of you," Brooke says, shivering, and it's an odd choice of words, considering that I'm the one who's really trapped—that she was lucky enough to find any kind of freedom in her father. "My therapist suggested I should distance myself from things that remind me of the past. And you . . . you're one of those things."

I want to be mad. I want to punch the table. I want to throw my chair. I want to show her how much this hurts and how ridiculous this sounds and how unfair she's being.

But I can't. I have no strength.

"So stop texting me!" she snaps, her breaths shortening. Grief is clouding her eyes. Pain is twisting her features. "And f-find somewhere else to park at night so I don't have to see you across the street every time I close the shades. I n-need distance . . ."

She slaps both of her hands over her face and makes a sobbing noise.

When she lowers them, she's deadpan.

Brooke leaves. She just . . .

Leaves.

I sit there for a few minutes. Maybe an hour or two. Staring at the table. The blood rushing in my head has disappeared, leaving it devoid of everything but a buzzing noise. Somewhere in my daze, I wander to my car, where I sit for . . . however long. Whatever. Anyway.

Where to go?

I drive aimlessly through the pounding rain, weaving through the city without any destination in mind. I find my way to the high school. It's late enough that the skies are darkening and the after-school activities should be over, so I park near the front, squirm into my old cleats, and pluck my teal ball out of the back seat.

I head out to the soccer field. The gate is ajar—someone must've forgotten to lock it, so I don't have to climb the spiral metal fence to get onto the field.

I drop my ball onto the grass and dribble it around, rain dripping off of my hood and jacket. Each time my foot makes landfall, a puddle of water soaks my jeans. The rain is so heavy, I can hardly see, but that doesn't matter. I move from a light jog to outright sprinting, cutting a line down the field, pretending I have defenders flanking me. I dodge left, right, and the edge of my foot sends the ball careening into the goal.

Score. Yay.

I fish the ball out of the net, breathing heavily, and spin toward the goal on the other end of the field.

Do you appreciate anything I did to keep her off your back?

I guess I never said thanks. Not even once.

I punt the ball like Alice would have in goal, then race after it, catching it on one of the bounces and ripping across the field.

You're my big sister! You're supposed to help, not make things worse! You're supposed to protect me!

I don't understand. I was too busy retaliating against Mom to realize just how hurt she felt by my actions. In fact, part of me thought that by lashing out, by showing that I *wasn't* a doormat, maybe Mom would one day realize that she couldn't push us around and antagonize us without backlash. Maybe she would . . . ease up. If only to keep me from making her life a living hell. I thought I . . . could've made things better for us.

But no. I guess not. I guess the only thing I'm good for is making shit worse. I picture three defenders. But I can handle this. I kick sideways and spin around one of them, reclaiming the ball. I run faster, faster, the rain painting my face and dripping below my collar. I kick hard.

You made everything more difficult . . .

Maybe she's right. I don't know. But why doesn't Brooke understand that she always had it so much easier? That while Mom attacked us both, she was the golden child, and not just because she let herself get walked on. That there has always been something about me that Mom has despised, loathed even—something that Brooke was lucky enough to escape? Something surely to do with my father, a man who I subconsciously determined died long ago, considering Mom has never received child support from him, that he's never reached out, that he apparently has no family who knows about me.

Oops.

The ball isn't where I thought. My ankle folds sideways over it, and lightning hot pain slices up through the muscle. I collapse onto the sopping wet grass, then lie there, the rain a numbing roar in my ears, my clothes clinging to my damp skin. I try climbing to my feet, but fiery pain scorches up through my ankle, dragging me back to the grass.

I guess I should call someone. Do something about this.

I pull my phone out and try sliding the screen open. It's too wet to register my thumb. I try wiping it on my shirt below my jacket, but even that's too soggy and only smears the water around. After another minute of trying, I pocket it.

Okay.

I decide to lie there because there's nowhere else to go.

CALEB

My dad showed up for dinner, asked me questions about student council, *and* covered the check. Little steps, right?

I leave the restaurant feeling good. Now that homecoming is over and I'm not stuck taking notes at student council meetings, I got to study with Juliet at the library after school. *Alone*, finally, because Emma decided to meet up with her sister. There, we sat on a love seat, studying and chatting between subjects, lending each other colored tabs and highlighters and sticky notes. I'm pretty sure I'll never find anyone else with this level of commitment to organization again.

I coast to a stop under a red light next to the high school. My windshield wipers are at full blast, the rain smashing against the glass like bullets. Other than flashes of lightning forking across the sagging clouds, and the haloed red of other brake lights, the world is depressingly dark.

I glance out at the school looming to my right. The windows are black, the flag in the pavilion drenched and wrapped around its pole. The parking lot is empty, save for a couple of cars. Including . . .

A powder blue sedan with rust around the tires.

Huh? Hadn't Emma gone to get coffee with Brooke? That was the whole reason she'd driven separately from us today—so she could drive herself to the shop. I fish for my phone, texting her.

> You at school?

I wait for a response. Nothing.

I feel uneasy, so I throw on my blinker and turn into the lot. I drive carefully through the puddles of rainwater and slide into the spot next to her, squinting through the water dousing my window. Her lights are off—she's nowhere to be seen.

I text her again.

> Where are you? Tell me you didn't break into school to pull some she-nanigans.

I wait another few minutes, tapping my foot against the pedals. No response. Maybe I should take off, but something doesn't feel . . . right. Why is her car here? It's unmistakably hers, from its outer appearance to the clothes in disarray on her back seat.

Maybe her car died?

My shoulders sag with relief. That's probably it. Her car died, and Brooke came to scoop her up. Though, I'd spent a long time working on it to ensure something like that *wouldn't* happen . . . Maybe I'd done a poor job?

My hand moves to my gearshift, but I can't push the car into drive. Something's nipping at me. I try another text.

> Are you with Brooke?

I thrum my fingers against the curve of the steering wheel, waiting. More minutes pass. Maybe she's busy. Maybe I'm worried for no reason.

Hmm.

I zip my jacket to my neck and grab my umbrella, kicking my door open. I step into the rain and fold it open, then splash up the pavilion to the front doors of the school, tugging. They're locked. I tread around the perimeter of the building, lamenting the dampness seeping into my pants and tennis shoes.

Then I notice the gate to the soccer field. It's open.

I jog up the trail past the spiral fences and push through. The bleachers and sideline benches are empty, the scoreboard powered off. But there's someone lying on the field. Wearing a black bomber jacket.

Emma.

Emma.

I dash toward her, kicking up mud and dirt and grass behind me. I slip a few times on my way to her, but adrenaline and searing panic keep me on my feet. I skid up beside her and toss my umbrella aside, collapsing onto my knees.

"Hey!" I say shakily. "Em? Hey, can you hear me?"

She's soaked to the bone, her autumn-blond hair stringy and matted to her sodden face, her clothes thoroughly drenched. She blinks through the rain in her lashes.

"Oh," she says.

Thank God. I was about to measure her pulse. "What the fuck are you *doing*?" I demand over the rain, which is now permeating my clothes and dripping down my hair and face. I realize her teal soccer ball is lying just out of reach. Frustration grinds at my chest. "You came out here to practice during a *rainstorm*? You could break your damn ankle!" I snap, squirming my arm under her head to tug her upright. She remains like a rag doll in my grip.

"Sprained," she whispers.

I stare at her. Then my eyes trail down her jeans. Carefully, I tug up the cuffs of her pant legs to scan for damage. She's wearing socks and cleats, but I can see her right ankle is puffy.

I want to ask more questions, but right now, I need to get her to my car. I wrap my left arm around her back, scooping her into my chest, and then nestle my other arm under her knees. I hoist her up and climb to my feet while Emma stares at my chest, limp, dazed, like she's half-asleep.

Somehow I manage to not only get her to my car, but open the passenger door and settle her on the seat without dropping her. I dart back to the field to grab my umbrella and her soccer ball, then throw both in my back seat.

As soon as I slam the driver's door shut, everything becomes quiet. Water still pounds the windshield, and I'm trying to level my ragged breathing, but otherwise, the noise has all but vanished. I look over at Emma, goose bumps flecking my arms. She's shivering, her lips tinted darker than normal, her skin pale and smeared with mud. How long was she lying out there?

I fly out onto the main road, heading home. "Your car's going to smell like wet dog," Emma says.

Like that matters. She's still using that unnaturally emotionless voice from earlier, so I decide not to try and wriggle answers out of her for now.

Finally, we make it to the apartment. She's right—it'll smell mildewy and gross in here tomorrow, and I can't crack my windows to air it out—but that's the last thought on my mind. My heart still pounds at a frantic, unsteady pace from having seen Emma sprawled out on the soccer field.

I half carry, half limp Emma up to my apartment, flick on the lights, and guide her to my bathroom. Mom is at work, so we're alone. I sit Emma on the bathtub edge, then leave to invade Mom's drawers until I find what I need.

"Change into this," I tell Emma, handing her the clothing.

Emma looks down at the sports bra and shorts.

"Before I look at your leg, you should clean up and get warm," I explain, unexpected heat tingling in my cheeks. "A shower is probably better so you don't have to, like, sit in the muddiness. But it'll probably be difficult to stand without . . . someone to lean on . . ."

Emma stares at me blankly. My face heats further.

"Sorry," I say. "Maybe that's too invasive. We don't have to—"

"I'll change." Her voice quiets from its former monotony, but her face is still uncharacteristically flat.

"Let me help with your shoes." I kneel on the tile floor and undo her laces, then tenderly pry both cleats off her feet. Emma winces as I roll her drenched socks off. I place my palm over my eyes, and say, "I won't look."

I hear a small puff of air that I think, briefly, might be laughter. I hear her squirm around, and wet clothes flop onto the floor next to me. A minute later, she mumbles, "I'm good."

"Okay." I offer my hand to her. "Let's get you cleaned up."

Emma

I guess I don't expect him to actually get in the shower with me. But I'm still trying to awaken from the complete, total numbness that's been encasing me for hours, so at first, I don't register it.

"Are you sure this is okay?" he asks, standing with me in the empty tub. He moves my hands to his shoulders so I can keep my weight off my ankle. I'm still ice cold, but his house is steadily warming me. "If you're uncomfortable, I don't have to be here."

I'm always comfortable around him. "It's fine."

"Is it okay if I touch you?"

Anywhere. Everywhere. "It's fine."

Caleb stretches over me to grab the showerhead, then aims it at the drain until the water is warm enough to place it back in its position above us. It trickles soothingly over my head and down my bare shoulders.

Several seconds pass in which I simply stare at him, and he glances awkwardly around the shower, still dressed in his shirt and pants. They cling flatteringly to his frame. Caleb isn't a burly, jacked guy, but his lean body is still relatively toned. Probably from scrubbing so hard at stains and dirt every day.

Steadily, my present situation sinks in. I'm standing in a shower in a sports bra and shorts with Caleb Daniels, watching water dribble from his matted hair to his soft jaw, gripping his shoulders to keep from falling over. Caleb Daniels somehow found me on the soccer field, even though I hadn't been able to call him. He carried me to his car like we were newlyweds because I couldn't be bothered to move.

The heat comes back to my body all at once. I wrench my eyes away from his probing blue ones.

He reaches for his face wash. "Close your eyes."

Thank God, because I don't know what to look at. I close my eyes, waiting.

"I'm going to touch you now."

Why does he sound nervous? I hear him lather the face wash in his hands, and he begins to trace circles around my cheeks, chin, forehead, temples, and nose. I really hope he'll discard the flush in my cheeks as my body reacting to the temperature of the water.

But of course it's not that. I'm standing in a shower with my exbest friend. My first crush. The first person who I really . . . loved.

Of course I'm still in love with Caleb. I thought it might get easier—that time would help my aching heart move on. God knows I tried, jumping from relationship to relationship to feel *something* for somebody else.

But every time I watch him saunter by with those ridiculously long legs, my chest stings. Anytime I see him talking with Jas, or the student council, or his lunch table, my eyes burn. He's so close but so far away.

I hoped I could make it to graduation. Then, I'd never have to see

Caleb again. But in came Juliet—beautiful, kind, her smile brighter than the flaming ball of hot gas in the sky. A person who could finally give me closure and spark my desire to fall for someone else.

Except that plan is failing miserably. I'm no closer to being their girlfriend than I was when I first met them, and worse, being around Caleb again is causing my latent feelings for him to rekindle. Now, when I watch him interact with Juliet, I can't tell where my jealousy is coming from. Is it because I don't want him getting close to Juliet? Or because I don't want *her* getting close to Caleb?

What a goddamn mess, this bitch-ass heart of mine.

"I'm going to rinse your face," Caleb warns.

He does, then gingerly pats my eyes dry. I keep them closed, though, afraid that if I catch his gaze again, I won't be able to look away.

"Arms next," he says. "Is that okay?"

"It's fine," I say mechanically.

He squeezes bodywash into a cloth—something citrusy and musky—and runs it up my arms, my shoulders, my neck, my collar. The pleasant feeling causes butterflies to tingle in my stomach. "Okay if I wipe your legs?" he asks.

Part of me wants to poke fun at him for continuing to ask. But he's being a gentleman, like always, because he wants me to be comfortable. He wants everyone to feel comfortable around him. He doesn't like being in a crowd, but he's a people person, whether he knows it or not.

"It's fine," I say.

He crouches, beginning just above the knee in his venture to scrub the grass and mud off of me. He's gentle, far gentler than he is with his cleaning supplies. I've seen him rub a cloth against a mirror hard enough to burn a hole through his reflection.

Ever so carefully, he makes scraping motions across my swollen ankle, light enough that I can barely feel it. I resist the urge to open my eyes and watch.

"Now your hair," he says. I almost blurt that I can do it myself before realizing that no, I need both hands for that, and they're currently propped on the only thing keeping me from tipping over.

So then he's massaging shampoo against my scalp, all sweet and soft and careful to avoid knots, and I can't help but open my eyes. He's investigating my hair thoroughly, clearing it of mud, like he used to whenever I got wood chips tangled in my locks from the playground.

Briefly, he catches my eye. His jaw shifts, and he tilts my head back, rinsing the shampoo out. "Em," he says, so quietly that it wets my eyes. "What happened?"

I should tell him. He deserves the truth, and so much more. "Brooke," I murmur. "She's . . . cutting me out of her life. I was practicing on the field to distract myself."

I can almost see his palm beginning to curl, leaving one finger out to reprimand me for impulsively heading to the soccer field in the pouring rain. But he refrains. Instead, he whispers, "I'm sorry." He massages conditioner into his hands, then runs it through the ends of my hair.

"Hey, Cal," I say.

His palms falter. "Hmm?"

There are so many things I want to say. I'm not ready for any of them. All I can muster is a quiet "Thanks."

His fingers graze the back of my neck. "Always."

My lips tremble, and I resist leaning against him. Fuck this.

Caleb helps me dry off, then limps me to his room and gets me a T-shirt and pajama shorts. He leaves me to change, which is an arduous task, and takes a shower himself. I check my phone while I wait—thankfully, it still works. It's not like I plunged it into a pool, but I held it in the rain long enough that I was worried it was broken. Considering my luck recently, I'm surprised it didn't. I'm still on my mom's phone plan, probably only so she can call me to yell at my voicemail whenever she pleases, but I'm not sure she'd be willing to replace it after how I left last time.

When Caleb returns, he's wearing a tank top and boxer shorts and has supplies—an ACE wrap and bag of ice wrapped in paper towels. His brown hair glistens with dampness, and his skin is shiny from whatever moisturizer he uses.

He sits cross-legged on the bed, then tentatively lifts my leg up beneath my knee. His long tentacle fingers can basically wrap all the way around my calf and shin. He tilts my leg—the shadow of a bruise is already blooming around my ankle—and says, "I'll wrap it."

"You know how?" I ask, before realizing what a ridiculous question that is. Caleb knows how to handle every situation without fail.

He gives me a skeptical look, then goes to work. I watch his hands, normally so big and clumsy, treat me as gently as they did in the shower. I don't realize I'm staring at him like a mesmerized infant until he catches me.

"What?" he asks.

I want to say, *Nothing.* What comes out, though, is "Why?"

He pops a thick eyebrow at me. "Why what?"

Shit. Why do I keep backing myself into a corner? I steer my gaze away and say, "Like. After everything." My voice is barely above a whisper. Probably because I'm hoping he can't hear me. "Why do you show up for me?"

I know why. It's because Caleb is a good person. Too good. For the world. For me.

"What kind of question is that?" he demands.

I blink at the sharp edge in his voice.

"You think just because we stopped being friends, I'd stop caring about you?" he asks. He seizes the pillow next to me and props it under my ankle, then presses the bag of ice against it. I wince as it makes contact with my skin. My ankle is throbbing, but the pain isn't as stabbing as before.

"You should've," I mumble.

"Don't be annoying. You were . . . my *person.*" His cheeks flush as he says it, which nearly makes my throat close up. "You were always there for me. When people picked on me, when I was lonely, when I was back and forth about my dad. You were there. Every day."

Now I'm really sniffling up a storm. How can he say all of that, like I left more of a positive impact on his life than a negative one?

He can't see how detrimental my presence was to him.

After a moment of silence, he retrieves a glass of water for me, then gives me ibuprofen to help with the swelling. After twenty minutes, in which we both sit there awkwardly looking at our phones, he takes the ice bag to the sink.

"I'll let you sleep," he says, heading for the door.

"Wait!" I blurt, and he pauses in the frame. "This is your bed."

"I sleep great on the couch."

"Just stay," I plead. I should know better than to sleep in the same bed with him, but guilt is basically dripping out of my pores. "The mattress is big enough to share."

I hear him clicking his teeth, see him tapping his thigh in deliberation. He says, "Okay," then flicks off the light and closes the door, plunging us into darkness. I watch his shadow fumble for an extra pillow in his closet, then approach the bed.

"Figure I shouldn't sleep with the blankets on my ankle?" I ask.

"Here." Caleb untucks the comforter and folds it in half, then drapes it over us, so I'm covered from my shoulders to just above my ankles. He leaves briefly to visit his dresser, then pulls a giant fuzzy sock up my left ankle. "To keep your foot warm," he explains. "But we probably shouldn't touch the other one."

He climbs under the comforter, wearing socks of his own. Why doesn't he just get under the sheets? Is this for solidarity? Most of his lengthy legs stick out of the covers, whereas mine are concealed nearly down to my ankles.

He'll just say something weird if I bring it up, though. I close my eyes and prepare for a long, sleepless night. Several minutes pass in which I lie in his bed, warm, blinking slowly at the ceiling. Trying not to imagine what it would feel like if he turned over and draped his arm over me. If he rested his head on my shoulder, his slow breaths grazing my neck. His legs tangling with mine.

I scowl. I wish I'd offered to take the couch. Not that he would've let me.

I try to imagine myself with Juliet instead. Lying next to me, an arm draped around me, her smooth skin resting atop mine. My stomach flutters, which is good.

I have feelings for Juliet. I can't forget that.

"Em," Caleb slurs suddenly, jolting me. He sounds half-asleep. "Do you still . . . Were you really in love with me?"

My heart skids to a stop. My muscles and veins snap tight. What?

He doesn't say anything further. His body rises and falls steadily under the comforter.

What?

I shut my eyes, pretending to sleep. Not that it matters—I'm pretty sure he's talking in his sleep and isn't awaiting a response. But his question tumbles between my ears, burning away any thoughts of Juliet I was valiantly clinging to.

How does he know?

I try imitating slow, quiet breathing, but I feel like my airway is pinched. How *long* has he known? Unless . . . he's just dreaming? Muttering nonsense in his sleep?

As I expect, it's another long, sleepless night.

Emma

BACK THEN

Emma was used to letting herself into the Danielses' apartment. She'd been doing it for six years, ever since the second grade, when she'd stood up for him against those older bullies, so she didn't hesitate to do it once again. What she didn't expect, though, after her half-hour walk to their apartment complex, was to find an outrageously tall man in the kitchen arguing with Caleb's mom.

Neither of them noticed Emma tromp into the entryway. At the sound of their heated voices, she froze.

"And when have you been there?" Ms. Daniels asked, angrier than Emma had ever heard her. Her beautiful face was gnarled with a scowl, and her tense posture gave the impression she was moments away from swinging a fist. "My *son* hasn't become strong and independent because of you. He's become that way in *spite* of you."

Emma felt her blood temperature drop. This man . . . was Caleb's father? He had a towering build, sure, but with his sandy hair, golden tan skin, and harsh facial features, he looked nothing like his son.

What did this shitface want? Over the last year, Emma had been working hard to help Caleb let go of this man who rarely gave him the time of day. He'd been doing so well lately . . . What was going on?

"Why are you really here?" Ms. Daniels demanded before the man could get a word in. "Your new girlfriend have a thing for hot single dads? The only reason you ever come back is when it benefits you."

"That's not true," the man said fiercely, slamming his palm flat on the kitchen countertop. "I love him. I *care* about him."

A wry smile came to Ms. Daniels's face. "What's his favorite subject in school?"

Math, Emma thought immediately, though the man looked bewildered. "What the hell does that have to do with—?"

"It's math," Ms. Daniels snapped. "What's his favorite sport to watch?"

None of them, Emma thought with amusement, and the man said, "I don't know. Baseball? What does it matter?"

"He hates watching sports." Ms. Daniels crossed her arms, glaring. "Who does he have a crush on at school?"

Emma blanched. What? Caleb . . . had a crush on someone? Or was that another trick question? A few months ago, Caleb had admitted that his "crushes" were really just people he liked a little more than others. People he was interested in being friends with, but not attracted to. Maybe he hadn't told his mom yet?

"How should I know?" Caleb's father asked irritably. He straightened his posture, his face becoming colder, angrier. "Look, you can't blame me for not asking him every damn detail about his life. I'm a busy guy, and he doesn't *do* anything. I love my son, but he's not an exciting kid. I mean, he spent ten minutes the other day talking about how effective his new brand of shower cleaner is. Do you know how hard it is to keep up a conversation with him?"

Ms. Daniels was nearly trembling with rage. Whatever she said next, Emma couldn't hear, because the blood boiling between her ears was louder. Did he have any idea of how much he'd hurt Caleb? Did he care, even a little, about the toll he'd taken on Caleb's heart?

How dare he say such nonsense about her best friend? Caleb was *extremely* interesting, thank you very much. He was a little obsessed with cleaning and organizing things, but he was the kindest person ever, and he gave you so much love you didn't even know what to do with it all. Caleb cared and cared and *cared*. He was smart and funny and he listened and . . .

Emma was so angry, her eyes were moistening with tears. "Piece of shit," she snarled under her breath, her words choked and haggard. "You'll *never* deserve Caleb."

Ms. Daniels and Caleb's father whirled around, startled, to find her seething in the entryway. Maybe she'd spoken louder than she realized.

"Who's this?" the man asked coolly at the same time Ms. Daniels's face softened and she said, "Emma, honey."

Caleb's father observed her with a condescending grimace, like he would've rather been anywhere else right now. "Don't deserve him, huh?" he grumbled, a vein bulging in his temple.

Abruptly, he swiveled to the front door and tramped toward it, swinging it open and glaring down at Emma, before giving a cutting glare to Ms. Daniels. "Fine. When Caleb asks why I don't come around anymore, you can tell him what this little brat said."

He slammed the door behind him, rocking the whole complex.

As soon as silence reclaimed the apartment, Emma realized her mistake. She kicked her shoes off (not wanting to mess up Caleb's floors), then inched toward Ms. Daniels, wincing, preparing to be scolded or yelled at. "I'm sor—"

Suddenly, the woman scooped her up into a giant, rib-crushing hug. "Oh, honey," she said softly, fingers working through Emma's hair. "Thank you for defending that sweet boy."

Emma was a solid mass, trying to comprehend this. Ms. Daniels wasn't mad? No . . . she was *thanking* Emma? "Um," she said into the woman's tank top. "You're welcome. Though I really didn't mean to say it that loudly. Is Caleb home?"

"He ran to the grocery store to pick up some fruit while I cleaned the house." She drew Emma back and gave her a knowing wink. "He wanted to do the cleaning, but I figured this was the only way to get him out of the house."

Emma nearly laughed. Caleb was so predictable. "Can I help?" she asked.

Ms. Daniels peeked around her apartment, then smiled. "Sure. Thank you. Would you like to unload the dishwasher?"

"I got it," Emma said, grinning. At this point, she knew where every dish and utensil belonged, so it was no problem. She squeezed past Ms. Daniels in the kitchen entryway and got to work while the woman dusted the living room. As Emma moved around, putting away plates, bowls, drinking glasses, and the like, she felt Ms. Daniels sneaking glances at her. Was something on her mind, maybe?

"How are things?" Ms. Daniels asked finally.

"Fine." Emma decided not to mention the reason she'd come here out of the blue, which was that Mom had kicked her out for the afternoon. Emma never knew where to go in those moments, especially when Brooke wasn't around to join her outside and give her company. So she came here. She always came here when she didn't know where to go.

"Brooke doing okay?"

"Yep. She joined the art club, so she's been sketching and painting at home."

"Good for her," Ms. Daniels says brightly, fluffing the couch pillows. Looking at her, Emma couldn't help but feel aggravation swirling into her chest. The voices of kids and their parents around school were a buzzing annoyance in her ears. Even Mom liked to mutter cutting insults about Ms. Daniels whenever she picked Emma up, targeting her clothing and sultry voice. It made her want to get violent all over again.

"How do you do it?" Emma asked suddenly.

Ms. Daniels lifted one bewildered eyebrow, and Emma felt her face redden.

"Um." She coughed away the hitch in her throat. "Sorry. I just . . .

how do you put up with people who are mean to you without punching them in the neck?"

Ms. Daniels was clearly startled, but she laughed nonetheless. "I guess . . . because I know my worth, and that doesn't change even when people have words about me," she said warmly, running the feather duster carefully along the coffee table. Emma had to resist telling her that she wasn't being thorough enough and Caleb might notice.

"So . . . when did you, like, learn your worth?" Emma asked.

"It took a while," Ms. Daniels admitted, her smile saddening. "I had a . . . well, let's say my household wasn't a supportive place to grow up in."

Oh boy. Emma knew the feeling. "Did your mom hate you too?" she asked solemnly.

Ms. Daniels's face flashed with brief, horrified dismay, like Emma had said something strange. Before Emma could apologize, though, she continued talking. "They didn't hate me," she said, tentative. "It was just . . . strict. My parents were devout Christians. They believed in modesty, covering up. Especially women."

"Ew." Emma's lip curled with annoyance. Why did girls always get the short end of the stick in all this religious bullcrap? "So you didn't want to cover up?"

"I tried," Ms. Daniels said with a soft, aggravated sigh. "Lord knows I tried. But my body matured very young. I had trouble finding clothes that fit, and the adults around me always had something to say about it."

She shook her head, jaw tensing at the remembrance. Emma was nearly fidgeting with anger. Faintly, she remembered her mom yelling at her for wanting to buy a cute, teal two-piece bathing suit to wear to the pool. *You don't need to wear something so slutty,* she'd said with a scowl. *You'll be eye candy for all the creepy men at the pool.*

To which Emma wondered why creepy men were allowed at the pool and why it was her responsibility to make sure they didn't look at her.

"So what did you do?" Emma asked, leaning forward with anticipation. Hoping the answer was something like *I beat all of them up, of course.*

But Ms. Daniels's face was dimming with dejection. "I . . . became obsessed with hiding my body," she said softly. "But it didn't matter in the end. Even then, men came on to me, and everyone blamed me. Said I acted a certain way, spoke a certain way, whatever. And one day, toward the end of high school, I said . . . screw it."

Ms. Daniels gave Emma a wide, self-assured grin.

"You beat all of those men up?" Emma asked hopefully, despite knowing how unlikely that was. (Ms. Daniels was sassy and cool, but she wasn't a spitfire like Emma.) Sure enough, Ms. Daniels chuckled and shook her head again.

"Not quite. Basically, I figured out at some point that the way people looked at me wasn't my fault." She shrugged, leaning up against the back of the couch. "And if people were going to be pissed at me for being comfortable with my body, they weren't worth my time. So I let go of people's opinions of me."

"And . . . um, did it help?" Emma asked, twiddling her thumbs.

"My family shut me out and disowned me." Ms. Daniels winked. "But yes. It was the best decision I ever made."

Wow. Emma . . . didn't know what to say. As much as she loved Ms. Daniels, she knew very little of the woman's life. She hadn't known it was possible to admire Caleb's mom more than she already did.

"You're amazing," Emma breathed. "Holy shit, you're so *cool*."

Ms. Daniels chuckled and ambled over, ruffling Emma's hair fondly. "Not as cool as you. I mean, look at how you just stood up for your best friend."

"It was nothing," Emma said, but she felt her stomach flutter with pride.

The front door jingled, and she spun toward it, preparing her fists for Caleb's father in case he'd decided to come back to hurl more insults. But it was merely Caleb with two bags from the grocery store in hand, his dark waves rumpled from the wind. "They were out of red grapes, so I got green," he called out, trudging to the kitchen. "I got some mangoes—Emma's been really into those—"

He sputtered off when he nearly ran Emma over. She grinned up at him, glad to see him after all the nonsense she'd just heard from his dad.

"Oh," he squeaked, his face reddening. "Hi, Em."

"Wanna go on a walk?" she asked. "I know you just walked from the grocery store, so it's okay if you don't want—"

"No, it's fine! I just. Um. Wasn't expecting you to be here." He scrambled to put the groceries away in the kitchen while Ms. Daniels dusted the rest of the living room, smiling to herself. Emma felt like she was missing something but decided not to ask.

"Be safe, you two," Ms. Daniels said as they exited the apartment and hobbled down the staircase. Together, they began to stride toward the city, the muggy heat of summer curling the tips of their hair.

"What happened?" Caleb asked eventually. He could always tell when Emma was trying to hide something.

She caved so she wouldn't have to put up with his finger. "Mom kicked me out of the house for calling her a bitch. To be fair, she was being a bitch."

Caleb exhaled with frustration, which made Emma feel guilty until he reached out and settled his ever-growing palm on her head. It was a simple movement that probably didn't mean much, but she found her body heating up anyway. Why was she becoming such a pathetic mess? Sure, she'd recently discovered that she loved him in the more-than-friends way, but did that mean she was going to act and feel like this *every time* he got close to her? How gross.

"Your mom is horrible," Caleb said, his voice softening. "But she has power over you because she's your mom." He gave her temple a gentle flick. "Maybe you could ease up on yelling back.

I worry about you. Every day. What if she throws you out in the middle of the night or something?"

"I'll just walk to your place," Emma said, and though she meant it teasingly, Caleb massaged his jaw with contemplation.

"I'll give you a spare key for the apartment so you can get in if I'm ever gone," he said earnestly. "And I'll keep my phone volume on. So if that ever happens, call me. You shouldn't walk alone, so I'll ride my bike to you."

Emma looked up at Caleb, warmth spreading through her chest in tendrils, her eyes glassing with water. He looked so sincere about it, and he was mumbling to himself now, like he was coming up with other ideas of what they could do in the event that her mom randomly kicked her out at night. Even though she was a shitty mother, Emma didn't think she would cross that line. Caleb probably figured that, too, but there he was, preparing anyway.

Emma really wanted to kiss him. She wanted to kiss him so, so badly, she would've done just about anything.

And so . . . she did. She kissed him.

One moment she had been standing there, wondering what his lip balm might taste like, and the next she was gripping his T-shirt in two fists and hoisting him sideways toward her. Suddenly, she was closing her eyes and smashing her lips up against his with no thoughts, no preparation, no *anything*. She was just *doing it*. Caleb made a squawking noise against her mouth, but he didn't rip away. He merely stood there, hunched over so she could reach him, still as stone, heat radiating from his face.

What the hell was she *doing*?

Emma tore herself away in horror, staggering backward, her heart throbbing in her ears. Caleb's eyes were two massive discs. His lips were still puckered, like his face had been frozen. He was strawberry red.

"Ah!" Emma screamed, because words weren't her forte.

Caleb didn't respond. Just stared at her.

"I'm sorry!" She stumbled farther away, mortification ripping through her. She knew she was impulsive, but she'd never done something *that* impulsive before. "I just . . . tripped! Onto your face."

Again, he didn't speak. She couldn't blame him. What kind of excuse was that?

She ran with it anyway. "I grabbed your shirt for support and dragged you down," she wheezed out, pretty sure her whole body was flaming red. "Thanks for catching me! Uh. Sorry about the accidental kiss. Weird how that happened."

And then she ran.

What else was she supposed to do? Wait for his face to twist with disgust, for him to smear her off his mouth? Fluster herself all over again by thinking about how soft and gentle his lips were?

So she left him there, frozen on the sidewalk, as she sprinted all the way home.

When she next saw him, on the first day of eighth grade one week later, neither of them spoke about what had happened.

And so it remained a brief, inexplicable moment that would stay in the past.

Emma

Caleb has crutches from when he sprained his ankle walking down some stairs (naturally), so I use them to hobble around school. The throbbing pain stretching up my ankle diminished overnight, so hopefully the swelling goes away soon. The wound Brooke left carved in my chest is more painful anyway.

I exit the bathroom beside the cafeteria during lunch (pissing with crutches is a trip). Jas, Caleb, and Alice are already seated at our table. My lunch account is frozen thanks to Mother dear, but I have enough cash to last another week before I have to stop home and replenish.

As I deliberate which line to get into (do I want to be healthy or violently inhale pizza?), my weight suddenly shifts, and I stagger, stepping on my bad ankle. Ow. *Shit.*

Someone just kicked my right crutch.

I whirl on the perpetrator. Lo and behold, it's Ian Summers, his narrow gray eyes glinting with malevolence. "Ew," I say, and I start to crutch away, but then he kicks the left one, upending my balance again. I spin on one foot toward him and snarl, "Back up, or I'll beat your ugly ass with these crutches."

His smirk widens into something nastier. "Go ahead. You're the one getting expelled."

My muscles stiffen. Faintly, VP Adams's words ricochet between my ears. *One more suspension, and we'll hold a disciplinary hearing to discuss expulsion.* Had Ian somehow found out about that, or was he just threatening me?

"I haven't gotten back at you for what you did," he says, leaning his burly figure against the wall like he's some hot villainous shit.

"You mean when I punched you and whacked your balls," I clarify.

He scowls, but quickly reclaims his menacing, amused atmosphere. "Keep acting like an invincible bitch, Jones. You'll regret it when there aren't teachers around."

"Emma!" a voice says before I can retaliate, and suddenly, Juliet is standing next to me in a cinched autumn-orange dress and massive hoop earrings. Caleb drove me straight to school today, so this is the first time I'm witnessing her beauty. "Thought you needed help getting food from the lunch line," they say, looping their arm through mine and guiding me away from Ian.

"Coming to the rescue?" Ian asks snidely behind us. "Cute."

Juliet pauses. Slowly, her head turns, and her stone-cold eyes meet Ian's. A smile devoid of warmth comes to her face, and she speaks to him for the first time. "I know someone who will fuck you up if you speak to me again."

Ian's face twists with angered disgust. He opens his mouth, but nothing comes out of it aside from a few frustrated growls and cuss words. Juliet places their palm on my back and nudges me into the nearest lunch line. Pizza it is.

"Wow," I say when we're beyond hearing range of his incessant cussing.

She clutches her chest with a gasping breath, and I realize there's a bead of sweat on her temple. "Oh, I hate confrontation. He can suck it, all of it, everything, *fuuuck*."

I toss my head back and laugh. When she sees my expression, a tiny, pleased smile furls her face. "Who is this *someone* who's going to fuck him up?" I ask with intrigue.

"Charles," she says.

". . . Your stuffed penguin?"

"Obviously."

"My mistake," I say, nodding with admiration. "You know, that was pretty damn brave of you."

"I guess." She sighs, her eyes darkening. "Whenever I'm around bullies, I . . . sort of freeze up. I think it reminds me of the things my old friends used to say to me." She gives my wrist a brief squeeze that causes my heart to skip. "But recently, it feels like there's nothing they can say to really hurt me. Because if I can have friends like you, Caleb, Jas, Alice . . . I must be a pretty great person to be around."

Her smile widens, and she twists her waist, causing her dress to twirl.

I want to hug her.

The urge catches me off guard. Over the last several weeks, Juliet has made my stomach flutter, my breath quicken. I've pictured myself cuddling with them, tucking their hair behind their ear, pressing them against a wall and kissing them deeply. I've wanted to hold her hand, to frame it around my face or peck her knuckles while gazing into her eyes. I've wanted to fall in love with her.

But that's not what's happening, is it?

No. In fact, these urges are coming less and less the closer I get to her. That's not to say I'm no longer attracted to her, because she's one of the most stunning people I've ever met. But . . . more than anything, I just . . .

Want to be her friend.

Ah, fuck.

Juliet's head slants to one side, and they examine me with concern. "What's wrong?"

". . . Nothing." I clear my throat and try to perk up. "Thanks for getting me out of that situation. I can't afford to throw one more punch."

Juliet's smile widens. "Always happy to help!"

Always and forever.

I tear my eyes away, swallowing hard.

CALEB

I bake sugar cookies. Whip up buffalo dip. Pack my least embarrassing pair of pajama shorts. I'm a tingling bundle of nerves, because not only am I about to sleep over at Juliet's, but their parents are leaving tonight to visit family friends.

We're going to have the house to ourselves.

And it's *gorgeous*. Despite meeting her frequently for carpooling, I'd never been inside. Her living room ceiling arches high above me, where a massive chandelier drips with crystals. Her TV is basically the size of a theater screen. There's a whole aquarium that acts as a divider between the living room and kitchen, which is rife with freshly painted cabinets, sparkling granite countertops, and a cabinet stocked with crystal.

"Thanks for coming," Juliet says brightly when I first enter, and they plug my Crock-Pot in, leaving it on the kitchen island to heat up. "Buffalo chicken dip is my favorite. It's almost like you've been stalking me."

They say this right as their father—a bald, lanky man who's even taller than me—comes to shake my hand. I laugh awkwardly as he fixes me with a suspicious glare. "It's one of my specialties," I say squeakily. "No stalking involved. Though I'm aware I may give off that vibe. Anyway, nice to meet you, Mr. Higgins."

"Likewise," he says in a smooth, calculative voice that tells me if I pull anything, he has ways to ensure I won't ever see the rising sun again. "I see you're rather early for the party, boy. Are you that eager to see my daughter?"

His eyes narrow further, to the point where they're nearly shut.

"Oh, I don't . . . I mean, I'm—"

"Caleb is just like that," Juliet says, squeezing my arm with a beaming smile. "Always more punctual than he needs to be!"

I nod adamantly along with her, though I'm caught up on her father's words. He said *party*. Did Juliet tell him there were multiple people coming so he wouldn't be upset with her for having a boy over?

"Leave the poor boy alone, Ivan," a voice groans, and a woman pops out from behind him, her hair puffed out in a curly 'fro, her lashes nearly as long as my fingers. She's wearing a suit jacket, which seems a bit formal considering they're about to take a road trip. "Lovely to meet you, Caleb. I'm Tina."

"Hi, Mrs. Higgins," I say, because no way in hell am I about to call Juliet's mom by her first name, especially not in front of her husband.

"You two have fun! Try not to get too toasted," Mrs. Higgins says, and she pushes her husband forward, forcing him toward the front door while he continues to hold my stare, his brows pinched with suspicion. "Baby, we'll see you when we get home Monday night."

"Try not to hit any pedestrians," Juliet says cheerfully like that's a normal occurrence, allowing their mother to kiss their forehead.

I help pull their suitcases out the door and pack them into the car (might as well leave as good a first impression as I can, especially if I end up dating Juliet). We wave to them as they drive off, and Mr. Higgins continues watching me through the window until he nearly rear-ends my parked vehicle, to which his wife smacks his shoulder and points at the road, yelling something unintelligible as they drive off.

"They seem nice," I say, her father's lethal stare seared into my mind.

Juliet pats my shoulder comfortingly. "My dad's a softie. Don't let him fool you into thinking he's some badass. He and Terrell are the biggest cowards I know."

"I mean, I still want him to like me," I admit. Especially if he's going to be my father-in-law ten years down the road.

"You're a polite, responsible boy with a big heart and soft skin. What's not to love?" Juliet gives me a playful smile that makes me so giddy I want to squirm.

We head inside, and I rejoice in the fact that we finally have the house to ourselves with absolutely *zero* interruptions.

You might imagine my surprise, then, when the front door swings open five minutes later while Juliet is in the bathroom, and standing there is not her parents returning for something they forgot, but Emma Fucking Goddamn Jones.

We stare at each other, her in the doorway, me on the giant sectional couch.

"Oh," she says flatly.

"Sleepover?" I ask wearily, already knowing where this is going.

"Sleepover," she confirms, gesturing to her T-shirt and sweat-pants.

Ugh. *Why?* Part of me wants to dissolve into frustrated screams at the fact that my plan to be alone with Juliet has obviously been foiled. But . . . another part of me, strangely, lightens at the sight of her. Maybe it's just an old reaction—I always used to get excited when she came over. Seeing her in the doorway is probably why I suddenly feel so comfortable, because it reminds me of back then.

"You're . . . not using the crutches?" I ask awkwardly.

"Foot feels okay." She flexes her ankle. "I think I just rolled it. The crutches are in my trunk, whenever you want them back." Silence befalls us again, and she steps into the house with a back-pack, eyes roving the place with fascination. "How did you find out about the sleepover?"

My brows inch together on my forehead. "I could ask you the same question."

"I invited Juliet to hang out, and they told me to come over and bring pajamas."

"I . . . Yeah," I say, defeated. "Same."

Emma slaps a palm to her face with irritation. I guess that's what we get for no longer talking about our upcoming plans around Juliet, for fear that the other person will try to infiltrate them.

"You're here!" Juliet says, appearing behind me so suddenly that I nearly launch myself into the chandelier. She changed into an oversize, sparkly pumpkin sweater and leggings. "Do either of you know what you want to do tonight? I was thinking we could have drinks, maybe watch some movies or a show, order a pizza . . ."

"Sounds good," Emma says, wandering over to the couch. "I'll go easy on drinks, though. I have an interview tomorrow, so I should probably look alive for it."

This piques my interest, despite knowing I shouldn't care. "When? Where?"

"Ten thirty. It's at the local movie theater. They're even offering higher than minimum wage." As she speaks, her voice fractures with apprehension. "I probably won't get it, considering my shit luck with interviews."

"Let's practice," Juliet chirps.

Emma's eyes shoot wide, and she throws her palms up, like she's warding us off. "Absolutely not! We're here to have fun, not study for my interview—"

"Emma," I say sharply.

She looks at me, eyes shimmering with uncertainty.

"We'll get you a job," I tell her.

Juliet nods enthusiastically. "I know two people who can help!"

The doorbell rings, a melodic hum that echoes through the house. Emma and I glance at each other with arched brows as Juliet skips off to answer it.

"I was told my presence is required," Jas says desolately.

"Let's get fucked!" Alice cries out.

Because why not?

X●X●

"And what are your strengths, Miss Jones?" Jas asks in a robotically professional voice, peering over the dining room table at Emma, her thick black hair twirled up into a chaotic bun that most managers wouldn't get away with.

"Well." Emma folds her hands politely in her lap, as I taught her a few moments ago so she'd stop waving them around like an elderly Italian woman. "I'm not afraid to speak my mind. I don't take shit from anyone—"

"*Beep, beep.*" Alice, our red flag detector, speaks up.

"What now?" Emma demands.

"Don't swear. Also, employers want to know you *can* take shit," I point out, combing through a knot in her hair. She shudders away from my touch, and I wince, backing off. "What makes you fit for working on a busy night?"

Jas poses the question again through a mouthful of chips and buffalo dip. "What are your strengths?"

Emma corrects her slouch (excellent), then says, "One of my best qualities is my ability to keep a level head when confronted."

Alice snorts loudly enough to startle us. Emma glares at her, continuing.

"I . . . can prioritize my duties to avoid getting overwhelmed." She glances at me, her hazel eyes seeking reassurance. I nod with an encouraging thumbs-up, ignoring the unexpected twitch in my heart. "I'm quick to learn . . . and don't need people to hold my hand. I'm . . . good at being organized—"

I choke on a laugh.

"—and consider myself very approachable."

Everyone snickers.

"*You fucks!*" Emma snarls.

"You're doing great," I say, handing her a cookie. She cusses at me but munches it anyway, cooling down.

We press her for an hour, looking up questions, teaching her "professional" etiquette and differentiating between the truth and what they want to hear. She's been attending interviews with the mindset of "I'll be myself." Which . . . isn't necessarily beneficial when you're a fireball without a filter.

After torturing Emma long enough, we sit on the fluffy couches in the living room, deliberating what to watch. None of us have any strong opinions, and Juliet is starting to squirm, so I ask them if they have anything in mind. Of course they do.

"Okay," she says with hesitation, "so there's this show. It's the love of my life. Some people think it's for kids, but the themes are so mature, and it has amazing character development, and the world-building is so complex! My old friends thought it was too childish . . . even though I came up with a drinking game . . ."

They smile uneasily.

"I know which show you're talking about," Alice says seriously, "and I absolutely *have* to know what your drinking rules are."

The rest of us look around at each other in bewilderment, shrugging. Juliet is nearly hyperventilating with excitement as they type their show into the search bar, reiterating once again that "we don't have to watch it. If you hate the first episode, we can find something else. Don't feel obligated just because I love it—"

As it turns out, Juliet's rules cause her, Alice, and Jas to get drunk on sweet wine from the rack in the kitchen way faster than intended. Emma and I are drinking water because she doesn't want to get wasted before an interview, and I . . . Well, I'll feel bad if she's the only sober one. Hopefully she'll ace that interview and she can start saving money so she's not reliant on her mom.

Oh, and she'll stop spending as much time with Juliet.

I would've liked to sit next to Juliet, but Alice and Jas flanked her when she centered herself on the sectional couch. Which left Emma and me sitting perched on the love seat, keeping close to the corners so we won't accidentally touch each other.

"Thanks again," Emma mumbles as the three of them giggle and talk over the "worst episode in the series," according to Juliet. She swirls ice in her glass, her expression forcibly level.

"We all helped," I say, but she shakes her head.

"Not just for the interview advice. For . . . carrying me out of the rain. Wrapping my ankle. Fixing my car." Her throat bobs with a swallow. She's purposefully avoiding my eyes. "I want to pay you back."

I resist the urge to tuck her strawberry blond hair back so it stops curtaining her face. "I don't need payment."

She sips, and I try not to notice how softly the glass touches her mouth. "You're always doing things for others," she says quietly.

"I feel like . . . people rarely do things for you. I was thinking last night, and I had an idea."

She finally looks up at me, her expression pained, broken, tired, defeated. Why does she look like that? What can I do to make things better? Or rather . . .

Why do I care?

But then she says something that erases all thoughts from my mind.

"I'm dropping out of the competition for Juliet."

Emma

It's not a difficult decision. Not really.

Caleb's eyes are bugging out of his head. "Huh?"

"I was thinking about it last night," I say, focusing on my lap so I won't have to see his expression. "You're right. I *do* steal people from you. Not that I was consciously trying to, but . . ." I heave a sigh, burying my face in my hands. All the names he rattled off when we proposed the competition . . . I only just realized how little I remembered about them, and how *much* I remembered the fact that Caleb was constantly around them. Until he wasn't. Because I was jealous.

I snuck in between him and any potential partners he could've had. Dating is so *hard* for someone like Caleb, and I made it nearly impossible by sliding in and making moves before he could. How fucking disgusting is that? That I stole away everyone he was interested in because I couldn't stand the idea of him caring about someone as much as he did me? Yet, selfishly, I'm also the person who cut him away, all in the name of trying to benefit him.

I've continued to treat him like shit and ruin his life even when I thought I was doing him a favor by breaking things off. Because that's what I do. Take, take, *take*.

Caleb deserves someone like Juliet.

I have to stop being around him. For both our sakes. The more time I spend with him and Juliet, the more I fall deeper into my feelings. The more I unearth memories I've kept buried for years.

"I'll hang out with them when you're not around, and I won't pursue romantic feelings for them," I explain, swallowing hard. "I'll tell them you and I aren't comfortable around each other, and hopefully they'll stop inviting us to the same places. I'll stop sitting with you at lunch. I'll stop carpooling with you."

Caleb looks like I told him I just ran over someone's puppy on the way over. Then he snaps, "You can't."

My eyes veer up to his. "Huh?"

He glances warily at the others distracted on the adjacent couch. "If Juliet picks me, she should pick me because she likes me. Not because I'm a second choice to someone she really wants. Besides . . . don't you like the dynamic here?" He gestures around the room, looking strangely desperate. "Isn't this . . . good? Is it just that you can't stand being around me—?"

"Of *course* it's because I can't stand being around you!" I snarl.

The room falls silent, save for the show playing in the background. Juliet, Alice, and Jas look between each other like they don't know what to do. *I* don't know what to do. Did I have to blurt that for all the heavens to hear?

"This puke is coming at a great time," Alice says, and suddenly, she lunges up and staggers off.

"Bathroom's this way!" Juliet scrambles up as well, guiding her through the kitchen.

Jas stares at us. We stare back at her. "I . . . love watching people vomit," she says, and she too gets up, following awkwardly after Juliet and Alice. Leaving us alone. For a minute, we watch the TV, listening without comprehending.

"So, are you just leaving it like that, or . . . ?" Caleb's voice is bitter, his arms are crossed tightly, and his mouth is screwed into a scowl.

My heart feels like it's twisting itself into a tornado of misery and frustration. "The problem is me," I say, my voice wobbling despite my attempt to sound neutral. "Being in your life. Holding you back . . ."

"From what?" Caleb swivels to face me, sounding incredulous.

I'm not ready to tell him, so I stumble to my feet and seize my overnight bag, then head for the door, sliding into my shoes. "Going to prepare more for that interview," I mumble. Suddenly, though, he grabs hold of my bag, pulling it from my clutch and tossing it aside. A spark of anger lights in my chest, and I whirl to tell him off, until he nudges me back against the front door and peers down at me.

"Just talk to me," he pleads, his prickliness bleeding away into exasperation.

What am I supposed to say, exactly? That I can't be around him anymore because it's intensifying the feelings I tried abandoning years ago? That the whole reason I ended things between us was because I was an anchor around his foot, preventing him from moving forward and growing as a person? That if he and Juliet *do* get together, I won't be able to handle seeing it? That he's the best thing that happened to me, and I'm the worst thing that happened to him?

Frustration scorches through me, causing tears to burn my eyes. His own are so vibrant, digging into my heart, petrifying me to my core. I whirl and snatch the door handle, swinging it open, about to tromp into the evening without my overnight bag.

"Is it true?" he demands as I'm halfway out onto the porch. "The other night. I asked you something."

My blood crystallizes into ice fragments, and I stagger to a stop. His slurred, sleepy voice from the other night echoes between my ears. *Were you really in love with me?*

The rush of emotions is becoming too much. I'm angry at him for persisting. Grateful that he cares enough to ask. Sad that I have to relearn how to let him go all over again, when I never quite got it down the first time. All of this culminates into one massive, writhing mess in my head, and one emotion storms forth, overtaking the others.

"What *difference* does it fucking make?" I yell.

Caleb totters backward, alarmed.

"I mean . . . why does it *matter*?" I demand, trembling violently. "You don't love me back! You never will! *And even if you did, I wouldn't let you!*"

The tears are now freely falling down my face. I have to get away. This is humiliating and pathetic. So I storm out onto the porch, fumbling for my car keys. But I hear thunderous footsteps behind me, and Caleb lunges around to my front, blocking my path. Suddenly, he has both of my shoulders in his powerful grip, and he's leaning over me again.

"How does it change nothing?" he asks fiercely, our seething faces mere inches apart. *"You were my first and only love, you fucking doorbell!"*

I fall still. What did he just say?

"You're the reason I found out I was demisexual!" he cries out, his cheeks turning a radiant pink. "I didn't understand why, of everyone, *you* were the only person I was attracted to. I never had more than surface level feelings for anyone else!"

He pauses to gulp in a breath. I can't move. I feel like he just set my head ablaze.

"The only reason I knew what attraction was was because I felt it for *you*," he continues, giving me a frustrated shake. The moonlight reflects against the glassy water in his eyes and causes his face to glow paler. "I thought about you every day. When you weren't with me, I wished you were. When I made you lunches, I wondered what you'd wear to school that day. When we played soccer, I was terrible. But I didn't care, because all I could think about was how you looked when you were excited . . ."

His trembling hands slide down my shoulders, my elbows, my forearms, until he's clutching at my palms. I leave mine limp in his, because I can't muster the strength to move any part of my body. His voice tumbles through me, each syllable grinding into my heart like jagged pieces of glass. How could someone so loving, so dedicated, so kindhearted, so *perfect* ever have feelings for someone as selfish as me? I've ruined so many lives. My mom's. Brooke's. *His.* So what . . . why . . . ?

Caleb waits for me to respond, his grip rigid on my palms. I can feel each heated breath against my upper lip.

I offer him the same thing I gave him during our duration as friends. Nothing.

We hear a scuffling noise and look into the house. Jas is peeking into the living room, clearly hoping we'd settled our dispute so she can return rather than watch Alice empty her stomach.

"Let's go," Caleb grumbles, tugging me back inside so he can squirm into his shoes and toss me my jacket.

I don't have the mental fortitude to fight him, so I follow out to his car parked on the curb. His lights flood the street as he unlocks the doors and opens the passenger side, allowing me to crawl in. He does the same on the driver's side.

"Where are we going?" I ask, frowning. His silence is unnerving. When he's mad, he shows it in his hands, contorted facial expressions, and chiding words. Now, though, everything about him is glacial and stiff. He doesn't answer—just swings the car around and guns it down the suburban road.

I decide not to ask any more questions.

Emma

BACK THEN

Brooke was making a peanut butter and banana sandwich. Interesting. Emma thought the flavor might be good, but bananas were too mushy for her taste.

"How hard is it to clean your room? How many times do I have to ask you the same thing?"

Peanut butter and jelly was the shit. Caleb made them so good, they were like drugs. He even cut them into fourths for her, so long as she promised to eat the crust because she was *thirteen* and should've been *mature enough* to not throw it away. Well, just because she was older didn't mean that it tasted better, but she appeased him.

"You're a teenager and you can't even make your bed? Should I give up on you?"

Emma wondered what Caleb might make tomorrow. He'd been getting into soup recipes lately, and Emma wasn't complaining.

"Hello? Am I talking to a wall?"

Emma stood to walk back to her room. Now that she was pondering it, she wanted to ask him. Sometimes she helped with meal prep after school, but it was Sunday, and he was spending the day with his mom. A *mother-son day*, he called it. The thought of having one of those with her own mother made her shudder.

Emma was wrenched back to the couch cushion, and she blinked in surprise, looking up into her mom's beet red face. Oh. Right. She'd been getting yelled at.

"Where are you going?" the woman growled. Brooke was still working on her lunch in the kitchen, sneaking them bothered, tense glances, like she thought they might start throwing fists. That wouldn't happen, of course. Mom always prided herself on the fact that she never physically punished her kids.

"I was going to talk to Caleb," Emma said flatly.

Mom barked with laughter, tossing her head back and causing her stiff blond bob to fly with it. "Yeah? The boy you treat like your servant?"

Don't listen. Caleb had told her that before. But Mom was very, very loud.

"Caleb and I are friends," Emma said, crunching her hands into fists.

Mom's golden brown eyes glinted with amusement. "A friendship is two-sided. What have you ever done for that poor boy other than drag him into your problems?"

Emma opened her mouth to yell back—she could only tolerate so much before damning the consequences of being thrown out—but her mind drew a blank. When she realized this, the panic settled in. What *did* she do for him?

Caleb acted as a goalie so she could practice soccer, even though he was terrified. He made lunches for her. He calmed her down and helped her study when she was ready to throw her books at the wall. He learned how to braid so he could help Emma keep her hair out of her face. He went to her soccer practices and games. For years, Caleb had given her kindness.

But Emma . . . Was there anything she did to return the favor? She'd stopped people from bullying him, but he was growing taller and more confident, and people weren't picking on him much anymore. "I'm his friend" was all she could say.

Mom laughed darkly. "Sure. And does he have any other 'friends' to compare to? Or did you scare them away?"

Emma's heart took another plunge. She knew she was intimidating. Caleb, though, was more approachable, with his rounded features and gentle blue eyes. But . . . were people avoiding him because he was always around the school's troublemaker?

Don't listen.

Would Caleb tell her if she was a burden?

Don't listen.

Of course not. Caleb would stay friends with her even if she was the worst thing that happened to him. And . . .

Don't lis—

Maybe she was.

Emma found herself standing on the front porch in her winter jacket and boots, watching snow flutter from the ice-gray sky. She wasn't sure if she'd walked out or if she'd been kicked out. She looked down at her phone messages with Caleb. Every time she blinked, there was a new one written in the text box she hadn't remembered writing.

Do you like me?

Do you think you'd have friends if I wasn't around?

Would your life be better if I disappeared?

She erased them. Her chest nearly exploded when a text from him arrived, like he'd sensed she was thinking about him.

CALEB

My place tomorrow after school? We got mint chocolate

chip ice cream I'm not going to eat lol

Yes. Anything to get away from here. Anything to eat ice cream with him.

He preferred vanilla bean.

Had Emma ever bought him vanilla bean ice cream? She couldn't remember.

She texted back, **Sorry, busy.**

CALEB

BACK THEN

Are you okay?

Answer my call please!!

Is this about your mom?

What can I do to fix this?

I'm sorry if I've been a bad friend.

Are you mad at me? Please just tell me.

Stop avoiding me at school!!

Brooke says you're not home. Is that true?

It's been three days.

Mom tried calling you. It's not going through.

"Don't talk to me anymore" ?? Is that all you can say?

This isn't fair. You won't even tell me what I did wrong.

Am I too much like your mom? I know I can be annoying.

I'll try to be a better friend. Please give me a chance.

Can you at least tell me if you're getting these?

Mom stopped by your house but nobody answered.

Are you okay? Please answer.

Please?

Fine. Fuck you.

I don't mean that.

I'm sorry for being like this. I wish I wasn't like this.

I guess that's it then?

Fine. If you're sure. I'll stop texting you.

But you can change your mind.

I'll be here.

I'll wait for you.

Every day.

Every month.

Every year.

Always and forever.

CALEB

I don't know where I'm going until we get there. I climb out, then circle my car and swing open Emma's door. She stares at the playground, her eyes glittering under the yellow streetlamps. "Here?" she asks skeptically.

"Where better?" I ask through clenched teeth. I'm still bitterly angry. For so long, I've waited for answers. For any logical reason that Emma left me. Now that she's given me a hint, I can't let her sprint away without explaining.

Emma leads the way to the swing set. There aren't overhead lights, so we're basically stumbling our way through the wood chips, bypassing the merry-go-round, play structure, and monkey bars. Emma plops onto her favorite swing, and I take the one next to her, then swivel toward her and dig my feet into the wood chips to anchor myself.

"Well?" I ask irritably. "If you loved me, why did you run away? I thought . . . I'd done something unforgivable."

Emma hangs her head. The cool evening wind bites her cheeks, turning them a shade of crimson I can faintly see under the suburb lights behind the playground. "You've never done anything wrong," she mutters. "It was . . . me."

I knead my forehead. Why can't she spit it out without me having to pry the answer from her? "What do you mean?" I press.

Her grip tightens on the swing chains. She keeps her focus on the wood chips she's nudging around with her feet. "You're . . . perfect," she whispers. "You care so much about others. You're kind, thoughtful, considerate. Somewhere along the way, I realized you deserve a life that gives you this same happiness. And you'd never find it while I was clinging to your ass."

She kicks hard, sending a clump of wood chips and soil flying. Her expression remains impassive. I think mine does too. I'm too busy processing her words to figure out how I should be feeling about them.

"I became a burden." Her voice breaks over the last few words. "You were always so busy looking after me that it hurt you. I never reciprocated your friendship. You put in so much effort, and I took it for granted. You gave, and gave, and gave. I took, and took, and took." She pauses, clamping her eyes shut and chewing her lips. I can almost feel how painful it is for her to say this, but I . . .

I don't understand what she's talking about. Never reciprocated? A *burden*?

Emma looks like she's trying to crush the chains to powder in her fists. Part of me wants to reach out and loosen her grip—to take her hands. To drag her chin sideways and force her to look at me as she says all of these nonsensical, ridiculous things. But I can tell she's not finished, so I remain still.

"I thought maybe I could step it up, but I'd already fallen so far behind," she says weakly. "I'd already damaged your shoulders.

And you didn't even know, because I was your only friend. You accepted my failure as something normal because you had nothing to compare me to. It was . . . toxic."

Maybe Emma feels the intensity of my gaze, because she tilts her face farther away, strands of strawberry blond hair concealing her expression from view. The only disruptions to the silence are the faint, distant noises of the city—the cool wind threading through the skyscrapers and alleys, the hum of car engines, the occasional horn or police siren.

"I was weighing you down. I knew if I let you go, you'd thrive. And you did." Faintly, I hear her sniffle. "You have people to sit with at lunch. You're the student council secretary. You're standing up for others. For yourself. If we'd stayed friends . . . who knows how far behind I would've held you?"

Emma throws her head back to release an irritated sigh at the cloud of light pollution hazing the night sky. The moon washes over her skin, emphasizing the glaze of dried tear streaks on her face.

"I loved you," she breathes. "That's why I left. Because if I kept you for my own benefit . . . What kind of love is that?"

Finally, she twists in the swing to pin me with a fierce, solemn stare.

"I'm sorry."

I lean up against the right chain, feeling like I haven't slept in thirty-six hours. So that's the reason for all the turmoil, the tears, the broken heart. I faintly hear her ask what I'm thinking, and it's a valid question. So many things, yet also nothing. My mind is a rotating galaxy of words and emotions. It's also a void. I'm thinking about everything and nothing. Among the chaos, though, comes a string of words.

"I'm going to commit a murder."

Emma deliberates her response. Then, "Make it quick."

"Not you," I clarify.

Emma's face pales, but she doesn't respond. That's fine. Slowly, my voice is coming back to me, along with the anger. The hatred. Sitting on this rusty-ass swing isn't helping, so I lunge to my feet, beginning to pace. It doesn't take a genius to figure out where this idea came from—to know who put these thoughts in her head.

"I told you not to listen to her," I say sharply, glaring down at her.

Emma's jaw flexes with annoyance, and her eyes harden. "She was right."

"Shut the fuck *up*."

Emma reels back in surprise, but I'm too pissed to consider apologizing for cussing at her. It's taking all of my strength not to hurl my fist into the play structure behind me and break every bone in my hand.

"Holding me back? Not *reciprocating* my friendship? You, my best friend for six years, being a *burden*?" I demand, curling my lip in angered disbelief. The words feel so slimy and thick in my mouth. "If I thought that was true, do you think I would've gone out of my way *daily* to see you?"

Emma wrenches her eyes away and grumbles, "You didn't know what real friendship was. I was your only example."

Another flash of white-hot ire courses through my blood. "Quit talking about me like I was some useless child who didn't know any better!" I howl. "Do you know how *insulting* that is?"

Emma winces, though I don't think it's because of my volume. I hate seeing her so . . . frail. Timid. The only time she ever acted this way was when she was too drained to combat that disgusting woman. I *hate* it.

"So what if I made you lunches and bought you ice cream and practiced soccer with you?" I ask angrily. "I *cared* about you. I never needed or wanted payment. And not that it fucking matters anymore, but you *did* reciprocate."

She offers a sardonic smile that only further stings me. "Yeah? Enlighten me."

"You looked out for me!" I cry out, my fingers curling when she rolls her eyes. "You helped me see value in myself. You say I thrived without you? That I became the secretary of student council, made friends, put myself out there because you left me? Bullshit. I did all of that in *spite* of losing you."

Emma looks ready to protest. She doesn't. Good, because I'm far from finished.

"I had to accomplish these things without you," I say, frustration giving way to exhaustion. "You were my rock. You helped me believe in myself. How to shake off negative personal thoughts and stand taller." I falter to draw a gasp, because I've been rambling without taking a breath. "Just because they weren't always physical, like making me food, doesn't mean you didn't benefit me. You shaped me into the person I am today. You helped me figure out the kind of person I wanted to be."

By the time I'm done, Emma's lip is trembling, and tears are dribbling from her eyes. "Caleb," she croaks. "You can't . . . I don't . . ."

"Why are you crying?" I demand, reaching out and knocking her chin up with my index knuckle. Forcing her to look at me. "You're Emma Jones. You're the strongest person I know. You don't take shit from anyone, least of all your mother." I yank my index finger out and jam it in her face. "You drink baby tears for breakfast and punch through anything that looks at you the wrong way. What reason do you have to cry?"

Her mouth twitches, like she's about to laugh, but she shoves her face into her hands. "Fuck you," she whispers. "Fucking dick. You piece of shit asshole."

"That's better," I say, smirking.

She wipes her face, returning her hands once more to the swing chains. I try not to wonder how many germs she just scrubbed into her eyes.

"You split with me without even *talking* to me," I say, folding my hands over both of hers. Her palms are quivering, and she flinches, like she wants to yank them away. But she doesn't. "Why didn't I get a say?"

"I . . . I don't know," she breathes, blinking her wet eyes frantically. "I'm sorry for leaving and making you think you did something wrong. I'm sorry for fucking up."

"And?" I ask sternly.

She looks at me, clueless.

"For listening to her." I bend down so I'm closer to her. Her eyes flash with guilt, and she backs her head away, putting more space between us. When she doesn't speak, I wonder, then, if she's not convinced of everything I said. The distance between us right now is more than physical.

Maybe I've done what I can, but there's something missing. She doesn't just need me. This is beyond our relationship. I . . . can't give her what she needs in this moment.

But I know someone who can.

"Let's go," I say, tugging her to her feet. I draw my handkerchief from my pocket, then fold it into a triangle and dab at her wet face, which she allows (though she doesn't look pleased about it). I guide her back to the car, and she climbs in, watching me warily. I close the passenger door and walk a few paces away, pulling out my phone.

I have a call to make.

Emma

I've been waiting for five minutes, watching Caleb speak muffled words into his phone. The one time I try to climb out and ask what's going on, he slams the door in my face and points his finger in a *behave* kind of way that makes me want to bite him.

I slump in my seat, scowling. His words from earlier are burning in my brain. I'm not sure what to believe, what's true and what's been exaggerated. Why would Caleb credit me with his growth, like he wasn't the person brave enough to undergo it? So he saw my false self-confidence and imitated it until it became real, but he did that himself. Maybe he used me as inspiration, but that's as far as I contributed.

I'm so deep in my thoughts that Caleb startles me when he flings the door open and clambers in. "Who was that?" I ask, narrowing my eyes as he swerves the car around and takes off. Away from Juliet's. Toward the city.

"Someone you should talk to."

"And that would be . . . ?" I squeeze my fists in my lap, antsy.

"Not saying. You'll whine."

I pinch my eyebrows, but he doesn't spare me a glance as we move farther into the city, the buildings beginning to crawl higher toward the sky. I huff, directing my gaze out the window. It's so late that the usual pack of wanderers have disappeared, leaving the streets abnormally empty. The streetlamps downtown are wrapped in orange lights, and several storefronts are decked out in Halloween merchandise, from mannequins to window stickers to glowing pumpkins.

When I see where we're headed, the blood drains from my face. A glowing sign out front states the establishment name, coupled with a neon-lingerie-clad woman. "Come on, Cal," I mutter, but he doesn't respond. Merely drives us through the loaded parking lot and swings around the back, pulling up to the staff doors.

I want to go back to Juliet's, I nearly say, but it's too late. Ms. Daniels is leaning against the brick wall, and she breaks into a wide smile when she sees me.

"Go on," he says.

"You're not coming?" I ask fearfully.

"I don't need to, Em." Suddenly, he's resting his hand atop my knee. I hate the reassurance that floods through my body from his mere touch. I hate that I want to flip my palm and lace our fingers—to cling to him for another minute, maybe five.

The feeling makes me desperate enough to exit the car. It's beginning to drizzle. Ms. Daniels waits under the awning of the building, dressed in a V-neck top and ripped jean shorts that cling to her curves, her dark hair twisted into a ponytail.

"I don't know why I'm here," I admit.

She nods thoughtfully, slinging her pale white arm around my shoulders. "You need a reason to see me?" she asks, winking.

"I . . . uh . . ."

"Let's head inside." She swipes her employee card at the back entrance, and we step into a brightly lit hallway. She steers me into a private lounge area with a coffee pot, kitchenette, and plush furniture, all lit by multiple golden lamps. She seats me on the left cushion of a love seat, then takes the right. A soft haze in the room smells of smoke, proven correct when I notice an ashtray on the table before us.

I brace for whatever she's about to say. She opens her mouth, and asks, "Mint?"

I blink. She's holding out a rectangular wrapped chocolate mint. "Thanks," I say, plucking it from her fingers.

"These are Caleb's favorite," she explains as I unwrap it and sink my teeth into the delectable bar. "Well, they're the only brand of mint chocolate he willingly eats."

"You must like it, though," I say.

"Meh. Not my favorite flavor."

My heart palpitates. The reason I assumed Caleb kept around the mint chocolate chip ice cream in his freezer was because his mom liked it. If not, why . . . ? It can't be because of me, right? Just in case I ever . . . ?

Great. My eyes are burning again.

Ms. Daniels turns to face me, and her friendly smile becomes more somber, like she's preparing to give me bad news. The sight of it immediately puts me on edge.

"Mind if I poke at your thoughts?" she asks, tentative. "I took my break early, so I have twenty minutes to kill."

"I . . . don't have anything to say," I mumble.

"Are you sure?" There's this knowing twinkle in her eyes, like she can see past all of my uncertainties and insecurities, like she knows my deepest thoughts and feelings. Like she knows . . . me.

"I'm sure," I say, though the words are feeble. But it's true. Why am I here? What was Caleb thinking?

"Sounds like you're having a rough night, maybe," she says, folding her hand over mine. Her thumb strokes the back of my palm, and it's such a kind gesture I feel a hitch in my throat. Of course my night is horrible, but I'm not willing to talk about it. Especially not with her, the mother of my first love. The mother of the boy I abandoned.

"Can I admit something?" she asks.

". . . Sure." I can't exactly say no.

"I broke our promise," she says softly, looking at me with apologetic, bright blue eyes, so much like his. "I told him you loved him."

I already assumed this, considering Caleb had to hear it from somewhere. And yet, the confirmation makes me feel like there's a soccer ball inflating in my airway. "Oh," I choke out.

"I couldn't stand to hear him talking about you as if you hated him," she whispers. "I'm sorry for betraying your trust."

"It's fine," I say, and it is, though I don't know why. Maybe I should be pissed, since I said it in confidence, but . . . I can't be. Not at her.

"I miss you, you know." Again, her smile weakens, and her palm moves away from mine so she can brush my hair back behind my ear. "You're a funny kid. I've never heard a little girl talk the way you do. The way you brought Caleb crawling out of his shell . . . it was amazing. After he met you, he was talking more. Opening up. He wasn't afraid to go to school anymore." She cocks her head at me. "Having you in our lives was the best thing that ever happened to us."

I stare at her in bafflement. It's clearly an exaggeration, but hearing it causes warmth to tingle in my chest.

"One more thing," she says. "There's something I never got to say to you before. Something I wish I had."

The soccer ball in my throat is big enough to block any words from getting out. Including my plea that she doesn't continue because . . . I don't know if I can handle whatever she's about to say next.

"You can come to me anytime." Ms. Daniels levels me with a stern, but tender look that begins to melt away the steel walls I've been maintaining for the last several years. Just like that. "I'll be here waiting. A call, a text. I'm here to chat, hug you, braid your hair. I'm here to take you clothes shopping, or buy you dinner, or offer you a warm bed. I'm here to talk boys, girls. To talk."

She shifts to grip both of my hands.

"I'm here to help you schedule doctor appointments, to nag you about your homework," she says quietly. "I'm here for movie nights, for venting, for anything and everything. I'm busy, yes, but I'll always make time for you, Emma. Always. And forever."

When I blink, I can't see her anymore. My eyes are flooded with tears, which are rolling down my chin, dripping onto my jacket. What am I supposed to say? How can she make these things sound so menial, when my own mom would've acted like she was getting scalped for spending more than three minutes around me? This . . . is what it really feels like to have a mom that *cares*?

I stumble to my feet, though I'm not sure why. My first instinct is to run. But Ms. Daniels rises with me, and suddenly, she's pulling me into a bone-crushing hug, her arms wrapped firm around my back, not allowing any release. I bury my face into her bare shoulder, raked with sobs, shaking wildly. "I'm here," she whispers, pressing a palm to my head. "I'm here, Emma, honey. I'm so sorry that I let you slip away from me. I tried to contact you when you left . . . texting, calling your mother, coming to your front door . . . I should've tried harder—"

"Don't," I choke out, holding her tighter. How could she possibly be apologizing for the fact that I ignored and avoided every chance she took to check in on me? I feel whole around Ms. Daniels. I feel like there's nothing I can do to make her turn her nose at me, or snap at me, or hate me. She loves me, all of me, even the flaws and the missteps.

Leaving her behind was almost harder than leaving Caleb. I've never met an adult who looks at me the way she does. My entire life, authority figures have loomed over me, glaring, scolding me for being me. Ms. Daniels is the only one who's ever stood at my back, her hand a comforting weight on my head.

"I've got you," she says gently, allowing me to rub my tears all over her shoulder. She's still so warm, and though her skin is sticky from running around during her shift, she smells of lavender lotion. She smells like . . . home. "I'm here. My sweet Emma."

I cling to her harder, and suddenly, everything Caleb told me makes sense.

I believe him.

I don't know what any of this has to do with what he said on the playground. There are a lot of negative internal thoughts I'll need to untangle to truly accept his words—that I'm worthwhile. But as I hold fast to Ms. Daniels, my heart fills with a sensation I've never experienced fully until this moment. Something soft, kind, loving. Maternal. I never want to let her go.

Ms. Daniels draws back and smooths her thumbs across my cheekbones, wiping my tears away. Her eyes are watering, but she's wearing a small, affectionate smile. I grip her hands around my face, hoping she'll hold me like this forever.

She can't, of course. She's a working woman, and Caleb is waiting in the car.

But it's enough. For now.

She draws me in, kissing my forehead. "I love you, baby girl," she says gently.

I give her another hug because I can't help it. "I love you too . . . Ms. Daniels."

I don't admit that I almost called her *Mom*.

CALEB

I've reread the text about sixty times. It's still not sinking in.

DAD

I want to fix some things. Want to try moving in for a few
weeks?

I should be happy. And I am. I think. I wouldn't see Mom as frequently, but we rarely see each other anyway, so not much would
change. It would be difficult to hang out with my friends on random weekends, and it'd be a hell of a commute to school . . . but it
could be worth it to spend time with him.

I tuck my phone away, because I don't want my thoughts
clouded with this. My passenger door swings open, and Emma
crawls in, her hazel eyes swollen. I've had my handkerchief at the
ready, so I hand it to her.

Emma smiles. "Fucking dork," she whispers, using it to wipe
her eyes.

At least she's smiling.

I peer through the windshield to find Mom standing in the
doorway of the staff entrance, one hand on her hip. We meet eyes,
and she gives me a wink that tells me everything I need to know,

which is absolutely nothing. I'll thank her more properly later for working her mom magic.

I turn the car around and begin back to Juliet's. Emma and I have been alone before, but something feels . . . different. The tension, which was previously thick enough to slice knives through, is barely noticeable. Emma's shoulders are straight rather than slouched, like she unloaded something from her back while she was inside.

"Thanks, Cal," she mumbles.

"I didn't do anything."

"You knew what I needed. You always know." Her hand flinches in my periphery, like she's about to reach out and touch me. But she grabs her palm, keeping her hands in her lap. "Thank you."

My stomach twists up like a swirl of ice cream. The ride back to Juliet's is quiet, aside from rain pattering against the windshield. We pull up to the curb, then sit there in the car, my headlights burning two trails through the rain.

"I'm dropping you off," I say eventually.

There's a flicker of disappointment in her eyes. "What?"

"I . . . need time," I admit. I have too much to think about to enjoy a sleepover. Even if it's with Juliet Higgins, the person I'm supposed to be wooing. Everything Emma told me . . . I need to process it. The reason she broke our friendship off. The fact that she loved me. The fact that she still might. The fact that I do. I still do.

I need to think.

Emma swings the door open, allowing the sound of rain to flood into the car. "I'll text you when my interview is over," she whispers.

"Okay," I say, trying to force optimism into my weary voice. "You'll do great."

There's a long, quiet moment. I'm not sure what either of us expect, if anything. But then Emma moves, cutting through the potential, and rises to her feet. "Bye."

"Bye."

She shuts the door, then stands there a few moments too long in the rain, her palm resting on the handle. Eventually, she ambles up Juliet's driveway. I don't leave until she's safely inside. As I do, I notice Jas watching from the front window, frowning. She's been texting me, but I don't have the mental capacity to answer.

So I go home. When I'm in the sanctity of my apartment, I throw off my clothes and take a shower, letting the heat soak into me as my thoughts and frustrations take center stage. I'm still angry. I'm *so angry*. But I'm not sure if it's at Emma, Ms. Jones, the situation, or myself.

I know her mom always had too much sway in her head, but Emma seemed able to push aside accusations involving me. I guess Ms. Jones's words sank deeper into her head than I realized, and saying, *Don't listen* wasn't enough. But what else could I have done? If I tried showing her the ways she benefitted my life, would she have seen them?

No . . . I shouldn't blame myself. Doing that will fuck with my head when the real culprit is her mother. Her own *mother*, who beat her down daily, hammering into her that she provided no light, comfort, to anyone.

I thought I'd seen through all of Emma's masks. Apparently not, because I'd never known just how deeply these insecurities ran through her blood. And love . . .

You don't love me back! You never will! And even if you did, I wouldn't let you!

Emma loves me. But she thinks I should pursue someone who can . . . what? Give me something she can't give me? It's bullshit—Emma has always given me everything I could want. Never did I feel like something was missing.

When Emma left my life, she took half of me with her. For years, there's been this emptiness lurking under my skin, in the vessels around my heart, in the essence of my soul. Whether it's platonic, romantic, whatever, Emma is my other half. She'll always have bits and pieces of me that I can't reclaim unless I'm with her. And maybe . . . I have bits and pieces of her, too.

Even if that's true, can I forgive what happened? Six years of friendship, and she strangled it without consulting me. It's not *fair*.

I'm never going to stop loving Emma. At the very least as my ex-best friend. At the most . . . I don't know. Are we compatible? I find myself seeking her out, watching her when she's not paying attention, thinking about her, but does that mean we can work things out? Or are we too frail to try again?

I wish I'd brought her home so we could figure things out. But

I should sort out my own emotions and thoughts before taking that step. I swipe away Jas's messages and climb into bed fully unclothed and damp from shower water, curling my arms around my second pillow. I know I should be alone.

That doesn't stop me from wishing she were next to me.

Emma

I spend the night in Juliet's guest bedroom with Alice. I don't tell anyone about what happened. It's been such a long night, and I have so many thoughts, I don't have the strength to reiterate it all. Even if they're palpably curious.

When I wake early to leave for my interview, the smell of sausage wafts through the air. I tug on the outfit Juliet prepared for me—black slacks, heeled shoes, and a striped blouse. When I enter the kitchen, I find her wearing . . . Oh my God. The cutest pink flower-patterned apron I've ever seen in my goddamn life.

"You'll need strength to kick your interview's ass," she says brightly. They're wearing a pink silk hair wrap that matches the apron perfectly. Not only have they been cooking sausage patties, but there's a platter of fruit and a plate of chocolate chip pancakes on the counter.

"Juliet," I whisper, approaching them with an open mouth. "You didn't have to do this."

"I was planning on it anyway, since this is the first sleepover I've ever actually enjoyed." She winks, flipping the patties. "How'd you sleep?"

"Your guest bed was comfy" is all I can say. To be fair, I'm not picky about the mattresses I sleep on. "And . . . I'm sorry for last night." I touch their shoulder lightly. "How Caleb and I snuck out like that."

"Don't apologize." Their eyes glitter with warmth. "I know you and Caleb have a romantically tense past to work out. No need to explain."

Oh no. How deep did her conversation with Alice and Jas get yesterday? "How much . . . do you know?" I ask weakly. I mentioned that Caleb and I used to be friends, but I sense she's more knowledgeable about it now than she was when we ended that conversation.

"Jas and Alice filled me in while you were away," she explains with an apologetic smile. "It was a gripping tale of passion and betrayal. I cried three times."

"Ah." Fucking traitors.

"We talked about a lot, actually." Juliet grimaces down at the sausage patties when she flips them again (they're burnt), then plates them. "I didn't know Alice played on the varsity soccer team with you."

"Oh, yeah. But she quit after I . . . also quit."

"You mean after you got suspended?" Juliet asks, eyes glinting with amusement.

Fucking *traitor*. But I'm beyond the point of saving face in front of Juliet. Maybe I don't mind them knowing these things as much as I did when I first met them. "I decked a teammate for insulting Caleb," I explain.

She grins with a hint of pride, then slides me a plate, which I begin to load with pancakes and sausage. (*Don't forget your fruit,* Caleb's voice nags in my head, and I sigh, grabbing a few strawberries as well.) I drench the pancakes with syrup and begin to chop into them with my fork.

"Incredible," I say through a mouthful of fluff.

"Don't lie," she scolds. "They're burnt."

"So? Gives it more flavor." Not that it's a good flavor, but I won't tell her that. "Caleb always has good pointers with this stuff."

Whoops. I hadn't meant to say that part out loud.

"Maybe I'll take him up on cooking lessons," Juliet says with a small laugh, hopping onto one of the stools around the kitchen island. "My dad is the chef of our family. I try helping, but he always shoos me away because *you forgot to spray the pan first* or *how did you set the stove on fire boiling fettucine?*" She shrugs with a sigh of exasperation.

The thought of Juliet fumbling around the kitchen with oblivious cheerfulness while their father gets exceedingly frustrated makes me laugh. Juliet smiles, but it slides away as they bring the pans to their sink. Maybe they're more upset about Caleb and me ditching their party than they're leading on.

I understand when she next speaks.

"Emma . . . I know we met a few weeks ago," she says quietly, scrubbing at the grease in the pan. "And I understand if bringing this up is crossing a line. But . . . I'm here for you. I know Alice is your best friend, but if you need someone to vent to, or if you need a place to escape, I'm here."

Ah. Alice must've spilled more about my life than I thought. "Thanks," I murmur. "Alice told you about my mom, then?"

"Just enough to piece things together." Her palms tighten around the soapy scrubber. "I know it's not nearly the same thing, but . . . I told you about my previous friends. I didn't realize how toxic they were until I moved here." She cocks her head over her shoulder to give me a frail smile. "Terrell was always there for me. I don't know what I would've done if I hadn't had a safe space to run to after they treated me like that. So just know that I'll always be there for you. Okay?"

She's sweeter than the syrupy breakfast I just inhaled (burnt though it may be). I bring the sticky plate to the sink, then nudge her shoulder with my elbow. "Thank you," I whisper. "For breakfast and for saying that. I'm glad I met you."

Their eyes widen, and they drop the pan, causing it to clang against the inside of the sink. "Ah! Sorry. So, that's what it feels like when someone whispers in your ear? Very stimulating!" She swivels toward the griddle and grabs it, continuing before I can even process what she said. "Anyway, you should head to that interview. You'll be amazing!"

I stare at her in puzzlement. Did I just . . . fluster her?

"Remember," Juliet says after I've brushed my teeth and buttoned Alice's formal jacket over my waist. They clasp my shoulders and peer into my eyes. "Just tell them what they want to hear. Kiss their hands. Slurp their asses. I believe in you."

I nod with determination. "Thanks."

I slide into my car and hit the road. Juliet's encouraging thumbs-up and confident grin from the porch fuel me.

Time to get myself a fucking job.

✗●✗●

My only reservation when I walk into the theater is that I see a boy preparing popcorn at the concession stand who looks an awful lot like one of Ian Summers's cronies. When I get closer to ask where the interview room is, I realize it is, in fact, a crony.

"You're the person they're interviewing?" he asks with a skeptical smirk.

I approach the help desk instead. No way will I let thoughts of Ian sway me away from a successful interview. I just hope that guy isn't close to the managers, or I can kiss this opportunity goodbye.

The manager is what I expect—a pleasant middle-aged balding man who spends the first ten minutes telling me about the importance of customer satisfaction before asking a single question. I nod along, keeping my posture upright as Caleb suggested. My voice wobbles when I speak (I'm nervous as shit, okay?), but I keep to the script. I tell him I want to work here because of the energetic environment and I can bring a lot to the table with my patient yet persevering personality. I hope I give the impression that I'm a calm, level-headed individual and not a perpetually ticking time bomb.

By the time the hour is up, I've ejected so much bullshit I'm surprised the room doesn't smell. He extends his hand over the table and says, "You're a delight, Emma. Why don't we get you in next week for your orientation?"

I stare at his palm. "I . . . got the job?"

"If you want it," he says, smiling cordially.

"Yes!" I lunge out, shaking his hand, my heart pounding in my ears and my armpits sweaty and gross. "I'd love to. Anytime. Uh, after school, of course."

"Of course." He begins to file papers into a folder for me and rattles off a rehearsed spiel about how I'll love being a new team member and that I can bring the paperwork back when I'm next here. He walks me to the front doors of the theater, and all I can say is thank you, over and over, until he leaves me.

I have a job. I can watch movies for free. I get food at a discount. I even get tips.

I have *a job.*

I know I can't survive on the pay, but I won't have to fully rely on sneaking home to steal from my mom. I'll have an income that ensures I can pay cash if my mom freezes my account. I can gas up my car, go out with friends. I push through the doors, resisting a scream of relief. Best to keep it professional if that manager is nearby.

My eyes rove the parking lot, and the first thing they find is him.

Despite everything, Caleb Daniels is here for me.

He clambers out of his car, dressed in dark pants and a checkered shirt. He cups his hands around his mouth and yells across the lot, "*How did it go?*"

I laugh, the warmth ballooning in my chest. Oh, God, how I want to kiss him. I take a few steps into the road and take a deep breath to yell back.

The car hits me before I can utter a word.

CALEB

It happens in a blink. Emma is walking toward me. Then she's on the ground.

The car barely taps her. Just enough to get her to stagger sideways and lose her balance, then collapse. Her first reaction is to lunge upright and whirl toward the driver to flick them off, so I know she's okay. But then I see who's sitting in the driver's seat.

It's Ian Summers.

He's laughing.

My breath catches in my throat, and anger shudders through my body. The edges of my vision bleed red with hungry vengeance. I watch, trembling with fury, as Ian climbs out of his car and grins at Emma like he's just committed the final, fatal blow in their short-winded rivalry.

"Next time you try to get in my way," he says to her in triumph, "or humiliate me, or even *talk* to me, I'll do something way worse. Got it?"

Emma's chest is heaving. She looks like she wants to hurl herself toward him, or walk away, or scream in his face, or bite her tongue.

She doesn't get to decide which urge to follow through on.

Suddenly, I'm across the parking lot, and then I'm seizing Ian Summers by the collar of his T-shirt and slamming him up against the side of his car, seething in his face. "*Touch her again*," I say in a low growl, "*and I'll break you.*"

Ian's mouth gnarls into a loathing scowl. Maybe I shouldn't have reacted so instinctively by putting my hands on him, because even though I've got superior height, he's got a lot more girth and muscle. But seeing him so delighted in hitting Emma . . . *my* Emma . . .

Before I can even react, he's shoving me onto my back on the street and clambering on top of me. I try to writhe, to upend his balance, but there's a forty-pound difference between us.

"You? Break *me*?" he shrieks, hurling his arm forward and slamming his knuckles into my temple with enough strength to briefly blacken my vision. Part of me wants to revert to being the little boy from the playground—to curl my arms over my head and retreat into fetal position—but the image of Emma hitting the asphalt keeps me pushing back.

"*You think that was funny?*" I shout as he lands a blow on my jaw, snapping my head sideways. "*You're a piece of shit!*"

"*It was just to scare her, you fucking idiot!*" Ian roars, and he grabs my shirt and yanks, then bashes his head so hard against mine that white dots explode before my eyes.

"*Get off of him!*" a voice screeches, and suddenly, Emma's using her whole body weight to tackle Ian sideways, throwing him off of me and sprawling him on the ground. "*Back up, you dick! I'll pull the blade out—don't fuck with me!*"

And then she has her sheathed pocketknife out, and she's standing over me protectively, snarling with hatred.

"Jesus *Christ!*" Ian scrambles backward, his eyes popping wide with terror. "You can't threaten me with a knife! *That's illegal!*"

"Yeah? You going to report me to the police?" Emma asks snidely, her whole body quaking with wrath. "While you're there, are you going to mention that you deliberately hit me with your car and scratched me up? Or should I tell them myself?"

Ian stiffens, his eyes flickering with fiery anger. "Fuck you, you crazy bitch," he snarls, and then he scurries into his car and slams the door. The tires screech as he peels away, tearing toward the main road.

Emma sags with relief. I stay in the road, catching my breath. My face is throbbing—I can already feel my jaw and temple swelling.

"Up you get, brave little soldier," she says, offering her hands.

Always the first to recuperate, this one. I take her palms, allowing her to hoist me to my feet. My brain pulses from Ian's headbutt. "Where are you hurt?" I ask, scanning for damage.

"Scratched my hands and knees when I fell, but I'm fine." She gives me a playful smile. "No worse than when you bodied me in the parking lot a few weeks ago."

"You grabbed my dick!" I squeak.

"Accidentally." She shrugs, still grinning. "I deserved the shove."

I can feel my face heating up from the recollection, so I take her palms, flipping them to assess. Thankfully, most of the scratches didn't cut deep enough to draw blood. There's a dark spot on her left pant leg, though, that tells me her knee is bleeding. "Sorry," I whisper. "I'm terrible at fighting."

To my surprise, Emma laughs. It's a soft, pleasant sound that warms my stomach. "You're not a fighter," she says, cupping her hand around my face, her thumb gliding over my cheekbone. "You're a healer. You're not meant to swing your fists."

I stare at her in bewilderment. Her hazel eyes are gleaming, emphasized by the sunlight raining over the parking lot. I think I want to kiss her.

I definitely want to kiss her.

"Come on," she says, her hand dropping from my face, leaving my cheek cold and sore in her wake. She gathers up the folder she dropped during her fall. "Let's go to your place. You'll have what we need."

I'm not sure what we need, but she's right. I probably have it.

"Why do you have a pocketknife?" I ask, hoping to steer my thoughts away from kissing her. It's the second time I've had to bear witness to it. "You . . . I mean, you weren't actually going to use it, right?"

"Of course not," she snips, giving me a skeptical look. "I've never even unsheathed the knife before. But I can't wander the city streets alone without protection, so I always have it on me in case someone wants to test my patience."

"Why are you wandering the city alone?" I ask sternly.

"Boredom."

"Well, next time you do, invite me. I'm a shitty fighter, but I look intimidating."

She gives me a teasing smile that tickles my lower abdomen.

"Never thought you'd be desperate enough to take me on long walks through the city," she says mischievously.

"I don't mind."

She seems skeptical, but my fierce expression must be genuine enough to convince her, because her face softens. "I won't wander the city without you," she says, lifting her hand in Boy Scout fashion. "As long as you don't bitch and moan at me while we're walking around."

Hmm. I do love bitching and moaning. "Fine," I say nonetheless.

We climb into our cars, and she follows me through the streets to my apartment complex. As soon as we're inside, Emma pulls out ice packs from the freezer and wraps them in paper towels. "You first," I tell her, retrieving gauze and antibiotic ointment from the bathroom. "Sit on the couch."

"It's just a couple scratches," she says, but when she sees my stern glare, she sighs and collapses onto the living room couch. She rolls her pant leg over her knee, revealing the patch of bleeding skin from hitting the asphalt. After washing my hands, I take her foot in my lap, dabbing away the dried blood before smearing antibiotic cream over the gashed skin. As I secure cotton to her knee, she nestles an ice pack against my jaw.

I glance at her. Her face hovers inches from mine.

"You're swelling up," she explains. "We shouldn't wait to put ice on it."

Right. I fold my hand over hers, keeping it positioned atop my aching jaw. A long moment of silence stretches between us, in which we merely look at each other, searching eyes, glancing at lips, heat flourishing in the air. I know what I want, but what does she want? Normally it's easy to read her thoughts, but now . . . she's an enigma. Is this a good idea? Probably not. Do I care? Also no. Her skin looks invitingly soft, her hair shiny, smoothly brushed for the interview. Easy to run one's fingers through.

"Caleb . . . are you still attracted to me?" Her voice is a nervous mumble. "I know we've grown apart, so . . ."

"I am."

Her cheeks flush. "And you still . . . even after everything . . . ?"

"I'll always love you, Emma," I tell her, nudging my index finger against her chin.

Her eyes are watering. Her lip wavers, and she whispers, "It's hard to think . . . I'm worthy of that. Of *you*."

"I know. But we can work on that, yeah?" I fold my available palm over her unscathed knee, heart pounding in my chest, itching for more. "So stop thinking. For now."

Emma's eyes wander between mine, like she's seeking permission. If I don't do something, she'll pull away, so I frame her face in my hands, keeping her focus on me. My thumb strokes a gentle path over her pale, slender brow. This moment . . . feels right. Despite knowing we have so much to work through. It's just her and me, alone, the lingering hints of adrenaline still burning in our veins, our breath quick against each other's lips. My fingers creep backward, sliding through her hair, encroaching along the nape of her neck. Her exhale hitches.

I draw her in, erasing the distance that's stood between us for the last four years. My lips land on hers, careful, tentative, but I can feel electric tingles twisting up my spine. My fingers lock along her hairline, drawing goose bumps, and I tug her deeper into a kiss. Her reluctance dissolves; her posture loosens. She's letting go of whatever inner turmoil is tumbling around in her mind.

I grip her beneath her knee and hoist her into my lap. Her legs cross at my waist and her hands clench fistfuls of my shirt. My chest rises and falls out of sync with hers, the fabric of our clothes scraping together with each shift of our bodies. I'm reclaiming parts of me I lost years ago—filling the holes that have echoed within me like whistling tunnels. My palms scrape a trail down her back to the flair of her waist, and I find her belt loops, pulling her against my front.

I've thought about this before. I've fallen asleep wondering what her lips taste like—imagining her waist fitting between my arms. Being attracted to Emma isn't something I've ever fully acknowledged until now. Picturing us partaking in . . . lewd activities was something I brushed off as pubescent hormones.

But it's more than that. No matter how many years we spend apart, the fact that she was my best friend, my first crush, my person, will never change. Beyond what she's done for me, I've admired her. Her loyalty, courage, ability to stand up for people and things she believes in, to speak her mind, unfiltered.

I want Emma. I want to feel whole again.

Emma's hesitance to engage has fully evaporated. She yanks my shirt, causing me to collapse on top of her on the couch. I almost make a quip about her lack of patience, but her tongue scrapes against my lip before I can form the words. Another time, maybe.

I tangle one hand in her hair, the other pulling the crook of her knee around my hip, and *God*, I never want this to end. Her shirt rumples up against her rib cage, and I don't know what it is about midriffs (girls wearing crop tops, guys stretching to reveal their stomachs), but they're the most likely body part to drive me feral.

Emma tugs the back of my shirt, and it begins sliding over my skin. Is she trying to pull it off? The thought sears my skin hotter.

But then my phone rings. I want to ignore it, but my brain is already diverting attention to the sound. Is it Mom? If so, I can't let it go to voicemail. Ever so reluctantly, I peel myself away from Emma. "Sorry," I say, gasping for air as I fumble for my phone. "Just double-checking . . ."

"All good," she says breathlessly.

When I see the caller ID, I have to blink three times to fully register it. "Dad?" I say when I answer the phone, just to make sure.

"Hey, kid!" His voice is its usual eager, confident tempo. "What are you up to?"

Making out with my ex probably isn't the right answer. "Sitting around."

"Next weekend, Jennifer invited me to visit her family in Ohio." I can tell he's speaking through a grin. "I'm trying to make a good first impression, and you've got a steady head on your shoulders that I think would impress them. I can swing by and pick you up? It'd be two nights."

Oh. Wow. I'm supposed to hang out with Mom on Sunday, but . . . an opportunity to spend a weekend with Dad? Maybe it would be a good test run for if I decide to try living with him. "Yeah!" I try toning back my enthusiasm. Play it cool, Caleb. "That sounds great."

Emma's brows are furrowing. I try to ignore it—I can already feel my annoyance at her reaction beginning to swell. I don't want him to come here to pick me up, since Mom always gets this disgruntled, spiteful atmosphere around her, so I suggest that he pick me up at a nearby coffee shop I can walk to with my suitcase.

I lower my phone to my lap, resisting a smile.

"Your dad, huh." Emma's voice is frustratingly stiff. "What's the occasion?"

Maybe she's looking for an excuse to rag on him, but I tell her anyway. "He's picking me up on Friday to spend the weekend with him and his girlfriend in Ohio."

"Oh."

That's all she can say. Not *It's nice to see him making an effort* or *I hope you have fun.* I shouldn't entertain her thoughts, but the question escapes me before I can swallow it. "What's the problem?"

She gives me a weary sigh, and her voice comes in a grumble. "I've just . . . seen you go down this road before."

"Years ago. I told you, he's different," I say in frustration, retreating to the corner of the couch away from her. "He even invited me to try living with him."

Emma's eyes widen, and I hope she'll say something more encouraging. Instead, "It's really going to hurt this time when he falls through."

"He *won't*."

"It's the same pattern." Her voice sharpens, and she twists to stare at the black TV. Back to avoiding my eyes, then. "He lures you in. He makes you promises. Makes you believe he'll be there for you. Just when you sink into his lies, he rips the rug out from under you. I don't have to see him to know nothing's changed."

Anger tightens my jaw. What right does she have to make accusations like that when she hasn't seen the progress he's made? But the fact that she can act so confident and condescending, like she knows more than me . . .

"Just because your dad never came back for you doesn't mean mine can't come back for *me*!" I spit out.

Foreboding silence seizes the room. Emma goes rigid. A storm of emotions writhes within me, so powerful and confusing that I can't risk opening my mouth again. Emma stands, gathers up her jacket and keys, then walks to the door, far calmer than I expect.

"You want to fall for it again, fine," she says coolly. "But I won't be there to watch."

She slams the door, leaving me alone with the strawberry taste of her lip balm.

Emma

It's the worst time for me to go home. Which is why that's where I'm going.

I don't know what I'm looking for. A fight, maybe? I'm seething, my palms vibrating around the steering wheel as I jerk through the neighborhood. I have to blink several times to see through the white rage clouding my eyes. Or maybe it's tears again.

Just because your dad never came back for you . . .

Fuck you, Caleb Daniels.

Mom's car is in the driveway. I screech to a stop and throw my vehicle in park, then storm to the door. My key still works in the lock. How fucking merciful of her.

I slam my way inside, and she startles upright from the living room couch, dropping the magazine propped in her lap. Judging by the pile of square papers, she was cutting coupons. The sight of such a leisurely activity boils my blood.

But when my voice comes, it's strangely calm. "Why?"

My mother examines me. Her blond bangs are pinned back, giving me full view of her disgruntlement, and she's dressed in a worn, casual sweater and jeans. "I hope you're here to apologize," she says stiffly.

Please. "Why?" I repeat.

"Why what?"

"Why do you hate me?"

She startles into a tense standing position, like I just reeled my fist at her. I know better than to hope she'll respond with anything other than an accusatory tone. "What the hell did you say?" she barks.

"Why," I ask calmly, "do you hate me?"

My mom's honey-brown eyes widen with disbelief—her fingers curl up into her palms. "You're my daughter! I could never hate you," she snaps, but she makes no effort to wrap me in a hug, like Ms. Daniels would've. Her eyes, which should convey remorse or affection, are devoid of anything but irritation.

I decide not to meet her combative air. "I ran away," I say, maintaining my level tone. "It's been a year. Why don't you text me to ask where I'm spending the night, how I'm doing, if I have enough to eat, if I need money for my car, if there's anything you can do to bring me home?"

Every word saps the color from her pale cheeks. "You're accusing me of being unloving because I allowed you to learn independence?" she asks in a breathy hiss.

Independence. Of every excuse, that's what she went with. "So you're fine not knowing if I'm lying dead in a gutter or getting mugged in an alleyway or starving. Because you're *allowing* me to be independent."

Mom actually bursts into laughter. "I know you're fine because you're spoiled," she says, insufferably amused. "Whatever food you don't get from my fridge, you take from someone else's. If you're not sleeping in my house, you're using someone's bed. If you aren't stealing money from me, you're forcing others to pay for you."

"So food, water, a bed, money . . . those things make me *spoiled*," I say coolly.

"Of course."

It's my turn to laugh, though whether it's at her ridiculous words or this whole situation, I'm not sure. "You giving me basic necessities isn't *spoiling* me," I mutter, clawing into my pant legs. "It's providing for your child. It's what every parent on this fucking planet should do, even if their kid is a brat."

She has the nerve to roll her eyes. "What would you know about the difficulties of raising two daughters without support—?"

"You have always made me feel like I don't deserve my life." There's a tremor in my voice, but I'm loud enough to silence her midsentence. Her nostrils flare with indignation, but for some reason, she doesn't try to speak over me. It's usually what she does the moment I raise my volume, so I'm not sure what's different. "That I don't deserve these basic things, that I don't deserve love. For a while, I believed you." I quicken my blinking, hoping to dry my eyes. I won't cry in front of her. "Because if my mom was saying these things . . . the person who's supposed to love me more than anyone . . . they must be true."

I feel like I'm choking on my words, but I press on. I'm not sure I'll ever be able to do this again.

"I'm not a burden," I whisper. "And existing doesn't make me one, even if my mother never wanted me. I deserve food, a warm bed, clothes, friendship, love. Even if people think I'm a piece of shit who only takes and takes. And I . . ."

My back straightens, and I speak with my whole chest.

"I *deserve better than you.*"

Mom's jaw is trembling with rage. "How dare . . . ? You think you can just say whatever you . . . ? You little . . ." I guess she can't decide on the right insult, because her voice dissolves, allowing me to continue.

"I'm coming home," I say fiercely. I come to the decision abruptly—in fact, I'm not even expecting it to flee my mouth like that. But there it is, so I can't retreat. "I'll eat your food, use the shower, and sleep in my bed. Because that's the least you can provide for me."

I take a hesitant step toward her. At first, she mirrors my action by backing away. But the second step I take, she remains still.

"I know . . . you had a rough life," I continue, softer. "I know your parents damaged you and beat you down in more ways than one. But you can't use that as an excuse for your behavior toward Brooke and me. Just because you don't hit us doesn't mean you're still not abusing us in other ways."

She's technically taller than me, but I feel like I'm finally the one who's towering over her. God, it feels *good.*

"Until you learn how to properly love me through therapy or something, I won't talk to you," I say sternly. "Yell at me if you want, but I'm not going to listen anymore. If you ever try to kick me out again, I'll call the police, and you'll *lose* because I'm a minor. The moment I can financially provide for myself, I'll be out of here for good."

Her body language tells me she's livid, but her sudden silence conveys something else. Maybe . . . she's listening? I don't want to entertain the thought, but it's the first time I've acknowledged that she had it hard, too. Her outlook on life . . . it obviously came from them, and she never fully healed from that.

"When I turn eighteen in April, you can legally do what you want," I tell her, wringing my hands because I'm not sure what to do with them. "Change the locks, disown me, whatever. But if and when that happens, I won't feel bad asking for help anymore. Maybe I'll still feel guilty, because you burned that into me. But I know what I deserve now. And so . . ."

I swallow with difficulty and force the words out.

"I'll take. And I'll take. And I'll *take*."

My mom's every inhale is a gasp, and she's still shaking wildly with anger. Her mouth moves into different shapes, like she's trying to speak but her voice won't come to her. I don't know if it's because she hates me so much, she can't even find the words to convey it, but I consider her flustered response an improvement. Maybe later she'll find the gall to cuss me out, to tell me I'm no longer her daughter and that I've caused her immense suffering. But it doesn't matter.

There's nothing she can say to hurt me anymore.

I return to my car. I shove my toiletries, clothes, and miscellaneous items into the baskets Caleb provided, and I take multiple trips to the house, carrying everything to my room. I shove my dirty clothes in the washing machine and pour in a healthy dose of detergent. I return my pillows to my bed, move the storage boxes out of my room. I use a feather duster to clear the dust from my drawers, headboard, and shelves, being thorough enough that Caleb would be proud.

I fling open my window, allowing a cool breeze to sweep away the stale air. I vacuum my carpet and fold my clothes into my dresser. I take a long, forty-five-minute shower, in which I deplete all the hot water. When that's done, I go to the kitchen, where I make a hearty lunch.

Mom leaves the house with her hand cupped over her mouth like she's having trouble breathing. She offers nothing but silence. But something in the air has changed. It's still tense and furious on her end, but . . .

For the first time, I'm not sure it's toward me.

As I brush my teeth, my thoughts wander toward Caleb. I won't give him all the credit—it took plenty of bravery to stand up to her—but he's why I could do what I did. Not just because his rage-inducing comment gave me gusto to charge into my house, but because . . . he's been teaching me for years that I *am* worthy.

He helped me realize what I deserve. And it's not sleeping in my rusty-ass car.

I won't tell him about my accomplishment until he acknowledges his mistake. I hope I'm wrong about his dad, but . . . even if the guy is trying harder this year, that just means it'll hurt even more when he inevitably falls through. I won't *ever* forgive that man for the insulting things he said about Caleb.

When I have everything reorganized, I take the longest nap of my life. In my bed, under my sheets, on a mattress, for the first time in a year.

I fall asleep within minutes.

CALEB

I don't talk to Emma for the next week. I regret what I said about her father abandoning her, but . . .

I'm *angrier* about what she said.

This is something I've wanted for years. A chance to connect with my father, even if he's been neglectful in the past. Shouldn't Emma be happy for me? He's making an effort, and maybe . . . maybe after this weekend, I'll see the sides of him he's kept closed away from me.

At lunch, Emma and I sit on opposite sides of the lunch table. For solidarity, Jas sits with me, and Alice sits with Emma. Juliet rotates between us daily, and though they don't say anything, it's clear everyone is uncomfortable with the energy.

"This is ridiculous," Jas says on Thursday through a mouthful of potato-and-spinach pancakes, her dark brown eyes sharp enough to rip through my organs. Juliet is in conversation with Alice and Emma, her worried gaze flitting between us, like she's hoping we'll pounce across the table and sob for each other's forgiveness. "You're both being clowns. On *purpose*."

"I'm not allowed to be hurt by what she said?" I demand, stabbing my pen into my notebook.

"Feel what you want, but you're stuck in your own perspective,"

Jas snaps, poking her fork at me. "Haven't you thought about why Emma said what she did?"

"Should I?" Don't see why it's my job to justify her behavior.

"Stubborn fucks," she grumbles, throwing one of her thick braids over her shoulder and smacking me in the face with it. "She's worried about you because she's seen you get hurt. Because of that, you're refusing to talk to her and pretending like you didn't just tell her you love her."

My face reddens with mortification. I wish I hadn't told her what happened after Emma's interview. "When she apologizes, I'll talk to her again," I say irritably.

"And if she doesn't?"

I twist my pen deeper into my notebook, causing the inkblot to widen. If anything, maybe this is proof that Emma and I . . . maybe we aren't . . .

Jas whispers something that sounds a lot like "guillotine me."

X●X●

When Friday comes around, I'm so nervous I have to change my shirt three times while I'm packing. My clammy body clearly doesn't know how to react to this make-or-break opportunity that's been giving me heart palpitations. This trip to Ohio with Dad . . . it's going to make a difference.

"He's not coming here?" Mom is leaning in my doorframe, dressed in a fluffy robe, hair twisted up into a towel. Getting ready for her shift.

"He's picking me up at that coffee shop down the street," I say, tucking two extra pairs of socks into my suitcase (I'm not sure what Ohio is like, but best to be prepared).

"Oh."

There's something in her voice that gives me the same irksome feeling I got when Emma asked about my dad. "What?" I ask wearily.

"Nothing. I hope you have fun." She steps into my room and pulls my shoulder down so she can kiss my cheek. She lingers for a moment, then says, "Text me how things go. And . . . try not to expect too much, honey."

She leaves before I can scowl at her. If everyone around my father has this little faith in him, it's no wonder he's had such a hard time changing. But I see his effort, even if it's tiny steps. I'll show him this weekend how much I appreciate it.

When my suitcase is nearly exploding, I lug it down the apartment stairs and roll it to the coffee café—a quaint shop with wood-paneled walls, scattered tables, and jazz music. I'm fifteen minutes early.

And so I wait.

Emma

I'm supposed to be studying my textbooks, not the fucking clock. It's 7:45 p.m.

"Our short answers are due Monday," Juliet says, eyeing the blank questionnaire on my lap. We're slumped in beanbag chairs beside Alice in her gaming room, listening to lo-fi, doing the opposite of what we *should* be doing on a Friday night (which is anything but homework). Jas is at a volleyball game, and Caleb . . .

If all went according to plan, Caleb is on his way to Ohio with his father and some blondie the guy is calling his "girlfriend." Sometimes I can't help but wonder what a fun-loving, sassy woman like Ms. Daniels saw in him. But I've never felt it was my business to ask.

Just because your dad never came back for you . . .

I scrunch my nails into my jeans, scowling. Caleb's never said anything so cruel before. Sure, I haven't spoken to his father in years, but I've never had to in order to know the subtle, deep-rooted ways he wounds Caleb, tying him to the tail of his horse and dragging him through its shit on the trail of deadbeatery. It's so *clear* to me.

Though, my mother's tactics escaped my notice for several years. I guess it's easier to spot the patterns in someone else's life than it is your own.

Caleb's right. My dad never came for me. I don't know if it's because he forgot about me, if the thought of my mother keeps him away, or if he's dead. The only information I know is in the form of insults muttered under Mom's breath. My hunch has always been that he passed away, because he's never paid child support, which is something she'd *definitely* cuss about if he was evading it. On top of that, she's never seemed fearful, or hopeful, of his return.

I guess . . . a fragment of me is envious that Caleb has a father to connect with. Even if he's a flaming sack of shit. But I can't believe he'd think I would try to keep him away from his dad because I don't have one of my own.

Doesn't he know me at all? Have we grown too far apart to rekindle what we had? Sometimes, love isn't enough to get you through tough moments. We balanced each other well in the past—him teaching me to tighten my grip on life, me teaching him to loosen his—but that doesn't mean we're still compatible.

It's eight p.m. now.

"What are you still doing here?"

My steadfast glare breaks away, finding Alice's. She's chewing on her pen, her thin, dyed golden brows pressed together. "Huh?" I ask, though I know exactly what she's talking about.

Caleb has always been there for me. In times of doubt, sadness, excitement, frustration, he's there to wipe my tears, clean my messes, help me through bullshit I've dragged him into.

I love him. I always will, even when I'm pissed. So what am I doing here?

I thrust myself onto my feet. "I have to fix something," I say, to which Alice nods approvingly, and Juliet observes me in supportive confusion.

"Hell yeah you do," she says brightly.

I jog down the stairs and lurch into Morgana. In my heart, I know he's there, waiting. And . . . if that's what he wants to do, fine. I'll support him, even if I think his endeavors are hopeless.

But I won't ever let him wait alone again.

CALEB

Well. We all run late once in a while. We all get too busy to remember things. Like the fact that one's son is waiting at a coffee shop with his suitcase, too nervous to use the bathroom for fear that he might miss his window of opportunity to jump into his father's car as it crawls past the doors.

I hold my head aloft in my palms, blinking at the glossy wood tiles. I've committed each plank to memory. The sound of the blender whirring is a hum in my ears. I've grown so used to the ding of the swinging door that I can no longer bring myself to look up.

I should go home.

My phone is silent in my pocket. At first I kept it balanced on my knee so I could see it light up. I checked it time and time again, rereading conversations with my father on the rare chance I might've misremembered the day and time. I called him with no response. As the minutes ticked on, I couldn't bear to look at it anymore.

I'm tired. There's nothing I can think that I haven't reiterated to myself several times. There's no new curse word to mutter, no new emotion to navigate. Things are how they've always been, and I was too stubborn to see the pattern. Once again.

The door jingles. I don't look up. They aren't here for me.

But then a pair of worn sneakers with teal soles scrape to a stop under my hanging head. Emma Jones is standing there, holding a bag of Reese's Peanut Butter Cups. By the time I register her presence, she's setting the bag on the table I've been occupying, and she's pulling my head forward, hugging it against her chest. Her fingers comb soothingly through my hair.

I stay in her embrace, her warmth melting away my icy numbness. My eyes tingle with a familiar, moist burn. "What's wrong with me?" I ask.

Emma's fingers curl against my scalp.

"Why am I not good enough?" I cross my arms around her waist, pulling her against me, shivering. "I've tried everything . . . justified every behavior from him . . . given him chance after chance. What can I do . . . to make him care?"

Emma cups my chin, nudging my head up. Her face is a blurry smear of color in my eyes. "There's nothing you can or should *have* to do to make him care," she says gently. "This isn't on you. It was never on you."

Warmth escapes onto my cheek. Emma gives me a smile, a genuine one, soft and sweet. She pulls my handkerchief from my shirt pocket and pats the corner of my eye.

"He can't see the kind of person you are," she whispers. "You're . . . beautiful. You deserve everything good in this world, and the fact that he can't see that shows his own failings. Not yours."

I don't know why she's speaking so kindly. Shouldn't she be

resentful of everything I said? Yet here she is, providing her comfort like back then. "I'm sorry," I croak.

She bends over, brushing her lips against my forehead. She folds the handkerchief into my pocket, then sits in the chair next to me, plucks out a Reese's, unwraps it, and hovers it an inch before my mouth. "Open up for the buttercup."

I can't refrain from smiling. I do as requested, and she pops it in my mouth, then smears her chocolaty thumb against my lower lip. It's a sensation I've never felt before, and it causes my chest to surge with heat.

"Better?" she asks.

The chocolate peanut butter melts in my blissful mouth. "Thanks for coming."

She knocks her shoulder against mine, conveying those three words without saying them.

We linger, munching on Reese's, our knees leaning against each other, exchanging amused glances when there's an intriguing conversation nearby. Her presence doesn't make my father's absence hurt less. But it makes the pain . . . bearable. Like, she's helping me carry its weight, simply by sitting with me.

"Corner market?" she asks eventually, rising to her feet and offering her hand.

"What for?" I take her palm, and her fingers thread through mine as she pulls me up.

"A pint of vanilla bean ice cream to get you wasted."

I smile, this one wider than the first. But then the bell by the hanging door rings, and my father walks in amid a swirl of ice-cold October evening air.

He's . . . here.

The man zeroes in on my monstrous figure immediately, and his eyes glint with relief. "Caleb!" he says earnestly, approaching us. "You're still here. Good."

You're still here.

The words sink into my chest, already heavy with the weight of the last few hours. My shoulders slump, and my posture shifts—an internal attempt to make myself smaller. Emma's eyes are massive with disbelief as she watches him stop before us.

"Sorry for the tardiness," he says with that familiar, cordial grin. I've never noticed until now just how . . . cold it is. Friendly, but always distant. "Ready to go, kid?"

The question is so ridiculous I nearly laugh. That's it? No explanation for why he's three and a half hours late or why he didn't bother texting? I glance at my suitcase, which I packed, then repacked, then repacked.

"Let's head out," he says. "Jennifer doesn't like waiting."

The frustration and wrath curdles up in my stomach. I'm not sure what to say or if I should even speak. Suddenly, though, a Reese's cup pelts the center of his forehead, causing him to squawk and stagger back. "What the hell?" he demands, his amiable expression melting away.

Emma has the bag of candy in one arm, and she's trembling with wrath. She digs into it again, then hurls another piece at him.

I guess he doesn't expect her to do it twice, because he reacts too late, and it nails him in the face.

"Enough!" he yells, drawing several eyes from around us. "Who are you? This is a family matter, you little brat—"

"*Shut up.*"

My father's sentence fractures. Slowly, he turns his enraged eyes to me. "What did you say?" he breathes.

"I told you to shut up," I say calmly.

He's glowering down at me. No, he's glowering *at* me. How am I now just realizing that we're the same height? For some reason, I always felt like I was inches shorter than him—that when he stood, he loomed over me. But I'm looking directly into his face without having to crane my neck. We're on equal footing.

"You left me here for hours," I tell him, settling a calming hand on Emma's shoulder before she can throw another candy. "I waited. I called you. Texted you. And now that you're here, you haven't even told me why you're late. You're expecting me to go along without asking any questions."

My father's jaw is visibly clenched, and his fists are balled at his waist. "The reason I was late," he says, seething, "is because I—"

"Stop," I say, the warmth seeping out of my voice, leaving my words frigid and stiff. "Why should I listen to anything you say? When you care so little about me that you left me sitting in a coffee shop for hours?"

"I do care!" he cries out. At this point, everyone in the shop is staring at us and murmuring in horrified bewilderment. Normally having that many eyes on me would make me want to hide, but not now. Let the world bear witness to me finally calling my father out on his bullshit.

"You've never cared. Not enough," I say, my eyes lowering to the wood floor. "I'm not going to fall for this anymore. So don't contact me. No more texts, calls. No more asking for life updates so you can pretend you're some doting father in front of whatever woman you're involved with." I wrench my gaze back up to his, pinning him with a glare. "If you ever want to establish a bond with me, a bond where you're not just *using* me to look like some supportive single dad for every bottle blonde hanging off your arm, then . . ." I inhale slow and snap, "Prove you're a changed man and send me the receipts."

My father's mouth is agape. Like he can't believe I have the gall to say this. "How could you say I don't care?" he growls, and he begins to tromp toward me, stretching his arm out like he's about to grab my shoulder. I hold my ground, glaring at him. Knowing full well he isn't worth any other words I can spare. "After everything I've done to be in your life, *especially* over the last several months, how can you—?"

"*Fuck off!*" Emma screeches, and suddenly she's assaulting him with the wrapped chocolate rapid fire.

"*Stop!*" my father howls, but he's backing to the door, like the attack is too much to bear. "*Caleb, get this brat to calm down!*"

"Nah," I say, laughing so hard, I can barely get the words out. "Once my girlfriend gets going, there's no stopping her."

Emma whirls toward me, and her eyes shimmer with astonishment, delight, fondness, before they narrow back to slits and refocus on my dad. The man gives me a disgusted look that I burn into my head so I'll never forget it, then slips out the door.

Silence claims the shop, aside from Emma's gasping. Everyone around us, including a barista who looks suspiciously close to dialing 911, are whispering. I hate whispers. Usually. But right now, I can't hear them.

I pick up the wrapped chocolates from the floor and dump them into Emma's bag. She's still panting, flushed in the face, anger carved into her eyes. "Sorry," she mutters. "You were handling the situation so well, too . . ."

I scoop her face up and hoist her onto her tiptoes. "I love you, Emma Jones," I whisper.

I kiss her using all the zealous passion I imagined kissing her with years ago.

Emma

Kissing Caleb is a lot more . . . um. Interesting. This time. Every movement feels sure, intentional. At his apartment, things were great but clunky. Hesitation lingered in the air between us.

Not anymore.

Caleb clings to my hair like it's his lifeline, kisses me like it's our last day before he's shipped overseas to fight in the war. We make out in the back of my car, but he's so vertically excessive that he keeps hitting his head against the door, and the fourth time, he crawls away from me, and mutters, "Not good enough. My place."

Anticipatory heat claws into my stomach. I can't believe this is his reaction to me baseball-pitching candy at his father.

I drive him to his apartment, already aching from the absence of his lips on mine. We barely stagger through the door before he's wrapping me in his arms and hoisting me up with more strength than I knew he had. He sits me on the kitchen counter, slides my legs around his waist, and lurches into a kiss.

It's so *good*. He's not letting his teeth get in the way, but when he does use them, it's to tease my lower lip or nip my chin. I latch my fingers at the nape of his neck, drawing him in, pressing my tongue against his mouth. I roll my hips forward and knead them against his waist, which causes him to make a startled, cute noise against me. His grip tightens, though, so he must like it.

After a few minutes, we have to part to catch our breath. Caleb's forehead falls to mine, and we stare at each other, warmth beading at our temples. "We . . ." Caleb gasps another breath and whispers, "We have things to talk about."

I nod, though I'm gnawing on my lower lip, and he definitely notices. "Not tonight, though, right?"

He looks between my eyes, his own fiery and yearning.

"I know this is new . . . and fragile," I admit, curling one fist into his shirt, hoisting his chest against mine. Hoping he can feel the vigor of my beating heart. "So if you're uncomfortable, I understand. But I'd really like to keep kissing you. Maybe even without clothes."

Caleb actually chokes on his next breath. "What?" he squeaks, stepping backward.

Maybe I shouldn't have said the last part so candidly. Still, his reaction makes me laugh, and I tack on, "No pressure. But if you were interested in that . . . I'm on board."

Caleb scratches his collarbone, looking around the kitchen uneasily. I wonder if he's about to start panic cleaning.

"Hey, Cal. Come here." I wiggle my fingers at him, and he steps closer again, allowing me to scoop his palms up. I fan open his left one and kiss it gently, then move to each of his fingertips, which I curl so I can peck his knuckles.

"What are you doing?" he asks, his voice breaking. He's nervous. Ah, he's so damn cute, I can't even stand it.

"Exactly what it looks like." I wink, pressing another kiss to the back of his hand. "If you want to talk, we can talk. I'll just be down here." I kiss a small mole on the center of his arm, noting the goose bumps crawling up his skin.

"I want to keep doing what we were doing," Caleb mumbles.

"Okay." I smile so he knows I'm not disappointed.

"But maybe . . ." He swallows loudly. ". . . In the shower?"

I look at him in astonishment. "Um. Holy shit, yes? Let's go right now—"

Just as I'm scrambling off of the counter, Caleb tosses his hands up, causing me to pause. "Um, before we do . . ." He glances around the room apprehensively, wringing his hands. "I'm trying to re-member the last time I . . ."

Sigh. Of course. "You want to clean the shower first?" I guess.

He gives me a weak grin that confirms my suspicions. "Five minutes?"

". . . You have three."

Caleb sprints toward his cleaning supplies in the hallway closet, the air around him sunshiny and excited. Fucking dork.

When I get to make out with him again, four whole minutes have passed (I'm feeling merciful), and the smell of bleach fades to the edges of my subconscious. We stand in the middle of the bathroom, clinging to each other, and I realize I need to initiate the next step because he's too respectful to do it. I pull his fingers to my button-down shirt, guiding them downward until it's undone. I shrug it off my shoulders, then I go for his, wrestling it over his lengthy torso.

"You're sure this is okay?" Caleb asks, eyes gripping mine with an intensity that tells me he's avoiding looking past my neck.

"If you are."

"I . . . Yeah. I am." His voice wobbles, but it's not out of apprehension. He's eager.

"Well. It's sexy time, then," I say, kicking off my jeans. Which I guess isn't a particularly sexy thing to say, because Caleb laughs. You think I'd be an expert at this by now, considering I've been in my underwear around people I've dated before, but with him . . . it's not coming easily. Normally, flirting and sensuality are things I've prided myself on, but I'm feeling unexpectedly self-conscious.

Since when are my tits flatter than Caleb's ass? And . . . wait. Do I have curves? Like, even *one*?

By the time I decide I should tell him not to look at me in full, it's too late. He's already examining me. To my horror, he covers his face and groans. Oh God. Is he that disappointed in my pathetic, unsexy physique?

"You look really fucking good," he mumbles.

Oh. "That's a relief," I say with a snicker, drawing his wrists downward. "And just in case you need to hear it, you look really fucking good too."

I pull him into another kiss, releasing his hands so I can find the button and zipper of his pants. Then the shower is on, and the rest of our clothes are scattered on the bathroom floor, and I'm shivering and kissing him under the hot water, arching into his touch, letting his palms wander across me. He's so gentle but deliberate—his passion is love. It's simply love.

My hands don't stay at his sleek chest. They explore the sharp bones in his shoulders, the small of his lean back, the flare of his waist. He reacts with small, pleasant noises that test my restraint each time I hear them. At one point, when we're pausing to breathe again, I give him a knowing smile.

"What?" he asks, a little dazed.

"Just thinking." I tilt my head at him. "It's the first time we're using the shower for a purpose that isn't cleaning shit off each other."

Caleb hangs his head back with another laugh.

We stay there, wrapped in each other's arms under the showerhead until our goose bumps are from more than just touch. He draws me into his bedroom and crawls over me on the mattress, his fingers finding the gaps between mine. He presses a lingering kiss to my neck, then my jaw, then my earlobe. The sight of his fervor is nearly overwhelming, so I close my eyes, curling my hands tighter around his.

"Missed you," Caleb whispers, his breath hot against my cheek. "I've missed you so much, Emma. My Emma."

His words flush my face all over again. How could such a plain, simple sentiment fluster me like this? It's almost annoying, how easy it is for him to make me melt. "I'm sorry for running," I say quietly, loosening my palms from his grasp so I can lift his face and look into those baby blues. "I'm sorry for hurting you. I . . . really love you."

Caleb smiles, and God, it's so tender. He curls his arms around me, drawing me against his chest. I love the weight of his arm over my waist—the sturdiness of his other arm under my head. Now that we're not frenzied with passion, he seems self-conscious about where his hands are resting. It's cute and polite, so I don't tease him about being reluctant to touch my butt again.

"I . . . Did I make you uncomfortable earlier?" he murmurs, propping his head up on the same pillow as mine. His pale eyes have always been intense, but now I can't escape them. I don't even want to blink. "When I called you my girlfriend in front of Dad. I know we haven't discussed—"

I silence him with a quick, fond kiss. "We're lying naked in bed together. You're my boyfriend, whether you like it or not," I say sternly.

Caleb smiles so bright it's nearly blinding. This boy makes me ache in the best way possible.

Things aren't perfect. He's still wounded from what I did in middle school. I feel it in his desperate grip, like he thinks I might slip away while he's asleep. I have my own issues to work through. Therapy sounds like a great option, and maybe . . . I don't know. Maybe I could even get my mom and Brooke to go too. I'm going to need help if I want to rewire my brain so I stop beating myself until my self-assurance is black and blue.

But I don't care about any of that tonight. Right now I just want to be with him.

He strokes my hair until I'm half-asleep, and I rub his back, my forehead in his chest. I tell him that I confronted my mom and moved my things back into my house. As I explain, I feel his shoulder muscles relaxing. "I'm proud of you," he says softly. "And I'm glad she hasn't been yelling at you lately. Better that she's not talking to you at all rather than screaming at you."

"I think she's pissed," I admit. "But part of me wonders if maybe I got through to her. Somehow. I don't know. At least it seems like she's thinking about some things. We haven't spoken since I moved in."

Caleb kisses me between my brows.

"We should come clean to Juliet," I murmur before he can say something sappy and supportive that'll bring tears to my eyes. "You think she'll hate us?"

"Nah." Caleb gives me a teasing smile. "Don't you know her at all?"

I do know Juliet. Not as deeply as I'd like, but that'll come with time. I know they're a genuine, kind, cheerful person who spreads their light to everyone nearby. I know they like playing video games and watching streams while they do homework. I know her best friend is her big brother, and she watches rom-coms when she needs a good cry, and that, like the rest of us, she's healing. Slowly but surely.

I know that we're friends.

"Let's tell them." I graze Caleb's chin with my thumb. "Together."

He tightens his grip around me. I love the feeling of our legs tangling, our warm, damp skin pressed together, the intimacy of his bare navel resting up against me, the way I can feel his body and muscles shift with every breath.

We drift off together into a peaceful slumber.

CALEB

We don't linger in telling Juliet the truth. That, for weeks, we've been in competition to win them over romantically. I don't know if they even developed feelings for either of us, but it doesn't matter. They deserve to know. So we invite her to meet us for lunch, and she happily agrees.

When I open my bedroom door to sneak to the shower, I'm mortified to find a sock draped over the handle. "You did this before I woke up?" I snarl at Emma, who's instantly laughing hard enough to bring herself to tears.

"No," she wheezes out. "Th-that wasn't me."

Oh my God. The weight of humiliation nearly brings me to my knees. Mom must've seen our discarded clothes on the bathroom floor when she came home and assumed we'd . . . gotten nasty. "Why are you laughing?" I demand.

"I just love your mom," Emma chokes out.

I'm flustered and irritable now, but Emma cures this by drawing me into a sweet, yearning kiss. "There, there," she says, smoothing her thumbs over my cheeks. "Deep breaths, my love."

My love. My stomach tingles, and I find myself smiling reluctantly. "You always know how to handle me," I say quietly.

"Mm-hmm." She rises to her tiptoes so she can wrap her arms

around my neck. "We'll get you a Reese's cup for breakfast, okay?"

Sounds horribly unbalanced and perfect to me.

By the time I leave the shower, Emma has driven home to clean up and get ready for lunch. Thankfully, Mom doesn't wake before I leave, so I don't have to confront her amused energy or taunting quips.

As I drive into the city, my chest constricts. I know Juliet won't hate us, but that doesn't mean our trust won't be broken. They came here from toxic friendships and have been slowly opening up. Now we have to tell her we've been omitting the truth since day one?

I find a free street parking spot and collect myself. Emma's car doesn't appear for ten more minutes, but at least she's on time. We allow the hostess to seat us in a booth near the back of the chain restaurant.

"Who should be the one to explain?" Emma asks beside me. "No, wait, it should be you. You're better with words. And being calm."

"Being calm?" I ask skeptically.

"I mean, I know you lose your shit when someone isn't holding their mop at the appropriate angle—"

"*Don't patronize me.*"

The restaurant door swings open, and Juliet walks in, wearing a sparkly shirt, leggings, and knee-high boots. When she sees us, she gives a jolly wave. I hope it's not the last time I'll see it. "Hey!" they say, sliding into the booth across from us. She gives me a careful look. "Things fell through with your dad, huh?"

Oh. Right. I'm supposed to be in Ohio with him. The reminder makes my stomach sink, but not nearly as much as usual. Emma's reaction to him was incredible enough that thinking about last night makes me smile more than it makes me ache.

"I realized he has better things to do, so I decided not to go," I admit with a shrug. "I . . . hung out with Emma instead."

Emma's lips waver into a brief smirk.

"Sorry to hear that," Juliet says solemnly. "He sounded like a manwhore, from what Jas told me. Sorry if that's offensive. Anyway, I'm glad Emma was there for you."

Emma places her palm atop mine, and reassurance courses through me. "We decided to try . . . um. Dating," I say awkwardly.

Juliet's eyes sparkle, and a massive smile lights their face. "Oh, wow! Marvelous news. I offer you my congratulations!"

She says it with as much joy as I've ever heard, but her stilted language . . . Why does she not sound surprised? Before I can comment, the server appears to take our orders. Juliet skims the menu while I order a grilled chicken wrap and Emma gets cinnamon pancakes. When he leaves, Juliet turns their enthusiastic gaze back to us.

"I'm the first one who knows?" she asks.

"Yeah. Because we . . . wanted to talk to you. And. Sort of. Come clean?" I say, my voice weakening.

Juliet tilts her head, and there's something strangely anticipatory in her eyes.

Emma and I glance at each other with apprehension. And so, I begin the explanation. About how we were both interested in dating her and, because I accused Emma of stealing people from me, a proposal was put forward—whoever could get Juliet to kiss them first would be able to ask her out.

As I speak, with Emma filling in the occasional missing detail, Juliet's face becomes unnaturally impassive. Maybe she's just . . . taking it in? "So, Emma and I have been hoping you'd invite us to one-on-one events," I say feebly. "But we started getting closer to each other, and . . . yeah."

I feel the weight of my decision choking me. Saying this plot out loud to Juliet . . .

"It was gross and horrible," Emma says, looking with determination at her lap. "We understand if you feel betrayed or need time to process. But please don't think we didn't want to actually be your friend."

I feel like I'm shrinking, mostly because Juliet's expression hasn't shifted at all—not even a flinch to show me what they're thinking. After several unbearable moments of silence, they draw a slow, deep inhale, then lean over the table, looking between us.

"Come closer," she says.

Emma and I exchange another terrified glance but obey, leaning over the table. Juliet frames her mouth in her hands, so we'll hear her clearly. My muscles draw tight, bracing. She offers a sardonic smile and whispers with unrestrained intensity,

"Do you take me for a fool, you fucks?"

We stare at Juliet, startled.

"What?" Emma croaks.

Suddenly Juliet is laughing so hard into their palms that I can't even hear them breathing. Emma and I keep staring, trying to figure out what's going on. Did our revelation . . . completely snap her?

"Incredible," Juliet chokes out, wiping the tears of hilarity from their eyes. "Look, dipshits. Just because I'm a happy-go-lucky, peppy person doesn't mean I'm oblivious. You think I never noticed the way you fought each other around me? You really think I couldn't tell you were both trying to get time with me?" She gives us a deeply skeptical look. *"Please."*

My mouth hangs agape as their words crash through my head like waves of horrifying realization. Emma says what we're both thinking before I can.

"You knew we were competing for you?"

"Obviously," Juliet responds, smirking. "Jas and Alice have been nice enough to fill in the details about your relationship over the last couple weeks. I decided to come out point blank and ask them to confirm my suspicions about you two fighting over me. They snitched on you pretty quick."

I . . . can't even be mad. I'm so floored that I can only sit there, my jaw in my lap.

"You knew this whole time and didn't say anything?" Emma asks squeakily.

"Well. Not the *whole* time." Juliet stirs her straw in her drink with a furtive smile that somehow makes me even tenser. "I really started to understand what was going on after Emma told me you guys used to be friends. Again, Jas and Alice were really helpful in putting the puzzle together. From there . . . I came up with my own little plan."

Juliet giggles like a maniacal villain.

"Little plan?" I ask, gulping.

"Mm-hmm." Juliet grins in this way that tells me she's delighting in our paranoia. After allowing us to wait with bated breath a few seconds longer, she says, "I decided to try to set you up."

More silence. I think I'm slowly turning to stone.

"I kept inviting you separately to the same place," they explain, their smile unyielding. "And you were too stubborn to ever talk to each other, so you fell for it. Even though I knew about your falling-out in middle school, it was obvious you were into each other. I decided to have fun with it. So there you go. Now we're even."

She knew. Not only was she aware of our competition, but she was working behind the scenes to use it to her advantage. "So," I say slowly, "the dinner after your movie . . ."

"Oh, yeah. I made up the story about Terrell having big news," Juliet admits. "I asked you to order an appetizer so you couldn't immediately leave after I ditched."

"And the sleepover party," Emma whispers.

"Yep. Invited you separately. And then there was the time I 'forgot' my water bottle in the car and left you two to wait for me, and when I invited Caleb and Jas over to join us for Alice's stream." Juliet offers a mischievous wink. "Jas and Alice helped me coordinate things."

I want to rip my hair out of my head. I was so focused on beating Emma that I ignored the clear signs that these instances might've been intentional.

"It doesn't feel great knowing that you treated me like some prize," Juliet says firmly, wrapping a curl around their finger. "But you admitted to it and apologized. And I ran with it instead of calling you out. So, I'm willing to put this behind us if you are?"

They hold their palm over the table with a lighthearted smile. Juliet . . . is an amazing person. I shake their hand, and Emma does the same, sniffling. "Friends," she murmurs.

"And just for clarity." My knees twitch. Maybe I shouldn't ask, but my curiosity gets the best of me. "Did you ever feel . . . ? Like, was there ever a time where you . . . ?"

"Did I develop feelings for either of you?" Juliet asks, eyes twinkling with mischief. "Or maybe you want to know who I would've picked. Is that it?"

I swallow hard. Emma straightens her back in anticipation.

"I think you're both great," Juliet says. "You're genuine, kind, supportive, loyal. You both have qualities I love in people. But my answer is . . . neither."

She offers another chipper smile and says, "I'm aroace."

The words strike against my brain like a gong, disorienting my spatial awareness. "Aroace," I say, hoping the word in my mouth will help it sink into my brain.

"I'm aromantic and asexual," Juliet explains. "I'm not attracted to people. I know it's different for everyone, but I personally have no interest in dating." She waves her hand airily. "I don't get crushes. When people talk about kissing and sex, I don't get it. I mean, it's cool in theory! Which is why rom-coms are a comfort. Like, having a special person who loves you in such an intimate, wholehearted way . . ." She gives a dreamy sigh. "I love stories like that. But when I imagine it happening to me in a romance-y way, I get squeamish. If that makes sense."

"It does," I say, and I mean it. I don't like slapping labels on my forehead, but I've always assumed I rest on the ace spectrum. Watching my peers grow more interested in each other and move from one crush to another was bewildering to me.

Emma slaps her palms to her face, then whispers, "We're ass-holes."

And . . . yep. We absolutely are. Not only did we devise this competition, but we didn't think for a single *moment* that Juliet wouldn't be attracted to one of us, romantically or otherwise. How closed-minded could we be? Our casual aphobia makes me want to bang my head against the table.

"How long have you known you were ace?" I ask tentatively, because I can reserve the head bashing for later.

"I heard the word *asexual* a couple years ago," Juliet says, fumbling with her thumbs, a pensive smile lifting her cheeks. "I was like, 'Yeah, this is me.' I didn't have to do much soul searching to accept that, though I never told my friends. They would've said I hadn't found the right person or I was a late bloomer. Then around you guys . . ."

Juliet fades off, her expression lowering briefly with grimness.

"I knew you were both queer," they mumble. "But I wasn't sure that if I told you, I'd be . . . accepted. Some queer people don't consider asexuals part of the community. Because we don't *suffer* as much, because we don't face the same *problems*, because *lack of attraction* doesn't qualify as a sexuality, blah, blah, blah . . ." She sighs. "So I was nervous. But then I got to know you."

Juliet looks up at us with glowing eyes.

"I learned what it's like to have friends who accept me for who I am. Who care about me enough to listen to me ramble and rant, to let me drag them to the movies. You two, Alice, and Jas have taught me what it means to have friends. *Real* friends."

Her eyes are beginning to glimmer with tears. Still, like always, she manages a smile. That stunning, infectious smile I've grown to love.

"The kind of friends who last lifetimes."

CALEB

There are tears in my eyes. Real, actual tears.

"I'll stick my popcorn scooper into your eye sockets if you say I look cute," Emma snarls.

But she *does*. Alice is nearly hunched in laughter, and Jas bites so frantically on her lips to prevent smiling that I expect blood to start trickling down her chin. Juliet's eyes are glowing with happiness.

"You look ready to be a miserable adult, Emma," she says, leaning over the counter. "I love this journey for you. How's your first day going?"

"Mm . . . weird?" Emma squirms, and a single tear trickles down my cheek. *"Caleb, I will kick you in the mouth."*

That's fine. If this is the last image I see before death, I'll be satisfied. Emma is dressed in a purple apron that ties around her neck and reads *Ask me about our weekly special!* in vibrant gold. A baseball-style cap sits atop her two strawberry blond pigtails, which are draped over her shoulders. The disgust warping her face isn't enough to stop me from wanting to kiss every inch of her.

"So, about that weekly special," Alice chokes out, and Emma flips her off.

"Suck my ass."

"Is that how a working woman should speak on the clock?"

Emma looks ready to vault the counter and beat us to a pulp. It's a Saturday morning, her very first shift behind the concession counter, and I'm so excited for her that I can barely keep still. Not only that, but she doesn't even have to deal with Ian Summers's friend, who got fired when the manager discovered he'd invited Ian to come harass her after the interview. (I convinced her to snitch, obviously.) The boss has a "no bullshit" policy, which I hope will continue to work in Emma's favor.

"Well . . . even though you're being annoying, thanks for coming," Emma says with a sigh. "You're the first customers today."

Immediately, I snatch a bag of Junior Mints off the candy rack and toss them on the counter. "I'll take these."

"You don't like mint and chocolate," she says suspiciously.

"So? I want to be your first customer," I say, grinning.

Her cheeks lightly color, and she taps her screen, searching for the candy tab. "Um," she says. "Will that be all . . . sir?"

"Yes, ma'am," I say seriously, to which she scoffs. I hand over my debit card, and she takes it so carefully that I almost start giggling again. She's quadruple-checking everything she's doing to avoid messing up. By the time she hands me my receipt, I swear five minutes have passed.

I push the mints toward her. "Enjoy."

"What?" she croaks.

"A snack to get through the day." I wink. "Hide it in your apron."

Emma glances toward the concierge desk, where the manager

is chatting with the secretary, then suddenly stretches over the counter separating us and grabs my shirt collar, hoisting me closer to deliver a soft kiss to my lips. "Thanks, babe," she whispers.

We chat with her for another few minutes before she eventually shoos us off—she has "things to do in the back." I don't know what that means, but she's so earnest about it that it makes me chuckle. Seeing her so passionate about work, wanting to please her authority figures, is kind of hilarious. So we wander off, leaving her to it.

As soon as she's out of sight, I wish I could see her again.

Emma

Okay. I can do this.

I'm not sure I would've mustered the confidence without Caleb sitting in the parking lot with me for an hour, hyping me up. It'll probably be brief, but I'm glad she agreed to meet with me one last time. Beyond today . . . our relationship is up to her.

It's the same coffee shop we last spoke in. This time, I have a peppermint mocha so I'll have something to look at that isn't her accusatory eyes. I'm so deep in my thoughts as I sip it that I don't even realize she's here until the chair across from me scrapes backward.

"Brooke," I say, straightening up.

My little sister plops into the chair. Her bronze hair, normally kempt, is tucked in a scruffy bun, and the edges of her honey-brown eyes are bloodshot. She looks exhausted and thinner than when we last spoke, but at least she's here. "What is it?" she mumbles.

Seeing her again—*talking* to her and hearing her voice—automatically creates a lump in my throat. But I won't let my emotions get in the way of what I need to say. "Unless there's some emergency, this is the last time I'll talk to you for a while," I promise her. "But . . . I wanted to say my piece."

Her eyebrow arches. I notice her lip is quivering, like she's refraining from tears. I wonder what she's thinking. Is she happy to see me too? Angry that she's here? She's always been good at hiding her thoughts, and even now, I can't decipher them.

I take a steadying breath, reminding myself that Caleb is just outside, if things go south and I need to crawl under his shirt and disappear. But I guess things can't get *worse*.

"I know . . . you want to start a new life and leave everything behind." I keep my voice level, but my fingers are trembling around my cup. Why is this so damn difficult? I told myself I'd get through this without a hitch, but now that she's here in front of me, the possibility that I could lose her for good is becoming uncomfortably real. "Mom made life miserable. You always took the pacifist route, and I made that difficult. When she was angry at me, she took it out on both of us. I'm . . . sorry I put you in that situation."

Brooke looks over my face carefully, like she's committing it to memory. Like she's planning on this being our last conversation ever. "You shouldn't apologize for the way Mom treated us," she says, gentler than I'm expecting. I guess that means her earlier lip quiver wasn't out of rage.

"I know. But you're right. I made things harder," I say, shrugging.

Brooke doesn't reply. Unreadable as ever.

"I get that being around me makes you remember life in that house," I say, hugging my mocha to my chest. Part of me still wants to argue that it's not as black and white as she claimed it was—that I was treated worse than her regardless of how I acted, that Mom constantly compared us, that it's low for her to cut me out when I'm still trapped with the woman we both swore we'd abandon together.

But now isn't the time for that. I need to be levelheaded. Composed.

I need to be an older sister right now.

"But . . . we had good moments, too," I continue. "Like swimming in the neighbor's pool. Or when we'd bake cookies when Mom was at work or watch a movie that was so scary, you'd throw up. And when I got kicked out, sometimes you'd walk with me to the state park. You were always scared we'd get attacked by a bear."

The remembrance makes me smile despite the hammering of my heart. Brooke doesn't speak, but I notice the grimness dissolving from her tense face. That has to be a good thing, right? A sign that I'm not fucking this up?

"I'm happy your dad is helping you build a better life," I say, wishing the words didn't feel so thick in my throat. "But . . . I want to be part of your life, too. I want to build new memories with you, free of Mom. And while remembering the past can be painful, I . . . don't think we should pretend it never happened."

My hands squeeze my mocha cup so hard that the lid pops off. I have firsthand experience of the consequences of running away from my problems. The worst one being that I lost my best friend and a parental figure who actually cared about me. If there's a way I can prevent Brooke from making the same mistake . . . I should try, shouldn't I? Even if she resents me, she's right. I'm supposed to protect her.

So I'll do what I can.

"I moved back home," I tell her quietly. "I confronted Mom about the way she treated us, and . . . even though she hasn't spoken to me in weeks, things feel different. It's hard to explain." I smile feebly and scratch the back of my neck. "I'm not sure I got through to her, but maybe . . . if you're willing . . . I might be able to convince her one day to go to therapy. I know that's something you've been wanting for a while."

At that, Brooke's eyes widen, and her chest begins to rise and fall quicker. The irritation pulsing in the air around her evaporates all at once. Finally, I can read her.

"Just know that I'll always be here." I look at her with determination. "I hope one day you can acknowledge the pain Mom caused us. I hope one day I'll look at my phone and see a text from you. So if you want to reach out . . . I'll be waiting."

It's the only thing I can offer to her right now. Support. A shoulder. Something I should've given my little sister years ago.

Brooke gazes unblinkingly at her lap. Slowly, she rises to her feet and taps the sleek wooden table with one pink nail. "I'll think about it," she says flatly.

Then she abruptly swivels toward the doors to leave. But I can tell she's still clinging to something, and if I let her leave so easily, she'll regret it later. So I lunge up and catch her wrist, hoisting her backward. Before she can protest, I fling my arms around her and squeeze her against my chest. "Love you, Brooke," I whisper against the top of her head. Because I'm not sure I've ever said it before.

Brooke is stock still, like my touch has turned her to stone. We stand there for several minutes, the hum of the coffee shop a distant white noise, and I keep holding her, hoping she can feel all of my pain and regret and love in the way I grip her tightly. Hoping this won't be the last time.

She breaks into a tremor. Ever so slowly, her arms rise along my back, and suddenly, she's hugging me back, hard, harder than I've ever been hugged by anyone. Dampness bleeds into my plaid shirt, and I know she's crying.

"I'm . . . Emma, I'm . . ." Her voice is a broken rasp, softened by the cotton.

"You don't have to say it," I murmur.

"No, I . . . I'm *sorry*." Her fingers curl into the back of my shirt, and a sob flees her lips. She slumps against me, like she's having trouble keeping her weight up, and I let her. I can hold the both of us for now. I wish I'd known earlier just how much she needed me to support her weight. "Ever since we talked, I've felt disgusting and horrible . . . I probably hurt you so much . . ."

She grinds her face deeper into my collar—clutches me harder.

"I took advice and ran with it, hoping it would help me heal," she chokes out. "But I shouldn't have done that to you. You're the only one who gets it. You're the only one who helped me through it . . . You were the only *good* thing about living with Mom."

She yanks away suddenly and looks up at me with teary eyes, the tip of her nose stinging-red, her mascara smeared, and her tanned face wet from crying.

"I'm sorry," she breathes.

I'm not sure what I was expecting out of this conversation. But this . . . it makes me smile. Warmth is flourishing in my pounding heart. Finally, I've managed to penetrate every layer of that cool, unbothered mask my sister has worn over her face for the last decade. All I had to do was . . . be there for her. I pluck away a piece of hair glued to her cheek and tuck it behind her ear. "We'll make it," I say lightly. "We always do. It'll be okay."

She gives me a wobbly smile, and it's the last thing she can manage before she spins around and runs out of the coffee shop, leaving me standing there, overflowing with relief.

It'll be okay.

It wasn't *the last time* like I feared when I first walked in here to meet with her. In fact . . . it was the first time. The first of many, I hope.

I head outside to Caleb's car, willing myself to believe it. We'll figure things out, Brooke and I. Maybe Mom can join us in that journey, too, if she ever relinquishes her stubbornness and recognizes the fact that she needs help just as much, if not more, than we do. I'm nowhere near the subject of forgiveness, but I *am* willing to be there if she decides to nudge herself in the right direction.

Because I *do* want a mom. And if she can acknowledge that what her parents did to her was wrong . . . maybe she can also recognize, one day, that everything she's done to raise me and Brooke was wrong, too. A fool can dream.

Caleb crawls out of the car, and he immediately draws me

against him, hugging me, telling me how proud he is of me, how hard the last couple of weeks must've been on me. Honestly, I would've detonated from the stress if not for him keeping me cool and providing me pints of mint chocolate chip ice cream.

Caleb kisses the top of my head. "Have time to hang out with Mom and me?"

He asks this like I've ever had *things* going on, and I haven't spent my whole life wandering around, waiting for funny shit to happen. To be fair, I just worked my first few shifts at the theater, which means I now have to operate around a schedule.

"I think I can make room," I say, grinning.

He draws me back and gives my hair a playful, fond ruffle. "Let's go home."

Home.

I know Caleb and I still need to talk about things, like if we're ready to commit to a full-time relationship or if we should slow down and rebuild our friendship first. I don't have the perfect answers. I don't need them, either. I'll take this step-by-step. What matters is that I can continue to be with him in some capacity, whether it's as his best friend or his girlfriend (or both, ideally). I'll be happy regardless.

Because I love him. Because Caleb Daniels is and will always be my person.

And that's not a truth I'll ever run away from again.

CALEB

EPILOGUE

It's a good day.

I close my eyes, inhaling the sweet scent of sugar cookies wafting from Juliet's kitchen. The crackling fireplace and chatter are soothing—Alice is trying to convince Jas to wear reindeer ears, and Juliet is laughing in that way that causes the room to glow gold. Traditional Christmas songs play as background noise on the TV, and I can taste the cinnamon spice of spiked eggnog on my tongue.

A sudden weight falls in my lap, and I blink. Emma's sitting on my thighs, two golden bells hanging from her ears, her face full and flushed with a warmth that matches her holiday makeup. Her hair rests in wide, gentle ringlets around her chin.

"Falling asleep?" she asks, smiling knowingly.

"Just . . . enjoying the night."

"Right. Because it's not like you pass out a half hour into your first drink every time we all hang out, or anything," she says skeptically.

I narrow my eyes, and she grins wider, resting her lips against mine. She smells like vanilla.

A beeping sounds from the kitchen, and Alice screams, "*Cookies!*" before scrambling toward the oven.

"I guess I have to partake in the decorations?" Jas asks with a sigh, and Juliet wraps their arms around hers, hoisting her up.

"Come on, Jazzy. Just frost a couple candy canes and I'll release you from this prison."

Jas pops a dubious eyebrow, then offers us an accusatory glare. "You two can take a break from eye-fucking each other to help, right?"

"Like I'd miss the chance to paint blue balls on our snowmen cookies?" Emma scoffs, sounding highly offended.

Juliet drags Jas into the kitchen before she can offer another dry quip.

"Well?" I ask, circling my arms around Emma's waist and peering up at her. She's so gorgeous under this lighting, it's taking all my willpower to keep from tackling her backward into the couch and violently kissing every inch of her. "Shall we get up so you can frost those testicles?"

Emma smiles fondly, like I haven't just said the worst sentence in existence. "We shall."

She climbs off me, then takes my index finger and tugs me into the kitchen.

I've never had so much fun at a Christmas party. Usually, Christmas parties involved me tagging along with Jas to some popular kid's basement, where music rattled in my head long after leaving. I spent my time trying to look natural to prevent whispers.

Now I'm with a close-knit group, listening to jolly music, talking and singing as we spread generous layers of frosting and edible glitter and sprinkles across sugar cookies.

Emma smears frosting across my lips and kisses them in a sensual way that makes everyone groan, and I can't help but laugh. Her lack of restraint lately has been amusing. I don't know where the passion is coming from—maybe we're just in our honeymoon phase where everything is peachy and sweet. We decided in October to pursue a tentative romantic relationship, with the plan of reassessing a few months down the road.

Emma and I are opposites, but we're steadily learning how to control our more intense traits around each other. Emma knows that she's stubborn, messy, and impulsive, but she's been trying to keep an open mind, clean up shared spaces, and think things through more frequently. Similarly, I know I can be too nagging and meticulous, so I've been trying to ease up and go with the flow. Because it makes her happy.

More than that, we're learning how to use our strengths to each other's advantage. When Emma's wild side starts to take hold, I help keep her grounded. When my strict cautiousness starts to limit our enjoyment, Emma's spontaneity reminds me to ease my grip. It just . . . works.

Things have been good. Emma's raking up as much money as she can to pay for car repairs, and things between her and her mom are . . . different. It's not warm and familial in that house by any means—in fact, Ms. Jones tries to avoid Emma altogether. They have eons to go in their healing process, but the lack of screaming feels like a step forward.

My dad hasn't tried contacting me since the coffee shop debacle. I've come to acknowledge that I haven't done anything wrong—that I can't force him to change his priorities. Emma was right. I've done everything I can to establish a connection with him, despite the warning signs, and I've always ended up burned.

There's not always a happy ending for those kinds of relationships. But sometimes letting someone go is better for your mental well-being than continuing to cling to an ideal concept of them that won't ever come to fruition.

I want him to be my dad. I want him to *act* like my dad. But until he makes a conscious, long-term effort to change his ways, I won't let him occupy my time or heart.

And I'm . . . happy. I love having Emma Jones in my life. Even when she's shoving her blue-balled Santa Clauses into my mouth.

After our cookie frosting paired with homemade spiked eggnog, we cuddle up on the floor of Juliet's massive living room, watching movies while the multicolored Christmas lights around us blink and glitter.

Eventually, the room falls silent, and when I next blink through the weariness, I realize everyone has fallen asleep slumped over each other. Except for Emma. She's leaning against my shoulder, fumbling with my fingers like they're little toys keeping her entertained.

"Juliet said we could have the spare bedroom," I whisper.

"Mm." She draws a slow, lethargic breath. "Carry me."

I oblige and crawl to my feet. She helps by standing with me (lately, her rose-colored glasses have convinced her I'm some domineering muscleman rather than a gangly squid, but I think she's finally coming out of the fantasy). But I can still carry her down the hall, so I sweep her feet up and nestle her into my arms, bringing her to the spare bedroom. I plop her onto the bed, and we squirm around until we're covered beneath the blankets. She draws my arm over her and rolls against my chest.

"So," she mumbles. "We going to have our own party before Christmas?"

"Sure."

"We should . . . buy vanilla bean ice cream."

I think she's falling asleep, because her voice is slurring. "And mint chocolate chip," I say softly.

"I'll get a bag of Reese's . . . Make sure you stay pleasant . . ."

I snort with laughter. Always sliding in digs when she's acting too cute for me to be mad about it. "And we'll play soccer in the backyard," I say, knitting our fingers together. "I'll stand awkwardly in the goal and cry anytime you kick the ball at me."

She smiles against my neck. "And then we'll go eat your phenomenal sandwiches."

I've been making Emma lunches for school again. It's a return to routine I've dearly missed, and her look of anticipation whenever I hand her a lunch box brightens my day. "You might have to kick a bully's crotch on the way up, though," I say.

"And he'll deserve it," she mutters.

We dissolve into giggles. It's silly, but these shared moments are my favorites.

"And then we'll wash up and get into cozy pajamas," I continue.

"And I'll kiss you through every movie we try to watch," she counters.

"We'll order takeout and eat our ice cream."

"And then have premarital hoo-ha."

I laugh again—she's so damn unserious. "And then we'll have to wash up again," I say.

"And then we'll stare at your Christmas lights until we start to fall asleep," she says quietly, kissing my jaw.

"And then we'll go to bed, and I'll tell you how much I love you."

I lean over, pressing a gentle, earnest kiss between her eyebrows.

"Always and forever."

CREDITS

VIKING BOOKS AND PENGUIN YOUNG READERS

ART AND DESIGN
Anabeth Bostrup
Kristie Radwilowicz
Theresa Evangelista

CONTRACTS
Jennifer Skrzypinski

COPYEDITING AND PROOFREADING
Emily Lawrence
Alicia Lea
Abigail Powers
Marinda Valenti

SCHOOL AND LIBRARY MARKETING
Venessa Carson
Judith Huerta
Carmela Iaria
Trevor Ingerson
Summer Ogata
Gaby Paez
Maggie Searcy

PRODUCTION
Vanessa Robles

EDITORIAL
Dana Leydig

MANAGING EDITORIAL
Alexandra Aleman
Gaby Corzo
Ginny Dominguez

PUBLICITY
Lathea Mondesir

PUBLISHER
Tamar Brazis

SALES
Emily Bruce
Tori Cashman
Enid Chaban
Brenda Conway
Madalyn Dolan
Abby Fritz
Michael Gentile
Becky Green
Emily Griffin
Mary McGrath
Jenn Ridgway
Mark Santella
Amy Schock
Travis Temple

MARKETING
James Akinaka
Christina Colangelo
Alex Garber
Lisa Kelly
Bri Lockhart
Danielle Presley
Talisa Ramos
Emily Romero
Shannon Spann
Felicity Vallence

SUBSIDIARY RIGHTS
Helen Boomer
Micah Hecht
Kim Ryan

NEW LEAF LITERARY
Suzie Townsend
Sophia Ramos
Olivia Coleman

LISTENING LIBRARY
Kelly Atkinson
Emily Parliman
Rebecca Waugh

AUTHENTICITY READER
Shadae Mallory

Also by Amanda Woody

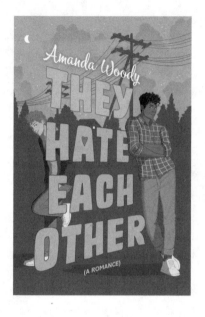

"Falling for your enemy has never been this entertaining . . . A complete home-run . . . Woody manages to take amazing tropes and make them even better, all on top of offering fully fleshed-out characters that will steal your heart from the very first page . . . An irresistible, delightfully funny, and emotionally heart–wrenching debut that's not to be missed!"

—The Nerd Daily